THE BEGINNING OF EVERYTHING

THE RISING SERIES
BOOK ONE

KRISTEN ASHLEY

ROCK CHICK

PRESS

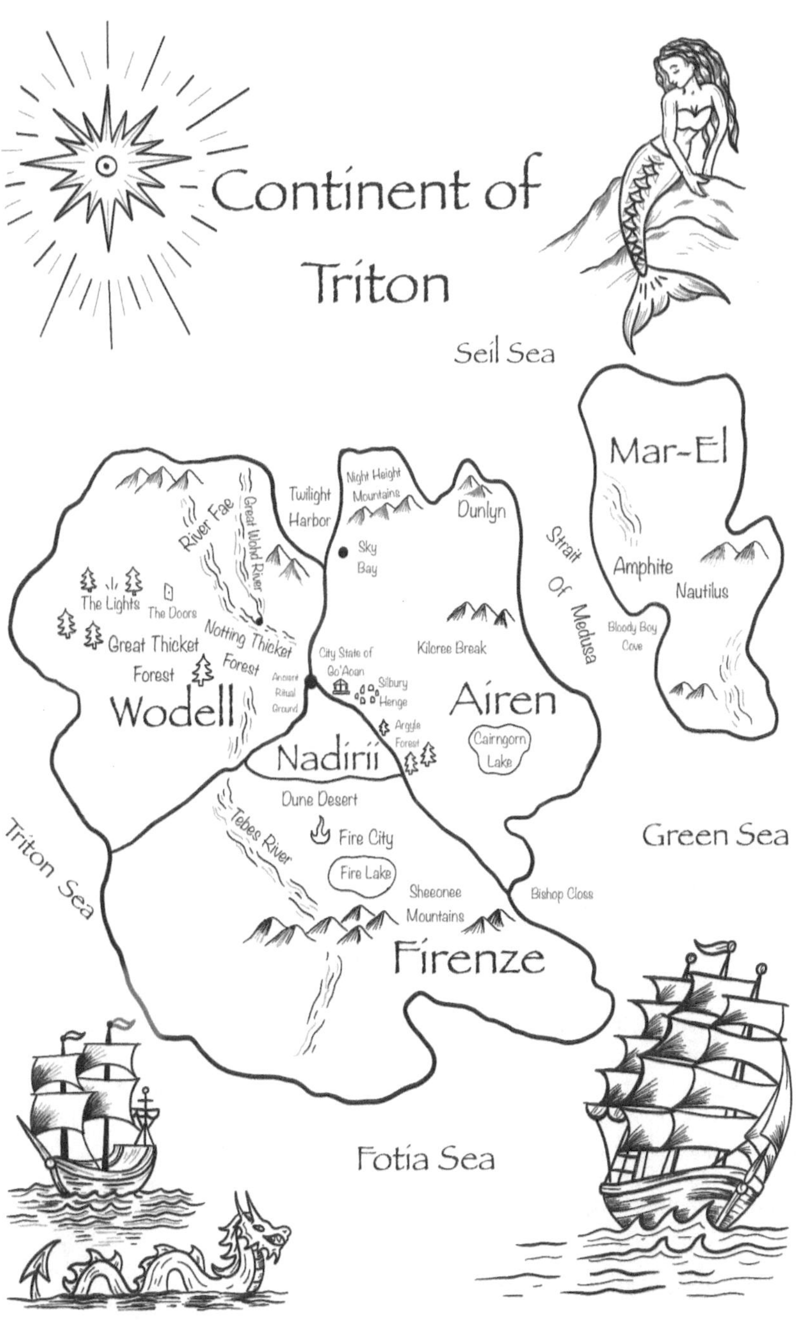
Continent of
Triton
Seil Sea
Mar-El
Twilight
Harbor
Night Height
Mountains
Dunlyn
River Fae
Great World River
Sky
Bay
Amphite
Nautilus
The Lights
The Doors
Notting Thicket
Forest
Great Thicket
Forest
Kiloree Break
Strait Of Medusa
Bloody Boy
Cove
Wodell
Ancient
Ritual
Ground
City State of
Go'Aoan
Silbury
Henge
Airen
Argyle
Forest
Cairngorn
Lake
Nadirii
Green Sea
Dune Desert
Tebes River
Fire City
Fire Lake
Sheeonee
Mountains
Bishop Closs
Triton Sea
Firenze
Fotia Sea

The Beginning of Everything

A LOVE IS EVERYTHING SAGA BY

KRISTEN

NEW YORK TIMES BESTSELLING AUTHOR

ASHLEY

PROLOGUE
THE PROPHECY

Once upon a time, in a parallel universe, there existed an abundance of beauty and riches on the continent of Triton.

Yet for millennia, the peoples within it knew nothing but mistrust and oppression and war.

Peace was not the destiny chosen by the rulers.

Differences were reviled.

Subjugation was observed.

Conflict was sought.

One cold night in Sky City, broken from centuries of exploitation, finding themselves without an alternate course, the women gathered their magicks and made the ultimate sacrifice.

They slayed the men who were their masters.

Leaving their sons and gathering their daughters, they fled the city and created The Enchantments of the Warrior Sisterhood of the Nadirii.

In the magical, green, sunny forest of The Enchantments, mighty trees charmed by their witches grew tall and strong, providing tree-homes for the sisterhood of the skilled warriors of the Nadirii. The sisterhood welcomed all who beseeched their Enchantments to escape their oppressors and thus grew and thrived through loyalty and trust.

And earned the wrath of men who sought to collect them.

The rest of Triton grew fractured, splintering into different realms.

There were the sun-drenched dunes and mountains of the wealthy, wanton and barbarous southern region of Firenze whose mines of jewels, northern fields of spices and rare silk made them the richest nation of Triton.

And their riches were coveted by others.

Then there were the wet, fertile, wooded forests, dells and plains of the virtuous northwest region of Wodell, whose sheep produced the best wool on the planet, and whose crops and orchards fed the continent.

And whose people tired of war and chafed under a weak king.

Further, there were the black crags of the northern shores and the rolling fields inland of the cultured nation of Airen, producing olives and wine and the best leather and weapons on the continent.

And populated by men who had not learned.

And there was the island continent of Mar-el. Its barren shores of rock and beach forced its people to live by the sea and become fishermen, sailors...and pirates. But within its boundaries, there was a secret.

And its peoples remained removed from the rest by decree of their king.

Last, there was the Dome City. Known for its resplendent golden domes, the city-state was the place of the religion and practitioners of Go'Doan. The priests and their mysterious female acolytes held fast to three sacred missions: education, healing, and most of all, extending their beliefs.

But even after the Night of the Fallen Masters that saw the birth of the Nadirii...

Dissension, assassination, rebellion and conflict reigned across the continent of Triton.

And then there were those...

Those who would see the dominion of all in all lands, the peoples of the nations of Triton cowed to their whims and controlled by new masters.

And it was those who conspired to reawaken the Beast, a fearsome creature who wrought tragedy and devastation across the continent who had been vanquished centuries before.

Foreseeing this, a powerful coven of witches proclaimed the prophecy.

Triton's four strongest warriors must wed its four most powerful witches, binding all nations together.

There is the quiet maiden, Silence, born of Wodell.

And the savage king, Mars, born of Firenze.

And the cold warrior, Cassius, born to Airen.

And the fierce witch, Elena, born to the Nadirii.

And the steadfast soldier, True, born to Wodell.

And the banished beauty, Farah, born to Firenze.

And the pirate king, Aramus, ascended in Mar-el.

To make the crusading Ha-Lah his queen.

If these men and women could see beyond their differences of culture and history, pride, politics and pasts—and love could prevail— their strength and magicks would flourish...

Then, they could face The Rising.

And perhaps defeat the Beast.

The time has come.

He has been awakened...

And he is rising...

I

THE FEEDING

The Priest
Ancient Ritual Ground, Lesser Thicket Forest
Wodell

He stood removed from his four brothers as they did their work.

It wasn't that he didn't have the stomach for it.

Well, not *this* part of it.

The part that had just been completed however…

The part that meant the virgin staked naked to the dirt, arms wide overhead, legs spread-eagle, was virgin no more. The seed of four men flowed from her into the earth.

That part he had no stomach for.

It was the next part he rather enjoyed.

He was happy to note she'd long-since stopped screaming.

"Continue," he commanded when one of the men who'd again donned his dark-gray robe turned his head the priest's way for instructions.

This was when it happened. When the ritual set his blood to quickening. His skin heating.

It was when the men approached her with their daggers drawn, and when they'd gained their places, they fell to their knees.

She had it in her for but a mere whimper when the first blade slid into her left side at her waist.

And then out, the blood swelling from the wound, rippling toward the earth.

Another, slighter whimper when the other blade slid into her right side.

And out.

The next slid precisely, nicking her heart, causing an actual gasp.

And then out.

And the next, her womb with an upward slice, and at that point, no sound at all.

The dagger was pulled out.

That was when the priest moved in his white robes toward her, his fingers wrapping lovingly around his own dagger at his gilded belt.

There was naught left of her to even turn her head and look at him, even if she still breathed. She did nothing but stare at the starry sky through the leafy trees. The pumps of blood surging from her chest slowing as that organ lost its strength were her body's indication of its desperate desire to stay bound in this realm, even if, perhaps, she did not share this wish.

She would find peace.

He did not know that for certain, but at this point, did it really matter?

He crouched close to her glossy brown hair that was now filled with dirt and mud and twigs and leaves, tangled, even ratted in places, due to her struggles that night.

She had been a spirited one.

The Beast liked those best.

"I'm sorry, my dear. We must feed the Beast," he murmured before he skated his blade across her windpipe, opening flesh and creating a surge of blood.

A gurgle from her lips.

Then two.

After that, the priest watched the light blink out of her lovely blue eyes.

He rose, stepped back, and commanded, "Untether her and turn her in order she drain direct."

The four men moved as ordered.

The priest stood separate, watching, waiting.

And when it came, it was more than satisfactory.

Much more.

The rumble, the growl, the roll of the earth under their feet so powerful, it almost took him off his own.

It had not been thus a fortnight before.

Most definitely not the fortnight before that.

Decades ago, when he assumed his role as the overseer of the ritual, there was barely a rumble, and no growl.

But now, it grew strong.

And hungry.

"My lord," one of the men called, eyes wide and on the priest.

"Not long now," the priest announced.

"Then every week," another of the men declared. "Centuries of the ritual. The sacrifices. So close. I can feel his strength. His hunger. Every week we shall join at this sacred place and—"

"No," the priest denied. "Every month."

"*Month?*" another man asked with incredulity. "It's been every fortnight for two and a half *centuries.*"

"You'll anger the Beast," the impatient collaborator snapped.

"He must understand who his master is," the priest reminded them.

"Who his masters *are,*" the man corrected him, and the priest narrowed his eyes.

When the Beast was his, that one would go first.

"Of course," the priest murmured.

"Every month seems—"

"*We* feed it. *We* nurture it. *We* give it what it needs. *We* make it grow strong. It will be *we* who liberate it. He must learn patience. He must learn gratitude. He must learn," he leaned toward the men, "*servitude.*"

The priest leaned back and moved his gaze through the four men, assessing each one.

He did linger on his favorite though, as was his wont, for there was much to linger on.

They had been chosen carefully. They had been trained accordingly. They, and those who had come before them, had lived, plotted, schemed, raped and murdered for one goal.

The goal they'd achieve while these men's feet walked the earth.

While *his* feet walked the earth.

And what he saw then was that these men knew it.

The priest would have patience. They would give it to him.

For if they did, they would all be kings.

(Save one, but he'd always been bothersome.)

"We have known, as our brothers before us, and those before them, and backwards for over two hundred years what we wish," the priest stated. "The lore is not lore. The Beast abides in the under-realm. Banished there after his last rising. He will rise again. He will be ours." He paused for effect, something he felt he was quite good at, before declaring grandly, "And then *Triton* will be *ours*."

There came a low "Huzzah" from his conspirators, but then again, a loud roar would not be the thing. They were deep in the forest. There was no one close.

But it wouldn't do for their sacred site that had stayed secret for over two hundred years to be discovered at this late date.

Obviously most especially after a ritual.

"She is surely drained," the priest noted. "Take her. Tonight, our work is done. We meet again in a month. And it's," his gaze fell on the impatient accomplice, "*your* turn to find the candidate."

His least-liked brethren gave the priest a look that said he wished to open his mouth and share something.

Wisely, he did not.

With ease borne of practice, the sacrifice was wrapped in a sheet, loaded on a horse, and with cursory farewells, three of the four men were away.

Leaving the priest with his favorite.

"Are you certain we should wait an entire month?" his chosen one asked as the priest drew close to him. "That growl seemed—"

"Open your robes," the priest ordered quietly.

Looking up, he saw his brother's eyes fire.

Gratifyingly, he then opened his robes and bared himself.

It was gratifying as it was so soon after he spent himself inside the vessel.

And it was gratifying because it was so beautiful to look at.

The priest dropped to his knees and took the shaft deep into his mouth.

And more gratification at the rumbling groan.

He tasted her for a but few strokes.

After that, he tasted only *man*.

Later, his snowy robes cast aside, naked on all fours in the moonlight, taking hard, thick cock through his arse, hands and knees in the blood-soaked earth, the priest's head jerked back, and he called his pleasure into the moonlit night as he spent his seed into the dirt.

His chosen one milked him dry before his thrusts grew in violence and he shot deep inside.

Finished, he ground there, murmuring, "Gods, but your arse is tight and hot."

"You really must remember to bring oil, Rupert," the priest muttered.

He felt his lover curl over him, still hard inside.

"You like the pain," he whispered in the priest's ear.

Indeed.

"Pull out. Needs be we're away."

Knowing precisely how he liked it, the end of the penetration was rough, making the priest moan.

"Oh yes, he likes the pain," was whispered above him.

The priest ignored that as he took a moment to rub his seed into the dirt.

There was no growl at that.

Just a hum.

And having done this, just like this (though with different partners), for over a decade, the priest knew he was the only one who felt the hum.

So he knew who the Beast's true master would be.

2

THE STANDING STONES

The Great Coven
Silbury Henge, Argyll Forest
AIREN

In the clearing of the forest, the first flash of light came before the first of the five standing stones.

It was marine blue.

As the woman stepped forward out of the flash, immediately, the stone next to her lit with red light.

And that woman stepped forward.

The next, the light was green.

And after that woman stepped forward, a flash of bright white.

That woman joined the others at the slab at the center of the circle.

A slab that in ancient times had known the blood of humans, then the blood of animals.

But for millennia, it had known no offering but the wind that shorn its edges curved and smooth, the rain that beat its height into the dirt, the sun that bleached its color.

Just as the standing stones around it. Once standing tall and proud over two stories toward the sky, now, they stood just over one, the edges dulled, one having taken a strike of lightning, weakening it, so a fragment broke off and plummeted, bedding itself in the earth by its sister's side.

The four women turned.

The fifth light flashed coral and through it came Ophelia, Queen of the Nadirii Sisterhood.

"Sister."

"Sister."

"Sister."

"Sister."

"My sisters," Ophelia murmured in greeting, taking her place amongst her sistren at the slab.

"Fare thee well?" Rebecca of the Dellish asked, her gaze sharp on the queen.

"Not tonight. The disturbance has occurred again, right on cue," Ophelia replied.

That was not the answer to Rebecca's question and Ophelia knew it.

Rebecca did not prompt.

"We have work to do," Lena of the Mar-el noted, moving closer to the altar.

The rest followed suit.

Lena began.

Touching the stone with her fingertips, she stated clearly, "The moon."

Nandra of the Firenz touched the stone. "The blood."

Fern of the Airenzian touched it. "The star."

Rebecca followed suit. "The dirt."

Ophelia went last. "The sisterhood."

A frisson of energy slithered up their arms, singing under their feet, vibrating in the stones, and the simple ritual complete, the circle united, the coven present, they took their hands away.

"They rouse the Beast," Rebecca told them what they all already knew and had, for some years now.

"They are cloaked. At the power of the last rousing, I spent the fortnight trying to find them and naught else. No sleep, no food, deep in meditation, casting spells that have not been attempted in centuries. And I could not," Lena declared.

"They have a powerful sorcerer among them," Ophelia murmured.

"Go'Doan?" Nandra asked bitingly.

Ophelia looked to her sister, sharing her dislike of the Go'Doan, at least some of them, (well, truly, most of them) but not showing it. "I suspect, but I cannot be sure. I cannot feel them either."

This was a surprise.

Especially after all these years of trying.

They were the most powerful witches of their lands, Ophelia by far the most powerful among them.

That was not strictly true.

They were the most powerful witches anyone of their lands knew.

At the now.

It would seem the others would need to be revealed.

"The prophecy must commence," Fern shared.

All the witches closely watched Ophelia after this was uttered.

But it was true.

When the Beast was banished, the coven had risen.

And every generation for millennia, the daughters were selected.

And the sons.

Just for this happenstance.

In order that they could banish it back.

"We can delay no longer, Ophelia," Rebecca said kindly. "We've all attempted to find them. We've all cast repeatedly to stop them. We've spent the last two years in these endeavors. It's come too far. The Beast has awoken. He rises closer to the surface. I no longer need to feel the earth move to know this is true. I feel...*it* when they feed him."

"You worry about your daughter," Lena noted, still regarding Ophelia closely.

"I worry about all of our daughters," Ophelia replied.

"It is too true. None of this will be readily accepted," Fern said under her breath.

"You mean none of *them* will be readily accepted," Nandra declared irritably. "As ever, it is the woman's wont to seek and build her place with the man. Especially in *your* land."

Fern looked away, color coming to her cheeks, but Ophelia spoke.

"We must not be cross amongst ourselves. It will serve no purpose. Fern, of any of us, even the Nadirii, is aware of what takes place in her land."

Nandra closed her mouth.

"Of the daughters sent forth, yours, I fear, my sister, my friend, will have the most difficult path to walk," Rebecca remarked to Ophelia. "We, none of us, have blood in this game. It is not one from our own wombs who go forth into this tribulation. Only yours."

"I am aware of that," Ophelia responded. "But my Elena will, as ever, walk with shoulders squared to make her sacrifice." Ophelia glanced amongst her sisters. "They all will. The lore has endured for millennia. The devastation the Beast wrought to this earth and its peoples may have become stories parents tell their children to give them a different type of chill on a cold winter night. But the Go'Doan will have felt it. The witches. The seers. The sorcerers. The veil of magic grows restless across Triton. Not one of them will desist. They will all agree. And it is not entirely a bad hand they've been dealt."

"You are, of course, talking about the warriors," Lena said tetchily.

"Or the warriors with staffs they only hold in their hands for personal purposes," Rebecca murmured.

Ophelia drew breath in through her nose as her way of affirming.

"We must toss the tiles, make the matches and be done with it," Nandra declared. "We all have rulers we must speak with and convince of their futures. And the tossing of the tiles will by far be the least onerous of our endeavors."

She was correct.

On all accounts.

Including the fact they must toss the tiles.

Ophelia felt her heart clench.

"The Head is already mated with The Crystal, so I shall not toss," Lena pointed out. "And it would best be remembered that has come about."

"And why is that?" Nandra asked.

"Because it shares that this is destiny. They were meant to be," Lena replied. "They mated without our intervention as, it could be, the others if given time would do as well."

Ah, Lena.

Brusque to the witness, but soft within.

She sought to make Ophelia dread less what might be coming, especially in her current state.

But there was naught which could make Ophelia dread less what might be coming, no matter what the tiles decreed.

She had hoped her daughter would succeed her.

Second born.

But born to rule.

"It's my understanding Aramus and Ha-Lah detest each other," Nandra returned. "Has your king even consummated the union?"

"Not for lack of trying," Lena retorted.

"His seed spent on his stomach is why we don't feel their growing power," Nandra observed.

"I'm uncertain when he spends his seed, it's on his stomach…at least not regularly," Lena muttered.

"That is worse," Rebecca uncharacteristically snapped.

"Ah, the Dellish and their quaint customs," Nandra muttered in return, her full lips quirking.

"Perhaps The Crystal will be more disposed to his charms if she knows mating with him will save the land," Lena rejoined swiftly before Rebecca could.

"I hear she's quite feisty, so even that might not work," Fern murmured while leaning toward Rebecca.

"Bring forth the tiles," Ophelia bid on a sigh.

Rebecca dug into the pocket of her skirts to find her tiles, her gaze on Ophelia, her tone again gentle.

"Would you wish to go first, my sister?" she offered.

"My daughter's match will be the last," Ophelia declined. "She will take what is left."

They all felt that was wise. If Ophelia tossed the tiles, the magic would make the selection, but it would be direct from her hand where the fates aimed her Elena.

However, before they could decide who would go first—Wodell, Firenze or Airen—Rebecca bumbled the tiles in her hand.

Or…

She did not.

Either way, they burst from her hold and clattered on the slab.

Rebecca and Fern gasped.

Nandra's eyes grew wide.

Lena smiled.

Ophelia watched intently.

Sparks of cool marine, bright vermillion, leaf green, striking white and deep coral danced as the rectangular cream tiles danced.

The one with the crossed bow and arrow imprinted in black on two sides.

The Warrior.

Signifying Elena of the Nadirii. Princess of the Sisterhood. Daughter of Ophelia.

The one with the diamond shape.

The Crystal.

Ha-Lah of the Mar-el. New queen to King Aramus of the island nation of pirates.

The one with the shroud.

The Shadow.

Silence of the Dellish. Countess of the Arbor. Niece of the king.

The one with the hand with the eye in the palm.

The Sage.

Farah of the Firenze. Daughter to a traitor. Stripped of status and possessions. Living in the desert in exile.

Then there was the one with the upside-down triangle in the circle to which at two sides there were wings.

The Head.

Aramus. King of the Mar-el. Pirate. Protector of the Seas.

And the one with one triangle over the other in a circle, around which there was a flower.

The Heart.

True. Prince of the Dellish. Heir to the throne.

And the one with the crescent moon at the top, surrounded by two circles, which was surrounded by lotus petals.

The Cock.

Mars. King of Firenze. Ascended the throne after his father's assassination. Ruled now beloved by his people.

And the last, another upside-down triangle in which was a flame over a lamp, boxed in a square, surrounded by a circle, out of which, north, south, east, west, sprung lotus petals.

The Balls.

Cassius. The Second Son. Prince of Airen. Born but a soldier and now heir to the throne.

With a clatter, The Crystal and The Head shot together, clacked loudly, sparked marine fire and dropped as one tile with now the crystal in the center of the insignia.

The others snapped and rattled.

And with a strike of vermillion, The Sage mated with The Heart and fell to the altar, the wise hand now embedded in the center of the triangle on the sign.

And then there was a flash of green, The Shadow united with The Cock and fell to the alter, the shroud gone, a face with eyes wide open, lips curved into a small smile where the crescent moon had been.

It was that which made Ophelia emit a hushed whine she could not control before the blaze of coral took The Warrior tile straight to The Balls, and with a muted explosion, they dropped to the slab, the candle gone, a unicorn now standing proud in the center of the symbol.

The magic receded, and the altar was lit only by moonlight as the witches stared down.

They knew Aramus and Ha-Lah.

But now it was Farah and True.

Silence and Mars.

And Elena and Cassius.

There could be no worse coupling for Ophelia.

For *Elena.*

It was her deepest fear.

Realized.

Rebecca spoke first.

"I am sorry, my sister."

"As am I."

"As am I."

"As am I."

Ophelia gazed at the unicorn on the final tile for long moments, hoping its magic and abundance signified something promising, before she lifted her eyes to her sistren.

"It is done," she announced.

It was not.

Not yet.

But it would be.

By every goddess and all things holy.

Ophelia just yearned deep into the core of her heart that none of those daughters suffered.

Overly much.

Especially her own.

But alas, for her own daughter she feared she would not be there to see.

3

THE SECOND SON

Prince Cassius Laird
Crown Prince's Bedchamber, Sky Citadel, Sky Bay
Airen

Cassius held his hand over the maid's mouth as he thrust inside her, his other hand tucked between her legs, his middle finger busy.

And effective, if the difficulty he was having containing her moans and whimpers and muted "*Pleases*" and "*Mores*" and "*Harders*" could be credited.

Fortunately, in short order, she climaxed.

Now, finally, he could see to himself.

This he did as swiftly as possible and with a grunt that he did not try to stifle and not only because it was not loud.

What had just happened had been...

Adequate.

He did not bow into her when he finished in order to recover, mostly because there was not much from which to recover.

Drawing breath, he pulled out, dropped her skirts that he'd been holding up with a forearm at the front, her hips had done that at the back, and stepped away from her where she held on to one of the posts of his bed.

He put both hands to the buttons of his leathers after he tucked his still-wet-and-hard cock inside. He'd wash her from him later, when she could not see.

"Your Grace," she whispered, her voice trembling.

"Thank you," he muttered, moving toward the door, continuing to button his trousers.

"Your Grace!" she called.

By the bloody gods, this was the part he hated the worst.

He turned eyes to her to see she had languid, but bright and hopeful eyes on him.

"It is...always so quick. I could...visit you in the night," she offered haltingly.

"No," Cassius declined abruptly, turned and strode from the room.

Only to practically run into Mac as he made his turn into the passageway seeing as his man was leaning, shoulders against the black stone of the citadel right by the door to Cassius's bedchamber, head turned toward Cassius, sly smile on his mouth.

"We should get you a professional, my brother. You'd climax a whole lot louder," Mac, or as his father had named him, Macrinus offered.

"I tire of my hand," Cassius murmured, continuing to walk down the wide passageway, his boots muted by the thick runner swirled in dark colors from black to charcoal to midnight with bare hints of silver.

If you had the time, which he rarely had, and you stood in the corridor and allowed your eyes to take it in, the long expanse of runner looked like a never-ending strip of the night sky.

In truth, all about him was dark. The black stone of the castle. The carpet. The wrought iron around the large, grand and ostentatious chandeliers dangling from chains along the ceiling. The long, heavy, midnight velvet draperies dressing the sides of the wide, spiked windows to his right. The black leather shirt, trousers and boots covering his and Macrinus's bodies.

Bloody dark.

The lot of it.

A physical metaphor for Cassius's life.

Mac fell in step beside him. "You know, it's not just a bodily function."

This he knew.

So very well.

Cassius just stopped himself from closing his eyes at just how much he knew precisely that and kept on without breaking stride.

Macrinus's tone was much altered when he began, "Brother—"

"Speak more on this topic, you'll be doing it through swallowing your teeth," Cassius bit out.

Mac gave it a moment, striding beside him, before he said, "I wasn't hanging about outside your room for an audible audition of the comely maid you've chosen, Cass. Your father sent me to get you."

At that, Cassius stopped short and turned to his friend.

"For fuck's sake, *why?*" he demanded.

"I don't know," Mac answered. "The earth is round. The sky is blue. His eggs weren't done to his liking this morning. He breathes. You breathe. I breathe. Does Gallienus need a reason to demand your presence?"

Unfortunately, his father did not and never had.

This being not only because the man was his father but because he was also king.

Cassius resumed walking.

Mac did as well.

"The tremor happened again last night," Macrinus noted unnecessarily.

"I know, Mac," Cass said on a sigh. "I felt it. The trolls and pixies and gnomes felt it. Even the mermaids and gogmagogs probably felt it."

"Well, my guess is, earthquakes don't happen every fortnight on the hour for months," Mac declared.

Not missing a step, Cassius spared him a glance, inquiring, "Do you think?"

Mac's heavy brows snapped together. "You're in a foul mood for a man who's just used a maid for good purpose."

Cassius stopped dead.

So did Mac and his brow had not cleared.

"You need to—" his friend began.

"Be careful how you finish that," Cassius growled.

"Cass, it's been six years," Macrinus growled in return.

Cassius turned fully to him, lifting his brows and crossing his arms on his chest. "And this? This is something you know? Is this the amount of time it takes to heal after watching your wife grunt and sweat and scream and push and pray and *bleed* as she expels your daughter into your own gods-damned *bloody* hands? And then the last thing on this earth she does is smile at her wee babe, smile in your face, and then *die?*"

"You know I have no wife and you know I can't imagine—"

"No," Cassius grunted, turning, dropping his arms and resuming his gait. "You can't. So cease speaking of it."

"Liviana would not wish for you to go on like—"

His friend didn't finish mostly because he had Cassius's hand wrapped around his throat and he'd been slammed against the black stone wall in a passageway of the Sky Citadel, the castle of the King of Airen, situated in the capital city of that great and terrible realm.

"Do not," he rumbled, his face an inch from Mac's, "speak of what Liviana would wish."

Mac didn't fight.

He also didn't give up.

"She would not wish it and you know it. She'd want you to find happiness and not with a bloody *maid.*"

Like what he did with that maid brought him happiness.

He hadn't been truly happy, sadly even in his daughter's presence, in six bloody years.

Cassius's fingers squeezed. "I'm warning you, Mac."

"And Aelia needs a mother," Macrinus spat.

Dear gods, he could actually *feel* the blood swarming in his head.

"For the gods sakes, would you two break it up," Nero called, and both men looked to the side to see their brother striding their way. "Gallienus is in a snit. Whatever this is, finish it later."

Cassius let his hand drop and turned away from Mac. "He sent you too?"

"He's called for all your lieutenants, and when you didn't arrive, oh, about two seconds after Mac departed to get you, he started getting testy," Nero returned. "Or...*testier.*"

Cassius's head turned again toward Mac. "You did not share this."

"Sorry, I was too busy being accosted to dive deeply into all of this morn's news," Macrinus retorted.

Cassius moved his attention to Nero who had joined them. "Why are you all there?"

"I've no clue. I also don't much care outside of having things to do this morning, wishing to do them, therefore also wishing whatever this is to be done so I can go about doing them. In other words, will you two stop dawdling?"

On that, Nero turned and prowled in the direction he'd come.

"We'll finish later, *not* with your hand around my throat," Mac muttered.

"We'll speak no more of it, with my hand at your throat or otherwise," Cassius muttered in return and resumed walking, now following Nero.

Macrinus was wise enough to keep silent.

Indeed, he was wise most of the time.

It would seem when he was tired of seeing his brother suffer that his wisdom receded.

In fairness, if the table was turned, he could see himself intervening with Mac.

That table, however, was not turned.

They descended the stairs, hit the grand entryway with its threatening, spiked, intricate, wrought iron candelabrum that was the breadth of two men—two *tall* men—hanging over it.

They turned left, as Nero had done, into the Great Hall where Gallienus held court, as his father had before him, and his, and depressingly for centuries before that, their fathers.

The king sat in the large, midnight-velvet-cushioned, dark-wood chair which was intricately carved, tall steeples rising high at each side, several feet over his father's head. This behind a long table set on a raised dais where, during feasts, or required dinners as summoned by the king (which were often), Cassius sat to his father's right.

And his three wives surrounded them.

It was nauseating, not only being in his father's presence during these times (or at all), but also that his father was a man who was so little of a man he could not find what he needed in one wife.

He had none of their love.

Just their greed, need for status, fear, or all three.

Fortunately, after his father's first attempt, he did not demand his granddaughter attend him there.

He had a second son, a spare to the throne.

When he attempted to make his rule include his granddaughter, he learned he would not have even that.

Gallienus never again made that attempt.

As he walked through the tables where the appalling number of courtiers sat to dine when his father was in full king mode, which was nearly nightly, Cassius saw that, indeed, all of his men were around. His personal guard. And this had been true even when they were but simply soldiers.

Then again, they each thought of all as their own personal guard.

As it should be with soldiers.

Macrinus, of course. Nero as well. Otho. Antonius. Severus. And Hadrian.

Every one a general.

Every one had things to do.

Cassius knew whatever was to come would not be a blessing.

He stopped directly in front of his father, absolutely did not bow, but instead noted, "You summoned?"

Cassius endured the flash of displeasure from his father's eyes and it was not difficult to do so.

"Before I even had breakfast served to me, the witch Fern demanded an audience," his father began.

"Is she still alive? Or have you had her beheaded for her insolence?" Cassius asked drolly.

"I can have you beheaded for yours," Gallienus snapped.

"The truth of the gods, I might welcome it for it'd put me out of my misery," Cassius murmured.

"And what of Aelia?" Gallienus pressed snidely.

Cassius felt a sharp pang rend his heart.

"She has six fathers. She'll be all right," he returned.

"This is not getting us to where I wish us to be," Gallienus noted hostilely.

"Please," Cassius rolled a hand, "do proceed."

"I'm delighted beyond measure I have your permission," Gallienus rapped out.

Cass sighed.

"The witch Fern has shared that the tremors mean the Beast is being roused," Gallienus announced.

Cassius's back shot straight and he felt the air in the room turn thick as his men went alert.

"You jest," Cass whispered.

"I wish I did. Alas, I do not. All of the witches have met. They've been trying to put a stop to it as well as discover who's behind it. Someone is rousing the Beast. They mean for it to rise. To surface. For what purpose, I don't know, and it doesn't matter. As it seems they cannot stop this from happening, we must be prepared."

"And how exactly do we prepare?" Cass demanded. "If lore is true, nearly the entire population of the continent of Triton fell to this Beast before they fled to Mar-el. It was only the Beast's aversion to water that kept them safe. But it's been so long, and there are so many incarnations to that story, we can't begin to truly know how it happened. Some say magical forces banished it. Some say the water injured it and it slithered home to recover. Others say—"

"I know the lore, Cassius," his father interrupted him. "I also know that the Great Coven was formed back then for this exact purpose. They've met over the millennia for other reasons, but there's a plan they concocted in that ancient time that they've carefully nurtured over the centuries. And the time is nigh for them to put it into action."

"And the plan is?" Cassius queried.

"King Mars will marry Wilmer's niece, a girl named Silence."

Cass did not at all like how this had started.

And he knew, irrefutably, that Mars was going to lose his mind at having to marry a Wodell.

"And how is this marriage—?"

"And Prince True will marry a Firenz woman called Farah."

Sad for True, who many said was deeply in love with the second daughter of the Nadirii.

However, he couldn't think on True because this wasn't getting any better.

"Oh shite," Cass heard Otho mutter behind him.

Yes, it was not getting any better.

Gallienus didn't hesitate.

But he did look like saying the words made him ill.

"And you will marry Elena, second daughter to Ophelia of the Nadirii."

He felt his brothers sidle closer to his back, but even so, there was no sound in a room that seemed stripped of its capacity to carry noise, so heavy was the silence.

Finally, Cass was able to control his fury enough to declare, "That cannot happen."

"Apparently, it must."

"She's Nadirii."

"Nauseatingly, this she is," his father spat. "And her sister killed your brother, my son, the heir to my throne."

This, Cassius could dispute and every man in that room, save his father, would dispute it.

Trajan died of pride.

Serena, first-born Princess of the Nadirii Sisterhood, had, indeed, inflicted a wound on Trajan that had ended being mortal.

But if he'd had it cleansed, stitched, tended, treated, and the proud fool had rested, perhaps a day, or better, three, or best, two weeks, he'd be of this earth.

Enraged Serena had wounded him, he'd refused even a cleansing, carrying on a battle that was entirely lost, doing this for three days, losing scores of men, eventually falling weak as the poison set in the wound, and after suffering greatly, dying.

Serena might brag as broadly as she could that she'd killed the heir to Airen, and she did brag, as was her way.

But Trajan had died, if not at his own hand, to his own prideful, reckless, unwise, irresponsible decisions, which was poetic, in its way, as in his life, he had made many.

There was not great love lost between brothers. Cass's brothers were not of his blood.

And they were all in that room.

But this meant Cassius Laird was not what he wished to be, a general in his father's army, free (for the most part) to live his life as he pleased without the yoke of his father's wishes weighing at his neck before the yoke of ruling bore down on it.

Now, he was heir to the throne and facing just that until his dying breath.

"I'll not marry her," Cass said low.

His father gave him a sick smile. "Apparently, she's a powerful witch whose power will grow momentously with the injection of your seed." His smile died. "And there is the matter of you siring me a grandson to secure the throne to the direct line for the next generation."

Aelia was bright, observant, learned quickly, was kind of heart, generous of spirt, sound of logic and thus would make a stupendous queen.

Cassius would never suggest that while his father was breathing, or he would indeed face a noose.

Or a guillotine.

"You suggest the next in line have Nadirii blood," he reminded Gallienus.

"At this point, I don't care if he has mermaid blood," Gallienus retorted.

"Nadirii don't abide male children," Cassius went on.

"She can't exactly put a future king in a basket and set him outside some cottager's home, now, can she?" Gallienus returned.

"They ceased doing that a century ago, Father. They've now learned to use magic to stop conceiving a male child."

"Well, you'll have to find some way to stop *her* from doing *that*, won't you?" Gallienus snapped. "And I daresay Fern can help you handle it. She knows to serve her king well."

She did at that.

Not a female in Airen didn't know exactly how to serve their masters well.

Even, and perhaps especially, a powerful witch.

"The Airenzian will never accept a Nadirii queen," Cassius pointed out.

His father flipped a hand. "They'll have no choice. They can accept her, or they can run from the Beast." He shook his head. "But it really matters not if they accept her. Once the Beast is dispatched, she can reside in the dungeons and her cunt will still be there. You can visit her, sire a son, take him, and she can rot there for all I care."

Cassius drew breath into his nose, and wondered, not for the first time, if his mother had found a man who looked much like his father and that was his true sire.

She was very dead, therefore he'd never know.

Oddly, Gallienus's tone gentled. "It is done, my son. There's aught to do about it. The others will have learned this news or will be learning it soon. We have no choice. We must ride for Firenze soon, leaving our staff behind to prepare for a royal wedding."

Trajan's decision to battle on wounded by a woman meant this was Cassius's life.

He had no choice.

In anything.

But with a fury beginning to boil in him the strength he had not felt since he roared his lament when the life left his wife's body, he realized he was heir to a bloody throne and yet utterly powerless.

Including who he would, or would absolutely *not*, take to wife.

4

THE BLUESTOCKING

Lady Silence Mattson
Study Corridor, First Floor, Bower Manor, The Arbor
WODELL

I walked down the corridor, my feet in their slippers silent on the carpets.

I'd felt it in the night, the tremor. It brought a chill of fear and foreboding, as it had done now for months.

Even as the sensation of the earth moving was getting stronger, these feelings normally receded, perhaps slowly, but they did.

This time, they grew. So much, I was not able to regain sleep.

Now it was early evening of the next day and my father's house had seen much activity.

Including a visit from a royal messenger, straight from the king, which caused a flurry of activity not only from the servants, but from my mother and father as well.

As usual, I had not been a part of it.

So, as usual, I had to use certain means to discover what was happening.

This I did, wending my way toward my father's study, where I heard his voice, always loud and thus it traveled, as well as my mother's, which was neither.

I heard this long before anyone I knew would hear it.

It was an oddity of mine, one of many, this unnatural hearing.

I'd long since learned to hide it, just as I had long since learned to do what I did once I'd stolen even closer.

Shifting into a recess in that corridor of my father's castle, one that held a table with a bust of some proud, puffed out, male ancestor of mine that for some reason commissioned a sculptor to sculpt him while his lips sneered, I focused my mind, experienced the tingle up my spine, and I drew my cloak over me.

It shimmered just a moment before I felt the ethereal shadow overtake me, warm and snug.

Truth, I would live shrouded by my precious shadow if I could.

Not to be seen.

Not to be known.

Naught to be expected of me.

Naught for others to be disappointed about in me.

And mostly, naught for me to be disappointed about in others.

"Johan, we simply cannot ask this of Silence," my mother said shakily, taking me from my thoughts, and I focused my attention on their conversation.

"We won't be *asking* anything," my father retorted. "It is her duty to her king, her father, her title, this very *house*. And Vanka, it cannot be borne that you don't realize how bloody opportune this is. The chit has demonstrated we'd never find her a match, until now, and not surprisingly, it isn't *her* who made it."

My breath snagged.

A match?

My father continued.

"Now she'll be wed to *a king*."

Oh, by the goddesses, *no*.

Was King Gallienus looking for another wife?

He seemed to collect them at an alarming frequency, each one younger than the last.

Could he—?

My mother interrupted my rampant thoughts.

"It's only in his father's reign before him that land has even become a degree of civilized. They're still barbarians."

But...what?

The Airenzian could indeed be considered barbarians, if pressed. Their treatment of females left quite a bit to be desired. If history told it true, it was actually worse now after the Night of the Fallen Masters those centuries ago, when the Nadirii Sisterhood was born.

But mostly, it was civilized. They had laws (however, not reasonable ones for women). They had taxes. Schools. Hospitals. And they had the best engineers and architects in Triton, so they even had running water in their abodes, and in some, you could turn a lever, and it would run *hot*.

I couldn't say in my several journeys there that it was not austere (though the countryside was lovely, the vineyards, olive groves, vast fields of grain, and the lovely, large Cairngorms Lake was astonishingly beautiful).

However, Sky Bay was actually quite terrifying, the whole city built from that glinting black stone. Of course, the buildings were beautiful, in their way, considering the talent of the architects that designed them. They were still frightening.

And the severe citadel carved into the side of the highest peak overlooking the bay was *definitely* terrifying (though also quite lovely, in a daunting manner).

But for all intents and purposes, Airen was even more civilized than Wodell.

Unless you were female.

Though, even females in Wodell (and, I'd heard, in Firenze) didn't have it like the Nadirii.

Ah, to be a Nadirii.

I'd often thought I'd do quite well with the Sisterhood.

Though I didn't reckon I'd be very good with a sword.

Or a bow.

Or a staff.

Or daggers.

Alas, perhaps the Nadirii was not for me.

"They're also the richest nation in Triton," my father said, interrupting my thoughts.

I blinked into my shadow.

The richest nation in Triton was…

"The Firenz don't practice fidelity to their mates," my mother remarked sharply.

…Firenze!

"Not the men, *nor* the women," she went on. "And they have those wretched communal baths where they all, *women and men*, bathe naked…*together*. They freely engage in that *terrible* smoke. And the violence practiced there is irrational. They fight amongst themselves, *liberally*. Since his ascendance, the king himself has quelled *three* coup attempts. These happening in the first two years after he assumed the throne. But even if in the last three there have been no rebellions, there still has been fighting. Their clans regularly—"

"*You* don't have to live there," my father noted.

Shockingly, my mother's voice was rising. "But *my daughter* will!"

"By the goddess," I breathed.

The messenger from the king.

I was to marry King Mars of Firenze.

Balls and begorrah!

How had this come about?

"By the goddess," I repeated on a whisper.

"Yes, she will," my father declared.

Oh, by the goddess.

I was to marry King Mars of Firenze.

"He will not take to her," my mother snapped, and my heart lurched.

My father had very little use for me.

This was because my mother could not give him what he wanted, a son, or even a second child who was more to his liking than me. He had tried, in his ways (which were not enjoyable), to make me the daughter he wished me to be, the Countess of the Arbor he felt fit the title.

But I preferred my own company, truth be told. Or if I had it, the company of my mother, who was dear to me and in her way showed I was the same to her. Or Estrilda, my Tril, who had been my lady's maid for years now.

I liked people.

I was heartened by companionship.

I just did not enjoy groups and definitely not crowds. It was fun to watch, for a spell, but after that, it became boring and sometimes could feel oppressive.

I therefore preferred reading to attending large dinner parties. I did not enjoy dancing a'tall. I further did not enjoy making banal discourse with suitors (or, really, anyone).

This, indeed, was perhaps my least favorite thing in the world. And I'd long since learned if I attempted something not banal, exposing I had read many books, traveled across Wodell, Airen, even had been amongst The Enchantments of the Nadirii once on a state visit with my cousin, Prince True. Or if I shared about the many times I had been in the presence or at the courtly affairs of our very own King Wilmer, and I had watched and listened well, learning much, my dinner or dance companions were shocked.

I had become known as The Bluestocking.

When I was not known as The Mouse.

I did not find this insulting (though, the second wasn't my favorite).

My father found it infuriating.

He wanted a bright, lively (but empty-headed) daughter who made a spectacular match to build the power of his title, which would carry forward to my child through me.

Instead, he got me. A quiet, watchful mouse whose head was far from empty.

But now it seemed even my mother did not think I could turn the eye of a king.

By the goddess, I wasn't that difficult to look upon, was I?

I thought my ebony hair was rather lovely. Very long, it wasn't stick straight, it had nice curls. It also had a rather impressive gleam.

And I'd always liked my eyes. Even my father said I had extraordinary eyes (albeit he said this grudgingly). I'd never seen my eyes in another's face, not *ever*.

Silver.

Not a blue that could be construed as gray.

Silver.

Polished.

Shining.

Dare I say my own self...*luminous.*

I knew the servants (and others) whispered some male ancestor of mine had been able to charm a mermaid (or, perhaps, more shockingly, my mother a mermale), for there was no other explanation for my eyes.

(I didn't mind these whispers, by the by. If I had mermaid blood, that would explain a lot.)

Not to mention my skin wasn't bad a'tall. Nary a blemish. Pale to porcelain, if I was out in the elements, or had made some effort, what I thought was a becoming rose would tint my cheeks.

I wasn't unsightly and the abundance of suitors I still had regardless of the fact I demonstrated I had a brain twixt my ears would demonstrate this as truth.

At least to my thinking.

"It's my understanding he has no choice," my father replied.

"The Firenz women are known for their shocking beauty. They are tall. Lush. He will not be best pleased with the beauty our Silence can give him, even if it is most remarkable in a variety of ways."

I settled as that kindness, coming from my mother, was not surprising and part of it not being surprising was that it was lovely.

My mother was often kind like that (and gentle and thoughtful), with me and everybody.

That was, she was like that when my father wasn't around.

"I prayed to the gods for years to give her at least another inch, though I would have preferred five," my father murmured. "At the best of times, you can barely see the girl."

Sadly, he had not noticed that this was due to an effort I made, not simply because I was petite.

But I had seen some Firenz on occasion, men, often with their women, who had come through Wodell to hunt or acquire wool or attend our merchants.

They were all uncommonly tall, like their brother nation of Airen were.

Indeed, although I had only seen him from afar—and even though True was exceptionally tall, his build was lean—therefore Prince Cassius, with his height and bulk, seemed like a veritable giant.

The Firenz men were just like that.

And their women were far from dainty.

"Though, if I know a Firenz, at the very least he'll enjoy her curves," my father carried on.

One could say I did have curves.

"Johan, I beg you," my mother did indeed beg. "Speak with my brother. Ask him to find someone else to make this alliance. I know he's angered King Mars..."

This he had.

King Wilmer, my uncle, had angered the King of Firenze. Repeatedly.

It was a daft thing to do.

Everyone knew their warriors were unbeatable. They might fight amongst themselves, but when threatened, their clans allied and the front they made was invincible.

Even Serena of the Nadirii, who didn't seem to have trouble picking a fight with anyone, wasn't stupid enough to go against the Firenz.

Uncle Wilmer picked fights with them all the time.

"...but the Firenz are boisterous and rowdy," my mother continued. "They have more celebrations in a month than both Wodell and Airen together have in a year. They live *so very differently* than we do. The shock of culture change would be difficult for our Silence to countenance. She would not fit. She's safe here, with me, you, Tril, her amusements. She's our daughter. It's our duty to keep her safe."

"She's our daughter. It's *her* duty to strengthen our title," my father returned. "But you heard the messenger, Vanka. The Beast rises. The coven has made the matches. It is out of Wilmer's hands. It's not even in Mars's hands. It's definitely not in *our* hands. She must wed Mars. It's not simply her duty to me, her king, her country, but to all of Triton."

I heard my father, but I was having difficulty breathing.

The Beast rises?

The tremors.

Oh *faith*, the Beast *rises*.

And I, somehow, in the misfortune that seemed to make up the entirety of my life, had to wed the king of a barbaric, but wealthy, nation in order to...what?

It was not lost on me I could hear quite well. I had also learned some time ago that I read more simply regarding a person's expression than anyone I knew. And testing this mermaid theory, I was, indeed, able to dunk my head in the bath and hold my breath for long periods of time.

And then there was my shadow.

But I was no Nadirii, that was for certain. That Sisterhood of Warriors carried most of the magic in all the land. They'd amassed it ages ago to instigate the Night of the Fallen Masters. Even the weakest of their witches was stronger than any sorceress of Wodell.

But it was not lost on me I held magic.

And this must be the reason why I was destined to be consort to a barbarian king.

"But we have an opportunity," my father decreed. "We will make the best of this match as we can. Our daughter will be his wife, and it is known wide, even if fidelity is not expected, a Firenz warrior dotes on his chosen one. We will make the most of this with Firenz rubies, saffron, silk. We will be the richest house in Wodell. She finally has come to mean something to my title, *her* title. And if this is true, if she can make an alliance that will somehow defeat the Beast should it rise, she, and this house, will be *legend*, my Vanka. Not to mention, we will also be *rich*."

"And you'd sacrifice your own daughter to such aspirations of *greed*," my mother stated with disgust.

There was a moment of silence before my father's voice came again, and now it was gentle.

Therefore now, I knew that he had approached my mother and was cupping her cheek in that tender way he had that, even with the difficult relations I shared with my sire, always melted something inside me.

"I very early came to love you, my beautiful wife," he said. "It was impossible not to, and not simply due to your great beauty."

Yes, I felt that something melt inside me.

"But you know, my dearest love," he went on, "that your father made that same sacrifice of you. Yes, he was king, but you were the seventh of seven daughters, his chest was running low due to war with the Firenz, and the Arbor is the richest estate in the land. No other of your sisters made a better match, even begotten by the king. Our marriage was arranged to further strengthen his house, his chest, his alliances, and thus, also his title. Now, shh..." he shushed her, and I knew she'd opened her mouth to speak. "It is how things are done and you know it. So think not of what may come for Silence. At the very least, fates are explained for she is no frivolous chit with no thoughts of her own. She is canny and vigilant. This will aid her in the months to come."

"This is true," my mother murmured.

"And she may be legend, and this might not be something she desires for herself, but I have seen her disappointment that she consistently disappoints me," my father continued. But this was not true. My disappointment was that *he* disappointed *me*. "She will be glad of this match. She will be glad she has something important to do. She will be glad she's of service to her parents, her country, her continent. She will do her duty, my dearest. And in however way it comes about, in the end, it will be fine."

To that, my mother whispered something even I could not hear, and I sensed their discussion was ending.

Therefore, I scanned the corridor with eyes and ears before I released my shadow, stepped out of the recess and my inanimate (which was often how I preferred it) company of the bust, and hurried along the hall toward the stairs to get to my rooms.

I did this not sharing my father's sentiments.

First, the Beast was rising and that took more than a few moments of reflection.

I'd heard tales of the Beast as far back as I could cogitate, these coming from my nanny (who was a harridan, for what nanny would share such stories with a wee child? I remembered being very happy when my mother sacked her, and I fancied myself kind-hearted, but I was not sorry to see her go). And then spoken of freely around fires for no purpose but for the teller to spook the listeners.

But such tales always ended with the fact the Beast would someday again be roused. He would rise. And he would feast on wee children and snack on the babes and tear the women asunder with his horrifying shaft and rip the heads from the men, drinking their blood from their necks and making the women weave the hair together so he could wear them as a necklace.

Larger than a gogmagog by thrice, faster on foot than an eagle in flight, able to spew venom from his mouth—venom that with a single drop touching the skin could stun entire villages into immobility for days, beings wasting away from no food or water, unable to save themselves, frozen in the poison as still as statutes.

His rising was not to be borne.

And apparently, I somehow played some part in stopping it.

Which, frankly, scared the knickers off me.

Far more than being wed to the barbarian King Mars of Firenze.

But it must be said, if not equally as terrifying (for nothing was as frightening as the Beast), it was still bloody terrifying.

I did not want to be legend.

I didn't like any attention a'tall.

It seemed I had no choice in that.

Worse, the king of a neighboring country who evidently didn't exactly get along with my king (it must be said, King Wilmer did some rash things, he truly needed new counsel, I knew that even before True shared with me his (vast) frustrations about this very topic) had no choice in it either.

This absolutely did not bode good tidings.

What was worse, when I entered my bedchamber, I saw Tril standing there, her pretty face pale, her chignon at the back of her head coming loose like she'd been worrying it, and her mouth instantly moved.

"I've had orders from your father. I'm so very sorry, but we need to make haste in a wedding trousseau, my lovely. I'll explain on our way, but we must needs get to town. We have lace, satin and velvet to look at and it will take far less time for us to go to them than for me to summon them to us."

I stared into her charming, but anxious, hazel eyes.

Balls.

And bloody *begorrah*.

5

THE DAMNED

King Aramus Nereus
Throne Room, Keel Castle, Nautilus
Mar-el

Aramus felt like a bloody damned fool sitting on his ridiculous throne.

He never sat his throne.

If he was not on his ship, marauding, or hunting, he was in a pub, drinking, or at a table, feasting, or at a wench, doing other things.

And it didn't help that his men stood around the foot of it—or the eight-foot high sirens-damned *pedestal* of the thing—bloody snickering.

"Be gone," he ordered.

"And miss this?" his man Bondi asked.

Fuck, but if he relished the idea of marking his wife's perfect skin, something he did not, he'd have the bitch brought up, tied to the pedestal under his ludicrous throne and order her flogged.

"Cap, not sure it's a good idea to sit your throne," Tintagel called up to his seat. "Also not sure I need to remind you she's not cowed by authority."

Ha-Lah was not cowed by anything.

At first, he liked this about his wife.

Being married to the bloody woman for six months and not even tasting her cunt with his tongue, not feeling its wet even on the tip of a finger, this feeling was waning.

"Tint, take the men and get out," he ordered his most level-headed seaman.

"Let's go, men," Tint said without delay.

There you go.

Level-headed.

"Tint, my brother, this is bound to be good," Oreti, Aramus's *least* level-headed seaman protested.

Xi was looking up at his king, thus catching his expression, and therefore repeating after Tint, "Let's go, men."

Aramus got looks from Nissi, Navagio, and Catedrais. They read their captain and king and spared no time rounding up the dissenters.

Aramus watched as they walked across the cavernous expanse of the room, their boots sounding, then echoing in the massive space.

He had learned, at his father's knee, a father who sat in that very chair with Aramus's arse on a cushion on the wide dais surrounding it, sheltered by the six colossal ibex-whale horns that formed the base which measured at least fifteen feet across, the ten-foot tall tips curved around it, that the throne of the King of Mar-el had been built to intimidate anyone who walked in that room.

Ibex-whales, outside angmostros (though, thankfully, those massive eel creatures did not have horns), were the hardest thing in the sea to kill. That throne up on its five-foot wide, eight-foot high pedestal carved out of coral (that also had the stairs up to the damned thing pared out) having the mighty horns of three of said beasts was impressive even to Aramus, who'd killed four times that many in his lifetime.

But this was lost on just about everyone, considering the only being on the mainland he liked was Prince Cassius, thus Cassius and his men were the only ones who'd walked into that fucking room, and none of that lot were intimidated by anything, so it was a waste.

Days of yore, all right.

Now it was just a place the bounden had to mop since now, they might accept visitors on their shores to attend their merchants or collect fish to take to the mainland, but no one not of Mar-el came inland.

And no one not Mar-el came to his castle.

On this thought, one side of the two enormous doors that were three stories tall and thus, if one of his men wasn't opening it, it took at least two bounden to do it, opened, and he saw the tall, slender, lithe, bloody-sirens-damned *regal* body of his wife wander through.

Born to be queen, if that body was anything to go by.

And her demeanor.

And bloody fucking *everything* about her.

She wandered amongst the four-story high columns that held up the domed ceiling, each column's width spiraled up with identical carvings of what looked like floating vines of seaweed.

And she did this like she had all bloody day.

The dress she wore clung to her body. Sleeveless. Sparkling. With some lace, some see-through sea-green at her calves, and a drape of netting at her middle that could be construed as being ready to cast for fish. But it was hung with some coins that flashed, torn in places that looked deliberate, and the whole fucking thing made a man wish to take long moments dissecting it visually before he ripped it off with his hands.

She stopped at the foot of the pedestal, tipped back her head, and the abundance of long, springy, soft, tight, black ringlets tipped back with her as she gazed up at him with her big, crystal-blue eyes.

"You've returned," she said in her siren's voice.

And *that*, Aramus had determined, along with her hair, those eyes, her elegant hands, her perfect *lait café* skin, her long-arse legs, and her rounded behind, had bewitched him.

Unfortunately for her, through her own endeavors, he was bewitched no more.

"A week ago," he grunted.

"Ah," she murmured disinterestedly.

Gods.

"We had another wave last night."

He noted the tension that hit her shoulders at his announcement.

This was because she knew, as they had, and those waves were difficult to miss. As they'd been doing for months, it came but minutes after they felt the tremor. Fortnight after fortnight, stronger and stronger with each wave hitting the western shores of Mar-el.

The cities, ports, and villages there had been built to withstand just that—waves, and the worst of storms. And his people had learned to batten, long before the regularity of the current strikes.

But even being hewn from the rock of Mar-el to withstand such occurrences, doors, shutters, windows, even latched strongly and barred even stronger, couldn't withstand a tidal.

And Aramus knew that was coming. Each wave higher and higher, it would take but months before they would face a tidal. Regularly. Every two weeks.

His people were seafarers. Their life was the sea. They could swim. Surf. Ride any wave in boat or by body.

They could not ride a tidal.

No one could.

"Lena has come to see me," he told his wife.

She could not hide behind disinterest at that, as she wouldn't. She was a bloody witch herself. The most powerful of her kind having an audience of the king, her husband, would be of interest.

"The Beast rises," he shared.

Her perfectly formed, puffy lips parted.

Right.

And there were those.

Those lips had bewitched him as well.

Bloody hell.

"It seems our marriage was not the greatest beauty of our island mated with her king, as it is now and has been for centuries. Apparently, the fates chose you for me, as you and I consummated will assist to beat the Beast," he declared.

With that, she shuttered herself away.

"This is not a tale I tell to pry open your legs," he bit out. "Lena spoke it herself."

"Then I'll need to speak with her," she replied. "For that's frankly ridiculous."

"Indeed," he agreed, staring down at her indifferently. "Great beauty, cold fish. My desire for your charms has faded as the months since our wedding have receded into memory and you've kept those charms from me."

If he was not wrong, those ringlets swayed with a slight jerk of her head.

Aramus no longer cared if he wounded her.

She was his wife and he knew the reasons she withheld were far more than "frankly ridiculous."

They were, if read a certain way, fucking treasonous.

"But friction, if not passion, will seal the deal," he concluded.

She had her side partially to him, but at that, she turned to face him full on.

"And as you rode the seas prior to your return a week ago, how many beasts did you kill?" she asked.

He sighed.

"Aramus, you sit on a throne made of the horns of the most magnificent creatures in all of Triton," she stated impatiently. "Perhaps all of the earth. Did you bring the oil and meat and bone for lamps and perfumes and candles and Airenzian corsets?" She tossed an elegant hand up his way as her crystal gaze heated with ire. "Those horns represent three *fathers*."

"These horns are five hundred years old," he ground out.

"So, five hundred years ago, calves went without their sires, as they probably went without their mothers, though no horns could be displayed from the mothers to pointlessly boast of the might of their murderers."

He sat back on plush cushions that were bunched at his back against the ornate gold that made his throne.

And he sought patience.

Finding at least some of it, he said what he had been saying most every time he was confronted with his wife.

And he decided to make one last go of it, therefore he tried to do it gently.

"Ha-Lah, it is not lost on you, since you are Mar-el and have lived on this isle since your first breath, this is the way of our people and has been since history has been recorded."

"And, Your Grace," he was not surprised she returned without a hint of patience, "it should not be. Not the whales. Not the dolphins. Not the octopus. I'm telling you, they do not only think, they *feel*."

"I have sailed the seas since I was a lad, wife, and this is not true."

"It is."

"It is not."

"Does a cow not keen when her bull is taken? When her calf is cornered?" she asked.

He shifted in his seat for the she-beasts did.

It was the most heinous thing he'd ever heard.

And every seaman knew, you did not take a cow if her bull was near, not of any type of whale. You'd lose your ship, and your life, if you enraged the bull when you were close.

"You stop the killing, you will find me not cold, my king," she shared, not for the first time. "And you stop the killing, I daresay you make allies of the sea you would never have imagined."

Now *that* was frankly ridiculous.

"And what will fuel our lamps, make our soaps, fertilize our soils, feed our people, our animals?" he demanded. "What will we sell to add to the treasury to keep our roads clear, roofs on our hospitals, arrows in our quivers?"

"Something else, something from the mainland," she returned. "They have oil. They have more animals who naturally make fertilizer. Grain by the bushel. Spices—"

"Cease," he bit. "We do not trade with them, they trade with *us*."

"But why?"

"You forget, my wife, my *sister*, they cast us to this isle years ago when *that* isle was *ours* and they conquered it and wrested it from us, banishing our people here and doing it *knowing* we would not survive. Mar-el's rocky shores dig deep inland. It does not have vast tracks to roam sheep and cow and sow seeds. We survived on the blessing of the great god Triton. His wife, our goddess, the beneficent Medusa. The spare sympathies of the sirens. They gave us the blessing of the seas. The bounty of the *whales*."

"The ire you hold is simply because we were defeated and you cannot abide the idea of Mar-el in defeat," she retorted on a lift of her chin.

There was the treason.

Aramus ground his teeth.

His wife was not done.

"But even if that is so, now, millennia later, you hold tight to these transgressions that did not befall you, or me, your father or my mother, your *grandfather* or my *grandmother*, but beings who are no longer even bones in the earth, but long since ash who have mingled with the rock and the mud. You do this when we hardly suffered. We not only bested their banishment, *we own the seas*. It was the *fates* who brought us to this isle, my king. It was the fates who brought us *home*."

Aramus didn't like it, but he couldn't exactly argue that.

They had not flourished on the mainland.

On this isle, they had grown prosperous and they had grown fierce.

His wife intoned just that. "We are the mightiest of all the kingdoms. We don't clash in their silly skirmishes, losing man and blade and blood. Our fleets grow larger, our men and women strong and healthy and *thriving*. They've long since ceased attempting to raid our shores, even find their way east of our island, for they can't pass our armadas *and they know it*. They can't even send a ship with their goods across the sea for trade *unless we allow it*. If a vessel from the Northlands or the Southlands from across the Green Sea comes, it is *we* who decide if they sail through our waters."

Aramus couldn't argue this either because it was all true.

Ha-Lah was not quite finished.

"We can use the bounty of our pearls, the treasure wrested by our raiders, sell the vast *fleets* of ships collected from the seas—"

He had to put an end to this.

She spoke blasphemy.

All of it.

"This is our insurance," he clipped.

"This is our *treasure*, our *due*, our *commodities*, and our *reward* for not allowing them to *best us*. You do not bow in victory, Your Grace. You crow it to the heavens and hold it over those defeated."

Aramus said nothing for part of him felt, uncomfortably, he couldn't argue that either.

It would seem when the fierceness went out of her beautiful features, and they gentled, his wife, too, had decided to seek patience and for the first time in their acquaintance, reach him a different way.

"I am not the only one who thinks this way, my husband," she said softly.

"And you touch the pulse of all Mar-el?" he asked curtly.

Though he knew she didn't, he also knew she spent most of her time out and about in Nautilus when he was gone (and even when he was ashore).

So she undoubtedly knew better than he.

She shook her head, which shook her shining curls. "No. But our coffers grow, and it takes months for a ship to cross the Green Sea and come back with coin for our goods, and different goods for our people. It takes nearly half a year to get to The Mystics."

"You tell me things I know," he replied.

"It takes less than a day to sail to Triton," she stated carefully. And even more carefully, watching him closely, she finished, "They banished us centuries ago. It is our king who keeps us banished."

His wife said no more.

But it was safe to say, especially with that last, he was now at his end.

He stood and walked to the edge of the dais, staring down at his bride.

"It is my duty as king of my people to keep them safe. To build their wealth. To protect our secrets. To guard our magicks. It is also my duty as king to provide an heir, which, wife, I will do, with your cooperation, or without. And now, it's my duty to shield them from the tidals, the threat of the Beast rising, and this I will do as well, sowing my seed *in you*."

She glared up at him, her exquisite face no longer gentle, but set.

"Lena shares that we will need to attend the weddings of the King of Firenze, the Prince of Wodell, and Prince Cassius of Airen, all happening to bring about the prophecy so we can know peace. *That* is what I will give to those who abide on the mainland. And I will only do it in order to protect my sirens-damned *own*."

Ha-Lah said naught, just continued to glare.

He continued to speak.

"Amass your chests with appropriate garments. Arrange for your servants to travel and attend you. We set sail in a week and we'll be gone months. And I'll warn you, you have until the time our feet hit Firenze to make your decision, wife. Or I'll make it for you."

She continued to glare up at him for long moments before she demanded, "Am I free to leave?"

He crossed his arms on his chest and jerked up his chin.

At that, she whirled and strode much faster, the skirts of her gown drifting like blades of sea lettuce around her calves and feet, and in far less time than she'd made the trek to his throne, she disappeared through the mighty doors.

To the truth, he didn't quite credit Lena's words of that morning, and wouldn't have, if the waves were not hitting with regularity, the tremors forewarning them.

But Aramus knew something not many did.

Something his father had shared with him very late in his training, in fact, close to the great last king's passing.

And that something was that the Beast did not make this isle those many years ago because water harmed it or because the Beast feared the salt, the wet, the ibex-whales or even the angmostros or sirens.

It was confounded in arriving at his isle for a wholly different reason.

And if his wife and he, Mars and his future bride, True and his intended, and Cassius and his female warrior did not mate...

They were all damned.

6

THE LORE

Frey Drakkar
Adela Tree Glade, Outside Fyngaard
Lunwyn
Northlands

Frey Drakkar stood in the snow, shielded by the elven mist, watching the adela tree before him glow as the diminutive shapes formed at its base, touched it, and grew to human proportions.

He looked to his left at his son, Viktor.

Vik showed no surprise at this magic, not anymore. As the next Frey in line, even if he didn't hold that Keerian name, his first, as his father did, his son had been attending his meetings with the elves for the last fifteen years, since he was ten.

Frey looked back to the elves who were now standing in the snow, with one having gotten close.

"My lord Frey," Nillen, the Speaker of the Elves, murmured.

"Nillen," Frey greeted.

Nillen looked to Frey's son. "My lord Viktor, my other Frey."

Vik grinned at the elf. "Nillen."

Nillen dipped his chin and stated, "Congratulations are premature, but I extend them to you for your upcoming coronation."

Frey drew in breath.

It was time.

His son was twenty-five.

When he turned twenty-six, he would become King of Lunwyn, taking over for his grandmother, who Frey himself had sat on that throne.

Queen Aurora was still sharp, and as savvy as she had been two and a half decades ago.

But Viktor Drakkar was ready to rule.

This did not mean Frey did not still see him as the dark-headed boy in short pants dashing around the decks of The Finnie with a wooden sword, learning swordplay from Frey's men...and his own mother.

It was just that now, he was as tall as his father, nearly as broad, the elves attended him, and they both had command of the dragons.

Not to mention, he had his grandmother's cunning, his father's strength, his mother's charm and the loyalty to his country of all three.

So yes, it was time.

Viktor gave a short bow. "Thank you, Nillen."

Nillen again dipped his chin then looked to Frey, and his expression had Frey bracing.

"I have news of great import," Nillen announced.

"And I have ears so let us hear it," Frey invited.

"The Beast rises."

Frey stared at the elf in his blue cap with its white feather, his icy eyes, his pointy ears, and he could not believe his own.

"Do you mean the Beast across the Green Sea?" Frey asked.

"The exact," Nillen confirmed.

"'Tis only lore," Frey stated.

"Regrettably, it is not," Nillen refuted.

"By the gods," Frey whispered.

"That can't be," Viktor declared.

"I am sorry, my young lord," Nillen said to Frey's son. "It can, and it *is*."

"It's been—" Frey began.

"Over three thousand years," Nillen finished for him.

Vik shifted beside him.

"What magic is this?" Frey demanded.

"We are unsure. He has been a mystery to us as well. We believe it to be a sorcerer, very powerful. So much power, he is hidden. Even from the elves. Feedings, as he did back then when he made the surface, blood, this through sacrifice. Torture, in this case rape—"

"Fucking hell," Vik bit out.

"Collaborators," Nillen carried on, "who performed these rituals for centuries, which did naught but stir the Beast. It is this sorcerer, his seed mixed with the blood, torture and sacrifice, that rouses the creature."

"And you don't know who he is?" Frey asked.

"We don't even think *he* knows who he is," Nillen answered. "Though we know he does not know what he does. We feel he thinks to rouse the Beast, surface him, and control him. But not even the elves could control that monster. Not the sirens or the fairies or the Green Men or the gods or goddesses of that realm. Certainly not the false gods of the scholars who reside there. And my lords, if he is not stopped, this time, he will traverse the sea."

"Bloody *fucking* hell," Frey clipped out.

"*Can* it be stopped?" Viktor queried.

Nillen tipped his head to the side. "There is a prophecy. It is our reading the witches of that realm have initiated its commencement. But we fear they don't understand where the true power lies," Nillen shared.

"And the true power?" Frey prompted.

"They facilitate the matings of the four most powerful witches of that realm to the four most powerful warriors," Nillen explained.

"This sounds bloody familiar," Frey muttered irritably.

"Indeed, but it is not the matings, my lord—" Nillen began.

"It's true love," Frey deduced.

Nillen nodded. "The passion they share will surely augment their power, all of them, in the females, their magic, in the males, their strength and invulnerability. But they must come to love each other, Frey Drakkar. Or all will be lost."

"And what are we to do about this?" Frey asked.

"You command the dragons. If the Beast rises, they will, as ever, be indestructible. But they alone cannot defeat him."

"And their fire, can it destroy the Beast?"

Nillen shook his head. "Slow it, perhaps. But if one should get within arm's reach, the Beast can send it nearly back to Lunwyn with one swing."

Slowing it wasn't much.

But it was something.

And they'd need something if even half of the lore of that Beast was true.

Including the fact it was immune to dragonfire. Not a being on that earth was immune from the fire of his dragons.

"Where the dragons go, I go. Or Vik goes," Frey reminded the elf.

Nillen dipped his chin. "This is so, my lord Frey Drakkar."

Well, one thing could be said about this, his gods-damned son and the future king of his country was not going to cross the bloody Green Sea.

One other thing could be said.

Finnie, his wee wife, Lunwyn's Winter Princess until Vik found a wife and made a daughter, was going to be all for a voyage across the Green sea.

Because no matter the venture, Princess Seofin Drakkar rushed to face it.

And further, she would never allow her husband to leave, even on the most dangerous mission, without her at his side.

Not ever.

Bloody.

Fucking.

Hell.

7
THE WARNING

G'Drey

Tent City of Travelers, Outside a Firenz Bazaar, Riverside of the Tebes
FIRENZE

G'Drey moved into the tent, eyeing the monster.

The desert he had traversed these past four days had been...hot.

The bazaar he had just attended had been...bizarre.

And this creature before him was...*mountainous.*

Drey's mouth watered.

He'd seen from his window in his rooms in Go'Doan when the Firenz warriors would visit the city.

Not to worship.

They had their own gods.

Not to study.

It was rare when any warrior of the Firenz came to read the tomes of history of the continent of Triton, or what they knew of the Northlands and the Southlands across the Green Sea, or what they knew of The Mystics across the Triton Sea.

Definitely not to attend the Go'Da, the university in Go'Doan that many from all over Triton attended. Mostly sons (and some daughters, but those were usually Nadirii) of aristocracy, some of the higher classes who did not have a lofty birthright but did have the ability to pay tuition. And some scholarships, gifted minds from the lower classes, who were usually eventually recruited into the Go'Doan Order.

No, whatever the Firenz were there for, Drey, as a Go'Tish, or training priest, had no idea.

And the Go'En, the high priests, did not enlighten him.

He'd been training for bloody damns ever. He was beginning to think you had to lick the arses of the entire rank of Go'En (and he'd done his fair share of arse licking, the kind he liked but mostly the kind he did *not*).

Now, after he'd waited so long, but with the worst possible timing, he'd finally been advanced to a Go'Ar, no longer in training, but not yet a high priest. And as such, sent on his first missionary assignment to the Fire City of Firenze, traveling through that realm to join his fellow priests there and take up his role.

This did not make him happy.

He did not like being away from his chosen one.

But in his travels, meeting this warrior with the bladed leather kilt at his hips, chest straps, forearm shields and mighty crossed broadswords at his back, he was beginning to rethink matters.

Especially when the colossal warrior unbuckled the strap at his chest and the broadswords fell with a heavy thud to the thick carpet that covered the sand and stone beneath their feet.

"*Toga, via,*" the warrior commanded, and Drey felt his rumbling voice, and his command, right through his arse.

His shaft was already hard and had been since before he entered the tent.

"I speak your language," he shared in Firenzii.

"Then take your robe off," the warrior stated in the same language.

With no delay Drey's hands moved to his gilded belt even as a small niggle of guilt slunk into his head that he was not being faithful to his chosen one.

This niggle vanished as the leather blades of the kilt fell to the carpets and he saw what was straining against the tight leather trunks underneath.

His belt was gone, and his bleached robe hit the carpet about two seconds after, leaving him only in his sandals.

The warrior didn't even look at him, which Drey did not like all that much.

The huge man moved around the posted mattress to a stand at the side of its head where he used his large hand to shove things aside. Jars, bottles, coins, wisps of parchment and other items Drey couldn't make out fell to the floor before he seized on one small bottle.

With his back to Drey, he heard as the warrior uncorked it and he saw the movements of his powerful arms as he poured something into his hand.

He replaced the bottle to the stand and turned, perfunctorily shoving the front of his trunks under his cock and balls, his hard, enormous phallus springing forth, and Drey instantly forgave the warrior for not admiring his (if he did claim so himself) trim and slight, but rather handsome physique.

And as the warrior moved, he was stroking that phallus, coating it liberally with oil.

Thus, when he made it back to the end of the long, wide, fluffy pallet on its high stand, Drey decided to take things in hand, figuratively *and* literally.

He moved forward, reaching out, getting close, touching the warrior at his waist and rolling up on his toes to seek his mouth.

"*No bocca,*" the warrior grunted.

"*Ma—*" he started. *But—*

Suddenly, he found the back of his neck seized and his cry of surprise was truncated when he was thrown through the air, landing facedown on the bed.

He did not protest his new position when his hips were jerked up and back, so that his knees hit the edge of the shockingly downy mattress.

He was not ready for the penetration when it came. Certainly with no preamble. And definitely not with the sheer size of the shaft he was taking.

But Drey was as he was and this mattered not.

Indeed, he came up off his hands with a *"Yes,"* in order to ride that brute.

Only to be shoved down to the bed, face first, a strong hand again at the back of his neck, and he was the one being ridden.

Hard.

G'Drey could barely breathe with his face stuffed in the silk, but that only heightened his arousal. And when he again met his chosen one, he would introduce this to their play.

Unquestionably.

And it might be he'd find climax simply with the drives through his arse and the fire coursing through his system due to his need to breathe.

Eventually.

But right then, he needed a hand.

When the warrior didn't offer one, Drey slid one toward himself.

He was close to his aching target when he took all of that big cock on a grunt from them both—the warrior's, of effort, Drey's, of pain—and then Drey's hand was slapped away.

"No," came another grunt from the warrior.

With difficulty, Drey forced his head to the side, he drew in a large breath and gasped, "But—"

And again with the pounding.

By the true gods, this beast was splendid.

He felt himself beading.

Maybe he *would* climax just from the thrusts.

"Labbra, mia gazzella," he heard murmured lovingly.

G'Drey blinked against the silk blankets.

His gazelle?

Yes, he did have a trim, lithe physique so he could countenance that.

But how could he give the warrior his mouth, *now*, when he was face down...

"Forte, mio toro," a woman's voice came.

His gaze jerked down the bed, and up as far as he could force it, as his arse took more, faster and harder, and he saw the be-ringed hands of a woman gliding around the warrior's wall of brown-skinned chest.

"Labbra." He demanded her lips, his word guttural as thumbs rubbed his nipples, and they were not the warrior's own.

"*Non dentro, mio amore. Solo per me.*" *Not inside, my love. Only for me.*

"*Sì,*" another grunt before he pulled out brutally.

He rolled G'Drey to his back, climbed over him on all fours, and held him by the throat in a powerful grip, his knees in Drey's biceps, pinning his arms to the mattress, as Drey watched, from very close, two hands stroke that mighty shaft, hers on bottom, his large one all but covering it.

And as he gasped, "*No,*" jerking his head side to side, trying to pull his arms out from under those sturdy legs, his body from that hold, when, with a manly, triumphant groan which did not quite drown out the female's delicate whimper, the warrior's seed flooded his face.

That was the injury.

The insult was the warrior shifting, moving his legs from Drey's arms so he could force his cock into Drey's mouth and stroke it through his milking while he kissed his woman deeply...

And Drey loving the taste of him.

And the feel of him.

And the sight of him (not including his tongue in the woman's mouth)

And the long, tight fingers still wrapped around his neck.

In the end he was sucking the softening member, his hand inching to his own cock.

Abruptly, the warrior no longer straddled his face, and his throat was used to tear him off the bed and send him reeling across the tent, landing hard on his hip.

"*Esci,*" the warrior demanded he leave.

Scrambling, the heat in his body rising from shame, but more with fury, Drey rushed to his robes.

He'd shrugged them on and was darting toward the flaps of the tent, pulling his gown closed at the same time trying to wind his belt around himself when he heard, "*Attento, falso prete.*"

He stopped dead and looked back at the warrior lounging negligently on the posted mattress, the bold-colored, sheer swaths of silk draping over it and all around, his woman draped on him. She was stroking his boxed stomach with one hand, her other arm around his back, her mouth in his neck, but her almond eyes were tipped G'Drey's way.

That was when he saw she was wearing the chain.

Delicate gold links starting at a small hoop in her upper ear, leading to another one in her lobe, it had some diminutive but shining rubies and what looked like amethysts dangling from the part that led from lobe to nostril, and then another length fed down to a small hoop at the side of her upper lip.

Right ear. Right nostril. Right lip.

Drey's focus honed on the warrior's lip and nostril.

He had the hoops.

He was just not wearing his chain.

They were married.

She was his wife.

Drey tasted bile in his mouth.

The warrior had said, *Careful, false priest.*

And then he spoke Drey's native language, the language from the Vale, that being Hawkvale from across the Green Sea. The language spoken throughout the Northlands, save Fleuridia. The language Drey had read all about in the history books. A language that had been brought over when a good number of Lunwynians escaped the ice centuries before when the last Frey before the one they had now betrayed the elves.

"Firenze is not safe."

"I think you've demonstrated *that*," Drey spat.

Those eyes under that heavy brow dipped before they lifted. "You are still hard, false priest, do not tell me you don't now go to your tent and stroke your own shaft, feeling me in your arse."

His woman licked his neck from collarbone to jaw then turned, snuggling in and smiling cattily at Drey as her husband rounded her lovingly with his beefy arm.

Enough.

He turned to leave, lifting his deep-edged sleeve to his face to wipe away the warrior's seed.

"That is not the safe I meant," the warrior called.

G'Drey whirled and snapped, "*What?*"

He then took a step back as he realized you did not snap at a Firenz warrior.

The large man's face was carved from stone and his enormous, muscled body was still in its lounge, but Drey sensed it alert for action.

"*Attento*," he growled at Drey. *Careful.*

"*Calma, mio amore*," she soothed her warrior.

"May I have your leave?" Drey forced out.

"Your hole was tight. I enjoyed it," the warrior stated. "For that purpose alone, I share, you are not welcome in Firenze. You will not be welcome in the Fire City. Firenz do not worship false gods. Be smart, false priest. Your teachings, your healings, we will accept. That is why you've been allowed through the fire. But do not press your gods on the Firenz people. They will not welcome it and our king will not abide it."

"I am a teacher," Drey somewhat lied, lifting his chin.

The dark eyes of the warrior assessed him.

"I hope so for you, *mio buco*," the warrior replied quietly.

G'Drey decided, with some trepidation—and feeling it, his fury rose —he didn't need the warrior's permission to leave.

He tore through the red silk flaps and stomped across the hard sand that butted the river tributary where the bazaar was located, thinking he would remember that face. He would remember that cock. He'd remember the woman. And he would not give warning when he was in the position he would soon be in and he used them both as he wished.

With her watching something that would *not* make her smile.

He made his white silk tent and tore back the flap.

He had six acolytes who traveled along to attend him, and the first, in her sheer white shift, who whispered, "My lord, we welcome your return," caught the back of his hand.

She cried out as she went to her hands and knees.

It was then she caught his sandaled foot at her mouth.

She flew to her back, blood spouting from her lips.

"*Draw me a bath!*" he roared to the others. "*Immediately.*"

They scurried to do his bidding, including the one, though she was much slower, who was bleeding.

Mio buco.

My hole.

"No warning," he groused, tossing himself to the white and gold cushions the acolytes had arranged for him when they'd made camp, as many of the Firenz nomads had done the same outside the bazaar.

He shoved his robes aside, caught his cock in his fist, and stroked.

Savagely.

"*No warning*," he groaned, engaging his other hand and squeezing his swollen sac as he spent himself magnificently on his robes, still feeling that Firenz warrior's cock moving through his arse.

8

THE UNICORN

Princess Elena
Balcony of Her Treehome
THE ENCHANTMENTS

I slowly opened my eyes and saw the rising sun as I sat cross-legged on the overhang outside my treehome.

After my meditation, I did not feel refreshed.

This was because I could not clear my mind.

And this was not surprising.

My mother had been much changed the last five days.

Further, she'd ordered a number of unusual things.

And as the queen asked, it was done.

This meant that five hundred of our warriors, the most elite, were daily doing formation drills on their horses and they were doing this for hours.

And all were conserving magic.

Neither I found comforting.

The only time sisters did formation drills was when we had a celebration or a rare state visit, sometimes a contingent from Wodell, more often priests from Go'Doan, or magic ambassadors from all the nations.

And as far as I knew, no state visit or Nadirii celebration was forthcoming, and even if there were, it might be fifty, one hundred warriors.

Not *five* hundred.

And the only time the sisters were asked to conserve magic was prior to battle or going on patrol.

Not that magic was used in battle. In an accord arranged by the Go'Doan, signed by our queen and the kings of Airen, Firenze and Wodell of three generations ago, no magic could be used in battle on any side—our warriors, their sorcerers and witches.

This was a good thing, considering battle magic was extremely fatiguing, and although could be useful, also left you vulnerable.

However, it made you stronger if you'd conserved it prior to going into battle, which obviously helped enormously.

So I did not understand the conservation of magic.

Making matters worse, I, personally, at my mother's decree, had been forbidden to use magic at all.

Not only conserve but meditate often and complete daily rituals that would build my craft inside me.

This wasn't concerning.

It was alarming.

Even so, at that moment, at the sun's rise, as I did every day after my meditation, I reached to my side and took up my cards.

My mind restless, not the best conditions to shuffle and move the cards in my hands, it took some time before I eventually felt it.

When it let itself be known, I pulled it from the deck facedown.

I set the deck aside.

And before me on my rug over the decking of my balcony, I turned it face up.

That was when I stared.

The Unicorn.

A high card.

One of the highest.

In all my days, since I could remember, I started my day meditating and then pulled my card, in the beginning, doing this with my mother at my side.

I had never turned the Unicorn.

If I was fully doing the cards, sometimes my own, normally reading for others, the Unicorn could make its presence known in the spread.

But not to start my day and share what I would face that day, or a forewarning of what I would face in future and must be prepared for, or ease away from.

In other words, a representation of where my life was...or where it was heading.

I stared at the white steed with its white mane, tail and coat, gold horn, proud head bowed, intelligent eyes serene, resting amongst the vines of wisteria, a night forest in the background, pixie dust glittering in the air as if those creatures had just flown through.

Magic.

Joy.

Serenity.

Fulfillment.

Change.

It was one of the only cards in the deck of any of the levels—high, middling, hushed—that was purely positive. No negative connotations, no warnings, no cautions, no calls to action, no suggestions of course alterations.

Just joy.

Peace.

Bliss.

"This...cannot be," I whispered to the card.

And it couldn't.

Those tremors.

Drills.

Magic conservation.

My sister constantly picking fights.

And my mother was dying.

"Elena!"

Quickly returning the card to the deck, I rose from my position and moved to the railing, looking down.

My lieutenant Jasmine was there.

I started to smile at my friend.

"The queen is calling you," she said.

"Well, hello to you too," I replied, now fully smiling.

"I've got to get to drills," she retorted. "I don't have time for drills *and* playing messenger girl."

No, what she didn't have time for was rising before dawn to be ready for drills when we were outside our patrol rotation.

Also, being ordered to stay inside our forest enchantments, rather than go to one of the villages outside and enjoy herself fully with one of her variety of admirers, drinking much wine, eating much food and enjoying much sex.

"I'm on my way," I told her.

"My day is complete," she returned, and I couldn't help but laugh.

She trudged with bow and quiver at her back, staff in hand, toward the arena.

I moved through the low hanging branches into my house.

Going to the staircase at the trunk of the tree that grew up the middle, I wound my way from the first level to the second and moved to the lump under the light quilt on the fluffy pallet there.

I pulled the thick golden hair aside.

"Dora," I called. "It's time to get up. Bathe. Dress. Get to your studies."

"Bluh," Dora muttered.

I grinned and leaned closer. "Theodora, up. My mother wishes my presence. You're going to have to do this on your own today without me winding up the stairs every five minutes to remind you to get out of bed."

She rolled to her back, giving me warm, sleepy brown eyes.

Those were her mother's.

My heart squeezed as it always squeezed when I wasn't braced to look into those beloved eyes.

"Queen Ophelia wants you?" she asked.

"Indeed she does. So up. Bath. Boots, casings and body stocking. Let's go."

I then leaned deep, touched my lips to her smooth forehead, and moved away, going to the stairs that wound up and up and up, to the eyrie, my chamber.

I'd already donned my lavender body suit. Therefore, I quickly wound the soft suede casings around my foot arch, my ankle, crisscrossing them up my calf to my upper thighs. I pulled on a short tunic, my belt and my low moccasins, and drew my daily band around my head, not the ceremonial one, not the patrol one, not the battle one.

A simple, but shining gold disk on which was printed a white oak leaf that sat in the middle of my forehead and lead to smaller gold disks that fed all around. I tied it at the back.

Not all sisters wore the headband on a regular basis.

Only three wore them.

My mother.

And the two Princesses of the Nadirii.

To finish, I yanked the suede armshields up my forearms and headed back down the steps.

Dora was at the pitcher and basin.

Excellent.

"I just adore you," I told her, still winding down.

"And you're just a big ninny," she returned.

I pursed my lips and blew her a kiss. She rolled her eyes. And I carried on winding down the steps until I hit the wide first level that held our tidy kitchen, our big living area, and our ritual space.

I didn't carry on down the steps.

I moved to the hole in the floor, grabbed the rope above it that dangled from a branch that grew through the room, and I slid down, landing soft on my feet on the forest floor.

I did this thinking, magic, joy, serenity, fulfillment, change.

The change I could understand.

Change was everlasting.

But with the sickness eating away at my mother that she refused to discuss, the unexplained tremors that shook the earth every fortnight, the disturbing vibrations I felt in the veil of magic, and the very presence of my sweet (and ornery) Dora in my treehome, I could not imagine I would ever feel joy and definitely not serenity.

I made my way through the trees, lifting my chin, or a hand, or calling hello to sisters I passed, pushing these thoughts into the back of my head.

I was not surprised to see Lucinda and Agnes, two of my mother's lieutenants, standing at the base of the grandly carved, wide wooden steps that wound around the trunk of the stately, tall oak tree where my mother's palace was built high amongst the leaves.

"My princess," Lucinda greeted when I stopped before them.

"My honored sister," I greeted back, not liking such a formal greeting from a woman who I regarded as an aunt to me, that me being a woman she regarded as mostly a daughter.

"My princess," Agnes said, and I felt the same about Agnes, and she me.

By the goddess.

What was happening?

"My honored sister," I repeated and looked up to the leaves. "She awaits me?"

"Rise," Lucinda answered.

I did just that, walking between them and rising to the palace on the grand steps.

I found her not in her personal chambers higher, but in the receiving chambers on the first floor.

This did not bode well either.

What made matters worse was that my sister was there.

Serena didn't look happy, but unless she was going for blood, or carousing, she rarely did.

We each had much of our unknown fathers in us, but you could tell our mother had a certain kind of male she enjoyed.

Our mother was petite, not frail, but not tall. When her hair was not white, as it was now, it had been an ash blonde. Her eyes were still a sharp blue.

My sister was tall, as was I. She had curves, as did I. Her frame had a willowy feel, even with her strong, toned, trim, fit muscles. As did I.

Her skin, however, held some freckles.

And her long, full hair was the color of shined copper, her eyes a deep, dark brown.

My hair was the color of honey, as was my skin.

My eyes were an unusual shade of violet.

We looked like sisters, even with the mismatched coloring.

And our polar opposite dispositions.

"Mum's finally in the mood to share her secrets," Serena drawled after I'd fully entered through the beaded door curtain to my mother's receiving chamber.

I took my gaze from my sister.

"Good morning, Mum," I said to my mother.

"My daughter," she murmured from her place on her cushion in her hanging basket.

I didn't look too closely at her. She got cross when I tried to read her state, this being the state of her health, something she flatly refused to discuss.

Instead, I again looked to Serena. "Hello, sister."

"'Lo," she muttered.

"I don't suppose you'd sit with me," Ophelia asked, mostly to her eldest daughter considering I'd absolutely sit with her.

I hesitated, not wanting to get whatever comment would come from my sibling if I did as asked without demur. I'd learned it wasn't worth it, and regardless, who wouldn't want to sit a morning with their mother?

Serena sneered at me.

She knew I wished to sit with my mother.

I sighed and moved to the deep-seated sofa basket that was much larger and sat on the ground but was of the same fashion as my mother's basket, the grand swoop of the top coming over the seat, the inside at the back fit with many comfortable pillows.

I climbed in and sat cross-legged, facing my mother.

Serena moved to the side farthest away from me and crossed her arms on her chest.

This was when my mother sighed.

She, too, had learned what was worth the effort with Serena, and what was not, for she sallied forth without delay.

"Six nights past, I went to the standing stones."

That got both mine and my sibling's attention.

It had been a night with a tremor.

And after the last, the strongest, Mother had given her orders.

"The Beast rises," Ophelia declared.

Both Serena and I jerked alert.

"Goddess be damned," Serena snapped.

Mother's face grew tight and she bit, "Do not speak such profanity!"

"That cannot be true," Serena retorted, unrepentant.

"If you can say that, then your senses are not opened, *and* your body's functions are not at their best for you cannot miss the vibrations of the veil *nor* can you miss fortnightly earthquakes," Ophelia returned.

As was my wont, I forged into the opening breach.

"Is this why you ask us to conserve magic and drill?"

Mother looked to me. "No. We travel to Firenze and perform in parade before all the kings and princes of Triton for Mars weds, True weds and Cassius weds."

I felt my heart thump hard in my chest.

True weds?

Who did True wed?

"Bloody *parade*?" Serena asked snidely. "In front of the entire *realm*?"

"Yes," Ophelia replied. "As celebration for an alliance unseen or unheard of since beings walked upright. The entirety of Triton merged in peace."

"Merged?" I whispered.

My mother looked to me and shook her head. "The nations stand. The Enchantments, my daughter, will stand. But forevermore, from these unions on, the blood of Firenze will flow through the royal house of Wodell. The blood of Wodell will flow through the royal house of Firenze. The blood of Airen already flows through all of Firenze. And the blood of the Nadirii will flow through the royal house of Airen."

Naught was said to that as both Serena and I froze in horror and shock.

Queen Ophelia did not take her eyes from me.

"You will wed Prince Cassius," my mother whispered.

Unable to stop myself, I burst from the basket, shouting, "No!"

"Dear goddess," my sister breathed.

Ophelia raised her hand my way. "My daughter, I know you hold feeling for True."

"I don't hold feelings for him! I'm in love with him!" I cried.

She shook her head again. "My darling, you don't know what love is."

"She cannot wed an Airenzian," Serena hissed into this exchange. "It's revolting. Vile. It cannot be borne. Especially not a *prince*. Not that blood. *Never* that blood. It's treachery."

"There has been much loss over the years. So much loss. It is time we lay down our arms, my daughter," Mother said to Serena.

"Really?" Serena rocked back on her heels, her eyes firing, her skin firing, everything about her firing. "And am I unaware, Mother? Have they recently passed a law that allows women to bear title to land?"

"Serena—" Mother began.

"Or that it's unlawful that a man raise his hand to his wife, his whore, his maid?" Serena carried on.

"My fierce daughter—"

Serena did not give up. "Or that he cannot discard a wife, a whore, a maid, turning her to the streets with no money and no possessions as he finds another to see to his needs?"

"*Serena*—" our mother kept trying.

But Serena spoke over her.

"And what of when he forces himself upon her? Wife, whore, maid, woman who is but a stranger to him that he passes in the street? Will he face punishment for such heinous violations?"

"Prince Cassius is much different than his father, or the father before him, or the one before him," Ophelia pointed out. "He took a wife. Only one and she was all he needed. It is told wide and with great heartbreak, stories of his open love and respect for her before she perished."

"So Cassius is going to be the shining star in Airen's sky who will change centuries of the degradation and subjugation, debasement, harassment, sometimes even *torture* and *death* of our *sisters*?" Serena demanded with open disbelief.

She did not wait for our mother to answer.

She drawled acidly, "Really, Mother, the Sisterhood was formed on the Night of the Fallen Masters. Spending decades amassing magic to put the males of Sky Bay to sleep so our sistren could slit the throats of their tormentors and steal into the night. It is direct of *your blood*," she leaned forward on that, then back, "and mine, that our great mother was *hung* for petitioning the crown *repeatedly*, and when that went to no avail, organizing the women to protest and revolt. It was her daughter, again our *direct blood*, who hatched the plan that found our escape, our freedom, built our sisterhood and raised The Enchantments."

"I do not need a history lesson, Serena," Mother sighed.

"Yes, well, thousands of their wretched men were assassinated that night, as was their due, and the Airenzian *still* did not learn. No, *Mother*, they punished the females left behind and continued their oppression," Serena returned.

"This happened two hundred and seventy-four years ago, my daughter," Ophelia reminded her.

"And there is not a patrol that returns who has not encountered a woman from Airen beseeching The Enchantments to let her in," Serena replied.

My sister warred. It was her way.

I patrolled the edge of The Enchantments. It was my duty.

And she was not mistaken.

Airenzian women did not come in floods, they couldn't. They couldn't get away.

But the ones who could, came.

Regularly.

And we let them in, without fail.

I moved to one of the glassless windows and gazed out unseeing at sunshine and green.

"Elena, do you have a bloody voice?" my sister shot at my back.

"He loves another," I said to the window.

"Another who is no longer of this earth," my mother said to me.

"They think Serena killed his brother," I shared again to the window.

"They are wrong, and I feel Cassius understands this," my mother shared with me.

Cassius was not yet king.

I'm in love with True.

It would seem that Unicorn was not about bliss.

Just about change.

But how could that be?

"Are we honestly considering this lunacy?" Serena demanded to know.

"We are not only considering it, it's done. The Nadirii ride for Firenze in two weeks. And it is my understanding, the others are already in route."

I turned at that.

Serena let out a grunt of anger.

Mother kept speaking.

"We present ourselves. We celebrate the betrothals. We attend the marriage of Mars and Silence…"

Silence?

True's quiet (but interesting and sharp, and when you spoke to her, quite lovely and spirited) cousin was going to marry the barbarous Firenz king?

Dear goddess.

"After that, Serena and I will ride home," Ophelia continued. "Elena, you will have your lieutenants and a guard of one hundred and ride to Wodell for the marriage of True and Farah of the Firenz."

I felt a stab wound to my heart.

Mother carried on, "You then ride to Airen for your own nuptials. Serena and I and the Nadirii contingent will join you there. And just so you're aware, the King and Queen of Mar-el, already wed, will be at all of these festivities."

"Dora comes with me," I declared.

"Are you bloody out of your mind!" Serena shouted, not to me, but to our mother.

But Mother said to me, "No, my daughter. It would be—"

"She comes with me," I said firmly, "I promised. I promised Tiana should she fall in battle, I would raise her daughter as my own."

"Melisse will—" Mother began.

Melisse, my mother's lieutenant, my beloved mentor, would be a magnificent surrogate.

But that was not what I promised my friend.

"She comes, Mum, or I do not go."

"You do know, it was one of Trajan's personal guard who struck Tiana low," Serena bit out. "And you'll be consorting with that very-dead arsehole's goddess-damned *brother*."

I looked to my sibling. "She is my daughter. You do not leave your daughter. And I will not leave Theodora."

"I cannot believe you're agreeing to this," Serena clipped. She turned to Ophelia. "And what does all of this have to do with the Beast?"

"These alliances, these matches, are prophecy," our mother

answered. "I do not know the outcome. But I do know it's our only defense. So we shall see."

That was not very much.

To commit me to an Airenzian, our mortal enemy.

To tear me from True, who I had hoped to find a way to talk my mother into allowing me to make him my chosen one, something no Nadirii did and ended that able to live amongst The Enchantments. If you took a male chosen, you lived in their land, not amongst the Sisterhood. You were not forsaken, but your male was not welcome.

True had been let in because, well...True was True.

True of word.

True of thought.

True of heart.

He was one of the only males, not of Go'Doan, who'd been allowed behind The Enchantments in nearly three hundred years.

And I had wanted him to be mine.

I turned back to the window.

"Elena will cow to your will, as ever, but I do not agree with this," Serena declared behind me.

I heard my mother's basket moving, and at the sound, I turned to watch her rise out of the cushions.

"You will, my daughter," she returned, her voice strong and unwavering. "You will ride to Firenze with your sisters. You will participate in the parade *precisely* how I tell you to. You will behave yourself amongst the people of Firenze, the kings and princes of the realms. You will act befitting the Sisterhood. You will represent your station, your mother, and your title *exactly* how I wish. Or I will banish you, daughter. I will give The Enchantments to your sister, and as she will be bound to the next King of Airen, *he* will have leave to lay claim to them."

I held my breath at these scandalous words.

"That's treason," Serena whispered.

"I will commit treason to see the Beast restrained," Mother hissed. "There will *be* no Enchantments, no Sisterhood, *nothing* if we do not *all* sacrifice. Elena sacrifices. I sacrifice. And Serena, *you will sacrifice.*"

She took a step toward her eldest and stopped, her face twisted, and at that, my heart did the same.

"Do you not think I die inside knowing she will be amongst them?" she asked softly.

Serena looked away.

She very well knew.

So did I.

"Mum," I called gently.

My mother looked at me.

"Much will be expected of you, Elena," she shared. "He has a daughter who cannot ascend due to her gender. He will expect an heir. And you should expect from him grave and vital change in his lands. But *you* will not have the power to do this. You will only have power over him. Perhaps. If you can earn his regard. That is," she returned her attention to Serena, "only if we defeat the Beast."

"So my virgin sister not only has to take his cock, she has to push out *a son*?" my sister asked with a sneer.

"Do you not think a future king of Airen, born of a man who has no love of battle, only duty, but who did have the love of a wife, something he earned, at the same time that son is born of a Nadirii, and raised by them *both*, will not much change the blackness of Airen?" Ophelia asked.

Serena saw the shrewdness of this, for she shut her mouth.

I only saw the impossibleness of this, and this was now my burden.

Direct engagement within the lands of Airen with that realm's bloody crown prince.

I drew in a deep breath.

Mother kept speaking.

"I regret this, my daughters, I truly do. But life often offers us limited choices. It is what we do with the cards that are dealt that is our measure."

The cards that are dealt.

Definitely a rancid fail with that Unicorn.

Probably because I could not clear my thoughts before it made itself known. The cards rarely were confused.

In times like this, however, it was not a surprise they were.

"Now, *sit*," my mother commanded, moving back to her cushion. "And I will tell you how my sisters, and especially my daughters, will share during that parade in a way it will be spoken of for centuries, the beauty of the Sisterhood."

I sat.

And Serena sat.

It was then I would know why I was ordered to conserve my magic.

And it was then I knew the Unicorn was an error.

Because when I left my mother's house, I was no longer simply alarmed.

I had a break in my heart.

And I was significantly uneasy.

9

THE LITTLE SISTER

Farah Magos

Front Gardens, Catrame Palace, Fire City

FIRENZE

I kept my head held high as I, and my mother, walked up the palace steps.

This was not a place I expected we would ever be again.

But two weeks earlier, the messenger had come, with the guards, demanding we pack our meager belongings from our adobe lodgings deep to the south of Firenze, and go with them to the Fire City.

They did not explain at all during that long journey why we had been summoned by the king.

My mother, I could tell, was terrified.

For good reason.

Therefore, I had to behave as if I was not.

Even though I was.

Outlandishly.

But in the rare rational times I had during the long ride across our grand, sandy country, I could not imagine Mars would punish us further than he'd already done.

Absolutely, the people of Firenze were shocked my father's sentence did not extend to my mother and me, as Mars's father would not have done, but his grandfather most assuredly would.

But we had nothing to do with what my father had done. It was proved. It was known.

In fact, King Mars had known it long before the investigation was complete.

So our punishment was just.

And all of Firenze agreed, calling this out with joyful voices, sending flaming missiles in the sky—because this stated their new king was the same as his father.

Just.

As his father had been, Mars was a much different sort of ruler for Firenze.

Innocents did not walk into the tarpits for no reason but to be a brutal reminder to anyone who might upset a king.

Maybe he changed his mind.

But I knew him well.

So very well.

And Mars had always been most decisive (like his father).

He was not the kind of man who changed his mind.

So I could not imagine, after nearly four years of living unmolested, but much more simply than we'd been accustomed to, stripped of status and most of our belongings, what this was about.

A male servant in the embroidered crimson tunic and loose pants of the adult staff of the Catrame Palace of the Fire City met us in the vestibule.

"*Ven, ven,*" he bid impatiently, but I sensed he was not impatient with us.

There seemed a good deal of activity in the palace.

In fact, there'd been quite a bit of it throughout the city from the moment we entered through the fiery gates.

We followed the servant, my mother close to my side, down a passageway we both had traversed thousands of times before.

A passageway that was taking us to what his father, King Ares, but mostly his mother, Queen Elpis, had fashioned into state rooms.

Before Ares, there were few affairs of state.

There was war.

And there were clan clashes.

When those weren't happening, there were celebrations, feasts, executions, games, parades and orgies.

There was still all of that, just not in the same abundance.

Save the celebrations, feasts, games, parades and orgies.

I heard my mother gasp, and I, too, was surprised when the servant didn't take us all the way to the end of the hall, where the throne room was, but turned right, where the informal receiving room was.

"*Mio re*," the servant muttered, bowing low at the waist.

I fell into a deep curtsy instantly, the side of my back leg flush to the floor, the knee of my forward leg tight to my stomach, my chin in my neck, my hands one over the other at my chest.

This was because Mars was lounging on the cushions of one of the divans under the burnished gold and vermilion, rich cream and olive-green drapings coming from a large, intricately carved chitai lamp hanging from the ceiling, crossing the room, and swathing the back wall.

"*Salir*, Farah, Sofia," Mars murmured.

We gained our feet.

After just a glance from the king's black eyes, the servant vanished.

Those eyes came to us.

"Come forward, my sisters," he said.

My mother took my hand and we moved forward.

"None of that, little mother," Mars said low, his attention to my mama. "I have passed my judgment. I learned at the foot of Ares. You spent much time with my father. You know better, no?"

"You did indeed, Your Grace, pass your judgment," I said to take his attention from my mother, who I could now feel was trembling. "Which was exile. So I do hope you understand why we're anxious as we thought never to see you or our Fire City or this great palace again."

He dipped the long point of beard at his chin into his neck and I tried not to look farther, even if there was much to look at.

It was known throughout the land that Mars Laches, King of Firenze, was the finest warrior specimen in the realm.

His father had been that before him.

His grandfather had not.

Well-chosen wives mated to seasoned warrior kings over centuries was what lounged before me in a pair of cream silk, paneled *ante* pants and nothing else. His feet bare. His wide, heavily muscled chest on display. His shoulders so broad and developed, the sinews overtook his neck. His stomach defined to such an extent, you could pour a river of wine in the indentations and it would run without crawling up the swells.

Long black hair cut in layers from crown to falling down his back.

A small gold hoop piercing his left brow. Little gold balls on either side of the bridge of his nose. An upside-down arch of diminutive Firenz rubies between his nostrils. A tiny asscher cut ruby in the indent of the flesh above his lips. Stout gold hoops in his ears. And a narrow gold hoop in his upper ear, his right nostril and just above the right side at the corner of his top lip, waiting for his wedding chain.

"I can understand this confusion," he said. "It is an important secret to keep, why you were summoned. And it will continue to be, for a time. But in that time, you must prepare." He dipped his chin, this time to two stacks of long, colorful cushions set beyond the low rectangular table inset with an intricate design of mother of pearl that sat before his divan. "Sit."

I led my mother to her cushions, and as she sunk to them, I let her go.

I then moved to mine and did the same.

"I forgot your grace, beautiful Farah," Mars murmured.

I put my hand to my chest and bent my head. "Your kindness warms me, my king."

At that, he roared with laughter.

My head shot up, I felt my eyes grow round, and I was too stunned by this response even to turn to my mother to assess hers.

Then again, Mars was always quick to laugh. He had a rousing sense of humor, both making you laugh (and laughing with you when he did) and finding a multitude of things amusing.

He was the easiest male I'd known in my life to be around. That laughter. The seriousness that would fall over his severe, but handsome face when you had something to say and he was listening. The tenderness that would invade his entire mammoth frame if he knew you were hurting.

It had been thus when he'd shared our sentence of exile, almost appearing as if it pained him more than it did us to strip us of all we had and all we knew, leaving us only with our names, before sending us away.

Though he did send us away with only meager belongings, all of those were of import. Heirlooms my mother had from her family's side, treasures it would wound me to leave behind.

And the modest accommodation he afforded us in our exile was hardly the home of paupers.

It was not a great dwelling the likes of which we were accustomed.

But although very small, very remote and very far away from all we knew, it was safe and snug and comfortable.

I should have known he would not change his mind and summon us to punish us further.

"All right, my little sister," he said when he'd calmed his hilarity. "Allow me to make this clear."

Suddenly, my back straightened and my skin tightened.

Because his handsome face turned simply severe as all humor left him.

And a humorless Mars Laches was not just a sight to behold.

It was a sight to fear.

"What your father did was not what you did," he stated, his deep voice rolling like sarsens toward our cushions. "I lost my sire, I watched my mother lose her husband, these are the only reasons I am more deeply grieved of that event than you. And it is not because you lost your sire or you," he turned to my mother, "your husband. For we all lost not only a king we loved, a man we loved more, but also much trust and any innocence we might have had left at the machinations of G'Dor."

I leaned forward. "King Mars—"

"I am Mars to you, Farah," he growled. "We sat at our cushions at our tables at our studies side by side. You bested me with the paint when I was seven and you were four, something you should be more concerned about at this juncture because I never forgot the humiliation."

I could not believe this, but I had the most bizarre feeling that I was about to smile.

Mars was not finished.

"The first boy who broke your heart, I broke his nose, *and* the second, and if memory serves, the third. You gave your heart too freely. It was a nuisance. And you spelled to sleep the first girl to break my loyalty in order that you could shear her hair. My father and mother lost my blood sister to forces they could not control or understand. *You* took her place."

I heard my mother's quiet sob.

I looked that way and my heart squeezed.

"Little mother," Mars said. "What was done to you had to be done. But truly, you must know your place in my heart."

"My son," she whispered.

She knew.

It was just beyond beautiful Mars still knew it too.

I felt like smiling no more.

Instead, I turned my head to hide the tears gathering in my eyes.

"Little mother, dry your eyes," Mars bid. "Farah, you as well."

I sniffled, controlled myself and looked to my king.

"Know this," he said when he caught my gaze. "Your father plotted to assassinate our king. This plot succeeded. He ended the life of the finest ruler this land has ever known. I can't even begin to understand how it would feel knowing the man who sired me did that. And he, his collaborators, and his warriors walked into the tarpits, my sister. They are gone. The Firenz know peace and further prosperity. It is done."

"So our exile is done?" I asked, my voice shocked, as it would be.

He was a ruler like his father, trained by his father to be fierce, but just.

It was still my blood and my mother's husband who killed the king.

He held my gaze and I noted he did not look at my mama.

"Not exactly," he answered.

Oh dear.

My mother spoke up.

"Mars, truly, with respect, my son, it's been two weeks. We've been most anxious. And—"

"Farah marries," Mars told her.

I did?

"She marries who?" Mama asked.

"The heir to the throne of Wodell. Prince True," Mars answered.

I blinked.

I then started when my mother clapped her hands and pretended to spit on the multitude of colorful rugs overlapping the floor before her.

"Wodell!" she cried in disgust.

"Little mother," Mars murmured, his lips twitching.

It was this I did not find funny.

I married a Wodell?

"They are *weak*," Mama snapped. "A Firenz woman does not open her legs for a *Wodell*."

"True is not like his father," Mars assured.

My mother sniffed and lifted her chin. "I can believe that. I can believe he's not even *of* his father. For that king has no balls and it would surprise me he even has a cock."

Mars chuckled.

I whispered, "*Mama!*"

My mother's head whipped to me. "We hear the stories, even in our banishment. Many of his men fall and fall and *fall* as he tries to steal our saffron, our tar, our *rubies*. We have been warring unnecessarily with Wodell for decades. *Centuries.*"

"The Firenz *did* steal that tract of land from the Dellish many years ago," Mars pointed out genially.

"Yes, and *we* have managed to *keep it*," Mama hissed at Mars. "But it was *ours first.*"

Mars chuckled again.

I sighed.

"I obviously have no power in this room, in this land, and definitely not sitting in front of my beloved king, a man I helped raise side by side with my sister-friend Queen Elpis," Mama began grandly. "But I can tell you, that ruby mine builds our armies and widens our roads. I know, Mars, like your father before you, you ceased taking the proceeds of royal holdings into your own personal treasury and added it to the treasury of the people. It is a blessing and the people know it, feeling of you like they did your father. That you are noble, adored and our true ruler.

The tar has *always* been of Firenze and *only* of Firenze. And those saffron fields are owned by *our king*."

"I do know this, Sofia, as I am that king," Mars muttered with amusement.

"And he *dares*?" she demanded.

"They are not as rich a nation as we," Mars explained.

"So...so...so...make more sheep!" she exclaimed. "That can't be hard. They rut. Another one comes. Even *I* covet Dellish wool."

Mars looked to me. "I forgot, as well, your mother's spirit."

"It's not spirit, it's loyalty," I returned.

"I did not forget that," he whispered, and I felt my throat close.

Instantly gone was her blustering affront, Mama emitted another sobbing peep.

Mars gave her a soft look before returning his gaze to me.

"This marriage is arranged, Farah, and there is no changing it. True rides here as we speak for parades and betrothal celebrations before you ride there for the ceremony." His voice dropped. "It's a good match, my sister. He is so not of his father, I would call him a changeling. At his last surrender, when his father again sent his son to command too few soldiers in an effort of folly, he knew it was lost before it had begun, and I could feel his frustration. He and his men fought with cunning and valor, regardless. His soldiers' loyalty to him is so strong, it scents the air. This match will mean an alliance between our countries. And I cannot say I do not feel some relief for it also means I do not have to defeat such a valiant soldier again."

One could not say I was overjoyed at the news that I would take to husband, a Wodell, prince or not.

What one could say was that I was being called to be in service to my people, and really, there was naught else that needed to be said.

"I will marry this prince, my king," I told him simply so he would know I would do it willingly, because as king, he did not need my assent.

But as the Mars I'd grown up alongside, he would desire it.

"And when you do, you will drip the finery of our great nation, my little sister," he replied.

I lifted my chin. "I already do."

My breath caught as Mars's eyes started to burn red.

I'd always loved his unusual ability to do that when he was feeling deeply.

It was a sight to behold too.

One of great beauty.

And one to fear.

~

King Mars Laches
King's Study, First Floor, East Corridor, Catrame Palace
FIRENZE

"LORENZ," Mars greeted, lifting his head from the papers he was studying as delivered of Lord Johan Mattson of the Arbor that were on his desk as his captain strode into his study. "You're back from your travels with Nyx so soon? I didn't expect you for another week."

Lorenz threw his large frame in a chair in front of the desk.

"I followed a Go'Doan from the bazaar at the Tebes."

Mars narrowed his eyes at his brother, asking, "And why did you do that?"

"Because Nyx was in a mood. This mood heightened when she saw him. And as her mood heightened, as it has a way of doing, so did mine. I took his arse for her. My wife was pleased. The false priest was not. And I thought nothing of it until the next day when his acolytes brought down his tent and one of them had a marked cheek and a swollen, broken lip."

A burn hitting his throat, Mars sat back in his chair.

"Did you ask what he was doing in Firenze?" Mars inquired.

"He makes his way to Fire City, obviously, since I'm here. And he says he's a teacher."

"Do you think he's a teacher?"

"No, I think he's a maggot," Lorenz said harshly. "And I think G'Dor was a Go'Doan before he renounced that faith to serve our king and marry Sofia. Though, it might prove true we would understand all too late why he didn't renounce the name they gave him. And I do not have to tell you, Mars, I still do not believe the Go'Doan did not have anything to do with the murder of your father."

"This was investigated thoroughly, Lorenz," Mars said low.

"And you don't believe they had nothing to do with it either," Lorenz replied. "This is why you have them watched."

Mars didn't say anything for there was nothing to say and Lorenz knew it.

This was why he had the false ones watched.

"I want to play with his priest," Lorenz shared.

"You only need Nyx's permission for that," Mars told him.

Lorenz curled out of his lounge, leaning forward, elbows to his knees, eyes on his king.

"I want to *play with him*, Mars," Lorenz growled.

"Will I have troubles with Go'Doan ambassadors with how you play?"

"Maybe."

Mars stared into his warrior's eyes.

"Play," he granted.

Lorenz smiled a smile Mars liked, Nyx would like more, this Go'Doan might not like at all (then again, he might), and his warrior pushed out of his seat.

He started to leave the room, but Mars caught him by calling his name, and he turned back.

"The Go'Doan are here to tend our sick and teach our children. They do not have immunity. I wish these acolytes to be watched closely. If there's another split lip or even a fucking bruise, Lorenz, I want the priest behind it brought forward on charges. And if the Go'Doan send an angry pack of envoys to argue their ways and that they should be allowed to practice them, even in foreign lands, I'll have an excuse to expel the lot."

"It's done," Lorenz returned.

"Gratitude, my brother."

Lorenz left.

Mars stared at the door.

Then he picked up his silver pen, dipped the quill into the ink, and struck out a variety of numbers written on the missive, changing their quantities greatly.

IO

THE DOWRY

Lady Silence Mattson

Throne Room, West Corridor, State Wing, Catrame Palace, Fire City

FIRENZE

"This is impossible to believe," my father hissed.

"Please be quiet, Johan," my mother whispered.

"I-I-I don't understand," my king stammered. "You have the fullness of the dowry you demanded when no dowry *should* have been demanded for I offer you my very own niece to quell the Beast."

"I do believe I changed the quantities," the King of Firenze noted calmly, completely ignoring my uncle's assertion a dowry shouldn't have been requested, considering I wouldn't be there if not for the fact that he and I somehow were meant to save the world.

This dowry situation, by the by, did not best please my father.

No, it did *not*.

Mostly considering my uncle expected my father to offer the lot of it.

And the lot of it was *a lot*.

I felt True shift, and he was so close to me, standing in a protective manner at my side and partly to my front (my *much* beloved cousin), that his arm brushed my shoulder.

I really wanted to look upon the woman with the lush exotic features, eyes that shone like topaz, and *such* finery on her body (but it was so strange, I couldn't believe).

The woman destined for my dear cousin.

The woman sitting on a pile of cushions at the king's side farthest from me.

But since entering the throne room of the Catrame Palace ten minutes before, a part of my uncle's somewhat large entourage (considering we were greeted solely by the Firenz King and True's intended), I could barely take my eyes off the brute sitting his throne.

Red, collarless, long-sleeved shirt, a black jacket that I would suspect, if he rose from his ruby embedded gold throne (something he did not do when we entered), would fall to his ankles, and it had no sleeves. Loose black trousers.

And bare feet.

This was interesting, as these were not the clothes of the males of my country (and no one in Wodell went in bare feet—and what feet! By the gods, who in all the lands had attractive feet? I'll tell you who—King Mars of Firenze!).

But truly, it was the rest of him.

The hair (so much hair).

The beard (*such* a full beard, and it came down to a *point*).

The eyes (so very black—pitch...or *tar*).

The piercings (everywhere!).

The slim scar that ran from his right cheekbone over the bridge of his nose.

The other one that ran under the swell of his left cheekbone.

And the sheer volume of his gargantuan frame, all of it made up of muscle.

He was the single most extraordinary being I'd ever seen in... my...*life*.

I could...

Well, I could gaze on him for *centuries*.

Sadly, it would seem, he could not do the same with me.

For when we arrived, and I was presented to my intended, he barely looked me top to toe before he turned his attention to my uncle. Though as was my way, I knew, even if his gaze rested on King Wilmer, his mind was attuned to True.

This would, of course, be smart.

Although my uncle had a guard in this very room that equaled sixteen in number, and another fifty stood outside the palace, I still would guess the only real threat was True (who I knew, because I heard, but I'd also seen him perform in the games, that he was a very good soldier, and he was renown as the best horseman in all of Wodell).

The King of Firenze was unarmed.

But there was a large, ceremonial broadsword hanging behind him studded with enormous Firenz rubies, even larger Sjofn ice diamonds, sparkling emeralds and beautifully-cut amethysts, which I knew were also mined in Firenze.

I further knew, from the stories I had heard as well as gazing upon him now, this king could have his hand around the handle of that sword in the blink of an eye and not give a thought to its pricelessness as he cut down my uncle's guard in a thrice and then turned to True.

King Wilmer should not have made True keep his personal lieutenants outside. They were like True. And I'd heard tell they'd die for him.

This thought made me get even closer to my cousin and rub my knuckles against his.

True took my hand.

The instant he did, the king's head turned, his face grew hard, and his eyes narrowed on our hands.

My heart skipped several beats.

Oh yes, he was attuned to True.

And perhaps even...*me.*

And right then, he was *terrifying.*

"You're aware," he said to our hands, "that no man, not her own, touches a Firenz bride unless given leave *by* the man who is her own."

"With respect, Your Grace, she's my cousin and not Firenz. I've known her since she was wee," True returned. "And I suspect this is a fretful occasion for her."

The king's gaze lifted to True's as he spoke again.

"You are aware," he said, much more slowly this time, and his deep voice seemed impossibly deeper, "that another man...does not touch...a Firenz bride...*unless given leave.*"

"I'm fine, True," I whispered, tugging my hand away.

I tore my eyes from the king to look up and see my cousin's jaw dancing as he scowled at the dark king.

True then looked down at me and he'd forced his expression to gentle. "You're certain?"

I swallowed.

True watched.

Then I nodded.

That muscle danced in his cheek again and he turned back to the Firenz king.

Doing perhaps the only wise thing he'd done in his life, my uncle interrupted this conversation.

"We've come bearing five hundred bushels of Dellish wool. Two hundred head of Dellish sheep. One thousand bags of milled Dellish flour, which you know, Mars, is the finest in all the lands. It makes the best bread and pastries in Triton. And also one hundred pieces of Dellish silver-pewter, which is *renown*. All of this as agreed."

"And I sent a messenger some weeks ago sharing I wanted one thousand bushels of wool and five hundred head of sheep," King Mars returned.

"That's outlandish," my father muttered under his breath.

"We received no message," my uncle said to the king.

"This is unfortunate," the king murmured.

"We cannot go back now. The ceremonies begin four days hence. The Nadirii already ride over Firenz land. And I'd hate to see what Serena would do if she rode all the way from The Enchantments only to have to turn back," my uncle warned.

"I care not what the copper one thinks," the king replied, and his eyes went back to True. "Everyone knows that gold is more precious."

I made not a noise as I shuffled closer to True seeing as that was just, well...*cruel.*

And thus, I stared now without awe (and perhaps there had been a wee amount of rapture) and instead gazed coldly at the king.

It would surprise me, and annoy me in that moment, that he actually *wasn't* attuned to True.

He was that to me.

I knew this when his gaze fell instantly on me the moment my expression changed.

"Have I irritated you, my intended?"

I glanced but briefly at the lush beauty on cushions by his side and I spoke no words about anything, specifically about the fact that my cousin was enamored of that "gold" that was more precious.

Namely, Elena of the Nadirii.

"Does she speak?" he asked someone else, for his words stated thus but his dark eyes never left me.

"She speaks," my father said, then turned, glowered at me and prodded, "The king asked you a question."

I drew in breath.

And then I answered softly, "I heard him."

"Well, *answer*," my father hissed.

I held the king's gaze.

"Silence," my mother whispered pleadingly when I said nothing.

"This is an odd name, no?" King Mars remarked. "And it seems she took it to heart."

"*She* is standing right in front of you, sir," I said quietly. "And *she* tends not to say anything when she has nothing to say, or nothing to say she wishes heard."

At that, to my stunned surprise, he threw his fearsome (but handsome) head back and the large room filled with the thunder of his laughter.

Oh *faith*, but he was even more easy to watch when he laughed.

That muscled throat.

What a bother!

I felt myself glaring at him and I had no idea what came over me because I had learned long ago to keep such to myself.

I could think things.

I could feel things.

I could not *show* things.

He was still chuckling when he caught my new expression and he leaned toward me. "Now I see I *have* irritated you, my little monkey."

One could say I did *not* enjoy being referred to as a *monkey*.

I turned my gaze to the lush beauty who sat on the cushions beside him.

If it could be credited, she appeared to be sending me the message that she felt for me, such was her rueful expression.

She got to marry True, who was the finest man I knew.

I was to marry this brute, who called me a monkey.

I didn't need her feeling sorry for me, or at least I didn't need to witness it, so I looked to the floor.

"*Piccolina,*" the king called quietly, and with nothing for it (he *was* a king, soon to be *my* king), I lifted my eyes to his. "A queen does not study the floor," he instructed, still speaking quietly. "Ever," he whispered.

"I'm not queen yet," I returned.

That was when his gaze took its time to traverse my face, taking in my hair, my neck.

It slid down my throat and lingered on my chest, which I had to admit, was much pronounced in the gown I wore of layers of sheer, sage-green chiffon that fell in a multitude of gathers from the off-shoulder neckline to a belt of the same material just above my natural waist. The gathers fell to a rough inside-out seam at my hips and then down in gracious folds to cover my feet. The lovely sleeves were wide and billowy and gathered just above my wrist.

It was lighter (and cooler) than my normal garments.

And I wore nothing to further adorn it but a sage satin ribbon in my hair, for I felt the simplistic wonder of that dress, and the sumptuous material, needed no accessories.

His eyes barely scanned my bottom half, and I could understand why, his lush companion was barely clothed (you could see her navel!—and her upper half was covered only in a bejeweled *brassiere*).

But it seemed, from the look in his eyes, a look that did something to my insides, he was pleased with my breasts.

I felt my cheeks heat even if I told myself at least that was something.

"*Rosa,*" he whispered, his gaze on my face. *Pink,* he'd said. "*Affascinante.*"

I suddenly found it difficult to breathe.

Because his last was *Enchanting.*

Oh *faith*.

His attention abruptly moved to my uncle.

"I'll take her," he declared.

It felt like there was a huge frog in my throat and something quite curious was happening in the region of my belly (and, truth be told, *below*).

My mother looked to me, pleased.

As did my father.

My uncle said, "Of course you do, Mars, to quell the Beast."

The Firenz king spoke as if my king did not. "You can send a messenger, have the rest of her dowry delivered while we travel."

"You said she pleased you. I don't under—" my uncle began.

"She pleases me, and I'll have her," King Mars announced.

Faith!

"But the dowry had already been agreed," King Wilmer repeated.

"The quakes, they've stopped, no?" King Mars remarked.

My uncle spluttered because they had. The last three fortnights there hadn't been one. And we were a week into the next and still...nothing.

"The prophecy must go forward. The witches warned us that it must be done," King Wilmer reminded him.

"And so you'll send the remainder of the dowry or, once we're wed, and my Farah is given to your Prince True, I'll have my warriors come into Wodell and they'll take it," he finished.

King Wilmer's face got red before he whirled to my father.

"Send a messenger, Johan, and have the dowry delivered," he ordered.

"At once," Father said, suddenly amenable and not quite hiding a sly smile.

I did not like his sly smile, and I was so much not myself in that moment, I didn't hide it.

It was when I felt King Mars's regard again that I noticed he was studying me.

When I caught his gaze, it went to my father, back to me, and he arched a heavy, black brow.

I pressed my lips together.

He studied me for an excruciatingly long moment, then his very full and attractive lips twitched.

"Perhaps I can have a few moments to get to know my own intended," True interrupted our silent exchange.

"Of course," the king of the Firenz agreed, standing (and I was right, that jacket fell down to his ankles, *and* he was taller than anyone, perhaps, *in history*).

He reached a hand out to the beauty beside him. She took it and gracefully came to her feet.

"The receiving room, my little sister?" he murmured, holding her long, elegant fingers (apparently, Firenz men didn't have any problem touching a Dellish man's intended—the cheek!).

"*Sì, mio re,*" she replied, looked under her lashes to True.

Then she sashayed out, full hips swaying, sheer burgundy skirts under a jewel-encrusted waistband floating (and her skirts were not sheer like mine, you couldn't see through the multiple layers of mine, you could most assuredly see her long shapely legs through *hers*).

True might be the only man who would follow that woman like he was heading to the gallows.

Something he did.

"I'm not thinking True got the short end of that stick," my father muttered to my mother.

I fought a roll of my eyes.

"*Johan,*" my mother hissed.

"We're finished," King Mars announced.

And with that, but without a glance at anyone (including me!), not to mention a word about our accommodations (which were supposed to be in that very palace), or refreshments (he hadn't even offered us a cool glass of water), with his long coat flying out behind him like a mantle, the mighty King of Firenze sauntered out of his throne room.

Farah Magos

Lantern Room, East Corridor, Catrame Palace, Fire City
Firenze

SENSING HIS MOOD, I did not take my intended to Mars's receiving room.

I wandered farther down the hall, beyond the vestibule, into the family's rooms, and I took him to Mars's informal sitting room.

It had always been one of my favorite chambers. The large lamp hanging low over the middle of the space had some clear, beveled glass panels, but these were mingled with artfully etched amethyst ones.

The many windows were shielded in screens of intricate boxes of exquisite scrollwork.

The floor was covered in thick rugs of cream and brown and taupe, there were large cushions to rest on flung about the room, woven rattan poofs to sit on or bring to you to rest your feet, and a divan in the corner with soft pillows to bolster you against the wall.

And Queen Elpis had put her array of iron lanterns here and there, which could seem odd, but gave the room a personal feel.

Once the Prince of Wodell had seen me inside the room in a gallant manner that reminded me of my own race, though much less showy, my intended had moved directly to the window.

A young servant boy had followed us in.

"Wine, my little brother," I murmured to him. "Cool water. Olives. Some shelled pistachios. And some cheese. Yes?"

The boy nodded and dashed out.

I turned back to my betrothed.

He had not been what I expected.

His frame was so straight, like an arrow. And it was tall, very tall. Much taller than I would have imagined. His shoulders were squared. They were broad. Perhaps not as broad as a warrior of my own kind, but they were broad. And his body was muscled, much leaner than men of my country, but there was something appealing about the economy of power, for even if he was lean, the power was not hidden.

His dark brown hair had a sheen to it. It was very thick and cut short. Not as short as an Airenzian, but it was definitely not long, as the men of Firenze wore it.

And it curled around his neck and ears in a manner that was also very appealing.

His features openly showed his aristocratic lineage, straight nose, square shaven jaw, high cheekbones, strong brow.

But the keen intelligence in his extraordinary green eyes was what had struck me upon sight of him.

The intelligence and the *feeling*.

He worried much about his cousin. Positioned to protect her. Indeed, his sole focus, after a scan of my king, and then of my person, was doing what a powerless man could do in an uncertain situation to offer her succor in a trying time.

Though it would come about that little mouse needed little aid.

A surprise, this coming from such a small woman. A woman of Wodell.

I suspected a good surprise for my king.

I moved across the room to my betrothed, watching him gaze out through the screens.

I stopped with my side to the wall and studied him further.

I did not have a good deal of time to do this for those green eyes came to me.

Truly, they were like emeralds.

"I've asked for refreshments," I murmured.

"I heard. Very kind," he replied.

And there was his voice. Deep and smooth, but muted. He was not a man who had to shout to be heard. People would listen simply because of his manner.

But he had understood my words to the boy.

This meant he spoke my language (as I did his).

"Your Grace—" I began.

"I think, Farah, as you'll be sleeping beside me the whole of our lives, that you should call me True, don't you?"

I felt a flutter in my chest.

But I nodded.

I dipped my voice and told him, "I know of—"

"Elena. Of course," he again interrupted me, not, I suspected, in a rude way. Instead, as if he wished to relieve me of saying something that was difficult to say.

He turned his gaze back to the windows and it was then I felt a tightness in my chest.

"We were not meant to be. We both should have known that. My father would never allow me to wed a Nadirii. And Elena would have died a new death every day if she had to leave The Enchantments. Her sisters. From the beginning it was futility."

"The heart knows nothing of futility," I shared.

Those green eyes again came to me. "I'm finding the heart knows nothing at all."

I wasn't certain he was correct.

I didn't debate the point.

"It's my understanding we face troubled times. I think, as we do, and as I'm finding you are, and I would hope you would find the same in me, that we could also find some sort of companionship, no?"

"Farah, I think you're very well aware that there are no times that aren't troubled."

It took a great deal of effort, but I did not allow my body to step away.

"You know of my father," I whispered.

With a single nod of his head, he replied, "I do. It says much of your king that you're standing right there."

At that, I felt a frisson of fear in my chest.

"You would not have done the same?" I asked hesitantly.

"I would not have banished you," he answered. "But I am not king. My father would have thrown you and your mother in his prison and allowed you to rot there, perishing in squalor, not thinking of you again. And King Gallienus would have had you executed. Also without thought."

It must be admitted that I could only agree with Mars that Prince True was not at all like his father. I'd noticed that quickly.

"Sadly," he looked back to the windows, "we suffer for our father's sins."

The skirmishes he was ordered to instigate to regain that tract of land.

Amongst, I reflected, other things.

It was shocking to learn that perhaps we had something very important in common.

"It will be good, through our union, that our countries will know peace," I remarked.

"Eight hundred and seventy-three men," he stated in a terrible, agonized way that made me hold my breath.

He looked again to me.

"All sons. Some of them brothers. Some of them husbands. Some of them fathers. All gone. And that was just in the *last* of our campaigns against Firenze."

Oh my.

I was seeing that I did not have on my hands a future husband who was a man of a neighboring nation that we did not get along with who also was in love with another woman.

I had a broken soldier on my hands who knew the precise number of his men who had fallen to his father's follies and he understood how terrible a price that was to pay in return for nothing.

It was at that my chest warmed, and I moved closer to him, reaching out a hand and wrapping my fingers on his biceps.

He looked down at it, and before I could speak, his gaze came back to mine, and he did.

"I know your nation's ways, Farah. And I will not ask you to betray who you are. Your customs, your practices, your religion. I have agreed to take *you* to wife, and in doing so, it is *you* who I will take, not a you I force into a mold that is not your own."

Could I believe what my ears were hearing?

He uncurled my fingers from his arm and then held my hand in both of his as he turned fully to me and continued.

"I will simply ask you to be of the Dellish in one thing. You will sleep beside me every night and you will take no other, except me, as I will vow to take no other, except you. I understand this is not your way, but it means much to me. I can imagine it is a great deal to ask, but I must ask you grant it. That I would know my wife was only my own, and I would give my wife the knowledge that I am only hers."

And it was at that, my chest did not feel warm.

It burned.

"I will grant that, True," I whispered.

And it was then, with his hands squeezing mine in an endearing way, I saw my betrothed smile for the first time.

When I witnessed that tender beauty, I was all of a sudden fiercely gladdened that this tall, straight man of feeling and character was only my own.

II

THE ARRIVAL

Queen Ha-Lah Nereus
The Plain, Dune Desert, Outside Fire City
FIRENZE

Aramus had forced me to ride to the Fire City in front of him on his steed.

And during our long journey by sea and by land, even if he had threatened other far more unforgivable deeds he intended to do to me, that was the only thing he forced.

When we were at sea, my mind was consumed with this threat.

And even though my accommodation was his cabin (and his bed in his cabin), although he was a large man, and the bed was *not* large, in the night when he joined me, he turned his back to me and slept without an inch of his body touching mine.

And he ignored me the entire voyage.

As I did him.

When we hit land, I was consumed with understanding the fruition to his warning was nigh, *and* the fact I would absolutely not forgive him if he carried it through.

But as we traversed that dusty, hot, bleak landscape, in the night I shared the pallet of my husband's tent, but that husband did not force his body on mine.

And as one day melted into the other (somewhat literally, this land was *hot*), I came to understand that his frustration at our conversation might have made him say the words.

However, that was not the man my husband was.

I also came to understand the significance of this.

And regrettably, it was then I came to understand that perhaps upon our marriage, I'd made a rather large blunder.

Now, as we made our final approach to Fire City, so much time had passed where I'd used righteous anger to make my arguments—arguments about things that held great import to me, and I felt I was right in them, but in doing so holding my husband at bay—I did not know how to break through the wall I myself had built between us.

I had spent more time with him these past weeks than I had in the whole of our marriage.

Through it, I saw how he was with his lieutenants. Boisterous and filled with humor and often-times rowdy. But there was genuine affection between them, and true loyalty.

Not to mention, he was a formidable captain. He expected order and compliance. He ran a tight ship and was skilled at it, but he was not dictatorial. He could be stern. If something was done wrong, he could be harsh. But wrongs were rarely done, and regularly he was attentive, had a listening ear, and was most the time jovial and approachable.

Thus, his seamen followed him due to respect.

And fondness.

Yes, I had most definitely made a blunder.

And I didn't know how to rectify it.

Further, it was important (but difficult) to admit to myself that there was not a small amount of pride that was holding me back.

In the course of my twenty-seven years of life, I had often found myself stumbling on pride, mostly around those times I had to admit I was wrong.

And this wrong was not about what was of great import to me.

But how I'd chosen to communicate it.

Therefore, we were currently riding to a great city in the richest realm of our land, I was soon to be faced with being introduced as the queen of my own beloved realm, wife to a man who was not truly my husband, this to kings and queens, princes and princesses.

And even as I sat in front of him on his horse, his arm loose around my waist, we were still oceans apart from one another.

"You speak to the dolphins," he grunted over my head (for he was tall and unless he dipped to my ear, that was the only aim his words could take).

I blinked at the sand before me.

"I'm sorry?" I asked, my frame tightening.

"I watched you. On my ship. You stood at the bridge regularly and you did it for some time. You weren't thinking. You weren't pondering. Dolphins swam with us. You speak to them."

He'd...

Watched me?

I felt something inside me flutter.

Though I could have no mind to it.

Because something else inside me was filled with fear.

"I—" I started.

"Do you speak to the whales as well?"

"My king—"

"It's naught to be concerned about," he declared. "It is not a magic we have in our land, but I know in the Northlands and Southlands, men speak with their animals, women speak with their own."

I continued to study the landscape as my breathing escalated.

His voice lowered.

"But I know naught but the mermaids who speak to the beasts of the sea."

Well...

Hmm.

"Do you have mermaid blood?" he asked.

One could say that.

"It would explain your affinity for these creatures," he stated. "Is this where your magic comes from?"

One could say that too.

Knowing what I knew of him now, I thought it safe to whisper, "Yes."

My husband had no response.

As he'd broken our very long silence, I searched for something to say.

Before I found it, he broke our current much briefer silence.

"Why did you not share this with me, wife?"

"We weren't exactly communicating very well, my king."

"No, we were not," he grunted. "Though it was not for lack of trying on my part."

Drat!

This was all too true.

"It is...the mermaids are..." I stammered.

"Greatly mythicized," he finished for me. "Even hunted simply for the purpose of study. And in olden days, when they were friendly, they were captured and held as pets, forced to perform for entertainment, or murdered and dissected to try to understand their magic. They learned, and they fled, hiding themselves away from beings of the land. And those who hold their blood hold this same allure, a fascination, an *other*, to be studied, prodded, tested."

"Yes," I whispered.

"And you did not think I could and *would* protect you from this if it was to be known about you?" he demanded.

I blinked at the landscape again.

Aramus kept speaking.

"You did not think I would accept you as wife, the King of Mar-el, the Protector of the Seas, you having the actual *blood* of the seas?"

Carefully, I noted, "You don't protect all beings in the seas."

"A dolphin does not sleep beside me, destined to bring me an heir, Ha-Lah," he returned.

Well, there was that.

It would seem it was high time I swallowed at least a bit of my pride and attempted real communication with my husband.

I had opened my mouth, determined to do that, though uncertain how I would, when I noticed it in the distance.

And my back shot straight.

Therefore, when the words came out of my mouth, they were not conciliatory. They were also not tentative appeasement or concession.

They were, "Wh-what is *that*?"

I was surprised when his loose arm at my waist became a tight one around my stomach.

"Do not fret, wife. It is the Wall of Fire around Fire City."

Of course it was.

I had heard of it.

However, seeing it, even from our distance, I could not credit it.

And as our horses drew closer, I feared it.

Aramus had brought five galleons with us. He'd left some men to guard the ships, but the rest he brought with us. Five hundred rode at our back, with his seven lieutenants amassed right behind our lead.

But I did not have good feelings about this, as we approached that wall of fire and it got bigger, and longer, and more frightening.

What magic was this?

I knew not.

What I knew was that it was grave, and it was powerful.

As if he read my thoughts, Aramus spoke again.

This time, he bent to do it in my ear.

"There is much tar under this land. Tar that burns lasting and hot. The logs are magical, my queen, for they never burn away. The tar is not."

I twisted in my seat to look up at him.

His visage and frame, from the beginning, had not been an issue.

He was not known amongst all as the most handsome man in our realm.

He simply was.

Large, bulky frame, massive shoulders, long trunks for legs.

His seemingly acres of skin the color of midnight.

His head was shaved, as all Kings of Mar-el kept their scalps, though his jaw was bearded.

His eyes were a warm brown.

His features broad and strong.

His teeth, so white and straight, the many smiles I'd seen him give his men over the past weeks made my heart feel oddly light.

And his scarrings were things of beauty.

They were the honored scars of a seasoned sailor.

And those of a ship's captain.

And those of a royal son.

And last, those of a king.

I could see them on his arms and I knew under his sleeveless, belted tunic, they rode up his back, over his shoulders and pectorals.

They were also across his nose, his cheekbones, and around his temples.

These last were the scars of a prince (nose and cheekbones) and later, after we lost his father, the ones of a king had been added (temples).

He was magnificent.

And although I knew the Firenz had ceremonial piercings…

And the Airenzian had ceremonial ink…

Not a being in that land who I'd seen had our skin.

Or our scars.

And I was suddenly afraid.

I turned forward and watched coming closer that great wall that seemed now to stretch left and right across the entire horizon, rose stories into the air, its fire burning high and bright, forcing the very air around it to dance.

And I made my decision, not for myself—for my king and my people who followed us.

Then I called upon it.

It was weakened when I was not close to the sea (and I was definitely not close to the sea).

But I had to do what I must.

The shimmer started as a feel at the small of my back.

It grew as it traversed up my spine, my neck, over my scalp.

I then cast it out and it flickered the air before us, going wide, bending back behind us, until all were shrouded with its invisible shield.

It was a great effort so it took more of just that to remain straight in the saddle before my husband and not whither with the sudden fatigue.

I had thought I was the only one to see, as I was the only one (I knew) who held magic.

I was wrong.

"Calm," my husband whispered in my ear, and at the sound, another shimmer slid down my spine, this one much different. "Wife, if we face other than we expect behind those gates, do you not think my men know how to use the swords and sickles at their sides?"

I stared at the wall of fire getting ever closer in front of us.

"We board ships, Ha-Lah," he told me. "And when we do, we do not use canons."

"Of course," I murmured.

"You will be safe."

"I'm not worried about me."

I felt his surprise.

Then I felt his arm ever tighter around my stomach and there was a growl to his tone when he said, "They will not accept us, wife. Prepare. They will find us odd. They will be appropriate, or they will court the wrath of their king. But they will look on us as curiosities. Hold your head high, my queen, for *you* know our beauty, our bounty, our loyalty and our strength. It matters not what they think. We will ride through their city to their palace and endure their stares and *we* will know the mightiest of kingdoms rides through. And *we* are all that matters."

I forced myself to nod.

He gave me a squeeze with his arm and for the first time since he knew me, his voice held humor. "But your magic is appreciated."

That was endearing.

As much as I wanted to think of my husband as endearing, I could not.

The Wall of Fire of Firenze was getting closer.

So I made myself nod again.

Aramus gave me another squeeze before I felt his lips leave my ear.

I found I was correct.

As we grew even closer, the Wall of Fire stretched across the horizon and rose three stories into the air. One could see it was made of great logs coated in glistening black beneath the red-hot flames.

And when we were but one hundred yards from the gates, with a mighty shriek, they started to open, still aflame.

I put even more effort into keeping my breath modulated as my husband held my back tucked tight to his hefty front and our steed did not falter as we rode through.

Once through, I saw it was unnecessary, as nothing could get over that wall, but it was there: ten-foot wide pits filled with bubbling tar abutted the wall on the inside. And if a being could jump that wall (which they could not, unless they had magic, or a catapult), they would not at first sink in that tar. The pits were covered with stanchions, the peaks of which were honed to lethal points.

So if you did not burn to death, or sink through the tar, you impaled yourself.

These fortifications told true the tales of this warring nation and its efforts to keep the citizens of this city safe.

I was so enthralled by all of this, I didn't notice at first.

And I might not have noticed it then if my husband's hand spanning my side did not grip my flesh in what felt like a reflexive gesture.

It was then I saw the people. People I had seen on occasion during our journey, nomads and much more populace around the many rivers, brooks and streams that snaked green with vegetation through the vast austere plains and dunes of sand.

Black hair, brown skin, tall, the adults pierced profusely, even the children had piercings in ears and nostrils.

And they were running toward us.

My body tensed head to toe.

And then the petals flew.

The cheer went up.

Some threw coins at our feet.

And men arrived with bows fit with arrows which made me gather my magic again, the small of my back tingling, only for their women to light parcels affixed to the tips and for the men to aim the flaming arrows in the air and let fly. Arrows that then exploded in mid-air with a small *pop!* before their shafts fell harmless to the ground.

"*Salu, Prottetori dei Mari!*" they shouted.

"*Salu, La Grande Bellaza del Mar!*" they cheered.

"Do you know what they're saying?" I whispered as I saw a young boy bend low and toss coins in our path as a girl at his side smiled brightly up at us as she threw crimson flower petals into the air.

"Hail, Protector of the Seas. Hail, The Greatest Beauty of the Sea," Aramus translated.

Clapping, cheering, coin and petal throwing and arrow releasing as more and more Firenz raced to line the road winding through the Fire City to watch the King and Queen of Mar-el ride through.

"They're celebrating us," my husband said, sounding even more surprised than I was at our reception.

"Yes," I breathed, smiling down at a small girl child who'd thrown a paltry amount of petals which was all she could hold in her little hand.

They barely lifted inches in front of her before they flew back in her face.

But she caught my smile, her face froze in wonder, then she whirled and shouted, "Mama! *Lei mi ha sorriso! La Grande Bellaza mi ha sorriso!*"

"She smiled at me," Aramus told me. "The Greatest Beauty smiled at me."

"I don't think we need my magic anymore," I muttered.

And then I heard what I had heard often during our voyage, but when I'd heard it, it was not something I had earned.

My husband's deep, silken chuckling.

I had liked it when it was unearned by me.

I liked it so much more when it was mine.

Oh, but I'd made a blunder.

I released my magic and we rode through Fire City, a phalanx that was testimony to the strength of our nation, and we did it on a path glinting with gold, silver and pewter, through air drifting profusely with crimson petals, to Catrame Palace.

I saw the palace was situated on a rise that was not far from the base of a high mountain that started dusty and beige, grew to lush and green, and spiked into the sky black with rivers cut through it of snow white.

As we approached it, riding through lush foliage to do so, I caught my breath.

It was fronted with wild vegetation all around, wide squat plants with large flat leaves turned face up to the sun, spiked greenery, gentle, swaying limbs that drooped at their ends with delicate crimson flowers. Large decorative urns set here and there. Big pots filled with thin, tall bamboo or bursting with ruby-red cyclamen. Crescent and star-shaped pools lined with dazzling designs of bright mosaic tile. And small streams of water flowing everywhere.

And in the center of the curved drive, abutted by a wide pentagram of artistically-laid tile, was a pool shaped of curves and points, inlaid with mosaics, with an imposing three-tiered fountain at the center.

It was exquisite, an oasis, and the palace that sprang from it seemed but a grand accompaniment to the garden's beauty.

The palace was not tall, only three stories.

But it was *long*.

The windows on the first floor were rectangular, and it would seem they all carried exquisite, scrolled screens.

On the second story, all the windows were of traditional Firenz. An unusual, but lovely, arch that had a steep point at the top, bulging out to a trimmed orb, the sides falling straight from that.

And on the third, the same but smaller.

It was built from burnished red stone that gleamed like a ruby muted by midnight.

And standing on its high steps was a warrior who was taller than my husband, muscular, but not bulkier. He was Firenz, fierce, but right then smiling broad and welcoming.

There was another warrior standing with him, wearing, oddly in that clime, thick black leathers—shirt, trousers, boots. He could be Firenz, but although he was as tall and broad as the other, his skin was olive, not brown. And his hair was black, but clipped short to his skull, not long.

And he had ink.

Not piercings.

Mars of the Firenz, the first.

Cassius of the Airenzian, the second.

We stopped, Aramus alighted and then put his hands to my waist to pull me down.

We barely turned before the King of Firenze was at the bottom step, but feet from us.

"My brother, my brother," he said, both of his big hands out, the smile still fixed on his face.

And it appeared genuine.

He took one of my husband's hands and clasped it, lifting the other to clap Aramus stoutly on the shoulder.

"I have desired long to meet you and to know you. Welcome to my lands. Welcome to my city. Welcome to my home. Many welcomes to you," his black gaze came to me, "and your beautiful queen."

Another clap on the shoulder before he released Aramus's hand, then to my shock, bowed at the waist, perhaps not low, but it was respectful.

He did this to Aramus.

And to me.

"Aramus," I heard a low voice murmur and the Firenz king moved aside as Prince Cassius took his place, and I was again shocked when they embraced, both clapping each other solidly on the back. They broke apart and Cassius stated, "Too long, my friend."

"Indeed," Aramus replied and turned to me. "Cass, Mars, my wife, Queen Ha-Lah."

Cassius also did a slight bow.

Having already bowed, King Mars smiled at me.

Then Mars clapped loudly. "Wine!" he shouted. "Food!" He started walking up the steps to the palace, but did it twisted at the waist toward us. "For you and your bride. Do not worry. We're prepared for your arrival. Your men will be settled and seen to." He smiled again. "Let the games begin."

Cassius fell back, and I heard him greeting Aramus's lieutenants.

Aramus took my hand in his and led us behind Mars.

"Aramus," I whispered.

"I must reflect," he whispered back on a squeeze of my hand.

He knew what I was saying.

Petals.

Coins.

Flaming arrows.

Hails to the King and Queen of Mar-el.

We were not curiosities.

We were luminaries.

So I had made a blunder in how I communicated with my husband.

And I knew right then he was reflecting on the fact that he might have made a blunder in not listening to his wife.

We arrived at the top of the steps, moved into a cool vestibule, and a variety of introductions were made to a variety of people that Mars clearly had very little interest in and even less respect for.

Save two.

Prince True, of Wodell.

And a strange exchange that seemed somewhat telling as he curtly introduced us to a petite beauty bizarrely named Silence.

His betrothed.

It was Silence I studied, doing this so intently, my head was turned to her even as my husband led us away, following Mars.

And I did this with the deepest shock I'd experienced that day.

Because she was Dellish.

And she was mermaid.

12

THE CAMP

Princess Elena

An Oasis, Dune Desert, Outside Fire City
FIRENZE

"Bid them to enter," my mother called.

"Yes, my honored sister," Lucinda answered and turned back to the coral silk of the tent flaps.

At who I knew was about to enter, my gaze went to Melisse who was sitting opposite me on the coral, purple, gold and silver pillows set on the rugs that covered the stone and sand of Firenze, and I gave her a disgusted look.

She shook her head at me.

My mother turned to Julia, another of her lieutenants, handing her some papers.

"When we return to The Enchantments, this must be discussed," she murmured. "We take in so many Airenzian, it's becoming difficult. Shelter. Food. Training in the craft. Finding ways for them to be of service to the Sisterhood. I'll want you all together in order that we can decide how to carry on."

"Melisse, as you know, has elected to be with Elena after Firenze," Julia reminded my mother.

"I'll speak with her before we take our leave," Mother replied. "This way, we will know her thoughts."

The flaps opened, and Julia drifted away as all eyes went there.

G'Seph of the Go'Doan came through followed by a slight man with straw blond hair, also wearing the pristine white of the Go'Doan robes. The second man had a gold filigree belt that said he was a Go'Ar, one of their learned priests who did missionary work, unlike Seph, who was a Go'En, a high priest.

"Seph," my mother greeted, pushing up from the pillows to take her feet.

I felt my mouth get tight and my gaze again went to Melisse.

She repeated the shaking of her head.

I understood her wisdom. I'd grown up with it. And she'd taught me much, including the fact that we had two eyes, two ears and only one mouth for a reason.

Watch.

Listen.

And then make your decisions or carry forth your acts.

But even though I'd spent a year in Go'Doan, learning Triton history and advanced ways of healing, and there were a number of the Go'Doan I liked, I still did not trust some of them.

Specifically, Seph.

I could not explain exactly why.

It wasn't that I was not fond his people felt it imperative to their religion to send missionaries wide in an attempt to convert others to their ways, and I did not understand the import of this.

Believe what you believed, and discourse and even debate of it was often enjoyable, and was apt to sometimes create converts, but the practice of diligently attempting to recruit others to believe your beliefs I found a mystery.

But it was their way and they believed in it, so it was not for me to say anything about it. Simply show them the respect of understanding their ideals but stay true to my own beliefs and leave them to who they worshipped and what they did.

It was also not the fact that in their temples across the various realms, they required weekly tithes, many of which were not kept in the local places but sent to the city-state, which was rather magnificent with its gold domes and tidy streets. Though, it was true that was this not only due to the duties they received from its worshippers, but also the cost of the education they offered to students.

This was again not my business. If their followers wished to do this, it was their coin. And the truth was, Go'Doan learning and healing was the best in all the lands (though the Dellish would argue that in regards to education), and their talents with diplomacy could not be questioned. They did provide many services.

And every being had to eat.

It wasn't even the fact that their gods seemed critical, often disapproving, and of what they disapproved, malevolent. If a follower did not toe the line, their punishments were severe.

They had three: Go'Bedi, the god of obedience, Go'Vicee, the god of service and Go'Chas, the god of faithfulness.

Though it seemed to me, Go'Bedi got the most attention.

But again, if that was what spoke to them, the path they wished to journey in their lives, it was not for me to say.

Importantly, outside of their arts of healing, their skill with diplomacy, their scholarly ways they shared well beyond the gold domes of Go'Doan, they were known to provide safe harbor in their temples, and if needed, arrange safe passage to those who required it.

And a goodly number of those were Airenzian women.

Mostly, I didn't trust some of them because their priests were oftentimes unnerving.

And my mother was a queen. The queen of a great nation. She was also ill, even if her stubbornness would not allow her to speak of it and she tried to hide it.

But we'd just been riding over desert dune and plain now for some weeks, and I knew she was weary, even if she tried not to show it.

Therefore, she should not rise for anyone, especially not a Go'Doan, and especially not in her state.

But she did.

And because she did, Melisse and I did as well.

One thing was good about this. Serena was not there. She was in her tent some ways away enjoying the Firenz servants that had been sent to attend our camp and she had far less patience for all Go'Doan (and, well, anybody).

"Ah, it is a miracle, the beauty and strength of the Nadirii Sisterhood just an hour outside the burning wall of the Fire City," Seph remarked, coming forward and taking both my mother's hands in his in a way I found too familiar. "Whoever would have thought this would come to pass?"

"Much is changing in our lands, Seph," Mother replied. She let him go and looked to me. "You remember Princess Elena?"

He turned my way and reached out both hands.

I hid my aversion and took his, wishing it was G'Jell who'd come to call. I very much liked Jell. He was genuine and kind and quick to find humor in a situation.

Mother had also shared that he was there, in Firenze, for the events and ceremonies.

However, he was probably doing what most Go'Doan priests should be doing at this time of night. Being at his prayers or being with his brethren or being asleep.

Not traveling an hour outside Fire City to disturb my mother for a good natter for no purpose at all when he'd see her tomorrow eve.

"Yes, of course," he said to me. "Your beauty continues to be unsurpassed."

As if I cared aught about that.

"Thank you, Seph," I replied. "And it's very good to see you again."

His words did not reach his eyes. "I'm honored you think so, Your Grace."

"And, of course, you remember Melisse," I noted.

He let me go and whirled to Melisse.

"The kind and wise lieutenant of a great queen. I knew not the fullness of privilege I'd have, walking through some silk flaps," Seph declared.

I took the opportunity of his obsequiousness to look to the man with him.

He was taking everything in with keen eyes and no expression, though I got the sense from him that he wished he was somewhere else.

Studying him, though, I felt a chill hit the back of my neck, and that, too, had no reason.

"Allow me to introduce my new G'Ar. This is G'Drey, very recently to this land and this is very lucky for he is here to witness these historical events," Seph announced.

G'Drey came forward and was appropriate during introductions, as the Go'Doan always were, with everything.

Outside of impromptu evening visits to a camp in the desert the night prior to the inhabitants of said camp performing in a massive parade and just hours after they'd made that camp after a very long journey.

Mother offered them pillows and called a trainee to bring wine, bread and cheese.

"The Fire City is abuzz, my queen," Seph launched in. "And has been for weeks. They are most excited about all who arrive here, those from these lands and ones far away. Much coin is being spent. Much revelry is in the air. And adding to this, the King and Queen of Mar-el arrived just today with great fanfare. He is fearsome, she is even more of a beauty than the stories foretell. The Firenz people rained petals on them, threw coins at their feet and shot flaming arrows in the air as they and their men rode through the streets."

I would have liked to see that.

I'd never met the King of Mar-el. He didn't often come to the mainland and the Mar-el people as a whole mostly kept to themselves on their vast island. But I heard he was just as imposing as he was easy to look at.

Indeed, because of their isolation, the whole of the Mar-el people were mostly a mystery. Simply their royals' appearance at these ceremonies was a strong shift in the way things had been for centuries in Triton.

I hadn't heard much about his wife, but I was curious about her.

"Of course, King Gallienus and Prince Cassius have been here for over a week," Seph carried on. "No fanfare with that, like brothers welcomed home, Cassius and his men instantly went off with some of Mars's lieutenants to hunt or fish in Fire Lake or," he flipped out a hand, "whatever men of that sort do."

"Indeed," my mother replied, caring not what men of that sort did.

G'Seph slid a glance my way before his attention went back to my mother and he carried on.

"And King Wilmer arrived just days ago with Prince True and Wilmer's little niece. So petite. I must say, Mars has displayed many qualities of his father. He's most patient and accepting, for a Firenz." This last was said with just a hint of abhorrence that I reckoned he thought he hid, but he did not. "But I cannot imagine he's best pleased with that waif. I've seen her wandering about the city with a guard of Mars's warriors as well as Dellish soldiers and there's barely anything to her."

Again, I looked to Melisse.

She was plucking at her casings like she'd lost track of the conversation when I knew she had not.

I drew in breath and with it, patience.

"I know Silence personally, and if Mars has persistence, he will find his match is most assuredly pleasing," my mother said.

"Yes, of course, as any sister would be," Seph murmured.

"And would it not be worth some thought that perhaps Mars would need to best please *his* mate?" Mother asked.

"It goes without saying, my queen," Seph replied.

I decided to turn my thoughts to just how long I had to sit there before it would not be rude for me to take my leave.

"Are you and yours quite ready to take the arena tomorrow night?" Seph asked.

"Yes, we are," Mother answered.

My sisters were.

Not only had they prepared before we left, we had stopped often on our journey to practice the drills we would be doing, becoming accustomed to the feel of the air, which was much different, and the heat, as well as allowing our horses to do the same.

Yes, my sisters were ready.

I wasn't so sure about me.

"Why don't we let you two friends speak," Melisse cut in, rising to her feet. "Tomorrow will be full so I'll walk my princess to her tent before finding my own."

By the goddess, I adored Melisse.

"My queen," she nodded to my mother. "Seph, as ever, lovely to see you."

"And you as well, faithful lieutenant," Seph replied.

I rose and said my farewells, giving more attention to Drey than Seph.

I did this wondering why he was in that tent. Assigned to Fire City, he should be involved in some healing effort, or at his prayers, not visiting queens.

I thought no more of it when Melisse took my elbow and led me to the flaps.

We hit the cool night air and cloudless starry sky of the Firenz desert and Melisse did not speak until we were well out of earshot of Mother's tent.

And then she said, "He has nothing to do and he's a gossip. He's probably beside himself, all these goings-on happening in the city where he's been assigned."

That brought forth an interesting point.

"Do you know why a Go'En of his stature was assigned outside the Dome City?" I asked. "It's unusual. A high priest of his standing, they normally reside permanently in the city-state."

"I've no clue and I don't care," Melisse answered. "The machinations of the Go'Doan have never been of much interest to me."

I wished I could agree.

For my part, I found them fascinating, but sometimes not in an enjoyable manner.

However, there were more important things to discuss.

"We must speak of Mum."

She patted my elbow where her fingers were still wound.

"Not to worry. I'll take you to your tent, then go back and talk with Lucinda and Agnes. I'll make certain they find a way to cut the Go'Doan's visit short. I'll see to it she has a potion. She'll be refreshed by tomorrow."

I stopped us and turned to my mentor, my mother's most trusted lieutenant, as well as her, and my, most trusted friend.

"The maneuvers she's designed—" I began.

"She'll be fine," Melisse assured.

"She simply watches them, but we'll have an audience of tens of thousands, and she'll—"

She rolled up on her toes and captured my eyes with her astute hazel ones.

"*Be fine*, Elena. Do not worry."

"It's impossible not to worry about my mother," I muttered.

She started us walking again. "And this is but a part of the plethora of beauty that makes you."

I wanted that compliment—a rare one from Melisse, who preferred to allow actions to speak louder than any words—to make me feel better.

But I did not feel better.

Tomorrow, for the first time, I would meet my future mate.

But before that, myself, and my sisters (but it was worth repeating, *myself*) had to put on a show for tens of thousands of people, including queens, future queens, princes and kings.

I cleared my throat and asked, "Do you know much of Prince Cassius?"

"I know he's a good strategist. I know that his father, like your mother, but for reasons *not* like your mother, protected his sons so if one was off to battle, the other was not. This he did to protect his heirs, not his sons, not his family, as your mother does when Serena goes to battle, but you patrol. Your mother knows Serena was built for battle, and you for patrol."

She stopped speaking as she often did during our talks to ascertain her point was made.

I nodded my understanding as I often did during our talks to assure her of that.

Only then did she speak again.

"I have also heard tale that his men are loyal to him, very much so, like blood brothers."

As we walked, she purposefully bumped into me.

"And I have heard he is extremely handsome," she finished.

I bit the inside of my cheeks.

Her tone gentled.

"You must let go your feelings for True," she advised.

"I've already done that," I told her what was mostly the truth, (actually, more like *partly* the truth). "I have meditated much on it, but as things stand, the simple matter of fact is that I have no choice."

"You don't, my sister-daughter," she whispered. "For that I am sorry. But I must say, as fine of a male as he is, I never thought he was right for you."

That made me stop us again.

"Truly?" I asked.

She nodded. "He is gentle. He is good. He is," a small, sad smile, "*true*. And because of that, there is no balance."

"But, we agree on all things," I told her.

At that, she shook her head. "I do not know. I take men for pleasure. I took them to have my daughters. I did not take one as mate. But I would think, especially for you, it would be most boring to spend your days with a mate with whom you agree on all things."

She started us walking again and kept speaking.

"You are Nadirii. You embody who and what we are, not simply because you are our princess, but because you are *you*. You are warrior. I know you and I know there will be times you'll wish to put your feet up and enjoy a glass of wine and harmony. But it is in your blood to fight for what is good and right and just and to know those around you know and respect your mind. And so I do not think an eternity of peace is what would fill your heart with gladness."

"I'm not like Serena. I don't need to be at odds with everyone around me."

"But you are like Serena in that you need things that you find challenging. True would never be a challenge to you. I fear, with the Dellish prince, you mistake friendship for passion." She paused before she concluded, "I also believe you will discover the difference very soon."

She couldn't be more correct in her thoughts.

For I had no choice.

"All will be well, my sister-daughter," she assured me. "And you will be happy."

I thought of the Unicorn card I had turned some weeks before.

"How can you know?" I asked.

I looked at her through the cool night air as she answered, "For you are you, Elena. I know you. You will find a way."

It was that compliment that penetrated.

And thus, we walked in silence the rest of the way to my tent.

Though the air was not silent as we approached.

What rose from my sister's tent, set not far from mine, could easily be heard.

Womanly laughter. Manly laughter. Groans. Grunts. Moans. And whimpers.

I looked to Melisse to see she had her brows drawn as she studied my sister's tent on our way to mine.

"It sounds, as ever, that your sister is seizing the opportunity afforded her," she murmured.

My sister, yes. As well as, from what I could hear, her lieutenants, Heloise and Genia, her mentor, Darma, with a few more Nadirii included.

Hours before, when we'd arrived at the area where we were to make camp, we found the King of Firenze had provided us a welcome gift.

Dozens upon dozens of baths set in crimson tents attended by Firenz men (or boy-men, for not a one of them was probably less than seventeen, but not a one of them was surely older than twenty).

These baths had clean, but fragrant milky water floating with petals and there were a plethora of jars and bottles of oils and lotions and salts and elixirs for skin and hair.

Precisely what a man would think a woman would want after a long ride.

It was true, of a sort. And because it was, I took a bath (without using the male servants to wash my hair, scrub my back and...*other*) and it felt nice. The selections I used smelled lovely, worked beautifully and helped to relax my muscles and take the tightness of the sun out of my skin.

But...

Please.

"I bid you goodnight here, sister-daughter," Melisse said on a squeeze of my elbow.

"Goodnight, my mother-friend," I murmured.

We touched cheeks and she gave me a small smile before she wandered away.

I watched her for a moment before I turned my attention to Serena's tent.

I had a mind to march over there, enter, and remind her I had an eight-year-old girl in my tent and I was not best pleased this was the lullaby she was hearing in a foreign land the night before we were all to enter a foreign city and attempt to win entire realms with drills and magic.

But I not only did not want to see my sibling as she likely was now.

I did not think I could keep my temper.

And my mother, and Melisse, had taught me well.

Therefore, I went to my tent and threw the flap back, only to have my own lieutenant, Hera, immediately approach me.

"Would that we were engaging in games on the morrow, not drills," she hissed. "I'd select her, unseat her and humiliate Serena in front of Firenze, Airen, Wodell, Mar-el *and* the bloody Go'Doan."

"How long has it been lasting?" I whispered back, my gaze flicking to the lump under the quilt on the pallet.

"An eternity?" Hera questioned in her sardonic answer.

"I'm sorry," I replied.

"You attended our queen," my friend said on a sigh. "And she is fine. She feigns sleeping, but Serena's ways are not unknown to her."

They were not, for the most part.

Though perhaps not *these* ways.

"Go, my beloved friend," I urged. "Sleep. I'll see you on the morrow."

Hera glared at me, glared at the pallet, glared at the tent wall beyond which was Serena, and then she nodded and took her leave.

I discarded moccasins, casings, tunic, arm shields, and body suit before I slid on a pair of panties and a shift.

I then climbed under the quilt with Dora.

She rolled and burrowed into me.

"My love," I whispered as I wrapped my arms around her.

"I'm never taking a man," she whispered back. "I'm going to be like Hera and find a sister to love."

Hmm.

"I'm not sure that's a choice, Dora, but if it is as you are, then I'll be glad for you and wish for you that you find your truest love and she has the truest heart," I said.

"All that grunting. And the cries," she said.

The damage was done. I could do naught about it now.

I still would have words with my sister tomorrow.

Theodora's next was tentative. "Does it hurt?"

"I don't know, sweets," I said. "Though Jasmine tells me it feels quite lovely and if times are right, it can be profound."

"*That* doesn't sound profound. It sounds painful and...*arduous*."

I listened for a spell.

It did indeed.

I sighed, pulled her closer with one arm and tugged the quilts over our heads with another.

Then I did what I never, ever would do.

Unless it was for Theodora.

I disobeyed my queen.

In so doing, I expended a little magic to drown out the noise.

And to add to it, I started humming, then singing.

I started with the sad notes of the "Song of the Lost Sons." The song about the Night of the Fallen Masters when our ancestors fled into the night, taking only their daughters with them, for their safety, and freedom, needing to leave all things male behind.

And when that seemed too melancholy to help my Dora sleep, I started to sing the "Hymn of The Enchantments." The story of my many-times-great grandmother raising The Enchantments in the forest we claimed that was surrounded to the northeast by Airen, the south by Firenze, the northwest by Wodell, and at its northernmost tip was the city-state of Go'Doan.

It told of how the trees in the forest grew ever taller, ever wider, the branches stouter in order that we could build our homes in them.

It told of the shimmering veil that could not be seen by man, only by woman. On horse or in carriage, a man could ride a straight line and not know it was not straight, but was bordering The Enchantments, for he could not come in or even know where The Enchantments began. But a woman, if her heart was pure, and her need was deep, could see them and beseech them for entry, relief and liberty.

Dora fell asleep during the fourth verse, and when I was assured her sleep was deep, I dropped my magic.

It took some time for my sister and her companions to cease their play.

Even when they did, I held my Theodora close.

But I did not sleep.
For the morrow would be busy.
And I had much responsibility.
Last, and weighing most heavily on my mind, on the morrow...
I would meet my mate.

I3

THE REASON

Lady Silence Mattson

Entryway, First Floor, Catrame Palace, Fire City

FIRENZE

"It is not you, *piccolina*," Farah said to me in a low voice as my future mother-in-law moved stiffly away after bidding a chilly goodnight.

We'd gone into the city with Queen Elpis, Sofia (Farah's lovely (but very sad) mother), my mother and my aunt, Queen Mercy.

As well as a guard of Dellish *and* Firenz.

We'd dined in an establishment where we sat on cushions on the floor (which I had discovered made up most of the seating options in this land) and women in much skimpier attire than Farah normally wore undulated around us with sheer veils over the bottoms of their faces. They did this while ringing little cymbals together on their fingers.

It was extraordinary and held much beauty, even if it made me feel fidgety in a way I didn't understand.

And the succulent spiced meat, flavored couscous, roasted vegetables, and flat pies filled with ground beef in a dense, tangy gravy were delicious (as all food in this land, I had discovered, was delicious).

I turned to my new somewhat-friend (only somewhat seeing as she and I had dined together every night since I had arrived, but other than that, I did not see her).

This night was the first with only the women (save Queen Ha-Lah, who had been invited, but word came from her husband that she declined).

The first night was the only night I dined with my future husband.

Though, on that night, he sat away from me, with his mother, and his friend, Prince Cassius, and totally ignored me.

Last night, and tonight, he dined alone with his men, Prince Cassius (and his men), Prince True (as well as his men) and King Aramus (and *his* men).

Indeed, in the three days I had been there, I had only seen King Mars four times (not including the throne room debacle).

That first dinner.

Once, when he had been standing down one of the *long* corridors of his palace, his head bent and listening to four men who looked much like him (but they were not as tall nor as handsome), Prince Cassius and some of Cassius's men.

He had not even noticed I was there.

But the next time I saw him was the worst.

I was coming up after dinner, alone, leaving my mother with Farah, Sofia, my father, Queen Mercy, King Wilmer, and my future mother-in-law, who was no less remote, and thus I felt the need to escape all of them (most especially King Mars's mother, who really did not like me).

Upon making the top of the stairs and before turning left to go to my rooms and Tril (who thankfully *did* like me), I had looked right.

Only to see King Mars striding down the corridor toward me in nothing but a pair of black silk pants that seemed to be made of flowing sheets wrapped around his legs and attached to his waistband...

And nothing else.

The colossal, defined wall of his chest was exposed. As were (obviously) his immensely broad shoulders. Equally obvious, his strapping arms and sinewy, veined forearms.

I could do nothing but stare.

It was true, I had seen men on our estate, workmen and farmers and Father's guard sweaty and dirty after being done with a day of work, and they'd pull off their tunics or shirts to dump a barrel of water over their heads.

But I'd seen nothing the likes of *that*.

When I felt something start burning deeper into my skin, I lifted my gaze from his chest and caught his black eyes searing into me.

It was then I rushed quickly to my rooms (trying not to look like I was rushing).

I shut the door...

And I bolted it.

He had not (thankfully, or perhaps...*not*, though I wasn't quite certain why I thought the latter) come after me.

The next day, I saw him again only for him to introduce the formidable and commanding King Aramus and his beautiful Queen, Ha-Lah. He did this in a way that indicated he was very annoyed with me when that could not be, for I hadn't been around him to do anything annoying (maybe he'd noticed I was, indeed, rushing to be away from him and his...*chest*).

And that was the last I'd seen of him.

One could say things were not going well at Catrame Palace for me.

Farah was lovely. Her mother as well (although, it was worth repeating, she was sad, and I felt this sadness had many facets, and part of it had to do with Queen Elpis, which was, from what I knew about that sorry situation, understandable).

And I could forget all of this during the excursions my mother, Mercy and I took in the city, which had proved to be full of wonderful smells, lively, friendly people, and fantastical happenings, not to mention enthralling goods and wares for sale, homes, tents, gardens, awnings and *everything*. All of it I could not hide my utter fascination with.

But back at Catrame Palace, even with its beautiful, exotic opulence, things were dreary.

"Pardon?" I said to Farah.

"It is not you she is being cold to," Farah said to me. "Her son has forgiven my mother and me. She is finding this more difficult."

This was confusing.

"Forgiven you?" I asked.

Her head tipped to the side and her demeanor grew wary.

"You do not—?" she began.

I lifted a hand. "No need to speak of it. I know."

And I did know.

Mother whispered it to me while we wandered a bazaar in the city the day after we arrived.

It was shocking, but I'd heard my father speak (and sometimes rant) often about the intrigues and violence of politics.

So it was shocking and it was sad, but it was not unusual for a plot to be hatched to assassinate a ruler (Mars himself (and I shuddered to think about it) had thwarted three such coup attempts during his short, five-year reign).

It was just unusual for it to come to fruition.

And obviously, I'd never met anyone even remotely involved in such goings-on.

Further, it was wretched when I met such persons, they were Farah and Sofia, who had not been involved, but they'd been swept up in the treachery all the same.

I dropped my hand and carried on speaking.

"But I hope it is not gauche, or offensive, for me to speak of it, fair Farah. I only do so to say I understand it, of a sort, for I do know my father would think the same, as would my king. This being that anything my father did was some extension of me, when it is not. He is his own being with his own thoughts and actions. But they do not reflect who I am and shouldn't for they are not my own."

She studied me at great length.

Then her beautiful face grew soft.

"True speaks highly of you. In the times you and I have shared together, I knew he spoke as he is. True. But it seems he was *very* true." She bent and pressed her cheek tightly to mine. "Goodnight, *sorellina*."

I felt warm in my insides for *sorellina* meant *little sister* and she had not yet called me that.

I liked it better than *piccolina* (*little one*), though that was also nice.

And obviously I liked it scads better than *little monkey*.

She pulled away.

"And all will be well with Elpis," she assured. "She is a good woman who is kind of heart and very generous. But she loves her son and is protective of him. More, she grieves her husband, a man she adored, and my mother and I being here I fear has opened a wound that perhaps she has learned to live with, but we remind her that it will never truly heal. It will take time, but you will win her, I'm sure."

I did not share her optimism.

Though now I was also concerned that Elpis would never allow these two ladies back into her heart, somewhere they wished dearly to be, and they were kind souls, so it would prove true that Elpis was generous if they could all become again what they once were.

Or a version of it.

I still smiled.

She smiled back and moved away.

"Silence, my dear, are you going up with me?" Mother called as I tore my gaze from Farah linking her arms with her mother and moving them both to the wide staircase.

"I'll be up in just a moment," I said to my mother.

Her brows knitted. "What will you do down here?"

"I haven't really had a full wander of the palace yet. I'm restless. Tomorrow is a busy day. I think I'll take this opportunity to have a look at the home that will soon be mine and perhaps a wander will fatigue me."

That was when my mother's face softened, she approached and touched her lips to my cheekbone.

"That will be fine, daughter," she whispered against my skin and then pulled away and looked into my eyes. "Enjoy your wander, but don't make it long. Tomorrow *is* busy, my dearest, and you need your sleep. I'll see you at breakfast."

I nodded.

She took hold of my upper arm and gave it an affectionate squeeze before she drifted away.

I watched until I could see her no more on the wide staircase carpeted in patterned rugs with fringe at the sides, and I kept my gaze there long after she'd disappeared.

After that, I wandered.

But when I did, I took nothing in.

My mind was too full.

I was trying not to think of my future husband wearing only those pants.

I could not, however, keep my thoughts from what it was seeming my life might be.

My husband had many men, and he spent much time speaking to them or behind closed doors with them.

Or behind them with King Gallienus. Or Prince Cassius. Or King Gallienus *and* Prince Cassius. Or King Wilmer and True. And now King Aramus.

Etcetera.

I had been told of all this. Or I had been told he was with his mother, or out in his city, doing king things that were not explained, or with his staff (and mother), overseeing the events and ceremonies that were to come.

Not with me.

True's attention was pulled by King Mars, King Wilmer, my father, Cassius, True's lieutenants that made up part our guard (etcetera).

But I saw him on occasion having a quiet moment with Farah, getting to know her, and I was heartened that they seemed to be growing an affinity.

I feared his heart was still with Elena, but Farah was lovely, and even if Elena was fierce of spirit and beautiful to behold, I did not doubt Farah would soon earn True's regard.

The same did not seem to be something my intended wished to earn from me.

These were my thoughts as I stared through the flawless scrollwork of the screen over a window in one of the less formal rooms to the east side of the palace.

What was beyond that screen were the formal palace gardens with their tiled paths, lush greenery, mosaic pools and flowing fountains.

In the time I'd been there, I had wandered them a bit.

And I decided, tomorrow, while everyone was preparing for the parade and the reception after, I'd wander them more.

Perhaps take a book. I hadn't had any time to read since we left Wodell.

I sighed, deciding my life would not be much different here than it was at Bower Manor, though my accommodation more opulent and with many more people about. Then, of course, there would be the fascinating city to discover. And the lovely palace gardens.

But in the end, without my mother there after she left, and Farah and Sofia being with True, I knew it would be far more lonely.

I whirled on this unhappy thought, made to stride, and slammed into a wall, nose first.

I drew back, my hand going to my nose as a blossom of pain bloomed behind my eyes, and with it surprise since no wall had been there before.

Quickly, the pain dissipated.

And when it did, I felt a hand flat on the small of my back, something hard pressed to my thighs and belly, and my eyes, that were right then encountering nothing but a large span of smooth brown skin, went up.

To see the black eyes of my intended scowling down at me angrily.

"First," he growled and his other hand (the one not at my back holding me to him) came to my wrist, his fingers winding around to pull it away. "We see to that nose."

And this he did.

He let my wrist go only to grasp my chin with the side of a finger under it and his thumb to the point whereupon he lifted my head, bent his deep, and studied that protuberance on my face.

Well, one could say this was humiliating.

And with that skin I saw, it was clear he was again wearing only those pants.

And I didn't know *what* to think about that, except it didn't bear contemplating.

Therefore, I didn't contemplate it.

He kept his fingers at my chin when he straightened and carried on scowling down at me.

"You are fine," he declared.

"Erm," I mumbled.

"You're also avoiding me," he declared irritably.

But...

I was not.

"Well, um..." I murmured.

"I do not like this."

He didn't like it?

I didn't see *him* striding our way as we stood in the vestibule, gathering together prior to leaving for dinner, doing thus to share he'd be joining us in the city that eve.

"Your Grace, I'm not exactly...I mean, you've been rather—"

"I'm not your Grace," he interrupted me. "I will be your husband. You will feel me between your legs. In your mouth. You will sleep under me."

I felt my eyes get wide.

In my...

Mouth?

My reaction made his eyes get angrier.

"You do not think to give this to me?" he asked.

"Well...I...in my..." I stammered and blurted, "What's my mouth have to do with anything?"

He blinked very slowly.

Then he relaxed, much more slowly, and took his fingers from my chin to drop that hand so he could wrap them around the side of my waist.

But as he did this, something fired in his eyes that did something discomfiting to my insides (specifically, regions *south*).

"My name is Mars," he stated in a much less irate tone.

"I know."

"You call me Mars," he ordered.

"All right," I said hesitantly.

"You also will not ever again run from me."

Oh balls.

I didn't hide that I was rushing.

"Well, you were then like you are now. Where you're not, really... erm, *dressed*," I explained.

"I know the Dellish, for whatever fool reason, men and women, feel it necessary to cover every inch of skin. The Firenz do not. And thus, this is the attire I wear at home when I'm at my ease."

This could be that in much of Wodell, for many months of the year, it got quite cold, and in Firenze, this did not happen.

I did not remind the dark king of that.

"All right," I said again.

"You will need to get used to it," he declared.

I did not think that likely.

"All right," I repeated.

"My land is not your land. You will need to get used to that as well," he went on being overbearing.

"I know this," I shared.

"And do it quickly," he decreed.

I pressed my lips together so I didn't say anything foolish.

"Tomorrow night, you ride at my side, and during the parade, you sit at it so my people can gaze on their future queen."

One moment...

Was he...

Mad?

I felt the length of my frame tightening.

"I cannot do this," I breathed.

His heavy brows shot together. "Why?"

"I...but...there will be thousands of people there."

"I know this."

"And you'll be the center of attention. Even, probably, for many when the Nadirii are drilling."

"I know this too. It is the way. I am their king."

"And if I'm to sit beside you as your future queen," I carried on, "they'll be looking *at me.*"

"I know this as well."

"But, I don't..." I shook my head, making an effort to pull myself together. "I'm not like that, my king, erm, Mars," I corrected when he looked to be getting irate again. "I dislike attention."

"In but a few days, you're to be made my queen."

"I know," I said softly.

"You cannot *not* have attention."

Oh by the gods, I hadn't thought of this.

And thinking on it now, I thought it was dire!

"You will need to get used to this too, little monkey," he proclaimed.

My attention was instantly pulled from my newest plight, to his words.

"If it pleases you, *my king,*" I said in a snappish manner that was not a'tall like me, "do not call me 'little monkey.'"

"It does not please me," he retorted instantly. "For you are my little monkey."

"I am not," I kept snapping.

"You are," he returned.

"Am not!"

Faith, my voice was rising.

He gave me a gentle shake and a less gentle squeeze, reminding me I was pressed to him (not to mention, he was a king so perhaps I shouldn't raise my voice at him) and that odd feeling hit my belly (and parts south).

"You are, *piccolina*, for you are adorable, as a monkey is adorable. So adorable, anyone who sees it forgets just how very clever it is."

My eyes got wide again as I stared up at him.

"You think I'm clever?" I whispered.

"You don't hold great affection for your father," he stated.

I lifted my chin. "My father is a good man."

He shook his head. "I admire your loyalty. It heartens me. But you do not truly believe this. You believe he is sly and grasping and is not a man who would thrust his body in front of an arrow to take that wound so his daughter would not. He would thrust his *daughter* in front of the arrow so he would not endure that wound."

My eyes slid away.

"And you are right," he declared.

I looked back to him and was again whispering when I said, "Please do not speak of my father that way."

He dipped his face toward mine and my breath stuck in my throat.

My, but he was even more handsome that close.

And more daunting.

But what he said next was surprising.

And, it must be admitted, warming.

Not the first part.

The last.

"I will make him rich, my little monkey. Beyond his imaginings. And I will do this so he will leave his daughter to my protection and leave *our* daughters to my protection. For, Silence, make no mistake, I would thrust my body in front of an arrow to suffer that wound for my child."

I stared into his eyes, unblinking.

But my heart was racing.

"And I will not have him interfering with you or using you for his own ends. I will make this clear to him. If he again comes to my realm to sit at my table, he will do it as your father and nothing else. Not a man who uses you as an instrument to further his own ends."

I didn't know how much time he'd spent with Father, I had not thought it was a lot.

But he sure had him pegged.

"My mother is lovely," I said softly.

"She is a woman torn between two forces. And she veers the wrong way."

I pressed my lips together again.

"Though, she will be welcome at my table at all times, *piccolina*," he assured quietly.

That was nice.

I did not share I felt that.

I just nodded.

His gaze held mine before it fell to my lips and his mood shifted so abruptly, and strongly, that it felt the air in the entire room shifted with it.

"It is but mine to teach you how you will use that mouth," he murmured like he was talking to himself, though his words (and the tone in which he stated them) made some things I didn't understand happen inside me.

And those things made other things happen to me.

Primarily, my frame relaxing in his hold, into his *body*, doing this languorously.

And it didn't seem I had the will to stop it.

"Mars," I whispered.

His eyes lifted to mine.

"You ride at my side, Silence, and you sit at it tomorrow eve."

It would appear I didn't have any choice in that.

Therefore, I nodded again.

"And you do not run from me, my bride, not ever again."

And no choice in that, either.

I nodded yet again.

Caught in the trance of his mood, I gave a small jump when his big hand swathed my jaw and I froze when the pad of his thumb swept my lower lip as his eyes watched.

All right.

That did something to my insides too.

They felt...

Melty.

"But mine," he said softly, as if mesmerized by his own movement—or my lips. "Only mine."

I then swayed when he let me go abruptly and stepped away.

"To your bed, Silence," he ordered. "Tomorrow is an important day and I'll not have you drooping during the Nadirii's performance, for if tales are true of Queen Ophelia, it is sure to be something."

And with that, he pivoted and prowled from the room, the panels of his chocolate-brown silk pants flapping against his long legs.

I stood where he left me, breathing deeply, and thinking I'd gone mad.

For it was dawning on me I didn't mind being a little monkey.

Farah Magos
Landing, Third Floor, Catrame Palace, Fire City
Firenze

We sat in the window seat of the back, center window on the uppermost floor.

All around us was dark.

We gazed at the moonlit gardens.

We were both twisted to the windows.

His thigh was up in the seat, as was mine.

Our knees almost brushed.

But they didn't.

Though I wished they would.

In the past days, he only touched me when he was being gallant.

Although this was often, as he was gallant in all things, I found I wished for other touches too.

These, I did not get.

"Would you like me to have a word with Mars?" he asked.

I studied the features of True Axelsson's handsome face, patterned silver in moonlight through scrollwork.

I had told him of Queen Elpis's remoteness.

And he would do that.

Talk to Mars.

For me.

For my mother.

Because I had learned very quickly that he was that man and he wanted nothing to weigh on me.

As he would want nothing to weigh on anyone who had even a modicum of his affection.

Oh, would that this man could truly be mine.

Elena of the Nadirii must be quite something.

"After Silence marries Mars, we're away to Wodell, True," I replied. "Mama is coming with us and staying with us. It matters not if Queen Elpis accepts us again. She will not be coming, and we'll be living on Dellish land, somewhere it is not likely she'll travel."

He turned to face me. "Her daughter-in-law will be Dellish."

"Yes, and if Mars takes his bride to visit her home, Elpis will not ride with them."

"Because of you?"

I reached out and briefly touched his knee before I said gently, "Because Firenze does not hold much interest in Wodell."

"Of course," he murmured, and I could see his lips quirking in the moonlight.

"I don't want to offend you," I told him earnestly.

He looked back out the window. "My father is of my grandfather. And my grandfather is of his. And so on, Farah. They have two things they are very good at doing. Selecting ill-chosen counsellors who advise them in all things and do it very poorly. And then they take this counsel and carry it out fully."

He turned his attention again to me, reached out and took my hand, but it wasn't briefly.

He held it.

He was good at that too.

"In other words, I'm not offended, sweets."

He'd begun calling me that yesterday.

I had marked the first time he gave that to me.

I did it not only because it was dear, but because I hoped he thought it to be true of me.

Carefully, I asked, "Did these counsellors advise your father to ride on Firenze?"

He squeezed my hand, let it go, but didn't take his attention from me.

"Three times. And if Rebecca, our great witch, did not share about the Beast, another campaign would have been forthcoming."

"Oh, True," I whispered.

He shook his head. "We are not a poor nation, Farah. We don't have the riches you do. We don't have the advancements of Airen. But our people are not starving. If we set the men we use to war on Firenze to training them in the engineering of Airen and bettering the piping in our homes, the irrigation of our fields, the improved passage of our rivers. If we were to build alliances with the King of Mar-el to allow our ships through to the Green Sea so our wool and grain and pewter can get through to Lunwyn, Hawkvale, Fleuridia, they would know better lives without ruby mines and saffron fields."

"I've noted King Wilmer has not taken this rare opportunity to sit with King Aramus," I remarked.

That made him look out the window. "It isn't rare. It's unique. And you're right. He squanders this opportunity when we have much wood that can build ships, and if we had passage, we could build fleets for merchants to deliver our wares to the Northlands and The Mystics." He turned again to me. "I do not know if my men would desire to be sailors. What I do know is that they would be gone from their homes for months, but they would return. And they'd do it breathing."

I caught *his* hand at that.

"Can *you* talk to King Aramus?" I asked.

He nodded. "I can and I will. Not now. Our relationship is new, and I don't think it'd be wise to ask for a concession when I barely know the man and he has no reason to grant it. He is warm to his men. He is warm to Cassius, who he knows. He is wary of everyone else and does not mind showing it."

I had noticed this myself.

True continued, "It's clear with my father and Gallienus, they're taking this opportunity not to worry about the Beast, but instead to enter into negotiations under the guise of diplomacy. I can't imagine they're missing the fact that Aramus is no fool. Though it appears just that is happening. However, we have months of travel together as we fulfill the prophecy. So I'll find my time. I just have to hope my father doesn't cobble my efforts before I find it."

"I've also noted he does not show great respect for the Mar-el," I murmured.

He took control of my hand so I was no longer holding his, but he was absently fiddling with my fingers in a way that I greatly liked, giving him something of mine to touch, hold on to, as he sorted important things in his head.

"His counsellor thinks Mar-el is not of great import, as he wouldn't, since he feels they can obtain an everlasting ruby mine and saffron fields. Though I'm uncertain who he intends to sell those rubies and saffron to, as, if we wrested that land back, the Firenz would embargo them, the Airenzian probably would too, and the Nadirii don't put much consequence in jewels. Therefore, we'd need to ship them to The Mystics or Northlands, and to do that, we'd need permission to sail through."

"This is *very* short-sighted," I muttered crossly, my gaze dropping to our joined hands.

Just in time for True to stop fiddling with mine and squeeze it.

"Ah, beautiful Farah. In our short acquaintance, I admit, I've wondered often if your beauty makes you beautiful, or if it is your loyalty that shines through and gives you beauty."

I stared at him, unable to breathe, for that was the highest compliment anyone could pay me.

"Perhaps both," he whispered, lifting my hand to his lips and touching them to it but briefly before he gave it another squeeze, let it go and rose from the seat. "Shall I walk you to your rooms?"

Apparently, our brief interlude was done.

This saddened me.

"I'm going to sit for a bit."

He bent, touching his lips to my forehead before he straightened.

"Sleep well, sweets."

"I bid the same to you, my True."

He granted me the gift of his smile in the moonlight.

Then I watched him walk away.

I looked out the window.

Tomorrow, I would see, and meet, this Elena.

Until then, I would hope that I would find it in me to like her for she was True's and I highly suspected he was a man who would not let go of anyone who had a place in his heart.

Even if what they'd wished to share, heart to heart—what *I* was coming to wish to share with him—would never be granted.

For any of us.

14

THE PLOT

G'Drey

Marital Bedchamber, Manor of Captain of the Trusted, Fire City
FIRENZE

G'Drey really did not wish to climax.

He really did not.

Not like this.

But he would, and he had, not frequently, but regularly, after the warrior had found him again in the city.

This time being the most humiliating.

And after it, he knew, he would vow never to come back.

But he also knew, when the crimson envelope summoning him arrived—becoming obsessed with these encounters like a man addicted to the effects of the *ashesh*—to get his experience, Drey would steal into the night from the Go'Doan temple and find their home. He would make his way to the back door, which would be opened for him, and eventually, after they used him as they would, he would climax...

Humiliatingly.

This time, his chin to the bed, his wrists tied to his knees, his knees staked open, tied to a brace, a leather strap along his forehead bending his head back as it was tied to the baton that was working through his arse, his aching, rock-hard member being sucked on by a *woman*.

All this while he was forced to watch before him, his noises muffled by a scarf shoved in his mouth—one of *hers*—as the warrior pounded between her legs, their lips hardly ever disconnecting, his grunts muted by her mouth, her whimpers the same by his.

And Drey watched the warrior's arse work.

He also watched his thick, veined, slick, rigid shaft plunging and retreating.

And he'd do anything for the opportunity to watch all of that.

Or the times the warrior would use that shaft on Drey.

Or the times he'd take a paddle to Drey after he'd filled him with something.

Or any of the attention the warrior gave to him.

Eventually, and simultaneously, Drey saw their heads snap back as the warrior roared his orgasm and his wife cried out hers, her hands grasping his muscled flesh, her nails digging, her long legs wrapped around the warrior's rutting hips.

G'Drey wanted to find it disgusting.

But the savage pounding in his arse and the talented suckling at his shaft, he could do nothing but buck into that mouth.

He lost the mouth and endured the mortification of being watched by the warrior and his wife as he was milked with her hand into some toweling over the bed under him while she used his arse brutally and he jerked and spasmed against his bounds as he poured his seed with muffled moans onto the bed.

"Take care of our girl, my darling," the warrior's woman bid and then it happened.

The female behind him was moved in front of him, her cunt shoved in his face, and the warrior fingered her to climax while his woman fondled his chest and he fondled their friend.

There was a good deal of kissing (this only on the mouth between the warrior and his wife, Drey had learned that was a boundary that was *never* crossed no matter who joined their play) and stroking and cuddling between the three of them that Drey was forced to watch before the women slowly exited the bed after lingering attention given to the warrior.

They left the room and the warrior flicked at Drey's bounds, releasing him, then offhandedly slid the baton from his arse and threw it on the bed beside him.

"We'll call for you when you're again required, *mio buco*," the warrior muttered. "Now you may leave."

He waited for the warrior to do the same before Drey tore the leather strap from his head, yanked out the scarf, and rushed to his robes.

These were not the ones of the Go'Doan. He did not wear those when moving through the city at night for these fetid (but titillating, and damnably fulfilling) assignations. He wore darker ones that were similar to the ones the priests and priestesses of Firenze wore.

He pulled them on, attempting (but not succeeding) in ignoring just how much he liked the feel of his used arse, his drained balls, his replete cock, and he felt the fire boil inside him.

They would all feel his wrath.

All of them.

Indeed, they would.

Eventually.

He wasted no time, stole into the night, keeping to the shadows as he moved through the quiet streets, returning to the Go'Doan temple, which, really, was an insult.

The city-state of Go'Doan was resplendent. The white stone. The blinding beacons of the profuse gilding of the doomed roofs. The snowy cobbles of the narrow roads that wound through the city. The glass of the windows blinking in the sun, perfectly clean under the constant ministration of their acolytes, the Go'Ella.

It was a place of inspiration, of great beauty, every corner affording an awe-inspiring vista.

Here, the Go'Doan temple was made of rusty stone with only one gold dome to say it was of the Go'Doan, a few spires, and the only good thing about it were its deep catacombs that went down five layers.

And as he snuck in, he was glad it was late at night and the royal celebrations that would span three countries and three months would start the next day, for everyone would be abed.

This was what he thought before, but two steps in, his head was knocked into the wall and stars exploded in his eyes.

Before he knew what was happening, or he could get his thoughts together, his head to stop pounding, the stars to recede, or his feet under him, he felt many hands on him and he was taken down, down, down.

And down.

Then in a room he'd never entered, not even after his extensive tour upon arriving several weeks before, a room lit only with candles and smelling profoundly of patchouli, his robe was stripped from him and he was forced to kneel on the stone floor. He was then bent over and tied bodily from neck to hips on a stone slab, his arms wrapped around its bottom and tied at the wrists, his legs bound to the legs of the slab.

And his arse was used again.

To take a lash.

His cries of pain had quieted to whimpers of agony and exhaustion when he felt the blood start to run down his thighs.

Only then was his hair seized and his head yanked back, and in a haze of pain and confusion, he noticed priests all around, their robes not white, but black, their hoods drawn up, their faces obscured, but he knew them...

He knew his brethren was around him.

And he could see right in front of him, Seph's face surrounded by his hood in the candlelight.

"You risk much to have your arse fucked," he bit out.

"My brother—" Drey tried.

Another lash across his arse and Drey's neck tensed, his teeth clenched, and they stayed that way for three more.

The whip stopped and Seph, who had not let go of his hair, started speaking again.

"Were you not, this very morn, in a meeting to finalize the plot?" he demanded to know.

"I was," Drey whispered weakly. "But, sir—"

More blows landed, and more blood started slinking down his thighs.

When they stopped, Seph carried on.

"The last attempt, our brother was forced into the pits." Drey's head was jerked back farther by his hair. "*Everyone* needs to stay sharp. There will be a time when these men will be at our command and you can get yourself fucked as often as you like by as many as you like. We will have Firenze. We will have Wodell. And once we do, Airen will have no choice but to fall. We'll burn The Enchantments and enslave the Nadirii and their magic to our will and Triton will be *ours*. But now, you have but one focus. You do...your duty...to...*The Rising*," he bit, slammed Drey's face into the slab and released his hair.

G'Drey was blinking away stars again when he felt Seph's presence had left him, but it didn't go far.

He knew this when Seph spoke to the others in the room.

"Leave him until morning in order that he can ruminate on his transgressions. Then have a recruit tend him. No Go'Ella see this," he ordered. "And do not allow Jell or Liam anywhere near. Both of them are of the old guard and will be on a horse to Go'Doan to report this faster than you can say 'Go'Doan Rising.'"

"Can those of us who want it use his arse before we go?" a voice Drey knew requested, and he winced when he flexed that area on his person as his answer to that.

"No," Seph thankfully replied.

"Can we use his face?" a different voice he also knew asked.

"For fuck's sake, fuck each other and stop bothering me with this absurdity," Seph said on a sigh.

Drey heard shuffling feet and whispering robes, some of the candles were extinguished, and when the noises were mostly gone, he heard Seph order softly from a new position at his other end, "The recruits don't enter until they have my leave."

"Yes, my liege," a voice replied.

Drey belatedly started trembling.

He heard a heavy door close.

But he knew he'd been left alone with Seph.

His liege.

At least...there. In Firenze. Where Seph was in charge of this part of The Rising.

There was silence.

Drey continued to tremble.

And he waited.

Seph finally spoke.

"You have a lover in Go'Doan, do you not?"

"Y-yes," Drey answered.

"He is of The Rising," Seph remarked.

"Y-yes. H-he recruited me."

His voice was contemplative when he noted, "Yes. Our brother G'Fenn. Alas, it is unfortunate Fenn will lose his hole."

After delivering that, an unmistakable noise came forth and Drey closed his eyes against it, thankful the flesh of his backside was so raw, he barely felt it, only felt the sting of the salt when Seph's seed he'd milked through his own hand landed on it.

"I own you now, brother," Seph whispered thickly. "I am no warrior, but trust me, I will use you well."

Drey said nothing but the trembling did not stop when he heard the heavy door open and shut.

But what he thought was that his lover was far more powerful than Seph.

And Fenn would not like his "hole" used and definitely not abused.

He liked Drey's bottom as it had been.

So when they were joined by Drey's chosen, they would see who owned who.

And G'Drey filed vengeance against Seph amongst the other transgressions that would eventually have his attention.

Not to mention, the two of his brethren who had sought to use him against his will.

But first, they had an assassination to carry forth.

For nothing was as important as The Rising.

15

THE PROCESSION

King Mars Laches

The Crown Prince's Bedchamber, Second Floor, West Corridor, Catrame Palace, Fire City

FIRENZE

"The queen, my king."

Mars looked from tying the laces at the side of his waist to the servant boy who was speaking.

"Allow her entry," he murmured, thinking that very soon, when anyone mentioned "the queen," they would be referring to a different person.

A Dellish.

His clever, little monkey with a soul of molten silver.

And he did not mind this.

On this thought, his mother moved into his rooms and he turned his attention to her.

Using the creams and lotions and elixirs of their land since she was a maiden, her beautiful face was nearly unlined, simply a few across her forehead.

However, two small indents at the bridge of her nose had appeared since his father died.

Her hair was mostly black, with but a silver thread here and there.

And for the night's events, she wore a long-sleeved choli top covered in a profuse pattern of jet beads, the same beads at her waist and hips, from which flowed the sheers of her skirt that exposed her legs encased in leggings that ended at her ankle. Her feet were in beaded, flat sandals.

All of this was black.

Mars most definitely tired of all the black.

The extravagant ruby necklace at her neck was the only thing Mars liked.

He did not share that with his mother.

When his attention returned to her face, he saw she was running her eyes over him as well.

"So, you've decided. You're changing the Firenz uniform, moving away from the blades," she remarked.

"We ordered a number of these," he replied. "They came with Cassius's envoy. Only my men for now. We'll then assess. But the leather of Airen is the best in all lands and they've made some improvements to their leather armor, which was already exceptional." As he caught the look on her face, he shared, "It's not as constricting as you'd think."

"I shall miss the blades," she murmured, stopping in front of him.

His father wore the blades, as did her father, as did her son.

It was time, in many ways, to move from olden things.

Ares had taught him that.

"It's handsome," she said, lifting a hand and resting it on his chest.

Mars couldn't argue that.

A sleeveless, sandstone-colored leather upper that had no collar and fit to his skin closely. He was able to don it by loosening the leather laces at the sides. Trousers of the same, though buttoning at the crotch, therefore no laces.

But he wore his sandals laced up the leather at his calves. He was not yet ready for the heat and rubbing of boots.

"And I quite like the mantle," his mother went on.

As did he.

A heavy crimson silk that went to his ankles at the back and cinched at his neck with a wide, gold clasp studded in the center with a large Firenz ruby.

The back of the mantle was embroidered with fire out of which rose the coiled Firenz black asp, its head raised, green eyes alert, mouth open, forked tongue snaking, fangs bared to strike.

The same snake was forged in gold with eyes of emeralds and these were affixed to his leather arm shields that were buckled to his forearms.

All in all, vastly different than the ceremonial royal finery of golden chest shields, thick leather blades tipped in gold and rubies dripping from his kilt, and helmets with plumes of vermillion feathers his father wore.

And a damned sight less heavy.

"We're to be away soon and I've been told the others are gathering in the vestibule," Mars noted quietly. "Did you come for an escort down the stairs?"

Elpis lifted her gaze to his.

"I hear the cheers of the crowd all the way to here," she replied. "The acrobats and fire eaters are already entertaining. Our people have something to watch so we have a moment before the procession. I'd like to take it."

He needed to take a moment for Silence before they left as well.

But he'd give his mother this as he would give her most anything she asked.

"Then do," he invited.

She turned, and from the folds of her skirt, took a long, thin box he hadn't noticed she carried when she arrived.

It was ebony, and as he moved with her to his bed, where she laid it, he saw on the top it was crusted with large, exquisitely-cut rubies and crescents of onyx.

It was seeing that, his gaze went to her face.

But he had her left profile. He could not see her wedding chain.

He heard the clasp release, looked back to the box she had opened, and felt his chest grow tight.

In a bed of black satin, two long, thin chains rested.

The top one: simple, minute, but brilliant gold links. Though there was a hoop studded in flawless rubies at the place where the chain hit the lobe of the ear.

The bottom, the same links, but at the lobe hoop of rubies fell three strings of gold links on which diminutive jewels dangled: one string with onyx, one of ruby, one of ice diamonds. The same size and type of jewels hung from the line that fed from lobe to nostril.

His mother's wedding chain.

And his father's.

"Mama," he whispered.

"It is time," she said to the box, then turned her brown eyes to him, and that was when he noticed she wore a new chain of only rubies with some emeralds, no longer diamonds and onyx. "And I've instructed the servants to move me out of my rooms tomorrow. I'll take others, in the east hall, not close to you and your bride. And I will remain in them for the time it will take to ready the relict house for me."

It was time. They both knew it.

In fact, Mars should have assumed her rooms on his coronation.

But he didn't have the heart for they were the rooms she shared with his father.

Mars didn't protest her offer.

He simply nodded.

"The day after tomorrow, so if she's in any discomfort, she won't feel it at the betrothal dinner tomorrow eve, I'll gather the women and we'll perform her piercing ceremony," she declared. "It won't be a lot of time to make sure the piercings are clean and no poison gets in them. But this is all going very quickly, and she wasn't pierced at thirteen to await her marital chain. We'll just have to hope for the best."

"It is good I have you to think of the things I have not," he murmured.

His mother searched his face before she whispered, "Does she speak to your heart?"

"You withhold from her," he noted instead of answering. "And not simply because she is often with Farah and Sofia."

He watched the flash of grief mixed with anger brighten her eyes at the mention of those two women before she repeated, "Does she speak to your heart, my son?"

"She has a soul of silver," he answered.

"Silver is bendable," she replied.

"Silver is luminous and precious," he returned. "And Father taught me bendable is not to be avoided. It's breaking that is."

His mother nodded.

She knew Ares had taught this lesson.

And lived it.

Mars carried on, "Though it is her wit I look forward to discovering."

Her wit and her breasts and that pink mouth and watching her abundant curves on her wee body as she rode his cock.

He did not share this last with his mother, however.

"I've not noticed much wit. She's very quiet," his mother remarked.

"She does not speak unless she has something to say."

Her head tipped to the side. "She told you this?"

He smiled at her. "Moments after we met. When I was demanding she say something."

It was then, he was glad to see a flash of humor in her eyes.

"Then it would seem, my son, she also has courage," she replied.

She might.

But she would not need it.

Nandra, their most powerful witch, had been adamant the Beast was rising, even after being questioned about this again once the tremors stopped.

But his wee monkey would not face these travails or any other.

He'd see to it his silver did not break.

It was what husbands did.

And as he would be husband to his tiny wife with her silver eyes, he would do the same.

"We must join the others," he said, before calling out to the servant boy who was always close unless he'd been dismissed.

The boy came forward.

"Lock this in the place I keep things most precious," he ordered, indicating the box with his hand.

The boy nodded as Mars took his mother's hand, lifted it to the side of his chest and began to move them from the room.

"We have not had time to speak of much more than planning the upcoming festivities, Mars, but you should know," she began. "I've decided I will not be traveling with you to the wedding of the Dellish prince."

She could not even speak Farah's name.

Mars sighed and replied, "I wish you'd rethink this. You'll be missed by Farah."

And Sofia.

"I would give you all things I have to give, as my son and my king," she returned as they moved into the corridor. "But that is not mine to give."

"Mama—"

She dug in her heels and he stopped, looking down on her to see her mood had swiftly changed.

"Farah, yes," she hissed. "She was of an age she was at her own pursuits and with her friends more than in her home with her father and mother. But Sofia slept at *his side*. She should have *known*. And knowing, she should have *warned us*."

"I do not wish to note this, but I will," Mars began. "He was in this very palace with you, and me, and *Father* the night before his blade struck treacherous and true. He was my second father. I spent much time with him the whole of my life. He was my father's most trusted lieutenant, and Father spent much time with him as well. And he, and Sofia, often joined you and Father in your bedchambers. And we, not one of us, understood his duplicity."

She turned a face set stubborn away from him.

"Just think on it, Mama, this is all I ask, and this will be the only time we discuss it."

Elpis faced forward and mumbled, "And for that last I will be glad."

Mars sighed again and moved her down the hall.

As they descended the stairs, he noted the vestibule was crowded.

All had gathered to begin the procession.

But his eyes searched for her.

And his cock made itself known when he saw her.

By the gods.

"Mars, may I have a word?"

He turned his head with annoyance when he had to take his gaze away from Silence.

Prince True.

"We have a parade to attend," he reminded the prince.

"One moment, and it's important," True replied, glanced at Elpis, gave a small smile with a small bow and then he looked back to Mars. "And with respect to you both, I need this moment to be alone."

"I'll make my way to my steed and ask the others to follow," Elpis said. "My son," she dipped her chin to Mars. "Prince True," she repeated the gesture.

With that, she waded into the bodies in the vestibule.

Mars looked to True.

"A moment," he granted.

True didn't waste that moment.

"Neither Farah nor Sofia will participate in the procession," he announced.

Mars stared at him.

True wasn't finished.

"My men have gone ahead to search for a safe place for them to watch the arena without anyone seeing them so they won't miss anything. But they won't be sitting on the podium. After this, they'll be escorted to the reception tent, again without anyone seeing them."

"Both Farah and Sofia enjoy Firenz events, True," Mars told him. "They've been away from them for years. But also, Farah is your bride, you're a part of the procession and you should sit on the podium with your betrothed."

"Your mother doesn't forgive them, which is understandable. But can you stand there and guarantee me that every citizen of Firenze does?"

Fuck, he had not thought of this.

And thinking on it, he saw the wisdom in True's caution.

However, in that moment, he had to assess the wisdom of trusting True with their protection.

They locked eyes.

"Your men will guard them?" Mars asked.

"My father's guard will be the Dellish representatives in the procession. Alfie, Wallace, Luther, Bram and Florian will remain behind to escort Farah and Sofia to the arena. They'll also stay with them."

Mars had met these men.

He had sat with these men.

They were True's entire personal guard.

True had Farah's best interests at heart.

And Sofia's.

And True mentioned it but made no judgment about Elpis's feelings on this matter. He simply made his point without driving it home in other ways that would not be welcome.

A good general.

A good diplomat.

Perhaps just a good man.

An oddity for a Dellish.

A boon for Farah.

Mars liked this.

"It will be done," Mars murmured.

"My gratitude, Your Grace," True replied, dipped his chin and turned, moving through the quickly clearing entryway on a path to Farah.

Finally, Mars was able to turn his complete attention to Silence and he did this as he walked to her.

She wore a gown not of Wodell. It was not of Airen. It wasn't even of Firenze.

He'd never seen anything of the like.

A red nearly the exact same shade of his cloak. It ran in gathers over her shoulders, covering her breasts (mostly, part of the swells down the middle could be seen). Under them, the cloth was attached to a wide belt of the same material that had horizontal gathers, rather than the vertical at her breasts and skirt. That panel molded to her midriff, stomach and upper hips and from it, the same silk floated down and swept the floor.

Her hair was up in a profuse bundle of loose curls that covered the entire back of her head.

But at the front and through the curls were threaded a multitude of gold chains that seemed to link in a knot behind her left ear. There, a number of strands tangled, falling down the wide path of bare, ivory skin of her front, between her breasts. The other he saw fell down her back, though he could not know how far they went, for she was turned to face him.

As he was noticing was her wont, she let simple (or in the case of that gold, subtle but extravagant) things make her point.

In other words, she wore no other jewelry.

She would wear her wedding chains beautifully against that pale skin and gleaming black hair.

But arriving before her, Mars decided she would take no other piercings.

Except, perhaps, one at her navel.

And one, like he had, in her tongue.

"Wee monkey," he whispered when he arrived at her, and he could sense her struggle with not, perhaps, rolling her eyes or uttering a retort.

This made him smile.

He took her hand and turned her to the line he'd prearranged to form before he led her to her horse.

"It's time to meet my men," he announced.

"All right," she said softly.

Her eyes. Her breasts. Her shining hair that looked soft as Firenz silk. Her wit. Her cleverness.

And her voice.

All of this he liked.

Very much.

"Lorenz, husband of Nyx, father of no one, my captain," he introduced Lorenz.

She bent at her waist and then held out her hand, murmuring, "Lorenz. My pleasure."

Lorenz took her hand and Mars heard her intake of breath as he pressed it to his heart and his stomach before releasing it.

This was also prearranged.

For traditionally, on such an occasion when a guard was presented in fidelity to the protection of a woman, the female's hand would be pressed to heart and cock.

However, Mars had recently learned his little one would most likely not react well to that.

And learning this, he wanted her small hand nowhere near another man's cock.

"My future queen," Lorenz rumbled.

She offered him a trembling smile.

Mars moved her down the line.

"Chu, husband to no one, father probably to many, though none known, my left flank," Mars declared.

"You are of The Mystics," she whispered, staring up at Chu with his deep-set eyes and sunflower undertone to the tan of his skin.

"I am, my future queen," Chu replied.

"I've not met anyone of The Mystics," she said.

Chu grinned. "You have now."

She held her hand to him as she bent at the waist. "My pleasure."

Chu took her hand and held it to his heart then his stomach before he released it.

Mars led her down to the next. "Guard, husband to Zosime, to be father to a daughter or son within months, my right flank."

"My future queen," Guard said as he took her hand and pressed it to himself.

"Many congratulations and a safe delivery of your child," she bid. "May he or she be vigorous and the gods smile down on them with abundance."

"And my thanks, my future queen," Guard replied on a grin, his eyes sliding to Mars, his gaze stating openly his approval.

Mars didn't need Guard's approval, if glad of it, so he nodded to his man and moved her to the next.

"Basil, not to be married, eventual father to orphans, if this is his choice, my rear flank."

"You...don't wish to marry?" she asked hesitantly, but curiously.

"I take only arse, my future queen. And that would be only male arse," Basil replied, and Silence gasped.

"She's Dellish, brother, remember this," Mars warned.

"My apologies, my future queen," Basil said. "Though, might I add, I wish to find but one arse I wish to take...eventually."

Silence blinked at Basil.

Mars looked to the ceiling.

"Dellish take arse, they just don't talk about it," Chu muttered, and Mars wrested his eyes from the ceiling and shot him a meaningful stare.

Chu grinned at him but spoke no more.

"Well, I, erm, hope you find the but one, um...*male* you like and adopt many orphans," Silence bid gamely, and Mars was forced to swallow laughter.

Though he did not stop himself from feeling the beginnings of pride.

The Dellish were known prudes.

This had been a concern before he met her, and then after he did with her attire, her stated inexperience, in times her manner.

Mars was glad to feel this concern fading.

"He's already found many he likes, *many*," Guard murmured.

Silence ignored this, and without hesitation offered a bow and her hand, and Basil took it, pressing it to heart and gut.

Mars led her to the next. "And Kyril, husband to no one, father also probably to many, my other rear flank."

"My future queen," Kyril said, sweeping her hand up to his lips while doing a deep bow before rising and pressing it to his heart and gut.

When he released her, Mars asked casually, "You'd like your head still attached to your neck tomorrow, no?"

Kyril grinned at him.

Mars ignored it and turned his bride to the fullness of line.

"These are the Trusted Ones," he told her. "Is this something you understand?"

She tilted her silver eyes from the line of his men up to him.

"I think so," she replied.

She did not.

"They are the Trusted Ones, Silence," he stated again. "Each Firenz king has them. They are trusted by me, and now you, in all things." He pressed his hand into the soft, warm skin of her back (for he had found, the ribbons of red led down to a waistband, exposing a strip of flesh that fell lower than her front, and the gold dangled all the way down her spine). "In *all* things, *piccolina*," he stressed. "Once you are my wife, they would lay down their lives for you."

There was a slight widening of her eyes, a brief nod, and she turned her attention again to his men, putting her hand to her chest.

"It is good to know you," she declared.

Simple words stated in a way she made clear she meant them.

That was when she received deep bows from the Trusted.

It was now done.

Therefore, it was time for the procession.

As he was moving to lead her out the door, he noted she slid her hand over the material at her chest, seeming to be trying to adjust it to more fully cover the curve of her breast before she noted his eyes on her movements and her hand fell away.

He took her other one, lifted it to the side of his chest and moved her out into the night.

They were to walk by Cassius on Caelus, his black steed as they made their way to the front of the large procession of men and women all of whom were already seated on horseback.

"Are you ready for tonight, my friend?" he asked Cassius as they passed.

"No," Cassius grunted, and he regularly looked ready for most anything, but now he looked ready for only one thing.

To kill something.

"Perhaps it won't be as bad as you think," Mars suggested.

Cassius's gaze slid to Silence before it moved back to Mars, but he made no answer.

Mars smiled at him and strode to the front of the group, finding he had to slow his gait and adjust his long strides for his little one's shorter legs.

This he did.

He made it to the Firenz bay he'd selected personally for her and was pleased to see she did not hide her delight in the fineness of the horse he presented to her.

Then she started to emit a surprised cry, something she quickly swallowed, when he lifted her into her side saddle.

That done, he swung up on Hephaestus, his own steed, as his men took their saddles.

Once mounted, the Trusted Ones assumed their positions: Lorenz at front, Chu at his left, Guard at Silence's right, Basil and Kyril behind him.

And the procession began.

They'd barely cleared the curve around the fountain in front of the palace when he noted his bride fidgeting.

He looked her way to see her hand was again at the material at her chest.

"It covers you," he told her, then decided to add, "And it's becoming."

"Mm," she murmured, quickly dropping her hand.

He studied her fully and remarked, "You sit a horse well."

"I'm not an out-of-doors woman," she replied.

This he did not like because he was an out-of-doors man. And an inside-doors man. And an in-his-bedchambers-with-a-woman man.

And he'd wish his wife as rounded in her pursuits as he.

"Though I like to ride," she carried on.

At least there was that.

"And garden," she said.

And that, though he did not do this, it was good she did.

"And read in the garden."

Also, there was that, and this was also something he did on occasion, just not in the garden.

"And I find it refreshing to take a long walk over the moors and by the creeks and streams, so I do this often," she carried on.

Mars grinned.

"And if there are games, I never miss them," she declared. "Even if they're villages away."

Mars chuckled.

She turned her head his way. "What's funny?"

"It might take less time, wee monkey, to tell me what you *don't* like to do out of doors."

Her chin lifted a bit and she returned, "I don't like to fish."

"Neither do I."

She faced forward, mumbling, "Well, I suppose that's good."

And her hand went back to fidget with her gown.

He clicked his teeth, tensed a thigh, and Hephaestus moved sideways, closer to her horse.

Her head twisted to him again.

"It is fine," he said softly. "So fine, Silence, in a week, half the women of Fire City will be wearing that same gown."

Her lips parted, and Mars was looking forward to having that all to himself and soon.

"I'm very bare," she whispered.

She was not.

Though she was much more bare than she was usually.

"As you've noted, Firenz do not mind bare."

"Yes, I've noticed this," she mumbled.

"Whose idea was that gown?" he asked with curiosity, thinking it was probably her father pressing her to do something she was uncomfortable doing in order to catch the eye of her king.

"Mine," she surprised him with this, saying it turning to face the road ahead. "I saw the fashions of your people, the colors of your standards, and I thought I should try to...fit in. So we went out and purchased some material today and Tril and some of your servants made up this gown from a design I sketched so I could...do that."

She wouldn't fit in.

She'd set the new standard.

"Silence," he called, and she turned her head.

It was then, he noticed the look on her face.

And it was then, she again spoke. "They'll all be looking upon me, Mars."

So, on hearing that, he leaned, reaching out with both arms, and she stifled another surprised cry as he plucked her off her horse and planted her side-saddle on Hephaestus before him, her legs draped over his right thigh, the skirts of her gown trailing down the side of his steed.

And having her so close, he found she also smelled very good.

Freesia.

Guard moved immediately to take the reins of Silence's horse.

"Faith," she for some reason whispered, staring with wide eyes to the road and sitting stiff against him as he tightened his arm around her middle.

He also bowed his back to put his lips to her ear.

"You are protected," he said there. "The Trusted you can see, but there are hundreds of my warriors at the arena, and there will be dozens around the podium, there to see to our safety."

"I'm sure, however—"

"And you are beautiful, in that gown, in the acres of material you normally wear, it is simply what you are."

Her frame tensed even further at that, as did her jaw.

But she had no reply.

However, he'd just paid her a compliment.

And a woman should acknowledge a man's compliment.

Especially if it came from a king.

So he squeezed her middle and prompted, "Silence."

"I do have nice hair," she said to the road. "And I have interesting eyes. And lovely skin, though it's much paler than your people. In other words, I know what I have, Mars. So do not lie. It is, I suppose, kind. But I know it's false, so it won't aid me in facing what I'm about to face."

Mars had to take a moment to calm his mind after his bride called him a liar.

He took that moment.

Then he asked, "And how do I lie?"

She twisted her neck and looked up at him. "I know I'm not beautiful, so saying such doesn't help."

He stared down into her silver eyes and took more time to calm his mind before he informed her, "Women who seek compliments are not favored by me, Silence."

"Women who..." Those eyes widened again before she carried on, but still didn't finish. "You think I...?"

With that, she faced forward and said no more.

Mars gave her another squeeze and called, "Silence."

"If you think that," she whispered. "Then you meant what you said."

"I always mean what I say."

Her chin lifted again, this time in a jerk.

But he also noted it wobbled.

"Silence," he growled.

"Thank you, my king, for your lovely words." She spoke in a trembling voice. "I think I now will feel much more robust about facing the crowds at the arena."

It was then, Mars understood their annoying exchange.

So it was then he straightened in the saddle, but pulled her closer and said over her head, "Once this is all done, you will need to talk clever and very long, my little monkey, if you wish your father to come back to my realm and sit at my table."

He felt her jerk around to face him again. "What? Why?"

He looked down his nose at her.

"Our daughters will know their beauty. They will never be in doubt of it, Silence. Not a single, fucking *breath* of their lives."

Those pink lips parted again, and she stared up at him in wonder.

Then she jerked back around and faced forward.

The sounds of the arena were getting closer.

Mars adjusted in his saddle and pulled her tighter to him, fitting her arse snug in his crotch.

His people were of the sand, the fire, the snake...

And of the horse.

They would expect their future queen to ride in, seated true in her own saddle beside their king.

But as they were right then was how his people would first see their future queen.

Held tight to her king, snug in *his* saddle, as the procession rode the edges of the field of the arena, before they dismounted and took their places on the podium.

And that was how they rode.

There was shouting.

Cheering.

The throwing of petals and coins.

And his future queen sat straight on his horse, held tight to him, her stature small, but her chin lifted, her shoulders squared, her baring regal.

She often waved at children.

And smiled at the elderly.

Mars had not put much thought into the prophecy and the need for his marriage to be arranged. He knew, if he didn't desire her, due to this being a marriage of arrangement, and not one of the heart, he'd simply sire an heir on her and find what he desired elsewhere.

And if his people did not accept her, he'd set her away somewhere she'd be comfortable and carry on with his reign as he saw fit.

But by the time Mars dismounted and pulled Silence wearing that splendid gown off his horse, he suspected she had a kingdom close to eating out of her hand.

He knew this as this was happening with its king.

16

THE PARADE

Princess Elena
Nadirii Sisterhood Procession to the Coliseum, Fire City
FIRENZE

"Still not talking to me?"

I was not, thus I didn't say anything.

"For the goddess's sake, I took my first lover at fourteen," Serena snapped. "Theodora should know the ways of things. It was good I did."

"Let us not do this now," I muttered. "There's much to concentrate on and none of it is you being thoughtless...again."

"You're right. There is," Serena agreed. "*Much* to concentrate on. For instance, how Cassius is going to take one look at you, know you're nothing like his very beloved, very Airenzian, very *obedient*, very *womanly*, very *dead* wife, want not one thing to do with you and then decide for the rest of his days to close his eyes and picture her while thrusting inside *you*."

I decided not to reply.

Regrettably, Serena was feeling chatty.

"Though it probably isn't such a bad thing, as you'll be closing your eyes, picturing True."

I again remained silent as we rode behind our mother and her lieutenants through the deserted streets of Fire City (indeed, the only beings that seemed to be about were the ones who opened the fiery gates to allow us entry fifteen minutes before).

We were on our trajectory toward the enormous, lit arena we could already see and definitely hear.

"I wonder what True's intended looks like," Serena pondered, unfortunately verbally. "She's Firenz. Their striking beauties are renown throughout all the realms. So I'm certain she's a stunner."

I drew breath into my nose and remembered the words Melisse often said to me about high roads and low roads and how you slept at the end of the day once you laid your head on your pillow, depending on which road you chose.

"And the Firenz are known to be more open sexually than even Nadirii. This means True's probably already had her."

At that, I started when a glimmer of coral shot between Julia and Agnes, who were riding in a line before us that included Melisse and Lucinda on the outsides.

It slammed into Serena's face, precisely her mouth, and my eyes flew to the front of the procession where my mother rode.

She was twisted in her saddle, her arm still raised to cast.

Her face was lethal.

Serena made a grunt.

Well then.

It appeared Mum wasn't feeling chit-chat down the line.

My gaze went to Melisse, who, along with all Mother's lieutenants, was turned in her saddle to see the results of her queen's craft.

Melisse caught my gaze, tipped her head to the side and the tips of her lips up, and then she returned to face forward.

Serena emitted another grunt.

"You must call orders, so I assume she'll end your silence eventually," I assured her good-naturedly, glancing sideways to see my sister looked murderous.

But she was silent.

That was all I needed in order to gather my magic within me and focus.

We proceeded, winding through the streets of a city that seemed to be made up of mostly squat buildings fashioned of rust-colored stone or the same colored clay. Night had fallen so the colors of awnings, the flowers in a profusion of pots, the paint on doors, the mosaics in archways, the rugs in courtyards were silvered and mostly colorless.

But I suspected it was quite something in the light.

Now, however, the din coming from the arena was growing ever louder and I had to quell my desire to look behind me, where Hera and Jasmine rode side by side with Serena's lieutenants in order to catch my friends' eyes and be fortified.

Theodora was riding at the rear with the trainees who would not be in parade. She would watch with them as we executed our exercises.

I told myself she would be fine in this land of an enemy who was not right then an enemy, but as an ally of Airen, they had been in the past, and it was understood they always would be.

I would also be fine.

My mother would be fine.

Melisse, Hera, Jasmine, Agnes, Lucinda, Julia and even Serena would be fine.

All my sisters would be fine.

We would get through this.

I would get through the reception after the parade.

And then I would face tomorrow...

Tomorrow.

As we drew ever closer to the arena, I noted that it was lit high up in the air by a long cauldron of fire that ran the length of the arched stands. This was held up by tall, tarred poles like those that made up the wall of the city. And this fire was screened at the back and top with polished steel, which directed the light of the fire down into the arena and on the field.

Clever, that, and a mammoth effort.

Though Firenz were known to enjoy a vast amount of spectator amusements. So many, I assumed, they wouldn't want it restricted to daylight hours.

We started to meet intermittent vats of fire set on the sides of the road that aided the moon in lighting our way perhaps half a kilometer away from the coliseum.

And about a quarter of one, we were met with two Firenz guards wearing bladed leather kilts, crossed belts at their bare chests, double swords at their backs.

This was not alarming because these guards were expected. They were to meet us, guide us to the arena and then open the gates for us to enter when it was time.

And thus, they twirled their horses when they met us on but a dip of the chin to Mother and guided the way.

The clamor was almost ear-splitting as we rode into a lighted tunnel that ran under the stands, and I wondered what was happening on the field to cause that amount of cheering, when the guards stopped at some gates.

Therefore, our line stopped.

It was only then I spoke to my sister, and I did it loud enough for only her to hear through the clapping, shouting and what sounded like pounding of feet.

"She's ill and she's using her magic to silence you, which will tire her. We will soon be parted, me from you, me from her. I would hope, my sister of the blood, that in future, or what she has left of hers, with me gone, that you take far better care of her than this."

I received a grunt in return.

An angry one.

But I didn't look at her and said no more.

I kept my gaze glued on my mother's back.

After a time, there seemed to be a quieting all around us.

Whatever they were viewing was over.

I watched my mother's back get straighter.

Therefore, I shifted my hold on my reins slightly and I felt my blue roan, Diana, bunch her back flanks.

Then the Firenz guards shuffled to the side, the gates before us flew open, my mother shouted her high-pitched Nadirii cry, and she burst forward, as did the rest of us.

But once in the stadium, Serena and I rounded our mounts to the sides, and the phalanx of sisters rode past us in a blur of horseflesh, streaming cloaks of coral or purple and flowing long hair of all colors.

And from the sidelines I watched as they raced—five abreast, one hundred precise rows—on the field around the edges of the stands, the horses so close, the riders' legs looked to be touching.

And the only sound I heard as the crowd was stunned silent at this sight (and perhaps sound) was the wail of the Nadirii cry rising into the night shouted by five hundred and nine Nadirii sisters.

With Mother at the lead, they'd rounded the entire stadium and past where Serena and I were waiting to go around one side of the oval of the coliseum again.

But at the front, where I could see a podium with no stands behind it, just a red, gold, and black striped awning over it and the roof of a large crimson tent beyond that (though I could see no one who was on that podium through the riders), the Sisterhood changed routes and cut their mounts down the middle of the field.

But when they arrived at the other side, they broke off, a row of five with coral cloaks going one way, a row of five with purple going the other.

They raced around the edges opposite each other, and I felt my lips curl up when they met at the other end, looking like they were going to crash into each other.

But they rode between each line so near, the snap of the material of cloaks striking against one another cracked through the air and a collective gasp went through the crowd.

Again at the middle of the stands opposite the podium, the riders cut down the middle, breaking again in half in front of the podium, streaming down the edge of the stands, meeting again on the middle in the other side, and cutting in again.

This time to take formation.

Intricately.

And perfectly.

When the five hundred horses and riders in five rows, one hundred across, faced the nine women spread at the front—Mother, her lieutenants, Serena's and mine—who had their backs to the podium, the Sisterhood facing it, the horses all stood in pristine lines, at sides, and front to back.

Lines so perfect, if you stood at the back, front or end, you could only see the horse and rider before you, not the ones beyond.

It was then, I heard my mother shouting, "*Staffs!*"

And every Nadirii sister pulled her staff out of its sheath at the back right of her saddle and whipped it in a circle in the air over her head.

They then pounded them down as one in the dirt at their right sides, and at each end, a flash of coral and purple sparks rose up high, glinting over the end of their staffs into the air, this to another, deeper gasp of the crowd.

"*To the left!*" Mother commanded.

Staffs lifted, every horse as one took one step to left, the riders circled their staffs over their heads and then pounded them in a shower of sparks to the dirt at their left.

"*To the right!*"

And again, this same routine, this time to the right.

"*Staff rest, Nadirii!*" Mother ordered.

All the staffs were lifted, twirled in a blur overhead, and again, and again. Then, in unison, elbows bent, and the staffs were twirled over the hind end of the horses again and again. And then as one they were brought to the left side and twirled again and again, and finally over the head where this was repeated to the right.

And simultaneously they were all re-sheathed, the collective crack of staff into scabbard breaking through the air.

"*Bows to the left!*" Julia yelled.

The entire left side of two-hundred and fifty Nadirii tore their bows off their backs.

"*Take aim!*" Julia shouted.

With precise movements timed to be performed as one, each of the left side of the Nadirii pulled an arrow out of her quiver, also at their backs, and fed the nock to the string.

The bows were lifted, aimed to the sky to the left.

"*Fire!*" Lucinda bellowed.

Another collective gasp sounded as the arrows soared into the air.

But it was calls of shock and cries of wonder when they exploded into bright, giant blooms of coral and purple sparks lighting up the night.

"*Bows to the right!*" Agnes yelled.

The right side of the formation responded.

"*Take aim!*" Agnes shouted.

They took aim.

"*Fire!*" Melisse roared.

And more arrows went soaring to the heavens before great star-bursts formed.

"*Fire at will!*" my mother thundered.

The Sisterhood complied, and the sky lit up in flashes of orange, coral, white, gold, amethyst and violet light.

The oos and ahs of the crowd layered over each other and didn't quite silence when Lucinda yelled, "*To the left!*" at the same time Agnes shouted, "*To the right!*" and the display overhead ceased as horse and rider of each company took five steps as ordered, opening a column in the middle of the formation.

The Sisterhood replaced their bows at their backs.

It was time.

Diana was ready.

As was I.

Collectively, the Sisterhood cried, "*Nadirii!*" ending this with our shrill war cry.

And Serena and I burst forth down the back of the line.

We turned at the open column in the middle and rode down, side by side.

I didn't have the chance to see who was on the podium, but even if I had, I did not have that in my head.

As we raced straight to our mother, sitting proud on her white steed in front of us, I thought nothing. I was nothing.

But the Sisterhood.

And my mother's daughter.

So when we made it nearly to her, we cut our reins and Serena went right.

I went left.

We speeded around the edge of the coliseum.

Moments before we would meet at the back, we pulled our staffs.

As we passed, one armed, we clacked our staffs violently at the front, the noise resounding through the arena, before we whipped our staffs around the smalls of our back, and traded them, staff for staff, at our backs.

I pressed over Diana's neck, the wind in my hair making it wing down my back, my thighs relaxed giving Diana her head, and I rode her at breakneck speed. When Serena and I met at the podium, right before our mother, we clacked our staffs at the front and returned each other's staffs at our backs.

And another race around the edge of the arena, holstering our staffs, but pulling forth our bows.

I reined Diana in slightly as we were about to make the turn down the middle then quickly looped my reins around the saddle horn.

All that I had just done was executed after a lifetime of training and was as natural as breathing.

This would take focus.

I closed my eyes.

Drew in a deep breath.

And when I opened my eyes, I pressed into my steed with my right knee and made the turn a half second after Serena, reaching to my quiver.

Serena let fly first, an arrow straight into the dirt before us

I aimed, let loose, and my arrowhead split her shaft down the middle.

Vaguely, I heard the simultaneous gasp from onlookers, but I'd already reached to my quiver, fed nock to bow, and let fly.

Serena's arrow split my shaft.

And again.

And again.

Digging my knees into Diana, we halted on a rear of our horses ten feet from our mother and Serena and I...one, the other, then the first, and the other, the movement of our arms but blurs, our aim always true, we embedded all the arrows in our quivers one on top of the other in the dirt a foot before my mother's unmoving steed.

I noticed when we stopped that the crowd was dead silent.

I replaced my bow to its hook on my back and again took up the reins.

So did Serena.

Then I clicked my tongue against the sides of my teeth.

As did Serena.

And Diana lowered her majestic neck as she gracefully fell to her cannons and knees before my mother.

I bowed my head too.

As did Serena.

Serena and her horse came up first.

Diana came up as well.

And as Serena screamed, "*Nadirii!*" Diana and I sprang forth, cutting left in front of Mother, down the front of the formation, the left flank, the back, the right flank...

But up the front, I pulled my feet from the stirrups, put the reins in my teeth, yanked my bow from my back, pushed up on one hand in the saddle, jerked up my knees, found my balance on my feet atop Diana, and stood.

Serena shouted, "*Standards!*"

And every Nadirii pulled her staff, thrust it high, and from it exploded proud coral or purple standards with a white oak leaf emblazoned on it.

And as I neared my mother, she tossed up her own quiver.

I caught it, yanked left with my teeth on the reins, tore down the middle of the formation while grasping the five arrows in Mother's quiver. I dropped it, sifting my fingers through the fletchings, setting the nocks to my string...

I pulled back, turned my bow horizontal, lifted up, aimed high...

I dropped the reins, screamed, "*Nadirii!*" and let fly.

The five arrows arced high into the air, up, up, up...

I closed my eyes again, feeling the prickles shoot up my spine like spasms...

I opened my eyes...

And the sky above the back of the stadium lit up with hundreds of blooms of coral, purple, gold and silver bursts.

Gasps and shouts and cries of delight rung forth as I dropped back into the saddle, returned my bow to my back and regained my reins in my hand.

I whirled in a tight turn at the end of the column, and as I galloped back up I closed my eyes again.

When I opened them the shouts and cries rung higher as the sparks exploding arrested and shot together in a glittering line.

The line swooped down over the stands, toward the field, zipping toward my back.

And when I stopped in front of my mother on a skid of Diana's back hooves, I pressed well forward as my mount's noble head, mighty chest and front legs reared up.

She struck at the night with her front hooves.

And the shimmers in a grand swoop up my back soared into the air, flying above the podium, only to burst right above it into thousands of magical butterflies that flitted peacefully away, disappearing into the night sky.

Diana and I dropped.

The air split open as the crowd boomed their accolades.

I looked up.

And that was when I saw Prince Cassius Laird, heir to the throne of Airen, sitting on the high podium, wearing black leathers, half his daunting face inked, staring darkly down on me.

And I fell instantly in love.

17

THE RECEPTION

Prince Cassius Laird
Royal Podium at the Coliseum, Fire City
FIRENZE

"Outrageous," his father hissed.

Cassius sat in his baronial, intricately carved chair on the high podium with his head turned left.

Away from his father.

The crowd was still thundering their applause for the Nadirii performance.

But as the Sisterhood trooped out of the coliseum, its upper echelon was assembling at that side of the podium.

He noted with approval the first thing they did was care for their horses, leading them to the barrels of water set about for that purpose.

He also noted that as her roan bent her muzzle to the wet, Elena rubbed her cheek down her mount's neck and drifted her fingers over the crest.

Watching this, oddly, Cass had to fight shifting in his seat.

And he had to do it again when she turned.

He had often seen the Nadirii fighting uniform, such as it was. And such as it was, was a body stocking under a leather breast plate stamped with an oak leaf and leather thigh, calf and arm shields. The only uniform he'd seen adorned in any manner during battle was Serena's, and her breast plate held a wide oak leaf formed of gold.

Cassius had never seen their ceremonial uniform.

It consisted of front-lace, slender moccasins that rode up the calf. Above this, stockings made of leather dyed purple that came up to a point edged in gold on the upper thigh. These held tight with silver ribbon casings criss-crossed about the thigh.

On the top they wore a silver tunic that came down to the knees, but it was split up the front of each leg, all the way to the pubis, exposing a silver body stocking at the join of the legs.

The tunic was topped by a hard-leather, fawn-colored, close-fitting bustier that covered the breasts and came down in a split plate, the front edge over the pubis, the sides over the hips. These slits exposed skin from upper thigh to inner hips.

On the front of the bustier were deep reliefs of swirls of gold that came up the ribs and rounded the breasts, bringing attention to that specific area. A Nadirii trait. They took every opportunity to glorify anything female.

Then there was a trim, dark-brown suede belt with a gold buckle at the navel emblazoned with a white oak leaf.

And from the chest and around the shoulders and upper arms, the coral mantle of the royal house of Nadirii fell down the back to the ankles.

Around Elena's forehead, as was around Ophelia's and Serena's (but it was only a band of suede with an oak leaf stamped disk at the front for all the other sisters, gold for the lieutenants, silver for the rest of the warriors), starting with a gold oval set with an oak leaf formed of amethyst in the center. This fed to smaller gold ovals that went around her head over her hair.

And Elena's hair was golden, falling past her shoulders, the ends of the thick locks mingling with the gold swirls at her breasts and midriff.

"That was an entirely obnoxious display," Cassius heard his father grouse as he watched Ophelia move up the steps to the podium.

But Cass froze, as behind the Nadirii queen, he saw Elena, who had been following her mother, turn abruptly.

Her face then lit with a bright smile and her arms opened wide right before a young girl with Elena's golden hair crashed into Elena's slender frame.

They wrapped their arms around each other and Elena gazed down dotingly at the girl who was jumping up and down, jarring Elena's body, the girl's mouth moving quickly in her excitement.

"She has a daughter?" he murmured, and felt Mac, who was standing at his back right, bend to him.

"Not that I know."

"She's right now embracing a daughter," Cassius replied.

"We'll find out," Otho grunted over his left shoulder.

At that point, his attention was necessarily taken with Ophelia making her way along the podium.

Cass noted the Nadirii queen smiled genuinely at Jell, but not as genuinely at Seph at his side and gave a curious look to the other Go'Doan that had arrived, G'Liam.

He felt his mouth tighten when Ophelia then smiled warmly at True, as well as Queen Mercy.

Though she did not do it nearly as warmly to Wilmer.

She showed clear respect for Queen Elpis, even lifting a hand up to hold to her chest as she nodded to Mars's mother.

She then again smiled warmly at Silence, who was sitting on high cushions stacked next to Mars, the Nadirii queen's face going so far as softening, before the guard came up over her features when her attention turned to the king at Silence's side and she assessed Mars openly.

She did the same when she was before Cassius, but to his surprise, she didn't linger long before all manner of expression swept from her face as her eyes lit on Gallienus.

Finally, speculation moved over her features as she took in Aramus and Ha-Lah, giving them both a regal lift of her chin.

After that, without a word, she rounded Aramus's chair, her lieutenants following her, and walked straight to the back, down the steps and into the waiting tent.

"Brother," he heard drawled in a female's voice, and he looked up to see Serena making her way across the podium to him, her brown eyes acidic, a supercilious smile curling her lips.

"Sister," he rumbled, offering the same medicine in return and watching those eyes flash with fury when he returned her jibe and she didn't like it much, before she strode in front of his father without even looking at him.

"Murderous bitch," Gallienus bit out.

But Cass had no time for his father or Serena.

Serena's lieutenants trailed her, and Elena was now in front of Silence, saying something to the girl.

Her daughter was not with her.

Silence's expression was openly friendly as she replied.

When she did, Elena smiled at her, and Cassius noted that her affect was entirely different than her mother's, or her sister's. Unguarded, sociable, informal.

She tipped her head to the side at Mars before dipping her chin deferentially, which Cassius found a surprise.

Nadirii did not bow.

Even in rare times of accord between realms, princess or mere sister, definitely not the queen, they did not bow.

What she gave Mars was not a bow, as such.

But it was the closest thing Cass had seen from any Nadirii.

At least to a man.

She moved to him and Cass felt a sudden burn in his gut when her gaze did as well.

By the gods, her eyes were...*violet*.

And they were roaming over his face in a way that seemed...*hungry*.

He fought shifting in his seat again.

"Princess Elena," he murmured, watching her move with an economy of grace that was the feminine version of the way any good warrior would use his body.

"Prince Cassius," she murmured in reply, her voice quiet, but surprisingly melodic, considering her sister's was lower and always held an unattractive vein of spiked steel.

Her attention went to his father, and although she looked him dead in the eye, there was no deferential tip to her chin.

Though she gave that to Aramus and Ha-Lah.

As she rounded Aramus's chair, Cassius turned his attention to her lieutenants, both of whom trailed slowly and had passed him, but were looking back, ignoring Gallienus, and openly studying Cass.

Not a surprise for it was definite all his men at his back had done the same to Elena and were doing it now to her guard.

Once the Nadirii delegation had disappeared in the tent, with no fanfare, Mars rose from his seat, taking Silence from hers beside him with her hand held in his.

He guided her around his chair and walked back to the tent.

Queen Elpis followed them.

"He could let his elders precede him," Gallienus complained, rising from his seat.

"And if it were me who had assumed the throne prematurely, and his father was still alive, and they were in Airen, would you wish me to allow Ares to precede me?"

Gallienus shot him a scowl before flicking his cloak back and stomping around his seat, his guard following.

Cassius rose, glancing at Aramus, who was guiding Ha-Lah to the tent, but his gaze was on Cass.

He was grinning broadly.

Cass did not feel like grinning, so he simply shook his head at his friend.

He then moved around his seat and his men surrounded him.

"Well—" Mac, of course, was the first to attempt to start in.

"Quiet," Cass bit.

He caught the men casting glances at each other before he focused on the stairs to the tent and moved that way.

His lost wife, Liviana, had auburn hair that she went to great lengths to tame, but it remained wild.

Their daughter had this same mane.

Liviana was also not tall, nor was she short.

Though their daughter was showing all signs she would be tall, like Cassius.

Liviana further had an overabundance of curves, a soft belly, full arse and thighs, and was feminine in all ways. Not to mention, having a mother who was Dellish, staunchly so, Liviana would blush simply exposing an ankle.

She would never wear garments that bared her upper thighs and seemed designed to draw the eye to tits and pussy, completely comfortable and in tune with her body, including having it on display.

And she'd had no idea even how to feed a bow, much less could split the shaft of an arrow at a gallop on the back of a horse.

By all the gods, even Cass couldn't do that.

Indeed, Liv grew timid just being on a horse, making her mount dance, before she found her bearing and was able to ride, though only sedately.

And she would drop due to vapors at the very thought of racing around an arena, or anywhere, like she was competing with the very wind.

And winning.

Soundly.

These thoughts plaguing his mind, he strode down the steps, through the tent flaps that were held open by servants, and when the young boy came to him immediately, he grunted, "Whiskey."

"*Sì, signore*," the boy mumbled and dashed off.

"*Cassius! Here!*" his father bellowed from his place in the middle of the crowded tent where he appeared to be attempting to hold court in a land where he had no courtiers to dance attendance.

And he'd decided not to bring any of his wives so they could perform that duty.

Therefore (likely due to habit, the man did it so bloody often), he wished to make his son dance.

Hearing his men order their own drinks around him, Cass muttered to any one of them who might be listening, "When was the last case of royal patricide in Airen?"

"History lessons are far past, Cass, but if memory serves, it's been over four hundred years," Hadrian answered.

The boy returned with his whiskey, Cassius took it, lifted it to his lips, but before he threw it back, he remarked, "I'm already making history, marrying a Nadirii. That said, I'm beginning to fancy lengthening my section in the Go'Doan history books."

Then he tossed back the entirety of his drink. That accomplished, he instantly put his bottom lip to his teeth and whistled low.

The boy, who was rushing away, darted back.

Cass handed the glass to him. "Another."

"*Sì, signore. Subito.*"

Cassius waited until his men had their drinks, and he had his own refreshed, before he moved with purpose, turning his back on his father and striding to a corner of the tent.

His men came with him.

"Even if you ignore her, she *is* still here," Severus noted as they all positioned, his men fanning out around Cassius, their backs to the tent, Cass's back to the corner.

"I'm well aware of that, Rus," Cassius replied.

Hadrian was studying him.

Cass knew what he saw.

And as was often with Ian, he didn't hesitate to share anything, including the fact he read Cassius well.

"You might never have seen her, but she's Nadirii. You had to know she'd be much different than Liv," he said carefully.

"I'm also well aware that I'll be bound in wedlock to a woman who is not my wife, Ian," Cassius ground out before throwing back a healthy dose of his drink, which was, owing to the astuteness of Mars's servants, twice the amount as his first one.

"Can we now talk about—?" Mac started.

"No," Severus, Hadrian and Antonius said at the same time.

"Right," Macrinus muttered, grinning into his glass of wine at his lips.

With a flurry of self-importance, his father joined their group, rounding his men to come to stand at Cassius's side.

"What are you doing standing here?" he demanded to know.

"Avoiding you," Cass told him.

Gallienus's eyes narrowed before he declared, "We must speak."

Cass lifted his brows when his father said no more.

"I'm sorry, are you asking my permission?" he inquired and watched his father's face start to get red as he went on, "For if this is so, please wait for me to find a scribe. This needs recorded."

Gallienus leaned toward him and bit out, "You can't marry that cunt."

Cassius felt his jaw set hard and his spine snap tight.

"That *display*," his father continued, flinging an arm to the back of the tent, indicating the field beyond, "was *obscene*."

It was far from obscene.

It was the most remarkable display of horsemanship and military drilling Cassius had ever witnessed.

"I quite liked the starbursts in the sky," Otho muttered.

"And the firm asses in the saddles," Mac added.

Gallienus ignored them. "This whole thing is *beyond* preposterous. It cannot be *borne*. And thus, we're leaving. Tomorrow. At sunrise. You will not wed that flagrant *tart*. I've seen better costumes on whores paid to play a role in order to stiffen a cock. It's coming quite clear as each night fades with no further quakes, this was all but a ruse for Ophelia to plant another Nadirii witch on Airenzian soil to cause strife and mayhem amongst my subjects. And further, by maneuvering these ludicrous alliances through marriage, she thinks to control all realms with the threat of the Beast rising and the use of wet cunt. A savvy ploy, but one destined to fail as it will fail tomorrow morning when we *leave*."

Cassius turned from his father when he heard Ha-Lah's voice saying, "Even a Nadirii could not cause those tremors."

Cass looked to the lovely Mar-el queen then up to Aramus, who was standing close to her back.

Aramus, as had been made clear these past days, was not at his most jovial in the presence of Cassius's father.

Though, not many were.

"She could if she had thousands of other witches with her which," Gallienus jerked his head to the back of the tent, "obviously, she does."

"To produce that magic, a quake felt in all realms, all the way to the shores of Mar-el, they'd need every witch in Triton, and after such a spell was cast, they'd be drained. They couldn't produce another for months, if not years," Ha-Lah calmly replied. "Certainly not every fortnight."

"You are witch so of course you'd defend them," Gallienus spat.

"You are old and pompous and not *my* king. In other words, be careful how you speak to my wife, Airenzian king," Aramus growled.

"You can't possibly be believing this rubbish," Gallienus returned to Aramus.

"I think the vastly more important subject we should be discussing is how Cassius's betrothed could clearly kick his arse all the way back to Sky Bay, if she had the notion," Mac jibed, most likely in an attempt to take the growing heat out of the discussion.

"I think it's more interesting that he never has to concern himself with clipping his own nails. Just ask his bride, she can shear them off from thirty feet with the point of her arrow," Otho ribbed.

"And I think it's very interesting…"

At the sound of the stately, feminine voice, Cassius's attention shot through what had been the wall of Otho's and Antonius's chests, both now turned toward the voice, as did all the men, and there he saw Ophelia, flanked by her daughters.

Ophelia seemed annoyed but collected.

Serena was clearly incensed and equally clearly having some difficulty keeping control. Of her mouth or a physical attack (or both), he did not know. Except in the presence of her mother, she was managing to succeed in this task. Barely.

But Elena…

Elena was looking at Cass's chest and she appeared…

Fuck.

Wounded.

They'd heard.

They'd heard quite a bit.

And none of it was about the most remarkable display of horsemanship and military drilling they'd ever witnessed, Elena playing an individual and extraordinary part in that.

"…that the Sisterhood trains since ten as horsewomen and archers and warriors, at the same time learning to harness their craft in ways great and wondrous that can be used at their command. We demonstrated that this eve. It was witnessed by all. And yet you speak of wet cunts and using our skills to trim nails," Ophelia finished.

Indeed, they'd heard quite a lot.

Fuck.

Gallienus pushed closer to the Nadirii queen.

For a variety of reasons, none of them familial, Cassius moved with him just as his brothers closed ranks.

"My son is not marrying your daughter," Gallienus declared.

"This will bring great relief as no Nadirii's *wet cunt* wishes to be tainted by Airenzian *limp cock*," Serena spat.

His father puffed up.

"Silence, daughter," Ophelia commanded quietly. But to Gallienus, she stated clearly, "It is your choice, and your son's." She tipped her head to Cassius. "But when the Beast rises, it will also be on your head."

"Where are the tremors, Ophelia?" his father demanded to know.

"I can't know, Gallienus," Ophelia replied instantly. "Though after the last, every nation moved to fulfill a prophecy that might serve to stop it. So perhaps those who call it have other things to do. Like, perhaps, preventing that prophecy from reaching its fruition. Which in turn might, perhaps, speak to how they fear the prophecy culminating which would share they fear it might work."

"Allow me to intercede." G'Jell of the Dome City suddenly sidled closer to the assemblage, and Cassius watched him with keen attention as he did.

This was because Cass trusted no Go'Doan. Not a one of them. And not for the reasons his father didn't. This being the fact that, years ago, and even in some temples today, they provided safe haven and assisted safe passage for Airenzian women who looked to escape the heavy hands of husbands, lovers and masters.

No.

A Go'Doan had killed the father he wished he had.

Ares.

And at suffering that monumental loss at the hands of a renounced Go'Doan priest, Cassius had no issue with distrusting the lot of them.

Not to mention, he felt they had something to hide, and the fact you rarely saw the scores of female acolytes who attended them laid testimony to that.

"Even the Go'Doan feel these unions are expedient," Jell continued. "Those of our own who study the magicks have sensed the instabilities in the veil. The prophecy was recorded centuries ago. And it is known by all that, if the Beast should threaten to be unleashed, it must be carried forward for the good of all realms."

Jell trained his eyes on Gallienus before he finished.

"And all realms agree. As they do, it's uncertain how they would feel if Airen refused when they each made their sacrifices, this refusal putting all at risk."

"The Mar-el make no sacrifice," Gallienus retorted, flicking a hand in Aramus's direction. "Their king is already wed."

"It remains to be seen what sacrifice Mar-el will need to make," Jell replied. "But you'll note the boots of the Protector of the Seas are deep inland on the soil of the mainland. For a Mar-el, this is already a grave sacrifice."

Cassius's father shut his mouth, for he knew this to be true.

G'Jell's attention shifted to Cass.

"Prince Cassius, it is your marriage, it is your decision," Jell said quietly.

"He is *my* son and *my* subject so it's *my* decision," Gallienus clipped.

"I will marry the Nadirii," Cassius declared, his gaze on Elena.

He got a hint of violet when she lifted her eyes to his, before she turned them away.

"This is good," Jell murmured.

"This is *abhorrent*," Gallienus retorted.

"This is unavoidable," Ophelia sighed.

"Perhaps, Gallienus, we can speak further of this over a glass of wine," Jell offered in an attempt to continue to diffuse the hostilities.

"I'm afraid not as I'm away to my rooms in the palace," Gallienus refused. "The company of this tent leaves much to be desired."

With that weak retort, he pulled his cloak forward at his front and shouldered unceremoniously between Ophelia and Serena, which caused Serena to tense as if she was going to pounce and Ophelia to put a staying hand on her daughter's arm after Gallienus cleared them.

"I need more wine," Mac muttered.

"Amen to that," Otho agreed.

"Serena, go see to the sisters," Ophelia ordered. "They camp in a garden not far from here that King Mars has offered for our use. I'd like to know they're settling."

Her daughter glared at her, turned her glare to Cass and his men, she shifted it to her sister, and then she turned on her foot and strode away.

Cassius felt his arm brushed.

He looked to his left and saw Hadrian there. His man widened his eyes at Cass then turned them to Elena with a jerk of his chin.

Cass looked to his intended.

She was bent to her mother.

"I'll go check on Dora," she said softly in her lyrical voice.

"I think, daughter—" Ophelia started.

Elena spoke over her. "I'll see you in camp."

"You're sleeping at the palace, Elena," Ophelia reminded her.

"I'll join you there tomorrow," Elena refuted.

Before Ophelia could say more, Elena turned to leave.

She took four steps away, winding through bodies, before Cassius shoved his glass at Ian, who took it, and he followed her.

"Elena," he called.

She was not far away, so she was sure to have heard him, but she made no indication she did.

"Elena," he repeated, closing in and reaching out a hand.

He caught hers and she stopped dead, turning to him and tipping her head back to look up at him with eyes now not violet.

They were brilliant amethyst.

It took him a moment to adjust to their luster, and as he did this, he was unaware his fingers squeezed hers.

The moment he'd accomplished that feat, he murmured, "We should talk."

"I think, for now, the words of your father and your men are all I wish to hear," she replied.

"I don't agree," he returned.

"That's funny," she stated, purposefully misinterpreting him. "Considering you moved to stand by your father's side and didn't make that clear when he and they were speaking. In fact, you were quite silent on *all* subjects."

He was.

Though she could not be aware that he'd learned over the years it was most often not worth the energy expended to say much to his father.

Or the fact a few of his men seemed to wish to act like lads until their dying breath.

No, she was not aware of this.

And apparently, with the pressure she was using to pull her hand from his, she was also not going to give him the opportunity to explain.

"Elena—" he growled.

With a forceful wrench, she tugged her fingers from his grip, took a step back, but that was all before she dipped her chin deep into her neck in a sardonic bow, and raised her head.

"Until the morrow, my prince," she whispered, turned, and pressed through the bodies surrounding her.

Cassius watched her go.

"That did not go very well, my friend," he heard Mars remark at his side.

Cass turned to his Firenz brother. "I note you didn't enter the fray."

Mars's lips were twitching as his head was shaking. "Since we were boys, you made it clear you preferred to fight your own battles."

"Perhaps," Cassius allowed. "When I was twelve and my father sent me to your father to train in Firenz tactics and every bully in the regiment wanted to take the Airenzian prince down a peg. And thus the Firenz prince coming to his aid would not have assisted in him making the point that needed made," Cassius rejoined. "This, my brother, is another matter altogether."

"Are you saying it's one you cannot best?" Mars asked incredulously.

"We all were not allied with winsome waifs with silver eyes we could set about charming or voluptuous beauties with sorrowful souls we could engage in healing," Cassius noted.

Mars sounded amused when he said, "Sadly for you, this is correct."

Cassius turned his head and watched as Elena abruptly stopped several feet from the flaps at the other end of the tent.

And his gut burned when he saw what stopped her.

Prince True was standing close, his dark head tipped to Cassius's betrothed, his face a mask of concern.

"Steady, friend," Mars rumbled low, no humor in his tone now when True lifted a hand and curled it around the side of Elena's neck.

Fortunately, his intended shook her head with agitation, raised her hand but briefly to squeeze True's wrist, but also to remove it from her person, and then she was off, disappearing through the flaps of the tent.

True watched her go.

As did Cass.

"He's growing to care much for Farah," Mars said, his tone now conciliatory.

Cass turned to his friend.

"This is good," he retorted. "In the meantime, either you tell him, or I will. If he puts his hand on my future wife again, he'll still have that hand, but it'll be cut from his wrist and shoved up his arse."

He waited only long enough to watch a muscle jump along Mars's bearded cheek as the Firenz king clenched his teeth to beat back laughter.

But yet again, Cass found nothing amusing.

Therefore, he pivoted, and the many bodies moved out of his way as he strode to the other end of the tent, out of it, and to his mount in order to swing astride and ride back to the palace and an entire bottle of fucking whiskey he could pour his gods-damned self.

18

THE THAW

King Aramus Nereus
Guest Suite, Second Floor, East Corridor, Catrame Palace, Fire City
FIRENZE

Aramus had not missed that, not long after the thaw that had started on their final approach to Fire City, the freeze in his marriage had swept up again.

Precisely at the time the servant boy had first shown him and Ha-Lah to their rooms at Catrame Palace, Aramus had left them almost immediately to meet with Cassius, and in doing so, he'd left Ha-Lah behind with orders not to leave that room.

He'd also left Nissi and Oreti guarding the doors to make certain that was so.

This was where she remained, unless there were official functions to attend.

And right then, the instant he guided his wife into their rooms after the reception, he saw that the guise of an allied front of husband and wife she'd put up for the procession, parade and reception was instantly dropped.

The freeze was back on.

He could even fancy he felt the chill.

"Ha-Lah—" he started on a sigh.

"I prepare for bed," she said coldly, moving toward their bathing chamber off which there were two dressing chambers.

One for him.

One for her.

He had now shared quarters with his wife for weeks, and outside seeing her in her sleeping garments, which were (in the current climate) frustratingly brief, he hadn't seen any more of what made his wife.

"I think it's time we talk," he said to her back.

She turned casually toward him, and when he had her front, he saw her brows were lifted.

"You do?" she asked.

"Obviously, I do," he asserted, attempting to keep hold on his temper at her manner. "You've said perhaps ten words to me since we arrived at the palace."

"Yes. I believe they were, 'Please, allow me to leave these rooms or I'll go mad.'"

That was eleven words, but he wasn't going to note that.

"There are reasons, and I told you those reasons."

"Ah yes," she nodded once, "how incredibly unsafe I am in a land where we were met with flower petals and scatterings of coins. I understand the force of your concerns, my king. For if I left these rooms, I might be murdered by adulation."

He really did not like to note his wife could be clever and amusing when she was also being aggravating.

"Ha-Lah—" he bit.

But he stopped himself from speaking when she uncharacteristically lost her temper, leaned toward him and spat, "*Spare me.*"

On that, she turned on her foot and fumed toward their bathing room.

Aramus drew a long breath into his nose.

Another.

Then he gazed about the room, with its large, posted bed on a podium, the posts draped in purple and red sheer silks. There were large rugs of bear hides on the floor on either side of the bed, these swathing down the steps to the podium. There were also chests and ornate lamps and gilded, tufted stools. A door to the left, behind which was where Ha-Lah's lady's maid slept.

And an opening with no doorway to the right, so you could see the rectangular, recessed bath tiled in blacks and purples with dense cushions on the sides. A bath that was always filled with clear waters that seemed magically heated to the perfect temperature.

His gaze swung from the bath, which he had used without his wife, to the bed, which he had used *with* his wife but not in all the ways he would wish.

He then walked to the door to the hall, flung it open, scowled at Xi and Cat, who stood at each side guarding it. He looked down the hall to the boy servant who was one of two always available should a guest in the east wing have some need.

"Rum," he ordered. "*Adesso.*"

Now.

The boy dashed down the hall toward the stairs.

Both Xi and Cat were avoiding his eyes and obviously fighting smiles when he ducked back into his chamber and slammed the door.

Storming to it, he threw himself on a divan in the corner, falling sideways toward the roll at the top, and setting his eyes to the bathing chamber.

It didn't take long before Ha-Lah wandered out in a satin shift the color of aqua that fell just below her arse, had thin straps, and that was it.

She had lovely legs.

He clenched his teeth.

His wife walked right in front of him, straight to bed.

There was a knock on the door and, bent over the bed to throw the silks back, she glanced that way as if she had the most minimal of curiosity for what was behind it as Aramus shouted, "Enter!"

The boy came in, found Aramus, walked swiftly to him and set the gilded tray he was carrying on a small table by the divan.

He hesitated a second, awaiting further instructions, and when he did not get them, he dashed out, closing the door behind him.

Aramus uncorked the bottle of rum on the tray, poured a healthy dose into the glass provided, set the bottle aside and took up the glass.

He swallowed all of it.

He had another glass filled in his hand moments later.

But his wife was under the silks and the lamp by her side of the mattress had been blown out.

"I'm your husband," he announced to the bed. "It's my duty at all times to see to your protection."

She did not reply.

He threw back the rum and poured himself another.

Holding it in his hand, he spoke again.

"It's also my duty to decide what the threats are, what they aren't, when a situation is uncertain, and precisely *how* you'll be protected from the former and latter."

Ha-Lah didn't move or make a noise.

Aramus tossed back the rum, set the glass aside and stood.

"It's for your own bloody sirens-damned good," he told her.

His wife made no response.

He glowered at the bed.

She didn't so much as twitch.

Aramus prowled toward the bathing chamber.

He stopped short when he heard, "Have you ever been locked in a room unwillingly with naught to say about it?"

When he looked back to the bed, he saw she still hadn't moved even if she had spoken.

"You're hardly in a dungeon," he retorted.

"That doesn't matter." She rose up to a hand in the bed and aimed her gaze at him. "Not even free to wander the palace, Aramus? Not even visiting with the women? Not even with a guard?"

Aramus stood, frozen in place, staring at her beautiful face that wore not an expression of mutiny or frustration, but hurt, and he had the sudden realization of something that made him excruciatingly uncomfortable.

He knew nothing about her.

She had mermaid magic.

She was beautiful.

She was stubborn.

She was strong in her beliefs.

She was appropriate in behavior when she stood beside him as his queen when they were in company.

She had been scouted when it was time for him to wed, found in a small, remote fishing village on the northeast coast of Mar-el, and brought to him to be his bride.

And he liked the gowns she wore, so she had good taste.

Other than that, he knew nothing.

And this nothing included how she would feel about having her liberty taken away and what she might need to do to occupy her time to make it the least enjoyable for her when she did.

Not to mention, being taken from her village and forced to wed the king in the first place.

Most women of Mar-el would find that the highest honor.

But he was finding his wife was decidedly not most women.

He turned back to the bathing chamber, moved to his dressing room, and changed into his short pants for sleep.

He then moved back into the bedchamber, shifting about it himself to extinguish the lamps, the last one at his side of the bed.

He lay on his back under the silks and stared at the dark ceiling.

He did this deciding how to go about doing what he should have started doing over seven sirens-damned months ago.

And what he decided was to tell her the truth, even if it frightened her, about why he was being so cautious.

"I know a raider of the Northlands, his name is Frey Drakkar," he said softly.

He sensed his wife tense at his side across the wide expanse of bed.

"He's a very powerful man, a good seaman. The best I've ever met who is not Mar-el. I grew to respect him very quickly."

Ha-Lah said nothing.

"He is a raider, but he is high born. Married to a princess," Aramus went on.

His wife made no move or noise.

"Tales were told wide about Drakkar and his Ice Bride. Many of them. They reached far. Their love, it is said, is unsurpassed. But not long after they were wed, in an intrigue that was not entirely out of his control, his wife barely escaped dying a violent death after she set aside a glass of wine she had not sipped that was poisoned."

He felt Ha-Lah's body tighten.

"Another woman mistakenly picked it up," he shared. "Her journey to death was not long, but it was violent, as she coughed up blood the entirety of it."

"Aramus," Ha-Lah whispered.

He turned to his side toward her.

"I do not know these women in this palace," he said. "I do not know the machinations of this land. You could take up a cup of tea but rooms away from me and be dead by the time I ran down the corridor to see to you."

His wife rolled to face him.

"But to lock me in a room?" she asked quietly.

"Everything you put in your mouth is tested by a servant boy before it's brought to you."

Her tone was sharper on this, "Aramus!"

"The men are at your door. We are on the second floor, but they also prowl under our window."

"Husband," she whispered, her tone on that much changed.

"I would have you safe, Ha-Lah. In his past, before they were wed, Drakkar had bedded the servant who attempted to murder his wife. He did not think she had that scheming in her. But she did. It was not his hand who poisoned his princess, but I can guarantee you, when he discovered whose hand it was, he felt as if he'd tipped the vial himself."

"You're close with Cassius," she said in reply. "It appears you respect Mars. Also Prince True. And Cassius clearly holds deep regard for you. How do you think Cassius would act if an attack on you, *any* attack, my king, was instigated?"

"I would not like to find out, not only because Cassius's sword would be mine in vengeance, and it would put him at risk, but because that might mean I had lost you."

He felt the silk rustle, he waited for her to reach out to him, but she settled before she did.

"How do you know him?" she asked softly.

Aramus wasn't certain, but that might be the most personal question she'd asked him throughout their marriage.

Or, perhaps, the only one.

And he gave her an answer without delay.

"Many years ago, when I was still prince, and very young, we were in a port city on the eastern coast of Airen. We were in a pub. We were at the rum. Cassius and his men were there, and they were at the whiskey. A game of tuble ensued. I beat him soundly and respected his and his men's manner when I did. None of us were near sober, it could easily have slipped out of hand, but his good-natured loss struck me. We decided to take our...revelry elsewhere—"

"With a visit to doxies," she murmured through the dark, fortunately sounding amused.

"Yes," he agreed through a grin.

"And as men in manly endeavors, bonds were formed amongst drink, gambling and prostitutes," she surmised, still sounding amused.

"Something like that," he muttered, and carried on, "He knew not I was prince, I knew not he was. As men do when a good time was had by all, we made vague plans to meet again a year after in the same place for the same festivities. I honestly didn't intend to go. And then I did, something drawing me to again spending time with him and his men. I did it thinking that he would not be there. But he was."

Aramus paused a minute before he finished.

"It took four such reunions before he admitted he was a crown prince. I was...affected by him sharing this about himself. It was something I well knew could put him in danger. But he trusted me with it. So I gave the same in return. And in our years of knowing one another, neither of us have given the other cause to regret it."

"He seems a good man to me," she remarked.

"He is."

"He is close with Mars," she noted.

Aramus nodded on the pillow until he realized his wife couldn't see him and he stopped.

"They are like brothers. Cassius came as a young man to train with Ares's armies. He is two years older than Mars. He stayed from age twelve to fifteen. After he left, Mars came to Airen to train with their soldiers. He was in Airen for two years. The bond was formed through that, but they already knew each other and played together as children when their fathers met for business between the realms."

"They look so much alike, you could think they were brothers. But they act like blood, so I suppose they just are," she said.

"They just are," he agreed.

"He has much the same with you, if not looking alike," she said, sounding like she was smiling.

"We do not have the history, but…" he hesitated before sharing, "he lost his wife, and when the babe she gave him as her last gift was old enough to sail, he came to Mar-el. He stayed some time. He could not be around things that reminded him of her. But I did not feel he shirked much grief when he was with us."

"That is sad," she whispered.

"It was," he replied.

"Mars greeted you as a brother," Ha-Lah noted.

Ah.

His beautiful, crafty wife.

"This he did," Aramus confirmed. "And I know where you're aiming with this, wife, but they are but two players on a board filled with many. There are those who are friends, and you're correct, those two are friends. But there are also those who are arrogant, those who are devious, those who are covetous, those who are cunning, those who are naïve, those who are imprudent. I walk that board, knowing who I can trust, and all the others I cannot. You do not walk that board, Ha-Lah. You do not walk it at all."

"I understand this, Aramus. Truly I do. But I cannot bear being locked in this room the entire time we're in Firenze. Or even consider how you wish to hide me away for my protection in the coming months as we travel Triton."

He heard her hand slide over silk his way, but it stopped before she touched him.

"And you cannot know this, but I'm a good judge of character," she said.

"How would you like me to put that to the test, Ha-Lah?" he inquired.

"Trusting me," she whispered.

Aramus fell silent.

Ha-Lah didn't break it.

Eventually, Aramus did.

"If I do that, and all does not go well, it is not my trust in you that will be broken. If others connive, the loss I could sustain is too precious to bear."

"For we couldn't quell the Beast?" she asked.

"For I would lose my wife," he answered.

He heard her soft intake of breath on his words, but she did not expel it to say her own.

"I would not be Cassius. I do not know you in that way," he told her. "But the two times of our marriage when you let me in, I like what I know. And I would miss it."

And I want more, he thought, but did not say.

Though he did not stop speaking.

"You did not know my father, my queen, and for this I am melancholy. He was a fine man. A proud father. But an inveterate pirate. He lived for the times he sailed the sea. Which was why he took a wife much later than the age I found you. He was fifteen years older than me when he made my mother his bride. But his love for her, like all the Nereus men, became legend. When his age meant he knew his life was in decline, he told me if he'd have known his world would be filled with her, he would have given up all his years at sea for just one more at her side. And when he died, it was not age that took my beloved mother. It was facing a life without him that did it. This was why I had our priests scour our lands for you so that I would not taste that regret. For I saw in both my parents that flavor was bitter."

Her tone was near-on gentle when she said, "Oh, Aramus, that is both beautiful and sad." And when he made no reply, for she was right, he heard her heavy sigh before she queried, "How do we find compromise, my husband?"

"You have a guard everywhere you go, until I say this no longer needs to be so," he answered instantly. "You allow a servant to taste your food and drink—"

"Aramus—"

He didn't allow her to cut in.

"I'm telling you how it will be for you to have what you wish, my queen. This is not a negotiation."

She again went silent.

"A servant tastes your food and drink and you don't put it to your lips unless one of my men says you can. You can spend time with the women. In this palace. Not in the city. Petals and coins are all well and good, but not every citizen of Firenze was on that street, Ha-Lah. It could be not conniving, but simply something someone says that would cause you upset, or a look they'd give that would be distressing, and I won't have that either."

"I don't know their language," she reminded him.

"As you've noted, many of them speak Valerian," he returned. "And all of Wodell, Airen and Nadirii have long since adopted that tongue."

She made no reply.

"We will talk," he continued. "You will share how you perceive these women. I will do the same. If we feel we've come to trust them, your guard will not need to be that close. But you are queen, Ha-Lah, you will always have one."

"All right," she agreed.

"All right about your guard, or all of it?" he asked.

"All of it, if I can leave these rooms, meet people, learn about them, see more of this land, even if it's simply the chambers of the palace of their king. Yes. I will agree. To all of it."

Aramus smiled and through it said, "Are you an adventurer, my Ha-Lah?"

"I don't know. I've never had the opportunity. But the little I've had, I know I like."

She had not had the opportunity.

Something else he now knew about his wife.

"Then we will see about making you safe so you can widen your adventures, wife," he decided.

"This would be appreciated, husband."

They both fell silent and Aramus determined that the next night when they were abed, he would not be sharing.

He'd be asking things about her.

In the dark of their room, as quiet fell over them, the entirety of the night and the rum and their agreement settled in and Aramus felt his eyelids getting heavy.

They opened when she whispered a drowsy, "Can we discuss putting boys in the path of possible poison again at a later date?"

At that, while smiling broadly in the dark, he realized he knew some other things about his queen.

And they were important.

She had a full heart, a bent of her own to protect things she deemed needed it, and the courage to stand and do that.

"Yes," he lied.

"Thank you, husband," she murmured.

"You are welcome, wife," he replied.

They again fell silent.

And again Ha-Lah broke it.

"I do not drink tea, Aramus."

He grinned.

Something else he now knew.

"And I know of Frey and Sjofn Drakkar," she carried on softly. "And I'd like to hear more of them from you."

Aramus drew in a mighty breath and let it out.

"And you will, my queen," he replied, just as softly.

"Thank you."

"It will be my pleasure," he murmured, meaning it.

She said no more.

Aramus waited until he heard her breath steady.

And then he let himself sleep.

19

THE RUBBLE

Queen Mercy Axelsson
Guest Suite, Second Floor, East Corridor, Catrame Palace, Fire City
FIRENZE

"Shouldn't we attempt to make headway with the Mar-el?" her husband asked.

"A waste of time," Carrington answered.

Queen Mercy of Wodell sat curled on the divan, fiddling with a fold in her skirts, her eyes on her fingers' movements, her attention on her husband and his counsellor.

"I'm uncertain. He's on the mainland. He's never on the mainland. We have an opportunity to have his ear," Wilmer replied. "True says—"

Carrington interrupted him.

And one could say Mercy detested it when Carrington interrupted her husband.

"Yes, and the love of your son's life is marrying an Airenzian. But she's besotted with your son. He holds sway over her. With her many..." Carrington spared a glance at Mercy, "*assets*, she could quickly gain sway over Cassius."

There was no one on this planet who could sway Cassius.

Except Liviana.

However, she was dead.

That said, with the way he had demonstrated he could care for a woman when he had his wife, if he were to come to feel that way about Elena...

This might be a rarity, Carrington making an utterance that held any merit.

Then again, if Elena remained enamored of True, Cassius would not miss that.

So there it was.

Carrington did not make an utterance that held merit.

"But Cassius has no sway over Gall. They don't get along. *At all*," Wilmer noted.

"Gallienus is weak. The soldiers of his army follow Cassius. And there has always been unrest in his realm. But he, like all his predecessors, chooses to ignore that every male in their land does not wish to look on their wives, daughters or sisters like chattel. I predict he'll be naught but a figurehead in a year. In fact, Cassius tires of him so obviously, he might force the man to make him regent."

"I can't imagine the Airenzian will blindly follow a man married to a Nadirii," Wilmer said something wise for a change. "In fact, that nation will see much strife due to this union."

That nation already had much strife and it wasn't simply the women who were far from fond they lived in a realm where the king and many of the male population had three uses for them: to bed them, to force them into service and to oppress them.

There were also men in that realm who thought this practice was repellant, men even back centuries ago, before the Night of the Fallen Masters, who felt their brethren got their just desserts.

And Mercy had long since suspected Cassius Laird was one of those men.

But those in power would do anything to keep their power.

She knew that all too well.

"And you don't think an alliance of the strategic mind and might of Cassius Laird and the magicks controlled by the Nadirii along with their prowess in the field won't quell said strife?" Carrington inquired. "You saw their demonstration tonight. It was breathtaking. And telling, as Ophelia meant it to be. It would be an extraordinary alliance. If it can be achieved, it can't be beat. Not even by the Firenz."

Ah.

There it was.

Mercy smoothed out her skirt.

"Not to mention, Cassius clearly has a bond with the pirate king," Carrington carried on. "This would mean Airen *and* Nadirii *and* Mar-el and most important, *Wodell* all allied against Firenze.

"This makes sense," her husband murmured.

Mercy quelled a sigh.

Cassius did have a bond with the Mar-el king.

But he thought of Mars as brother.

She did not enter this fact into the conversation. She rarely spoke when Carrington had her husband's ear.

She found it served her purposes much better to have her words in private.

"Our focus is Gall," Carrington declared. "Cassius. Ophelia. Elena. Even Serena, if we can manage to charm her in the slightest. She prefers Dellish men for her adventures. There might be a way we can gain some advantage of her there. Perhaps one of True's men?"

Mercy fought a roll of her eyes to the ceiling.

None of her son's men would touch Serena for fifty bags of gold.

And everyone knew, Serena was a use-it-and-lose-it woman.

As in, she used a shaft once, then she walked away.

"I don't think one of True's men would be wise," Wilmer murmured.

Mercy's lips curled up slightly.

"I'll think on it," Carrington replied. "But we persevere with our strategy. Wodell has had an alliance with the Nadirii for decades. If Airen has an alliance with the Nadirii, as well as Mar-el, Firenze will be left in the cold. We'll get that tract of land, Wilmer, and as planned, once we do, we'll push south."

Mercy faked a yawn.

"My wife tires, Carrington," Wilmer stated. "We'll take this up in the morning."

"Of course," Carrington muttered, sounding aggrieved.

Mercy lifted her eyes to him.

When he turned to her, his expression changed.

She found hiding her thoughts and feelings was most of the time wise.

With Carrington, she did not do that.

He had her husband's ear.

She had his bed and had given him an heir.

She had but to yawn, and her husband was dispatching his aide.

Even a fool like Carrington knew who rose to the top of that power structure.

And she enjoyed taking her moments to remind him of that.

He bowed smarmily and said, "My queen."

"Goodnight, Carrington."

"My king," he said to Wilmer.

"Carrington."

He took his leave.

Mercy stared at the door for many moments, cursing the thick carpets in the halls of the palace where you couldn't hear footfalls.

She'd had the carpets in the halls taken up in her own castle *years* ago.

It was a wonder Elpis didn't do this but an hour after her husband leaked his lifeblood all over the floor of his own study.

She tore her gaze away from the door when Wilmer got close.

"Would you like to prepare for bed, my beloved?"

"Leave True to his own engagements," she said quietly.

His head tipped to the side. "I'm sorry?"

"Carry forward your strategy, my love, and allow True to do what he will," she explained.

Her husband's back snapped straight.

He would, of course, take umbrage that his wife made a suggestion in the dealings of a nation (and he did, often, though she managed to handle that, just as often).

Sadly, things were not, amongst the other realms, *that* much different than they were in Airen.

Just as he would take ridiculous advice from a greedy man who had no battle experience, no diplomatic experience, and only came to them when Wilmer was younger and sang his charlatan's song after finishing a degree at the Go'Da.

Certainly, it was an advanced degree.

But knowing the precise date the Lunwynians arrived on their shores and intermingled their language that would soon sweep the continent, all except Firenze, as well as left some of their gods and goddesses with the Dellish. And knowing when the Mar-el expelled the dissenters who sailed the seas and started the nation of Maroo in the Southlands. And knowing precisely when the aqueducts were finished in Sky Bay did not make a King's Counsellor.

"True represents the crown in all things," her husband declared.

"Of course he does," she murmured. "However, when results are far from guaranteed, don't you think two negotiators attempting two lines of negotiation, both for the benefit of our realm, are better than all focusing on just one?"

Wilmer blinked and then appeared adorably befuddled.

Mercy waited.

He cleared that and stated, "This bears contemplation."

She waited again, hoping.

He dashed her hopes.

"I'll discuss it with Carrington tomorrow."

She again quelled a sigh.

"Are you coming to bed?" he asked.

"Of course, my love," she whispered, pushed up, and Wilmer shouted, "Helga! See to your queen!"

The door to the servant's chamber instantly opened.

Mercy moved toward the bathing chamber and her dressing room.

Helga followed.

Perhaps she'd be able to have another word with him before he breakfasted with Carrington like he did every day.

Or perhaps it was time for something else.

The tremors might have stopped, but the earth was still shifting.

And as seemed to happen with alarming frequency, Wodell was being relegated to the rubble.

Aramus wed the greatest beauty in his land.

Cassius got a princess.

Mars got a countess.

And her son True would be bound to the blood of a traitor.

The blood of a traitor who, no matter that Mars showed her deep affection any time he saw her (this had to be a ruse to keep True and Wilmer happy, she wouldn't countenance such a person her presence, as Elpis did not hide she had trouble doing), was first, a barbarian who barely clothed herself when out *in company*. And second, was so far from good enough for her son, the future king of her realm, it didn't bear contemplating.

Therefore, as usual, Mercy had to protect her husband.

She also had to find some way to strengthen the position of her son.

And last, she had to take care of her realm.

So yes, perhaps it was time for something else.

Something daring.

Something ghastly.

But something necessary.

20

THE BARGAIN

Princess Elena

Guest Suite, Second Floor, East Corridor, Catrame Palace, Fire City
Firenze

"At least he's handsome, I suppose."

"*Very* handsome."

"And tall."

"*Very* tall."

"Sadly, now I'm out of things to say about him."

"I'm not. He's gargantuan so she won't have to tip her head down to kiss him. That's important. I find it's a much more natural position to tip my head back when I'm being kissed."

"I prefer to tip it down."

"Of course you would, because Rosehana is shorter than you."

I studied myself in the mirror as Jasmine and Hera babbled from their positions on the bed in my rooms in the palace. This being beyond the screen I was dressing behind, both of them lying abed with Dora while I readied myself for the betrothal dinner.

I stopped studying myself and instead stared at myself.

Something was not right.

And it was not that the bloody corset I was wearing that was so tight, I could barely breathe.

It was also not the fact that I imminently had to face Prince Cassius Laird again and I wanted to do that about as much as I wanted my skin flayed from my body.

It was that I'd never dressed this way before.

Melisse had commissioned the garment and all its accoutrements. When she explained what it was, I'd balked.

She told me to trust her.

As I trusted Melisse in all things, I endured the fittings that carried on throughout our journey to and through Firenze (as we had two seamstresses in the squad who could fit it perfectly to me, something they did).

I was not trusting Melisse now.

For in the now, I wore a sheath of stiff black satin. It had no straps, the material running straight over my breasts (exposing some of them at the top) and that was that. The cloth hugged me to my lower hips where it flared out (fortunately, so I could bloody walk). There was a short train at the back. And from the hem of the train and all the way up the back were tiny, fabric-covered buttons.

Melisse had procured a necklace that wrapped around the column of my neck in five layers of small pearls. There was another of such around my wrist. And pearls in my ears.

And for some reason, I was to add long black gloves that rose nearly to under my arms (the bracelet was to be worn over the gloves—so odd).

This, I had just done.

But it wasn't just bloody uncomfortable.

It wasn't right.

I bent at the waist toward the mirror and felt the stays of the corset dig into my flesh.

I ignored them and stared at my painted face.

Jasmine had done this for me because she was good at it.

A hint of strawberry rouge on my cheeks.

A not-so-hint of red rose at my lips.

The edges of my eyelashes were tipped with a thin line of liquid black paint that sent wings out to the sides and my lids were shadowed with some pearlescent powder.

And she'd brushed some black substance on my lashes with a tool that looked like a miniscule auger.

I looked like me.

But I didn't.

My hair was down, falling over my chest and down my back and...

I turned to the tray of womanly wares Jasmine had brought with her.

"I think I'll start with the dark-headed one when I make my way through his guard," Jasmine said as I looked back to the mirror and bunched my hair up at the back of my head before reaching out to the tray.

But of course.

Jasmine didn't discriminate.

And thus she was planning her Airenzian sexual conquests.

"They're *all* dark-headed, save the bald one," Hera replied as I shoved a pin into my hair and reached for another one.

"Precisely," Jasmine returned as I fixed another pin. "I'll finish with the bald one."

"You can't like them all, Jazzy," Dora entered the conversation.

"I don't like them, little precious," Jasmine retorted. "And this is important, Dora, so listen. I don't *have* to like them."

"All right!" I called an end to that, shoving in another pin and hearing a giggle from Dora.

"You might want to know, you're fifteen minutes late!" Jasmine called back.

"Bloody hell," I whispered, shoved in another pin and then stared at myself.

Some tendrils were hanging down beside my face and along my neck, and turning my head side to side, the back seemed just to be a mass of messy curls attached to my skull.

But I didn't have time to do anything more and I didn't know what I was doing in the first place.

Though at least now you could see the necklace and the pearls in my ears.

I'd have to do.

"Come out, Ellie!" Dora cried. "We want to see you!"

I had buttoned and laced my own self in my clothing, and after besting that feat, I could just say it was good the Nadirii practiced intense stretching to augment range of motion.

I looked into my own eyes and whispered, "Nothing for it."

And there wasn't.

There was nothing for it.

By some twist of a malcontented fate, I was stuck with a taciturn betrothed who, when he deigned to look at me, studied me like I was some specimen he was mildly curious about.

A male who was also surrounded by arseholes (his father) and louts (his men).

And from this dinner forward, that would be my lot.

Mine and Dora's.

And for some reason that was *entirely* unexplainable, I was drawn to him so deeply, his inattention when we were in each other's presence cut like a blade.

I had slept not a wink the night before. I tossed and turned, my mind filled with his face (and his shoulders, and the way he filled out his leathers, and his short-clipped black hair, and his beard, and his tattoos, not to mention his sky-blue eyes).

Bah!

I had not spent much time with men (save True). They unnerved me (save True, and of course the ones I was battling).

So I'd never felt such as this in my life.

Even for True.

I moved out from behind the screen and stopped to look at the trio who were all belly down on the bed, side by side.

All of them were staring at me.

I put my arms out to my sides. "Well?"

"Holy goddess," Jasmine breathed.

"If I wasn't already in love, I'd be in love," Hera said. "With *you*."

"You look like a princess!" Dora cried.

I studied my girl a moment before my gaze slid to Hera.

She was pursing her lips.

I turned back to Theodora. "I'm already a princess, Dora. And darling, this is important. A gown does not make a princess."

"Yes," she agreed. "But now, you look like one who'll ride to her fairytale prince on a unicorn."

I opened my mouth to cease this bent, but Theodora wasn't done.

"You already ride faster than anyone, Ellie. Faster than *lightning*. And you can notch five arrows to a string in a *thrice* and let fly. *Five*. Even Serena can only do three. And Queen Ophelia told me that princesses are made, they are not born. So you can light up the night with starbursts and butterflies and ride Diana standing and wear a gown meant for a queen. Serena can't do *any* of that. And you couldn't do *any* of that when you were born. So you were *made* a princess. And how beautiful you are right now proves it, because you look this lovely, and you can *still* do all of that. No normal fairytale princess can do *any* of it, save the gown. So you're the real thing!"

Oh heavens.

Suddenly I felt like crying.

And I realized then I didn't need some male I did not know to be impressed I could notch a bow with five arrows while standing on my galloping horse and let fly.

All I needed was Dora to feel that way.

Clearly agreeing with me, Hera threw an arm around Dora and pulled her into a sideways hug.

I expended the effort to control my emotions before saying softly, "Come here, my lovely. I want an embrace before I attend dinner."

She made a show of being annoyed she had to climb off the bed and she made another show of how difficult it was to trudge the six feet to me.

But when she wrapped her arms around my hips, she did it tight.

I bent and said into her hair, "Love you, Moonshine."

She tipped her head back. "He's Moonshine."

I blinked down at her.

She kept speaking.

"You have to call me something else," she ordered. "I saw him on the podium, watching you. And he's dark. Like the night. So he's Moonshine. You're Sunshine. And that means he's *really* your fairytale prince because you can't have the sun without the moon and everyone knows, with every hero and heroine of a fairytale, it's about destiny. And there's no greater destiny than the sun leading to the moon and the moon leading right back."

I twirled a lock of her hair around my gloved finger and asked, "When did you get so clever?"

"When I was three," she answered cheekily.

I smiled down at her. "Well, smarty, be clever *and* good for Hera and Jazz. Eat all your dinner and go to sleep on time. Am I heard?"

She rolled her eyes.

"That isn't a response, Dora," I told her firmly, but I did it now fighting my smile.

"I'm always good."

She was not.

But I was late so I couldn't argue.

I bent again, gave her a kiss on her forehead which she tried to duck unsuccessfully. This left a rosy stain which I had to rub away with my gloved thumb, something she also tried to get away from.

"Okay, now you're twenty minutes late," Hera announced.

I looked to her.

She looked sympathetic.

She (and Jasmine) knew how badly I did *not* want to go to this dinner. And why.

She still said, "You best get down there, Ellie."

I nodded, tousled Dora's hair (something she also tried to avoid), shot my friends a smile I hoped looked confident and brave, bid my goodnights and walked out.

I wanted to drag my feet, but I couldn't. I was late (apparently, preparing for dinner like a woman not Nadirii took a great deal of time —how did all the Firenz, Airenzian and Dellish do it?).

I was also getting later by the second. And worse, it would already appear it was because I was avoiding this. If I was any later, it'd appear my wish was to avoid it altogether.

I was Nadirii.

I regularly clashed with brigands and highwaymen and sorcerers and Airenzian masters in search of their escaped wives (or lovers, servants, etcetera), and the like, all attempting to breach The Enchantments for nefarious purposes.

This could get perilous.

And Jazz, Hera and I always bested it.

Therefore, I could face a dinner with a man who did not want me, but had to wed me, doing this being scrutinized by kings, queens, princes and priests.

On my way down the stairs, I squared my shoulders, and I was ready by the time I turned left and made my way along the hall to where we were to meet for before-dinner beverages.

I moved into the room that had a low din of conversation and an overabundance of bodies, and at once, I longed for the forest.

There were a goodly number of Nadirii.

But we had a lot of space.

Regardless, if you were up in your tree, surrounded by green, you could fancy yourself the only woman in the world.

I did not look for him when I entered.

Instead, I searched for my touchstone, and found her.

My mother, standing covered in a golden tunic that went down to her ankles, but was slashed up each side to her knees. It had radiant coral beading from short sleeve to short sleeve across the split collar. She was talking with Queen Elpis and Silence's mother, Vanka Mattson.

Her hair was also up.

It was nice to know I made the right decision with that.

I moved farther into the room and stopped when a young boy asked, "*Bere, principessa?*"

"*Scintille, per favore,*" I ordered sparkles to drink.

The boy moved away.

I felt attention, turned my head cautiously, and saw my sister staring at me from across the room.

She had a curl in her lip.

The instant she caught my eyes, hers dropped to my hem, then came back up, and the curl deepened.

"Elena?"

I looked to my side at the call.

And up.

Directly into True's beautiful green eyes.

And immediately had the thought that I wished I'd at least kissed him before our dream turned to ash.

True was a gentleman to his bones. He would not take a kiss from a woman who did not offer that any sooner than he'd cut off his own arm.

Thus, I should have found the courage to offer.

Or stolen one myself.

All right.

Maybe I *couldn't* make it through this dinner.

"True," I whispered.

"By the gods," his eyes were moving down my body and he did it very much without a curl in his lip. They came back to my face. "You look lovely, Ellie."

"Thank you," I murmured, wondering if that boy would take very long with my drink.

This was difficult and awkward and definitely impossible without a glass of sparkles.

I sensed True go alert, and when he did, I focused on him again to see he was looking over my shoulder.

At the exact same moment, my elbow was seized.

Yes.

It was *seized*.

What on...?

I started to turn my head to see who had a hold on me.

"True," I heard growled.

I froze at the sound.

"Cassius," True returned, his face going hard.

I then found myself being marched right back out of the room with that hand tight on my elbow.

Once in the hall, I looked up at the stony face of my intended.

I had the side not inked.

It was still fascinating.

However, I could not dwell on that considering I was being towed not of my volition down a hall.

How was this happening?

I opened my mouth to speak at the same time I was going to pull my arm from his grip.

However, it was also the time he turned us, opened a door, tugged me inside, closed the door (or more accurately, slammed it), and he did not carry on pulling me into the room.

He shoved me to the side, against the wall by the door, stepped in so I had no choice but to retreat—this being nowhere as my back hit the wall—and he pinned me in with his body and his hands to the wall on either side of me.

"Did that...did you...did that just—?" I stammered angrily to his throat.

But I stopped speaking when I lifted my eyes to his furious face.

"And now that I have you to myself, we shall talk," he rumbled.

I was breathing heavily and wondering how appropriate it would be —during ceremonial events in royal palaces that marked historical happenings that were designed to save our continent and ally all nations—to attack my future husband.

The corset and long skirt would be hindrances.

But the strength of my determination to make a point would be an advantage.

I was deciding my strategy when his eyes dropped to my chest.

And suddenly, all manner of him changed.

Entirely.

His sky-blue eyes stared at my heaving cleavage and the anger blinked out of his expression as something else overtook it. That something else was so strong, it invaded the room. It felt like it seeped into my very skin. And I found it even *more* difficult to breathe in a manner that had nothing to do with my corset.

And his face was so very close, I could study his tattoos. The thick arches and curls and slashes and diamonds.

I knew of the Airenzian ink. How it told a story. How they used symbols of ancient runes to share tales of boon and loss, study and achievement, venture and defeat and victory.

It seemed in his life he had much story to tell.

And not even knowing what the symbols meant, I found all of it fascinating.

So fascinating, unconsciously, my hand was drifting up toward his face, and so deep in his study of my breasts was he, I'd almost touched his temple before he caught my movement and jerked his head away like my touch would burn.

My stomach dropped.

As did my hand.

At that moment, the door opened and we both looked that way.

Serena strolled in wearing her long purple tunic (though, unlike Mother's, the side slashes went up to her hips) that had coral beading across the neckline.

She shut the door behind her.

"Commendable, Cassius," she purred. "The pin-to-the-wall maneuver. Often quite effective, and apparently that's proved true for you. You obviously don't let grass grow."

"This is a private discussion," Cassius returned low.

It had been private.

But there had been little discussion.

"Oh, of course," Serena replied, not leaving but instead coming farther into the room.

It was then Cassius did something curious.

He took his hands from the wall and turned to my sister, but did it close to my person with his back mostly to me like he was...

Protecting me.

A Nadirii.

How strange.

"Though I'm a big sister. It's hard to get out of the habit," she went on. "And how you manhandled her out of the room, I hope you forgive me if I felt the need to ascertain if she's all right."

First, there were very few situations where I could not make myself all right (though, to the truth, this one seemed to be one of them), and Serena knew this.

Second, my sister never cared if I was all right.

"As you can see, she's fine," Cassius returned.

She bent slightly to the side to take me in.

"Very fine," she murmured. "Quite the becoming blush, sister."

"Serena—" I moved to round the prince.

But I stopped when his arm came out in front of me, wrapped around my belly, his hand curling around my hip to stay me.

Also protective.

And something that again made my breath uneasy.

Serena's gaze took in his arm and I saw the hardness form at the backs of her eyes before they went again to Cassius.

"Now how is this going to go, exactly?" she asked. She tipped her head to the side and finished cattily. "The widower and the virgin?"

I caught my breath.

Cassius's fingers dug deeper into my hip.

Well then, that awkward discussion no longer had to happen.

My future husband now knew I was untried.

Brilliant.

"The mingling of families," she carried on. "His daughter." She looked to me. "Your daughter." Her attention went back to the prince. "Though not her blood daughter, obviously."

"If you don't mind, Elena and I have things to say to each other," Cassius gritted out.

"Do you know of Theodora?" she asked with a faux curious tilt of her head.

"I know I'd like any further knowledge of my future wife to come from *my future wife*," Cassius replied tersely.

"Serena, really, it would be most—" I started.

My sister spoke over me.

"Sweet girl. So sad. Her mother falling in battle to Airen."

I closed my eyes.

Cassius's arm dropped.

I opened my eyes only to see he'd ceased touching me only to position more fully in front of me.

"You can leave, or we shall," he told my sister.

"Which one was it?" she asked oddly. "Of course, I know, as all know, how covetous your brother was of, well..." she tossed a hand his way, "just about everything that's you."

"Really—" I tried again, moving to get out from behind the prince only to have him shift to keep me blocked.

"Your skill on the field," she kept talking. "The sweetness and beauty of your dead wife."

Oh goddess.

She had to stop.

But before I could do aught about it, she carried on relentlessly.

"And the closeness you share with your guard."

Cassius started to turn to me, murmuring, "This is enough."

I absolutely agreed.

I shifted to move with him.

"It was Nero, wasn't it?" she asked, and Cassius's head whipped her way in a manner that made me freeze solid. "Trajan coveted your guard so deeply, he ordered his father to assign them to him. And he got what he wanted, of a sort. That sort being the charming way your father does things. He gave him just one. To be selected by you."

She shrugged, took a step deeper into the room and then turned back to us.

"Not easy, I would assume. Though it's heard, as is *your* way, you gave them their leave. They decided amongst themselves. Drew straws, was it?"

"It's clear you need to make your point and intend to make it," Cassius stated with resignation. "Therefore, cease the play and simply do that."

Serena didn't hesitate.

"It was Nero who struck the mortal blow to Tiana," she announced.

Oh, by the goddess, no.

No.

My throat closed, and I took a step back.

Cassius shot a dark glance at me before returning his focus on Serena, doing this with narrowed eyes.

"Oh yes, you don't know who Tiana is," Serena began helpfully. "Or *was.* She was Elena's dearest friend. Thick as thieves they were, mentoring together at Melisse's knee. Tiana was also Theodora's mother."

That was when I saw Cassius's entire frame freeze.

"We do that," Serena shared. "Those of us who have daughters and go to battle. We make arrangements, if we should fall. She fell. To Nero's blade. Fortunately for her, Elena had vowed to raise her daughter as her own. Though unfortunate in the now, as she's here. Dora. In this very palace. Right now. With the only mother she'll ever know. And also here, the man who killed her blood."

A sick smile curled her lips when she concluded.

"So I dealt the death blow to your brother, your brother not of your blood dealt the death blow to the sister my sister wished was blood. I am here. And Nero is here. This alliance, already interesting, just became more so. Don't you think?"

"Are you finished?" Cassius ground out.

She pretended to consider it and then said, "I believe I am."

"Then you wouldn't mind taking your leave," Cassius suggested darkly.

"I think I'll do just that," she replied breezily. "It's almost time for dinner and I'm *famished*."

And after aiming a contented smile to Cassius, shifting it to me, she sauntered to the door and through it.

The instant it closed behind her, Cassius turned to me.

"Elena—"

I looked him right in his eyes and declared, "We will have a son."

He shut his mouth and his bearded chin jerked into his neck.

"I will give you that," I told him. "And you will give me a daughter."

His voice was much changed, lower, softer, when he took a step toward me and said, "Elena."

I took a step to the side.

He stopped.

I did as well.

"If you have to close your eyes and picture someone else, that will be fine. I will endure," I announced.

Those eyes he would have to close narrowed again with his heavy brows drawing together over them before he whispered in a sinister manner, "*Endure?*"

I could imagine many found that expression (and his sinister whisper) most fearsome.

However, I had been trained not to find much fearsome.

And regardless, in that moment, I had to finish what I had to say, somehow manage to get through dinner sitting at his side, and then find a way to get through the next day, and the next, and the next.

Until he had his son.

I had my daughter.

And we were done.

"This will be our bargain, Prince Cassius of Airen," I proclaimed. "I will be your princess and when the time comes, I will do my duties as your queen. I'll provide you an heir and you'll provide me a daughter. I will love and nurture both with all my heart, as I hope you will as well.

But we will live separate lives in your black citadel, separate in all things, except where it pertains to our family."

Feeling I stated my case, I started to move to leave when his words came.

"I don't agree to this bargain."

"You don't have a choice," I retorted, turned to the door, but again found my elbow seized, my body moving not of its volition, my back against the door, and Cassius's visage all I could see.

Of all the bloody...

Did all men act in this manner?

I didn't get the chance to ask.

"You will give me a son," he growled. "And I will give you a daughter. You will be mother to my motherless daughter and I will be father to your fatherless ward. Then you will give me *more* sons and I will give you *more* daughters, however they come to us. You will sit at my side as I reign. You will *sleep* at my side as I sleep. You will move under me as we make our family. And when you do I will not..." his face got nearer, "close...my...*eyes.*"

Oh my.

He was not yet finished.

He got even nearer and the whisper he then gave me was a different kind of sinister.

"Also when you do, Elena, you will not endure. I'll make you enjoy every *fucking* second of it."

Oh my.

And still, he was not finished.

But fortunately, he moved away to say his next.

That was, he moved away...*minutely.*

"Together, we will force the dark out of that bleak place that is night even when it's day and we'll do this with the halls ringing with our children's laughter. We will not live separate lives, Elena. We will be prince and princess then king and queen. And we will be husband and wife in *all* ways we can be. *That* is our bargain. And on that, *you* have no choice."

"I—" I forced out that one noise through the hammering of my heart that was beating in my throat.

I got no further.

"Now, we eat," he concluded.

He then pulled me from the door, took my hand and curled my fingers around his elbow.

He wrenched open the door, his hand moved to clamp over mine on his arm, imprisoning it there, and he drew me out into the hall.

For the sake of dignity, if nothing else, with no choice but to walk with him, I lifted my chin to salvage some pride and hissed, "We will speak further of this sometime later."

"We will not," he retorted.

"You do not make decisions for the both of us," I returned.

"I didn't. Destiny did. And for the first time in a bloody long time, save your sister becoming my sister, and not because she wounded my brother, but because she's vastly unpleasant, I'm beginning to think the fates don't loathe me."

This declaration made me shut my mouth.

Because...

What did *that* mean?

I would suspect he said his next with careful timing.

This being just moments before we returned to the room he'd dragged me from.

"And mark this, Elena, if True approaches you again when I'm not at your side, whether you're in uniform or wearing the most comely gown I've ever gods-damned seen, this will not make me happy."

All right.

So.

Now he knew I was a virgin.

And I knew his man killed my dearest friend.

And perhaps I finally understood why Melisse had insisted I wear this gown.

He also knew how unpleasant my sister could be (though I reckoned he already knew she was thus just simply from her reputation, not to mention she dealt the blow that would eventually lead to his brother's death).

And he further knew True and I had feelings for each other.

To end, if I thought the night before that our relations weren't starting all that well, I had much gloomier thoughts about this subject now.

Though it would seem I was wrong, and he wasn't entirely disinterested in me.

And apparently, he liked my gown.

However, as he held my hand caught tight in his elbow tucked close to his side, which meant I had to be close to his side, as he led us directly to King Mars and Silence, I was wondering if this was a boon.

Or if the fates might loathe *me*.

21
THE DINNER

The Priest
Formal Dining Room, First Floor, West Corridor, State Wing, Catrame Palace, Fire City
FIRENZE

The last to arrive in the formal dining room of Catrame Palace were Prince Cassius Laird of Airen and Elena, Princess of the Nadirii

The minute both their feet stepped over the threshold, he felt it.

And feeling it, he took note.

Also feeling it, Ophelia's head twitched, and her eyes sought her daughter's.

Elena's head jerked, and her gaze sought her mother's.

Ha-Lah's curls bounced and she put her hand to her stomach in a comforting gesture.

Silence's eyes narrowed bemusedly.

Last, Farah's lips parted, and she looked to the floor.

For the priest's part, he felt his lips thin momentarily before he smoothed them and moved to find his assigned seat.

When he found his chair, he saw that he'd been relegated to a table with non-important personages.

This did not make him angry, as it used to do.

They would learn.

As he sat, he did it thinking this had been a nuisance, these alliances being made...and why.

Now it was *more* of a nuisance because he was concerned.

That vibration in the veil of magic, the strengthening, it happened simply with all of them together but without all of them being *together*.

What would come of it when they were?

There was nothing for it.

He'd had to cease the rituals so he could assess the possible danger of how the realms were aligning to beat the Beast.

Now, the priest would have to keep close in order to stop these alliances from coming to fruition.

A bother.

And a frustrating one.

Though it was his understanding he only had to select one and then all would be lost (for them).

He would do that tonight.

He dipped his chin to the boy who filled his wineglass, greeted his dinner companions as they joined him, and looked to the long table at the front of the room where the couples were seated all in a row.

Elpis was no fool.

There was a seat's-worth of space between each couple.

Privacy.

Time to get to know one another in a room full of people at a table shared by many.

Cassius and Elena to the left. Mars and Silence beside them. Ha-Lah and Aramus next. Ending in True and Farah.

The priest made his assessments and started with the least likely couple first.

Drawing it in, focusing on it, he felt the sensation grow in his lower stomach, and then he utilized it, honing on Mars and Silence, and using his magic, his ears took in their words at a distance he would not normally hear them.

"What was it?" Mars asked low.

"I don't know." Silence sounded disturbed.

"A tremor?" Mars queried.

"No."

"A draught?" he went on.

"No. Yes. What I mean to say is, it was a tremor, but *not* a tremor," Silence explained. "A...a *throb*. And it was not a draught. More like a wind. Not a breeze, a *wind*. Didn't you feel it?"

She was talking about the strengthening of the veil.

Though she couldn't identify what it was.

A boon.

"I felt nothing, *mia piccolina*."

My little one.

Yes, they were the least likely couple. They were already much drawn to each other.

And Mars had paraded his new bride in front of his people like she was a precious, priceless ruby extracted from deep in a Firenz mine and hewn to lustrous perfection.

The priest sensed, already, if she were to be harmed, Mars would turn every stone in five realms to find the culprit and exact his vengeance.

And if Mars were to be harmed, the waif had much magic. She might not yet know how to use it, but he did not like to think if she harnessed it through emotion, but without the knowledge of how to control it, what she would do.

And obviously the priest had to survive. Not only to bring forward the Beast, but to master him. He couldn't be hunted down by a barbarian or magicked to another realm (or the like).

No, that wouldn't do.

"Nandra, as you know, is here tonight," Mars shared. "After dinner, I will have her brought to me and I will ask about this."

"I'm not certain it was a bad thing, my king."

"We will *make* certain, my bride."

Yes, the least likely couple.

"Think no more of it. I will find answers," Mars stated and changed their subject. "Now tell me, do you worry about the ceremony tomorrow?"

The eavesdropper tensed.

What ceremony?

"I don't know, does it hurt?" Silence asked.

"It is a piercing of the flesh, Silence," Mars said gently.

Well then.

As they would do, they were preparing her for her Firenz wedding which was to take place three nights from that one.

She'd endure their odious piercing ceremony.

But of course.

"So it hurts," Silence murmured.

"Ice is used to numb the flesh. It's mostly painless at the time," Mars assured. "Though there can be some discomfort after."

"Well, everyone is pierced here, so it can't be all that bad," Silence stated gamely.

Mars's slow grin did not hide his approval.

The priest tired of their discourse, studied the couples, and turned his attention to what he perceived was the next least-likely pair, especially considering the pirate king's current demeanor.

That being, he was resting back in his chair, his large bulk shifted toward his wife, his long arm along the back of her chair.

"Of course you would think that," Queen Ha-Lah was saying, but she sounded amused. "You're a man."

"I am that." King Aramus also sounded amused.

"Though I cannot agree," she said.

"That I am a man?" he teased, raising his brows.

His queen gave him a small smile and an exaggerated roll of her eyes, answering his tease without words.

"They returned to the room with her on his arm, close to his side," Aramus observed, returning to their discourse.

They were discussing Prince Cassius and Princess Elena and the earlier shenanigans.

Really.

These Airenzian men.

Would they never learn?

That would not go well for Cassius.

But it might go well for the priest.

"They did, though he looked furious and she looked like she wished to whirl her Nadirii staff straight into his head," Ha-Lah retorted.

Aramus chuckled before he repeated, "Yes, wife, but he brought her into the room on his arm and *close to his side.*"

"I see this says something to you about Cassius," she noted, watching her husband closely.

Aramus's expression grew serious. "I worried about him most of all with these allegiances. He much loved his wife."

"And?" Ha-Lah prompted when he did not go on.

"Cassius is a man of honor. His father, and the brother he lost, were, and in his father's case, still is fond of war, whether it spills blood, or the wounds inflicted are unseen. Power. Control. Demonstrations of might. Conflicts to determine supremacy. It is, for them, an addiction. Cass is a man of peace. He is good at making war, even if he doesn't have the heart for it. But he still has Laird blood."

"And that means?" Ha-Lah asked.

"That means he might have found the kind of clash he cannot only stomach, but that he will enjoy."

"Ah," she murmured, grinning at the plate of food set in front of her.

Aramus captured a curl of her hair and wound it around his finger.

His queen seemed discomfited for a moment at this gesture before she hid it, and hid her fondness for his touch, as minimal as it was, by reaching toward her wineglass.

"There is more, my wife," he murmured distractedly.

He was speaking but he was much caught up in the twirling of her hair.

After taking a sip, her voice was husky when she asked, "There is?"

"My friend, he is a man lost."

Ha-Lah set her glass aside and turned her head his way, which took her tendril from her husband's fingers.

And they both looked like something was lost with that.

Aramus recovered first. "Tonight, when he walked in with his future bride, his eyes were full of fire. I have not seen that from my friend, not once, not in six years." He leaned toward his wife. "It brings gladness to my heart, Ha-Lah. For this means he might get found."

"Then it brings gladness to mine, Aramus," she whispered.

His eyes dropped to her mouth and he grinned.

With some clear nervousness, she faced forward.

Even if their words were amicable, they were not yet in full accord.

But they would be.

She had the beasts of the sea at her command.

He had a secret weapon.

No, it would not be wise to target either of them.

The observer shifted his attention to the left end of the table.

"My daughter is not here," Cassius was saying. "She meets us in Wodell. I didn't want her away from her studies for this long."

Elena did not reply.

Instead, she stared angrily at the plate in front her.

"But I will meet your daughter," Cassius declared.

"In a few days," Elena murmured, picking up her fork and knife.

"Tomorrow," he retorted.

Her head turned his way and her cheeks were flushed, not with her rouge, with ire. "Tomorrow is too soon."

"It's not too soon. What is soon is that we will be a family," he replied.

"Yes, and your man killed her mother. Perhaps you'll give me, oh... I don't know, *an hour* to come to terms with that myself," she rejoined.

One of his men killed her ward's mother?

Interesting.

Cassius dipped his head to Elena, and she braced, clearly wishing to pull away at the same time fighting to hold her stance for she didn't want to show the weakness of retreat.

"It was war, Elena, and I do not know the circumstances. What I do know is that it is likely it was him or it was her. And it is unspeakably unfortunate it was her. As it would be unspeakably unfortunate if it was him."

A wise response.

The priest knew that when Elena turned her attention back to her plate, set down her utensils and reached for her thin flute of sparkles.

She had no retort.

Not to that.

"It matters not. We cannot arrange a meeting for the morrow," she said before putting the glass to her lips. "The piercing ceremony is tomorrow."

With that, she took a sip.

"It's my understanding that lasts less than an hour," Cassius returned.

With but a glance at him, she fired back, "It's *my* understanding much bonding happens after it."

She then drained the last of her wine.

Cassius instantly put his bottom lip to his teeth and emitted a low whistle.

A servant boy came forward.

"Bring my intended another glass of sparkles," he ordered.

The boy nodded and dashed away.

And as he did, Cassius most definitely had the full attention of his betrothed again.

"Did you just *whistle* at a servant?" Elena snapped.

Cassius looked to her. "Tell me, is there anything I can do in this moment that will please you? Outside leaving your presence, of course."

"What you could do is not whistle at servants like they're dogs or order my wine refreshed. I can order my own wine."

"It is the gallant who sees to his partner's needs before she realizes she even needs them," he educated.

"I don't need a gallant," she returned. "I need a dinner partner who doesn't whistle at servants."

Cassius sighed, sat back and reached for his own wine, bringing it to his lips and murmuring to the rim of the glass, "Would that this was whiskey."

"Would you like for me to whistle at a servant and get that for you?" Elena asked archly.

At that, Cassius set his glass aside untasted and twisted his torso fully to her, leaning in.

He was very much larger than her, and looming that way, an immediate threat.

She again didn't retreat.

This time, it would be a mistake.

"You don't wish to know what I truly would like to do," he said low.

"Yes, I do. You're my betrothed. Obviously, it is my most fervent desire to know *everything* about you," she responded sarcastically.

"Trust me, this you don't wish to know," he warned.

"I'm no wilting violet, my prince," she stated unwisely. "If I haven't made this clear before now, you don't need to protect me from anything. I have traveled. I have studied at the Go'Da. I protect The Enchantments. I highly suspect I'm more worldly-wise than any female you've ever met."

"I am utterly certain that is not true," he murmured.

"Put me to the test," she challenged, again unwisely.

"Right then, my warrior," he rumbled, leaning ever closer to her. "What I would like to do is drag you from this room, take you somewhere dark, kiss you until you're breathless, also, importantly, *speechless*, and equally importantly, *soaked*. Then I would spank you until you beg me to stop and apologize for being bloody-minded."

Her brows were up in full affront. "Spank me?"

"Spank you," he growled.

As their eyes clashed, and this went on for long moments (very long), her indignation ebbed, she appeared to be fighting confusion, as well as (finally) considering the wisdom of her next.

She made the wrong decision.

"Soaked?"

He dipped so close, he had to avert his head in order to put his lips to her ear.

"For me," he purred. "Between your legs."

She jerked away, belatedly, and hastily took up her utensils again.

Cassius moved slightly from her but did it studying her profile.

"I see. *Very* worldly-wise, my future wife," he murmured, sounding a cross between contemplative, pleased, amused and titillated.

"You can stop speaking now," she declared, spearing something on her plate.

"I don't think I will."

"Then I'll stop speaking to you," she declared, shoving her fork into her mouth.

Cassius turned to his own plate as the servant boy set a new glass beside Elena's and whisked away her old.

He picked up his utensils, muttering, "If we cannot get along, at least I won't mind gazing upon you. Not to mention, life will be far from boring. Especially in bed."

Another flush hit Elena's cheeks.

The priest considered this situation.

One could say with some certainty they had no accord *at all*.

However, Cassius had already lost one wife to forces he could not control, thus no vengeance could be meted.

He desired the Nadirii.

Would Cassius Laird unleash wrath for a woman he simply wished to bed?

The listener did not think he wanted to test that.

He turned his attention to the final couple, finding them with his eyes before he did the same with his ears.

Only to see Farah of Firenze staring right at him.

He looked to his own plate.

"I say, are you with us?"

His gaze lifted to Carrington, the advisor to the Dellish king who was one of five sharing the round table with him.

"You've been miles away," Carrington noted when he had his regard.

"My apologies," he replied. "Much is happening. Much on my mind."

"Of course," Carrington murmured, reaching for his wine.

The priest did the same.

While doing it, he felt someone's regard and turned his attention toward that sensation.

Melisse, the queen's lieutenant, was studying him.

"You are well?" she asked quietly.

She did not care if he was well.

She might have sensed he'd been using magic. He had a habit of cloaking it, even around his own people. But he didn't often use it around a Nadirii.

Perhaps it was he who had been unwise.

"Quite well, my friend," he murmured.

She tipped her head to him and bent to her plate.

He took a few bites, a few sips, made a little conversation.

And only then did he look back to True...and Farah.

Farah was turned to her prince.

"I don't trust him," she whispered.

"The Go'Doan are harmless, sweets," True replied. "Or at least, he is."

"You know my father was Go'Doan," she returned.

"Don't put yourself in that place, Farah," he said gently. "They are all not your father."

"I also felt what I felt earlier, True," she declared. "Do you think this is a coincidence, what I felt coming from him, and feeling that earlier?"

"There are some very powerful witches in this room, as well as all who fulfill the prophecy," he noted. "That would be an explanation, wouldn't it?"

"Perhaps," she murmured.

"Emotions are heightened. Much is happening. It would not be outlandish to think you're responding to that," True assured.

"I suppose." Farah didn't sound convinced. "We'll talk more of it. Later."

"When he's not around?" True sounded teasing.

Farah smiled at him. "Just."

True smiled back.

She adjusted her attention and the priest sensed it was coming back to him.

So he returned his attention to his dinner companions.

He did it making a decision.

He would travel the astral plane that very night and tell his lover to continue with the rituals, simply without his attendance...for a time. The priest would return to their work in the forest as swiftly as he could when this threat was cleared.

As for the threat.

It would be them.

Farah and True.

Or, specifically...

Farah.

He took up his wine, smiled warmly at Johan Mattson, father of Silence, took a sip and set it aside contentedly in order to focus on his food.

He was starving.

22

THE RETRIBUTION

Princess Serena
Guest Suite, Second Floor, East Corridor, Catrame Palace, Fire City
Firenze

The Mystic withdrew his mouth from between her legs before she climaxed.

Serena did not like that.

Not at all.

He was talented down there.

Exceptionally so.

And she would have more.

"I'm not finished," she snapped, as he rose up to his knees between her legs.

"I am," he murmured, meaning what he had been doing.

Not what *they* were in the throes of doing.

She knew this when he reached toward her.

She reached toward him as well, but her aim was different.

Thus, she grasped tight hold of his hard cock, pleased to hear his pained grunt.

Keeping hold, she got up on her own knees and placed her face an inch from his.

She gave his shaft a rough tug, got another grunt, and staring into his unusually tilted black eyes, she demanded, "You will finish what you start."

"Yes," he replied. "I will."

Her wrist was then captured, and he pulled his hips away, freeing himself from her hold. He veered to the side as his other hand went into her back, shoving her down.

His hand at her wrist twisted it behind her back and then drew it up.

Harshly.

She gasped in pain against the silks over the mattress that were to her face as he kicked her knees apart with one of his own.

She'd assumed wrongly.

He was not a Dellish peasant, easily subdued and made submissive.

He was also not a Firenz servant, whose wish would naturally be at her command.

He was not simply a man confused at a strong woman who demanded her own needs be met and careful in his treatment of her lest he "harm" her.

He was one of Mars's Trusted Ones. The Firenz king's guard that was legendary throughout all the lands.

In other words, he was the best of the best of warriors in his realm.

As was she.

And as the pain snaked through her shoulder as he drew her wrist farther up her back, she was realizing her mistake.

She tried to push up on her free hand, but it caused significantly more pain.

Therefore, with only one hold on her, he had total control.

And when she felt the tip of his cock glide through her wet, she suddenly didn't mind.

He slammed inside.

Her hair went flying as her head jerked back.

Then he used her.

By the *goddess*.

He used her.

"Would you care to climax?" he asked casually, driving inside.

"Y-yes," she whispered, rearing back into his thrusts, her arm still caught behind her, her nipples hard, painful points, the walls of her tightening as his cock beat inside.

He pulled out, let her wrist go, twisted her to her back and caught her ankles tight in his grip, lifting them high so her arse left the bed.

Then he spread them wide.

He set one on his shoulder to put a hand between them, his long cock penetrated her again and she clenched her teeth at the satisfaction of having him back.

He took hold of the ankle he'd released, and she lost herself in the show of him thrusting inside.

No Dellish peasant had that chest.

Those shoulders.

Not even the pleasing Firenz servants had his magnificence.

And his face...

"Touch yourself," he ordered.

She...

Perform for...

Him?

"You," she returned the command, though it didn't sound very commanding, as it was breathless.

He let loose her ankle, reached between them and pinched her clit brutally.

Her lower half spasmed and her eyes rolled into her head in ecstasy.

Hand back to her ankle, he grunted, "*You.*"

Serena rolled her eyes again to him.

"No," she challenged, "You."

He pulled out, let go of her ankles, and she cried out when he reached to her, lifted her by the throat, whipped his legs around so that he was seated on the edge of the mattress, and adjusted his hold to the back of her neck.

She was then shoved face first into the bed, her bottom half over his thighs.

His hand came down and the crack to her arse broke through the room.

"*Oh my goddess*," she breathed, trembling at the same time pushing up at his hold on her neck. "Release me," she demanded.

He struck her again.

Her voice was thick when she repeated, "Release me."

And he spanked her again.

And again.

And again.

After more, Serena inched her legs apart in an eager invitation, feeling her wet dripping onto his thighs.

"Please," she begged.

She had no idea what she was begging for, but whatever he wanted, she knew she would give it to him.

It was then she found herself on her knees on the floor with the Mystic standing in front of her with legs planted wide, thrusting his cock into her mouth.

She wrapped her fingers around his arse and, in a daze, her eyes drifted up to his handsome face.

He took hold of her hair and rumbled, "You'll swallow."

She nodded her head, suckling desperately, clutching the tight globes of his sculpted arse.

He held her gaze as he used her mouth and only closed his eyes mere moments before he flooded her throat with his seed.

She swallowed it down greedily.

He pulled out, yanked her up with a hand under her arm and held her casually at the waist as he shoved his hand between her legs and worked her clit perfunctorily until she orgasmed.

Spectacularly.

Clutching onto him, crying out her pleasure, her knees weakening.

The best.

Rapture.

She was not quite finished before he tossed her to the bed.

He moved to his leathers scattered on the floor.

She pushed a hand between her legs and cupped there in an effort to hold what he'd given her to herself.

"I'll have you again," she whispered words she'd never said to a man in her life.

"Maybe." His eyes came to her. "We shall see."

He finished dressing and, carrying his sandals, he walked out of the room without looking back.

She felt the burn in her backside, the quivering at her nub, the wet between her legs, her blood still singing in her veins, her eyelids heavy, her mind hazed.

She would have him again.

Or allow him to have her again.

She would.

And she would do whatever she had to do to make that so.

Because...

She had to.

~

King Mars Laches
King's Study, First Floor, East Corridor, Catrame Palace
FIRENZE

MARS LOOKED from Cassius seated across his desk from him in his study to the door as Chu walked in, carrying his sandals.

Mars smiled.

Chu sat down in the seat next to Cassius, tossed his sandals to the floor between his feet, and stated, "She is mine," before bending to lace his sandals on.

Mars looked to Cassius.

Cassius was studying Chu.

"Just once?" Cass asked skeptically.

Chu did not straighten from his laces as he turned his head and twisted his neck to look up at Cass.

"Yes."

After that, he returned his attention to what he was doing at his feet.

Cass sat back and murmured, "The mighty Serena felled by one taste of cock."

"She did indeed have one taste of cock, and she swallowed my seed when she did."

Cass's eyebrows flew up.

Mars beat back laughter.

"Though, in her cunt, she had two tastes of cock, her arse took a tanning that had her dripping, so by the time I thrust in her face," done with his laces, Chu sat up, "she would have paid to gulp down my seed."

"You spanked Serena of the Nadirii," Cass said.

"Yes," Chu confirmed.

"You spanked Serena of the Nadirii," Cass repeated.

As his brother had answered that, he didn't do it again.

It was then, Mars arrested for Cassius started laughing.

It was not loud or raucous.

But it was genuine laughter and Mars had not seen that from his friend in six years.

Cass sobered and requested, "Please tell me she's not good in bed."

"She was greedy and selfish. Until I made her neither," Chu replied.

Mars grinned.

Cass grinned as well.

Something else, it being authentic, Mars had not seen in some time.

"In the end, she was passable," Chu finished.

"We'll need to ask you to go at her again," Mars told his Trusted.

"She has a greedy cunt, she also has a greedy mouth." Chu shrugged. "This will not be a hardship."

Chu turned his attention to Cassius.

"This transgression against you," he began. "How deep does it lie?"

"It isn't against me," Cass returned. "It was against her sister."

"It is known wide she inflicted the wound that killed your brother," Chu noted.

"It is also known wide that Trajan angled for that battle, hiring ten of the most powerful sorcerers in the land, at great expense, to cast in an attempt to bring down The Enchantments after the return was denied of five women who were lovers or servants of wealthy men in Airen. They had gone to the Nadirii for refuge. These women were not kidnapped and held hostage. They escaped to make themselves safe. It would have been easy to let that situation lie. He did not. He attacked. Thus he sealed his own fate. In a number of ways."

"So you seek retribution for a bride you barely know?" Chu inquired dubiously.

Cassius stared intently at Chu before he spoke.

"It is not my destiny to take a mate. It is my destiny to take a mate while I build a pre-determined family. I'd barely said a few words to the woman who would share my bed, give me children and be mother to my daughter, before Serena made a move to drive a wedge between us. Her venom was aimed at me, perhaps so her sister would not realize the extent of the envy she holds for her sibling. I did not miss this. Her attack was on Elena. I could countenance an attack on me and move on from it without a thought. But if you attack what's mine, if you attack my family, you will endure my retribution. It will be swift. Creative," he indicated Chu with a nod of his head, "if need be. And finally, it will be *thorough*."

"And what do you wish from this once I make her slave to my cock?" Chu asked.

"I've no idea," Cassius murmured. "Mars suggested you and your skills. It seemed a good suggestion for the likes of Serena. She would never see that coming. But I haven't thought that far ahead yet."

Chu stood from the chair, saying, "When you know, tell me. Now I'm off to test my tethers."

Mars chuckled.

Cassius grinned at his calf that was up, his ankle resting on his knee.

And with that, Mars's man strode out.

Cassius gave Mars his attention.

"How did you know that would work?" he asked.

Mars sat back. "I didn't know. But there are two sides to every coin. You can't know what you'll get when a coin is flipped. But there was no harm exploring. Fortunately, the coin flipped in our favor."

Cassius nodded before his expression turned severe.

"She will not relent on Elena," he said.

"Of course she won't," Mars agreed. "Her jealousy consumes her. I noted this during the parade when Elena rode on her own. Serena watched her with the ill-concealed need to control her bow so she didn't take aim at her mother's other daughter."

Mars watched Cassius's mouth grow tight.

He had not noticed that.

He had been too busy watching Elena.

"She knows her mother's favorite, Cass," Mars continued. "She undoubtedly knows, if the prophecy did not need to be brought about,

Serena would be relegated to general, and Elena would assume the role of queen. It has happened before in Nadirii history. They are not bound to whatever whims the fates decree for the ascension of a royal line."

"This is known to me, obviously," Cass muttered.

It would be.

It was known to everybody.

Though there might be something not known to Cass.

"I watched her tonight as well, Cassius. She's covetous of what her sister will earn from you. And I don't think it's the fact that, clearly, she wishes a man who can take charge of at least *some* things in her life."

Cass shook his head. "That's absurd."

"She would not make a good ruler. She is not a good sister. Or perhaps a good daughter. But she is a good general. As are you."

"So you think this draws her to me?" Cass asked with disbelief.

"I think I caught her watching you with Elena at dinner and I did it often. Silence saw me and noted it herself. You were involved with Elena. But we were not the only ones who noted it. Ophelia does not miss much. She did not miss that."

"Bloody hell," Cass muttered.

"Perhaps Serena knows she'll never have any kind of relationship with anyone meaningful in her life, man, mother or sister. She holds too much hate. For men, though Nadirii have long since started to take lovers, partners, even husbands. For her mother, for not loving her as much as her sister. And for that sister, for earning the love of the mother. And now, it may be, she's admired you from afar and it cannot be escaped she won't have you, but her sister will."

"Brilliant," Cass sighed.

"It is not lost on me, my brother," Mars started quietly, "that you share some of the same unrests in your life as your intended."

"Trajan," Cassius said.

"Yes," Mars agreed. "Your father did not demonstrate his preferences in a son, as probably Ophelia doesn't either. But if those preferences are strong, they'll be felt by a child."

"Agreed."

"And Farah and True share weak fathers," Mars remarked.

"I've noted that," Cassius said. "And what do you share with wee Silence?"

Mars shook his head. "I've no idea. My father was good. Her father is not. My mother is good. Her mother is torn. Though I have no siblings, and neither does she. But this is not a foundation for a strong bond, an understanding of each other, the basis from which to build something meaningful, as you have with Elena, as True has with Farah."

"I suppose you'll enjoy finding out."

Mars was enjoying quite a bit about his little monkey.

Thinking of his bride, he became serious. "Tonight, she felt unrest in the veil."

"All the intendeds are gathered, Mars. And tonight, for the first time, we were in close proximity for an extended period of time. It's my understanding this is what's supposed to happen."

"This is what Nandra says."

Cassius raised his brows. "You disagree?"

"It disturbed my Silence," he grunted.

Cass sat for a moment, immobile.

And then again came forth his laughter.

After he expended it, Cassius stated, "I've never thought on it. If I had, I would have pictured you with a lush Firenz beauty. Like the Marel, your finding the most exquisite female in your land and taking her to wife. Though now, I see, you found beauty of another sort from another land and you are glad of it. So I am glad of it for you."

"She is virgin," Mars told him.

"So is mine."

At that, Mars raised his brows. "Really?"

"As shared by her sister in an effort to humiliate her. She didn't refute it. And she didn't because it's true."

Mars watched him closely, remarking, "So True hasn't had her."

"He has not."

They stared at each other.

"She pulls at you," Mars whispered.

"We'll just say there's another Nadirii princess who earned a spanking tonight and I very much wish it was her who got it," Cassius replied. "Though, after that, our ending would have been much different than Chu's."

Mars grinned.

But his grin died and another expression altogether came over his face.

"I am glad of it for you too."

"The fates have not been kind to me."

"Then it is your time."

And yet another expression came over Cassius's face when he noted, "You found your father murdered in this very room, Mars. The fates have not been kind to you either."

"So it is my time as well."

"We go forth against the Beast with these women," Cassius said quietly.

"Our might will be enhanced, their magic. A witch does not fight a battle with a blade. We do. They'll be nowhere near."

"Says the man not marrying a warrior," Cassius murmured.

"Her sister was simply disagreeable, as is her way, and you sent in Chu. She'll eventually be humiliated by him. He will enjoy their play, but he will not form a bond with a woman like Serena. And she will be lost when he deems he's done with her. This, after one conversation of spite. You will find a way to protect Elena. And you will find a way to make her accept your protection."

"Perhaps the prophecy also gives us power to make miracles," Cassius joked.

"Perhaps it shall."

The men held each other's gazes.

Mars broke it off to call for some whiskey.

23

THE DETHRONING

Prince True Axelsson

Diplomatic Table, First Floor, West Corridor, State Wing, Catrame Palace, Fire City

FIRENZE

"I think, at this unprecedented juncture, all the realms together, as we have spoken much about a great many things that will ally our lands in ways beyond the matrimonial, an important issue has not yet been addressed," Gallienus began pompously. "This being the abolition throughout Triton of the bounden."

By the bloody damned gods.

True shifted in his seat, his gaze moving instantly to Aramus after Gallienus's proclamation.

Aramus was relaxed, his arm thrown over the back of his chair, his gaze steady on the Airenzian king, his expression bland.

"It is, of course, unconscionable," Gallienus went on.

And the king was, of course, correct.

But that wasn't the way to go about bloody doing something about it.

True turned his attention to Cassius, seated at corners at the table from his father.

The Airenzian prince was sunk so deeply in his chair, his head rested on the back of it, his hands were one on top of the other on his stomach, and he appeared to be napping.

Cassius Laird was not his favorite person at that moment.

And this had suddenly turned into a volatile meeting.

But seeing him thus, True fought smiling.

"All the realms, save Mar-el, outlawed the binding *two centuries ago*," Gallienus carried on.

True looked to his father, who was nervously adjusting the front of his shirt into his waistcoat.

This could be explosive.

But there was no help there.

He shifted his gaze to Mars at the head of the table.

The dark king was staring in a brooding way at his fingers, which were drumming a beat on the table.

Although war could very easily break out at that moment, True (somewhat) understood Mars's preoccupation.

Silence was being prepared for her piercing ceremony which would commence in an hour's time.

True had always admired Mars as warrior. And from what True had heard as Mars took up the mantle of his father's civilian advancements and the modernization of his realm, True admired that as well.

He still did not think Mars would make a good husband for Silence.

It would take more than a generation to wring the barbarous out of the barbarian.

He was being proved wrong.

Apparently, women did not attend a boy's piercing ceremony.

Men did not attend a girl's.

Silence was no girl.

But traditions were to be held.

Mars was brooding because he was worried about her. Silence was about to endure a ritual no one (outside the lobes of ears, piercings Silence did not have) did in her world, and it included pain.

When True visited Silence that morning, she didn't seem resigned to it. Nor did she seem to fear it. Perhaps she was not eager, though she was curious, as she had an active mind and was wont to be.

She was also keen to do something for Mars.

They seemed a good match.

Surprising.

But gratifying.

And this was where Ophelia was, and why she was not at that diplomatic table.

She would attend the ceremony.

But as she would just be an observer, and it didn't start for some time, there wasn't actually an excuse not to be there at the present time.

Thus True had the sense that something else was keeping her away.

"Well, is no one going to *say anything*?" Gallienus demanded with narrowed gaze at True's father.

True felt his jaw tighten.

He could not believe this.

Gallienus had negotiated something with Wilmer.

And his father had not shared with True what they'd negotiated.

This being a direct confrontation with a mighty king that was bound to bring discord.

It was just, without Carrington whispering in his ear, and in the face of uncertainty since no one else had backed Gallienus's declaration, his father was holding silent.

A gauntlet had been thrown on a table meant to bring forth diplomacy.

And it was not shocking that Gallienus had thrown it.

What was unknown was what would come of it.

And True did not have a good feeling about it.

"You do know, Aramus's great-great grandfather enacted the Those in Service Act," Cassius said to the ceiling, his eyes still closed.

"'*Those in Service*,'" Gallienus scoffed. "Is that a jest?"

"No," Cassius replied, opened his eyes and turned his head on the back of his seat to look at his father at the foot of the table. "The Act is relatively all encompassing."

"Binding is binding," Gallienus bit.

"For instance," Cassius went on like his father had not spoken. "You cannot take your hand, nor fist, whip, paddle, crop, or other to your bounden in anger, in punishment, in retribution, or for any reason. If you do, the punishment served will be jailtime for the proprietor."

"And I'll repeat, binding is binding," Gallienus decreed.

"You also can't force your intentions on a bounden, be you male or female, your bounden male or female. If you do, your jailtime is much increased. And if it's a child, you face a noose," Cassius shared.

True looked to Aramus.

He was studying the fingernails of the hand attached to the arm hooked on the back of his chair.

Cassius turned his gaze again to the ceiling and closed his eyes. "And if a bounden serves his or her proprietor for fifteen years, they can petition for liberty, which must be granted. They then are given any belongings they've collected, a new set of clothes, boots, a steed and a bag of silver. Or they could petition to stay in service as a paid servant. And a proprietor cannot sell or trade a bounden. If they cannot keep their bounden, they must free him or her."

"Perhaps we should ask a Mar-el bounden here, son, and he can lay testimony to his fair treatment," Gallienus suggested acidly.

Cassius turned his head again and the air in the room changed when he whispered, "I note you said '*he.*'"

Aramus chuckled.

Gallienus moved with agitation in his seat.

Cassius continued speaking.

"The Act also includes strict edicts on the provision of food, medicine, garments and housing. Bounden can marry at will. Spouses cannot be separated for any reason, not of their own choosing. And any child they produce is born free."

"So it's all right with you that any ship from the Northlands, the Southlands, The Mystics or *Triton* can sail through *Mar-el's* waters, be boarded and innocent people pressed into service for *fifteen years*?" Gallienus demanded.

His emphasis on the word "Mar-el's" was telling.

What peeved Gallienus was that the waters belonged to Mar-el.

He didn't give a damn about the bounden.

He wanted the seas.

However, how he thought he'd get them, or access to them, by possibly angering the man who ruled them, True couldn't begin to imagine.

"It is not unknown the perils of the sea, Father."

"How about this?" Aramus took his arm from his seatback and turned fully to the table. "The Airenzian give women leave to own property. To press charges and have them justly tried if anyone causes her physical harm, rapes or violates her in any way. And all are freed to the right of peaceable assembly should they wish to gather together to darn their husband's socks, organize to petition the king for better royal patronage of orphanages or say, *any reason*. In return, I will grant freedom to all bounden of Mar-el after five years of service."

"In a time where women were allowed assembly, they used that right to plot and connive and thousands of men died," Gallienus reminded the Mar-el king.

"They did indeed," Aramus agreed.

"Further, our women are not bounden," Gallienus spat.

"Are they not?" Aramus queried.

"An Airenzian woman does not *have* to marry her husband. She does not *have* to take his coin in return for cooking his food and cleaning his hearth," Gallienus retorted. "She chooses to and it is our custom that a man rules his house as he sees fit."

"Does she? Choose to, that is," Aramus asked.

"Of course!" Gallienus returned.

"I would not choose to clean anyone's hearth," Aramus noted. "I would do this only if I had to do it in order to eat."

"She has choices," Gallienus sniffed.

"Yes," Aramus agreed. "It's my understanding girls in your realm cease education at age twelve. They do this by royal edict. Hence, they are not allowed to be doctor, midwife, lawyer, teacher or merchant. So they do have choices. Service. Or whore, prostitute, doxie. Or wife, which is much the same depending on if her husband has some coin, much coin, or is a sailor."

Cassius and Mars both chuckled.

True clenched his teeth.

"You find this amusing, my son?" Gallienus asked.

Cassius, who had his eyes closed and was facing the ceiling again, turned his head his father's way. "Which part? You demanding the Mar-el free all bounden? Or Aramus defining the different types of working girls based on the men who use them?"

"Our women, indeed all our people, are *paid* if they serve," Gallienus declared.

"Barely," Cassius muttered. "Especially the women."

"And I'll point out, none of *my* wives are *whores*," Gallienus spat.

At that, Cassius straightened in his chair.

Bloody hell.

Cassius fully engaged in this conversation did not bode well.

"All of your wives *are* whores," he replied.

True was correct.

This did not bode well.

"You say this of your mother?" Gallienus demanded.

"My mother is dead. And I'm thankful for that for her. Entirely," Cassius returned.

Gallienus's face was getting red.

True looked again to his father.

His father was studying his lap.

There was nothing for it.

"Men," True said.

Everyone looked to him.

He looked to King Aramus.

"It was not presented well, but it is something to reflect on. No lands on this earth, since all in the Southlands stopped practicing it decades ago, except the Mar-el, carry on with enforced servitude. Your grandfather did a brave and noble thing. It was also wise. Change for the good, but not so much it would throw a nation into dissension. Perhaps the time is nigh for another change."

Aramus held his eyes a moment before he slowly dipped his chin.

True turned his attention to the rest of the table and continued speaking.

"However, there is much to concern ourselves with in the now. Changing ways of life and incurring strife inside our realms when the Beast awakes is not wise."

He looked to King Gallienus.

"But in the face of a danger that could destroy all realms, we all should take this opportunity in the calm before a storm to reflect on how we can better the futures of our people once we traverse that storm. *All* of our people. We can take the threat of the Beast as a warning. And we can take our current circumstances as more than mere coincidence. Instead as a lesson. We're in a realm that has faced decades of change. And with it, decades of prosperity."

"And Mars also faced *three* coup attempts in his first *two* years on the throne. And his sire was *assassinated*," Gallienus retorted. "I do not wish to face that." He tossed his hand to Cassius and carried on, "Or my son to do the same."

"It is your kingdom, Gallienus, it's not for me to say," True murmured.

"No, it is not," Gallienus agreed.

"Though, the last time one of your line, when your subjects were restless, who didn't listen to wise counsel or consider changes that were sweeping other lands, saw thirteen thousand of your males having their throats slit," True finished.

"Yes! Murdered in cold blood!" Gallienus cried.

"I could not imagine," True shook his head, "given no choice but to take a life in order to make my own livable."

Once he said this, he felt the increased focus from Aramus, Mars and Cassius.

"Son," his father joined the conversation by speaking one syllable tremulously.

"You speak treason to Airen," Gallienus warned.

"Oh for fuck's sake, Father. He just speaks truth," Cassius sighed.

Gallienus glared at his son. "So can I take that as *you* making Airen face decades of change when *you* take my throne?"

"Unquestionably."

Bloody *hell*.

"What?" Gallienus whispered.

"Un...question...ably," Cassius repeated a lot more slowly.

Mars and Aramus chuckled.

But True did not feel himself wishing to do the same.

This was good, of course.

Ideally.

However, if it happened, Airen would descend into civil war and who knew which side would win.

The gentry of Airen had standing armies of their own. Gallienus favored them not only for their high-born breeding and their chests, which he could tax, but also because, if he angered them, they could ally and depose him.

By force.

Which meant they could ally and wage war against Cassius if he made changes before these armies were disbanded, something Gallienus or one of his forebears should have done years ago. Weakening their gentry. But none of them had had the courage to do it.

In other words, one side had money, men and the power of the throne.

The other had a tactical genius as a general commanding a royal army that might be in disarray as the soldiers in it took sides.

"You know, my sister has a son," Gallienus threatened Cassius.

"Please, I beg you, I'll give you bags of gold, pass the crown to my cousin," Cassius replied. "He is weakly and can barely ride a horse, can't leave his hearth without catching a chill that sets him abed for three weeks, and eschews meat as it's unsavory to him that beasts are hunted. I think he'd make the perfect king."

Gallienus stood, announcing, "I believe diplomatic relations have just broken down."

"That's impossible, considering all nations for the most part agree, it's just you who's being stubborn because those men you protect have wealth and militias, wealth you tax and armies you fear, and you don't wish to make them angry. And further, if your wives had rights, it would be a spectacle, the king of the realm brought up on charges," Cassius stated drolly.

"I see my son feels his power growing with his alliance with a Nadirii," Gallienus said softly. "Careful, Cassius. The weight you carry at this table will not translate in Sky Bay."

"Why don't we test that when we get home, me riding into Sky Bay with a Nadirii at my side, the might of their warriors trooping at my back, indication that the sons of the poor will no longer fall to bloodlust and the whims of the wealthy when we repeatedly clash with a warrior nation? What do you say, Father? Shall we?" Cassius invited.

"You do not want to cross me," Gallienus returned, and Cassius's eyebrows shot up.

"Do you even know me?" he asked.

True bit his lip and lifted his eyes to the ceiling.

Mars and Aramus did not bite their lips.

Their amusement was auditory.

"I fear I won't be able to attend your nuptials, King Mars, for I'll soon be away to Airen," Gallienus announced.

"If you think to leave," Cassius started quietly, "and go home to amass support against the crown prince, I swear to all the gods, Father, I'll plan one last war. To usurp your throne."

"You never wanted it," Gallienus retorted.

"I've since received a promise from my magnificently comely bride to provide an heir. Thus I've changed my mind," Cassius fired back. "You will stay here, and we'll discuss you making me regent."

Gallienus's eyes grew huge.

The air in the room went static.

True noticed his father straighten in his seat.

"Drunk on a Nadirii?" Gallienus sneered. "Already?"

"Tired of your shite," Cassius returned. "A long time ago. Now sit. You aren't going anywhere."

"I'll go where I please," Gallienus rejoined. "My guard, my son, is five times yours."

"Mine is even larger," Mars drawled, and Gallienus's eyes shot to the dark king.

Aramus was back to studying his fingernails, but doing it, he said, "Mine is as well."

"Don't think to turn to the Nadirii," Cassius advised.

"Did you plan this?" Gallienus demanded of his son.

Cassius shook his head. "No. But you prod the bear, my king, you risk his claws."

"You are no bear," Gallienus spat.

"You're correct. But I didn't disrespect the diplomatic table of King Mars and I didn't challenge King Aramus. You did. But I'll remind you, my king, you cannot kill me, or you not only face the Beast, you face four nations who know *they* will have to face the Beast because of *you. That* is where my power lies. And you'd do well not to forget it."

"And on a whim, you're regent?" Gallienus asked disbelievingly.

"It would seem," Cassius muttered.

"This is preposterous," Gallienus huffed.

"And what do you think those of our land will think of you angering the Protector of the Seas by making demands of his rule when you barely know the man?" Cassius asked. "Aramus was not friend. Or not *your* friend," Cassius stressed, making his point very clear. "He was also not enemy. You sought to make him enemy. No land needs an enemy. Especially not a powerful one. Our armada is miniscule compared to his. He simply has to line our shores and strike a match to cannons and our ports would be gone. Warehouses. Homes. *People*. And I'll note, Father, you're standing there, blustering in fury, when the same type of demand was made of you."

Gallienus looked to Aramus, "If you so need your bounden, have them."

"My gratitude for your permission, but I think we've gone much past that, old king," Aramus murmured.

Gallienus's face was getting even more red.

And True's father was doing nothing.

"Let us stop here," True suggested. "Take a moment. Break for some luncheon. Cool heads. There is much more happening here than a single discussion can settle. But nothing is settled well in anger."

"I don't need a cool head to know—" Gallienus began.

True looked the king right in his eyes and said quietly and simply, "Gallienus."

The man shut his mouth.

"We can reconvene this afternoon," True continued.

"I'll be indisposed," Gallienus announced.

"Shall we accept Cassius as your proxy?" Mars inquired.

"I'll be here," Gallienus said between clenched teeth.

"Excellent," Mars murmured.

Gallienus moved around the table and swept out of the room.

True's father rose.

"Son, we need to speak," he declared.

True looked him in the eyes as well.

"We do," he agreed. "But not now."

"We need—"

"Not...*now*," True stated firmly.

His father stared him in the eyes.

This didn't last long before he said, "Gentlemen," rounded the table and swept out.

After the door shut on King Wilmer, Cassius quipped, "I'd like to have that ability. To say my father's name and have him shut his mouth and walk out of a room."

No one laughed at the quip as Mars said quietly, "Cassius. Regent?"

Cassius sighed, got up, went to the door, opened it, looked into the hall and jerked up his chin.

His man Macrinus entered and closed the door behind him.

"Shadow my father and his personal guard. If he sends a bird, shoot it from the sky. If he sends men, waylay them," he ordered.

"Why don't I have a good feeling about this?" Macrinus asked.

"Because I just declared my father make me regent."

"Gods-damn *fuck*," Macrinus hissed.

"Indeed," Cassius muttered. Though he did not mutter when he ordered, "Mac, get men to Aelia. Leave the city, send a bird, make certain she has guards we trust with her at all times. When my men make it to her, have them bring her to me wherever we are on our journey. But I don't want her traveling without members of my personal guard." He paused and finished, "Make one of those men Nero. When needed, he acts as her guard anyway. He won't balk at this mission."

"Aelia? Do you think he would—?" Macrinus started.

Cassius interrupted him. "I'm not taking that chance."

Macrinus nodded and said, "We need to—"

"Talk later," Cassius said low.

Macrinus nodded again before he moved out of the room.

Cassius walked back to his seat and took it.

When he did, True declared, "You'll have our swords."

Slowly, Cassius turned his head to True. "I'm sorry?"

"You'll have the swords of Wodell," True stated.

Cassius looked to the chair True's father vacated and back to True.

"You can make this assertion?" he asked.

"I think my men will be relieved if they march to a fight that is right and not a fight all know is folly," True returned.

Cassius considered this a moment before he asked quietly, "Are they *your* men, True?"

"They are the only thing I have in that realm, Cassius. My father, but mostly his advisor, might argue they aren't. But if he did, he would not like how that went," True answered. "My father assumed the throne at a young age. He never rode a horse to battle. But he does not mind sending them, and the men on them, to do just that. My sword has been bloodied. Repeatedly. I think you know what that means to a soldier."

By the look on Cassius's face, he knew.

"This will get ugly," Cassius warned.

"It already is," True returned. "Shall we rectify that?"

Slowly, Cassius smiled.

"You'll have my armada."

Both men turned to Aramus when he made this surprising announcement.

The Mar-el never engaged in the politics of the mainland.

But Aramus was looking at True. "And you'll have your five years, Prince of the Forest."

By the gods.

True stared at him.

Aramus murmured, "It is time." And as an afterthought, he went on, "And I suspect it will please my wife."

For the first time at that table that morning, True smiled.

"You'll have my horses, Cass," Mars added.

But at that, Cassius shook his head.

"You'll need them and the men on them. Your reign is not secure, my brother," Cassius noted. "You're enamored of her and it may be she's charmed your capital city, but you marry a Dellish. None of our peoples know the Beast rises. The panic which might ensue would not help matters. But as news reaches the ends of your realm, not understanding why you're the first Firenz king to marry a woman outside Firenze and do it with a female from a nation with whom you clash, this might not be popular. And you above all know the Firenz do not mind taking action when something is not popular."

"Nothing allies the people of a nation more than war, Cass," Mars replied.

Sadly, True thought, this was true.

"It goes without saying, you'll have the staffs, bows and blades of the Nadirii," True noted.

"I'm not certain anything goes without saying with the Nadirii,"

Cassius returned. "Especially when it comes to Airen. However, if Ophelia does not offer her warriors, there's no question she won't stand in my way."

True nodded.

"Talk with your men, meet with the Nadirii queen, plan your strategy, send your birds," Aramus said to Cassius. "And as you do, let it be known all the nations of Triton back the new Airenzian Regent."

The men sat silently at the table as Cassius looked at them, one by one.

Finally, he said, "It is done."

It was, indeed.

History was most assuredly in the making.

In a number of ways.

And True was honored he sat at a table during the dethroning of an unjust king.

Turning his head as the men exchanged glances, he knew he was in good company.

24

THE PIERCING CEREMONY

Lady Silence Mattson
Royal Palace Gardens, Catrame Palace, Fire City
FIRENZE

I t didn't seem a'tall bad, having a lovely, fragrant bath, my hair cleaned and brushed until it was shining, and donning the drape of orange silk edged in crimson that was tied at one shoulder (and thank goodness, pinned down the side for I wore nothing underneath!).

I thought this as I moved through the palace gardens on my bare feet to an intimate corner well to the back that was lush with foliage and pots brimming with greenery and flowers.

In that corner there was a rectangular pedestal that rose perhaps two feet from the ground.

It was draped in crimson silk with an edge of orange. It also had a small pillow at the top dressed in emerald green. And covering the entire pedestal as well as floating down to the silk that also swathed the mosaic tile on the ground, were crimson and orange and apricot flower petals.

This the women had done prior to me arriving. It was part of the ceremony, I'd been told.

No, this wasn't all so bad.

It was when I saw the squat gilded table at the top that had a bowl of ice, a bowl of clear liquid in which there were several needles, and a number of bright white bandages, I became nervous.

Queen Elpis sat on a cushion at the head of the pedestal, and next to her was Nyx, a Firenz woman I had met that morning, Lorenz's wife.

Behind the table, Zosime, Guard's wife, who I had also met this morning, sat on a cushion of her own.

And around the pedestal, all seated on pads, were my mother, Queen Mercy, Farah, Sofia, Ophelia, Elena, Ha-Lah and Elena's precocious ward, Dora.

I thought perhaps Dora shouldn't be there, but she was not my ward, so I said nothing.

As I'd been told to do, I walked to the end of the pedestal and Zosime and Nyx rose as I did.

They joined me there and took my hands as they helped me step up on it, turn, and then all the women reached out to assist me as I aimed my behind to the plinth.

Once I was down, I fell back, stretching out.

Apparently, what I lay upon was stone. I knew this because it was hard and not very comfortable, even with all that silk and the petals.

But the pillow was nice.

Nyx and Zosime moved to the head of the pedestal while Elpis arranged my hair over the edge of it, and the minute the two women sat, Queen Elpis started speaking,

"Silence of the Dellish, Countess of the Arbor, betrothed of the King of all Firenze, today you prepare to take the most sacred of vows you'll ever make. More sacred than those to your father. More sacred than those to your mother. More sacred than those to your children. More sacred than those to your nation. They are the vows you will take in joining with your husband."

I pressed my lips together and slid my eyes right, catching my mother's gaze.

She gave me a nervous smile.

I took a deep breath.

"This will be cold, *mia figlia*," Elpis murmured.

After she said that, I felt the cold of the ice all along my ear.

"In all," Elpis continued, "you stand by your husband. In all, you give him your ear. In all," I saw another hand come toward my face (Nyx's) and felt the ice held to my nostril, "you give him your thoughts. In all," another hand was added (Zosime's) and ice was held to my lip, "you give him your honesty."

Well then.

That was rather profound.

Not to mention beautiful.

"To remind you these are what makes a strong marriage," Elpis intoned, "you wear the wedding chain. You wear it daily. You wear it so your husband can see he can share anything with you, and you'll listen. He can be far away, but he'll be in your thoughts. And he can count on you telling your truths to him, so he can know your mind."

Yes.

This was rather beautiful.

"In turn," Elpis went on, "he will wear his chain as his vow to you to listen, to hold you in his thoughts and to share his soul."

Oh my.

Very beautiful.

So much so, I might even cry.

"You will take my son's chain at your wedding, and you will hold it dear. He will take your chain at his wedding, and he will hold it blessed. Until your last breaths, it symbolizes not your union to those who look upon it. But your intimacy toward each other. He will be but yours, and you will be but his, in heart, in mind, in speech, forevermore."

All right yes.

I might cry.

They'd told me how this would go (though obviously not the words).

But I hadn't asked if I could show emotion.

Therefore, I held back the tears.

"Do you understand this, Silence of the Arbor?" Elpis asked.

"I do," I answered, my voice sounding husky.

It was then, Elpis leaned over me and looked into my eyes.

Her thoughts had always been deftly concealed.

And they were right then.

Until they were not, and I saw tenderness sweep in.

"I am glad, *mia figlia*," she whispered. "Now you will be pierced. Are you ready?"

Carefully, so as not to disengage the ice held to me, which it must be admitted, was so cold, it was getting uncomfortable, I nodded.

"As this is so, we shall commence," Elpis told me. "All four. At once. So it will be over quickly."

I nodded again.

It was then I saw, for the first time, my soon-to-be mother-in-law's eyes smiling at me.

They disappeared.

The ice disappeared.

I heard the sloshing of liquid.

And then I felt the tips of the needles at upper ear, lobe, nostril and lip.

Faith.

I held steady.

"*Lei è coraggiosa.*" This came in a whisper, I thought, from Nyx.

She is brave.

How lovely.

I drew in breath when the needles pierced my flesh.

Quickly, they were drawn out and I felt the hoops slid into the holes, the one at my lobe the last, as Elpis was at my ear, Nyx at my nostril, and Zosime at my lip, and Elpis could not do both at once.

Not long after, each was bathed with something that stung.

A spirit to keep the poison out.

After that, the ice was back, covered in cloth and held to the piercings.

I barely felt anything.

Just a tinge then a sting.

Yes.

Not bad a'tall.

"It is done," Elpis announced. "Silence of the Arbor is prepared to wed a Firenz. She is prepared to be a good wife. She understands what will make a good husband. And they will serve each other in confidence and understanding for the whole of their days. Praise the blessings."

"Praise the blessings," the women around me murmured.

"Praise the oath of marriage," Elpis chanted.

"Praise the oath of marriage," all around repeated.

"Praise understanding," Elpis said.

"Praise understanding," everyone repeated.

"Praise harmony," Elpis finished.

"Praise harmony."

"Do you praise these things, *mia figlia*?" Elpis asked me.

"I do," I answered.

"*Bello*," she whispered. Then louder, "Bring the king's gift."

The king's gift?

What gift?

Should I have a gift for him?

Oh dear.

The ice was taken away.

"Sit up," Elpis bid. "We shall replace it when needed. And give you a small draught to help with any pain. And, of course, after you receive my son's gift, we shall smoke."

Smoke?

No one mentioned smoke.

I could not ask.

I'd sat up, and when I did, I saw Zosime was coming forward with what appeared to be a small cage.

She offered it to Elpis, who did not take it, she opened the door.

And I gasped in delight when a tiny monkey with a bushy face and a striped tail bounced out into Elpis's hand.

She offered the wee precious thing to me.

Instantly, I reached out and took him.

He wrapped himself around my finger, which was about his height.

"It is a baby and it will get no bigger than your hand, that would be even *your* hand, Silence," Elpis said. "From Mars, for you. His gift, after you gave him your gift of bearing his wedding chain."

Oh by the gods.

By the gods.

Yes, now I was weeping.

I looked to the queen.

"You must name it, *tesoro*," Elpis bid, and I noticed her eyes were bright with unshed tears too.

"Piccolo," I declared.

"It's a girl," Elpis murmured.

I grinned at her through wet eyes.

"Piccol*a*," I amended.

She gave me a soft smile in return.

I gave my attention to my new darling, bringing her up to my face.

"Allo, wee precious," I whispered.

She reached her teeny hand to my nose.

I started laughing and instantly fell in love.

With a wee monkey.

And maybe...

A king.

~

EVERYONE GIGGLED.

"It is not funny," Elena stated.

We were in the royal bath of the palace garden that was at the very, *very* back. It was somewhat opened to the elements (no ceiling, only the head and end of the bath walled, the rest was sunshine and shrubbery with some stout columns that held flowering vines). It was tiled in small diamonds of peach and green. And there were eight lounges facing it.

I was on a lounge with my ornate *fumaria* beside me (a glass contraption that looked like a bottle with an extravagant stopper in the top and a glass extension where you put your lips).

Smoke was lovely.

Smoke, outside my wee Piccola, was my new favorite thing *in the world*.

Elena was in the bath, wearing her body stocking, looking lithe and tan and like she could fell a whole regiment of Firenz with her trim, tall, athletic body.

To my shock, Zosime, Nyx and Farah were in the bath as well, and they were naked (even Zosime, and she was heavily pregnant!).

Ha-Lah, the Mar-el queen, was in it, and she was naked too!

And she was thus when her guard was not far away. If he looked (which I'd checked, and he wasn't), he could see his queen *in the nude*!

This, of course, led to Mother and Aunt Mercy vacating the premises.

But Elpis was there.

She wore a short sarong wrapped around her torso and hips, and she sat on the side of the bath with her feet in it, her own *fumaria* at her side, laughing.

Sofia was on the other side and down from Elpis, in her own sarong. She had a *fumaria* and was using it, but she wasn't laughing, or talking, just being with us...and smoking.

Dora had gone with Ophelia, but Elena's lieutenants were now with us and one of them, Jasmine, was *not* in her body stocking (though the other one, Hera, was).

Everyone had a personal *fumaria* (save Zosime, who told me she couldn't do the smoke when she was expecting).

And it appeared we all loved them.

"It *is* hilarious," Jasmine negated her princess's words.

"He's a lout," Elena declared.

"A handsome one," Zosime said.

"If I did not have my Lorenz or he allowed us to play with such as him, I would not mind this lout pinning me to walls and telling me he wanted to kiss me until I was *soaked*," Nyx added.

I giggled again from where I reclined still wearing my orange drapings, though I did not quite understand what this "soaked" business was that the ladies were tittering about.

I had flicked the silk off so my legs weren't covered.

My mother would be scandalized.

But the sun on my legs felt *wonderful*.

At my giggle, Queen Elpis turned her gaze to me and gave me an affectionate look.

By the gods.

It was true.

She liked me!

"You would never kiss him," Zosime said as if she was horrified.

"I would not," Nyx agreed. "But I wouldn't mind him threatening me with it."

Elpis threw her head back and shouted with laughter.

Then she lifted her *fumaria* to her lips, drew in and eventually popped the lavish stopper from the top, taking in the smoke.

When she did, I decided to do the same.

I just *loved* listening to the bubbles in the liquid at the bottom when I drew in.

"Those piercings are pleasing, Silence," Hera called after I'd set my *fumaria* aside. "I'm thinking of getting some."

"Oh, you should," I declared, as I'd been shown a mirror and saw the small, gold hoops in my ear, nose and lip, and since my to-be husband had the same (and more!), I'd *adored* them. "They're lovely."

With that, I got another affectionate look from my soon-to-be mother-in-law.

I settled in my lounge, feeling quite happy.

Though, they'd taken my monkey away.

If I had Piccola, I'd be happier.

And if Mars was close and I could show him my new gold, I'd be happier.

And if he was close and I could also tell him how much I loved my monkey, I'd be happiest of all!

With what sounded like care, Jasmine asked Farah, "Will True give you a wedding chain?"

Appearing like she was being certain not to glance Elena's way, she replied, "I don't know. It will be his decision."

"I think you should ask him to give you one," Elena said quietly.

Elena was so lovely.

Farah looked to Elena.

"I agree," Ha-Lah declared.

Ha-Lah was so lovely too. Her manner was regal, but kind. And her skin was the most beautiful skin I'd ever seen. And I envied her bouncing curls. And maybe a little bit, I envied her courage to slide into the water nude.

For when she did, she got this odd, fetching expression on her face, like she was coming home.

I felt that way when I was in water. I adored a bath.

But since I didn't have a body stocking and I wasn't brave enough to go nude, I was on my lounge in the sun.

Though I had my smoke. So this was all right with me.

Maybe another time. After I was wed, and I was Firenz as well as Dellish.

"He might not take one himself," Elena went on, her gaze kind on Farah. "But he should give you one with the understanding he gets all of that from you, and even if he doesn't wear it, you get it in return."

Yes.

Elena was so very lovely.

She was clearly not getting along with Prince Cassius (he should give her a monkey!), but she was being very kind to Farah about True.

"I will discuss it with him," Farah murmured, and Elena smiled.

"And he will then give one to you. That is True. If he has it to give, he will give it. But if he cares for the one who's asking, he will move sky and earth and sea to hand it to you."

Hesitantly, and what appeared hopefully, Farah gave Elena a return smile.

"As far as I can tell, you all are fortunate," Nyx declared. "Of course, outside the Beast rising. But *I* had to win my Lorenz and he did not make it easy. You were all *given* the finest warriors of your realms without any work involved." She smiled largely. "If I did not eventually win my Lorenz, I would be most jealous."

"There is naught to be jealous of," Elena declared. "For as mentioned, mine is a *lout*."

Everyone giggled again.

"I'm so very glad you've decided to join us these last days, Queen Ha-Lah," I called when I was finished chortling, and the queen turned her beautiful face to me. "We have much time we will spend together, and it is good knowing you."

"That is very kind, Silence," she replied in her extraordinary voice. "It is good knowing you too."

"Your husband scares me though," I shared.

It was then, she started laughing.

I did it with her, even though I had no idea why I was doing so.

"He is not such a brute as he appears," she told me.

"He is very large," I told her.

Her head tipped to the side and the curls she had pinned to the top bounced that way. "And your Mars is not? Though it would seem you don't find your king frightening."

I thought of this and burst into giggles.

"'Tis true!" I cried.

Everyone laughed with me.

"We *are* very fortunate," I declared when we were finished with our merriment. "In so, *so* many ways. At home, in my father's house, I had no one but my Tril. And sometimes, my mother. And now." I swept my arm out. "Look!" I cried. "I am surrounded by friends."

I smiled but I did not receive the same in return.

"You were that much alone in your home, *mia figlia*?" Elpis asked.

I shook my head vehemently. "It is not so bad. I like being alone."

"As do we all, Silence," she replied softly. "Until we don't wish that. And when we don't wish that," her gaze just glanced off Sofia before it returned to me, "we need our friends."

"And now you have them," Farah declared. "Not friends. *Sorelle.* That is what we are. *Sorelle della Bestia.*"

Sisters of the Beast.

"Hear, hear," Elpis called, lifting her *fumaria*.

"Huzzah!" Jasmine shouted, striking out to the side of the bath toward her own elaborate pipe.

I took up mine.

"To us!" I cried louder than I'd ever spoken before, lifting my *fumaria*. "Sisters of the Beast!"

"Sisters of the Beast!" the ladies called.

We all smoked (save Zosime, who just smiled).

Then we all giggled.

Outrageously.

And thus when we did, we did not notice the waters of the pool, the very earth underneath...

Rippling.

25

THE LECTURE

Lord Johan Mattson

East Corridor, First Floor, Catrame Palace, Fire City
Firenze

Really.

The man was vile.

This was what Johan thought as he strode down the corridor and his future son-in-law strolled toward him.

He wore no shoes.

And he was again in those leathers without sleeves that he'd worn to the parade.

They were practically sculpted to his skin.

It was obscene.

And his long hair...

Piercings...

Scars...

Johan could barely stand looking at the animal.

By the gods, even if his daughter was not destined to get his own name in the tomes of history (and he reckoned that the man was becoming so enamored with Silence, Johan would get that preposterous dowry back tenfold the moment he instructed Silence to ask for it), they'd be on their horses and out of this foul city before the boor could blink.

When they were near, Johan stopped and said, "I'll have a word, Mars."

The king stopped as well and lifted a brow.

"Mars?"

Johan didn't understand the question for, unless he had a twin, he was Mars.

The man did not hesitate answering Johan's unasked question.

"Did I forget giving you leave to use my given name?"

"You're to marry my daughter in two days," Johan noted with exasperation.

"Yes," Mars agreed.

He ignored this ridiculousness and stated, "We need to speak."

The large man rocked back on his (bare) heels and crossed his arms on his (massive) chest.

"And what do you wish to say to me, Johan?" Mars asked.

"*Lord* Johan," he corrected glibly.

He was not feeling glib but a second later when he could not help himself from recoiling when he saw...

Could it be credited?

A burst of actual red *flame* light in the king's eyes.

By the bloody *gods*.

"Let us not," Mars growled. "I've had a trying day. I missed dinner with my bride. It's late. I marry the day after tomorrow and there is much still to be done. If you wish to speak, do it," he ordered.

Johan lifted his chin.

"I have sent word for the rest of Silence's dowry to be delivered," Johan declared.

"This I know," Mars returned.

"I have showed you that respect," Johan told him.

Mars said nothing.

"My daughter is twenty-three years of age," Johan stated.

"Fascinating," Mars murmured, his gaze darkening, and Johan got the distinct impression the king was no longer even aware Johan was there.

He fought snapping in the behemoth's face and instead snapped with his voice, "Thus she is young and has been very sheltered."

Mars blinked back into the conversation but only visually, not audibly.

"She received these piercings of yours today," Johan reminded him.

"Did you stop me on my way to my bed to tell me a variety of things I know, and only one I did not?" Mars queried.

Johan was losing patience.

"She's showing respect to you as well," he clipped.

"It is our way."

"It is not ours."

"And thus I am aware, *Lord Johan*, that this is a gift she has given me. *She*. For it is her skin that bears the marital hoops that I will fill with my chain. What I'm not understanding is why I'm in the corridor discussing it with you."

"Then I'll explain. *I* would like respect returned by you not making my *sheltered, young* daughter do such as share a bath with women who wear no *clothes* while she engages in that vile *smoke*."

"This is of my people too," Mars replied.

"Silence is—"

"Enough," Mars whispered, and there was no flame, but his tone, his look, and the strange appearance of his body having grown several inches in both height and width made Johan fight taking several steps back. "I will give you what you desire, Lord Johan."

"I desire nothing but—"

"One small chest of Firenz emeralds."

Johan gasped.

That was...

Well, it was worth the entire dowry and then some.

"One large chest of Airenzian gold," Mars went on, to Johan's shock, for this was *far* more than ten times the cost of the dowry. "And a pouch of Firenz rubies."

Johan was suddenly feeling much more beneficent to his future son-in-law.

"I don't...that's quite generous...it's—" Johan stammered.

"It is not generous, although it is a fortune," Mars declared. "But it comes nowhere near the worth of your daughter, which is what, with that fortune, I'll be buying."

At this, Johan was perplexed.

"You already have her," Johan reminded him.

"After all the prophesied are wed and she and I come back to Firenze and we go about our lives, you will not see her, unless I allow it. Her mother will come at Silence's behest, under my guard. But you will not attend her. Is this to your understanding?"

And with that, he was no longer feeling beneficent to his future son-in-law.

No.

He was *enraged*.

"You...you intend to...to...cut me out of my daughter's life?" Johan stammered.

"If she never sees you again, this will not bother me. If she wishes to see you again, I will consider it. But I will not grant it unless I feel you can attend her without harming her. Now this is understood, no?"

"I would never harm my daughter," Johan snapped.

"She does not know her own beauty. And my mother spoke to me earlier this evening and told me Silence shared she has no companions in your land. She is close only to a woman who I'm told is her lady's maid. A woman of Silence's wit and charm should have more in her life than her lady's maid."

"She's an oddity."

Johan fancied a rush of hot wind hit his entire frame when Mars growled, "She is not..." he drew breath in through his nose, "*an oddity*."

"She's an oddity in our land," Johan hastily explained.

"And how is this so?'"

"She reads."

Mars blinked.

"She does not like to dance," Johan continued.

"I do not like to dance either, but I am not an oddity," Mars remarked.

"You are not a woman. Women enjoy these things. Fine clothes. Fripperies. Courtly advances. Flirtations. I don't know," Johan tossed out a hand, "kittens."

This seemed to concern the king for he asked, "My bride does not like kittens?"

"Yes, she does, of course, but not figurines of them scattered about her rooms."

It took a moment before Mars sighed a heavy sigh.

He then said, "You do not understand her."

"She is not like other girls," Johan returned.

"No, she is like your daughter. And there is no one, outside her mother, who should understand her better than her father. In twenty-three years of life, I would suspect there is much to know. For what I know, in just a few days, I've learned this is true."

Johan went still.

"Do you like to read?" Mars asked.

Johan felt his insides turn cold.

"Yes," he mumbled.

"Do you like to ride?"

"Of course."

"Your daughter likes to ride."

"Girls shouldn't like to ride in anything but carriages."

"This is how you harm her, Lord Johan. For I know of two things you enjoy that your daughter enjoys as well, and you do not share these with her."

Johan shook his head. "You must know, it is every aristocratic daughter's role to advance the means of her title and as she is, she was unweddable."

"She is not now, for she marries a king. And you will leave here with chests of riches," Mars returned. "And with that you can see, Lord Johan, she was not unweddable. It was simply that you did not value all she has to offer, you made that clear to her, but fortunately for your daughter, destiny led her to someone who does."

"I must think on this," Johan murmured.

"If you don't mind, I'll leave you to do so on your own," Mars murmured back, dropped his arms and started to move away.

"King Mars," Johan called.

On another sigh, Mars turned back.

"You can't possibly think I'll give up the right to see my daughter for a chest of gold."

"And you can't possibly think it's wise to barter for more treasure for this isn't an offer, this is a gift from a king on obeying a command."

A command?

He was not this king's to command.

By the gods, he'd take a moment to think before he obeyed his own king's command.

Johan was getting angry again.

"If you were going to give me so much for her, why did you demand such a huge dowry?"

"*That* was a barter," Mars explained. "And your king is not very good at it."

After delivering his parting line, Mars sauntered away.

And Johan watched him go.

As he did, he realized he was the father to a woman who would be queen in but days' time, and at the parade, he'd been relegated to the stands, not the podium.

And at the betrothal dinner, he'd had to sit with a Go'Doan and a Nadirii lieutenant and his king's counsellor, *not* at the table with Queen Ophelia and Princess Serena and his own king and queen. But the bloody wife of a *traitor* had sat with them.

Further, his daughter had had her flesh pierced and lazed about all afternoon getting fuzzy headed on *smoke*.

And he'd just been offered a payment in order never to see his daughter again, except at a foreign king's leave.

He'd also just endured a lecture from a man who wasn't even a bloody father on how he had not been a bloody good *father*.

He was Lord of the Arbor. He was an aristocrat. His very veins flowed with royal blood. And he was married to the daughter of a *king*.

Yes, Johan was enraged.

And he very much hoped his Silence and her brute, Cassius and his warrior, poor True and that slut he had to marry, and the King of the Sea and his bride could quell the Beast.

Because after they did, Johan was going to make a king *beg*.

And he was going to use his daughter to do it.

Though, as Johan stormed down the hall in the direction the king took, toward the stairs, he thought he would not wait for the defeat of the Beast.

King Mars was falling in love with his daughter.
And that gave Johan power.
And he was going to use it.

26

THE KING'S BEDCHAMBER

Lady Silence Mattson
*The King's Bedchamber, Second Floor, West Corridor, Catrame Palace,
Fire City*
Firenze

After dinner, when I walked up the stairs and arrived at the top, I did not turn left to go to my rooms.

I stopped and looked right.

Mars's rooms were at the very end of that hall.

Or what I knew were Mars's rooms, now, since I noted all the clamor of the servants when the queen had moved to our end of the hall.

And although I'd finally had a rather thorough tour of the palace and had been there for days, I'd never seen his rooms.

And the day after tomorrow, we would be wed.

He was behind closed doors in his meeting room, apparently something important (and time consuming) was happening, so he, nor any of the kings or princes or Queen Ophelia, had joined us for dinner.

I should not do what I was thinking about doing.

And in thinking about doing it, I could not blame the influence of smoke. It had worn off some time ago.

Though I'd had one more glass of wine than I usually did at dinner that evening.

But it wasn't that either.

It was about my monkey.

And the fact that the night after tomorrow, I would be married.

I looked left, then right again, noting, as guests were retiring, the servant boys were busy (thus not in the hall), seeing to bedtime needs.

This being the case, I quickly stole down the hall, checking over my shoulder repeatedly.

When I arrived at the closed door to his room, I knocked (just in case), quietly (because I didn't want anyone to hear).

His voice didn't come through the door telling me to enter.

I entered anyway.

And for a second, I was immobilized.

After I realized I was standing in his open bedchamber door, I shut it behind me and stood there staring.

I had a small bathing pool off my rooms.

But this before me...

This was not small.

It could have all the ladies in it, times about three!

It was tiled in black and emerald tiles, these tiles inside the pool and *all along the floor*. The walls around it were a warm peach. There were four lounges down the sides that were more like double-wide *divans*. There were also four pots with actual *trees* growing out of them (though they were small and artfully trimmed, they still were *trees*). Cushions scattered on the floor. Beautiful ceramic vases from which sprung fresh flowers.

It was enthralling.

Though as much as it was, I couldn't stand, staring at Mars's bathing pool, what would soon be *my* bathing pool.

I had to hurry, take my look and leave.

He could arrive at any moment, and even though I could easily call my shadow to hide me, I didn't want to take even a slim chance getting caught.

So I walked in, looked left through an archway, and I felt my mouth drop open as I wandered that way.

Opulence.

More peach walls. Fluffy divans. Cushions. Tables scattered here and there. Lamps scattered. Intricate hanging chandeliers. Silks and velvets and rich furs and flowing beaded tassels.

There were plenty of places to sit and read.

Plenty more places to lounge and have hundreds, thousands (more!) conversations between husband and wife.

Or perhaps I'd ask Nyx and Zosime to attend me and I'd share time with my new girlfriends there.

And there was a desk in the room at a corner facing out. It was not as large as the one downstairs in Mars's study. But it was large and ornately carved and kingly.

I moved to it thinking he could work while I read, and when we were done, together we could...

I stopped thinking beyond that and saw he did, indeed, work up here. There were parchments and scrolls on the desk, as well as two silver pens engraved with some designs, all of this scattered on top. Three inkpots. And four different colored waxes for sealing, one black, one red, one green and one gold. There were also two different stamps.

I lifted one and looked at the bottom. It was a snake. The other, a lick of flame.

I wondered what each stamp was used for and each color of wax or if he just used them at his fancy.

I'd ask.

One day.

And he'd answer.

Because I'd be his wife and I should know such things.

And I could not deny that this thought made me feel oddly *giddy*.

In that moment, however, I could not give in to feeling giddy. I had a whole other room to explore as Mars's rooms took over the entire end of the west wing.

I scurried across the room, seeing what I hadn't before, bookshelves encased on either side of the wall that led to the archway to the pool, and they were filled with books.

I smiled to myself, even more giddy in the knowledge that I would get to peruse those later, and darted across the tiled floor of the bathing room, through some sheer black curtains...

And I was in the bedchamber.

"*Faith*," I breathed.

An enormous bed on a podium up three steps. These steps were carpeted in a snowy-white fur. The bed had an overhang that came down from the ceiling painted in blacks and reds with accents of gold. From the corners of the overhang, black sheers fell, bunched to blossom a little more than halfway up the bedposts. An apricot velvet padded headboard. Dozens of pillows at the head. Luxurious furs as covers.

The floor was black marble and it gleamed so brightly, I fancied I could look down and it would mirror my face.

Tufted footstools. More divans. Mirrored chests. Vases with fresh flowers.

It wasn't opulence.

It wasn't lavishness.

It was *sumptuous*.

I quickly moved to the two arches on the wall facing east and shoved aside the sheer black curtains that covered one.

More sumptuousness.

A dressing room. Velvet covered daybed. Furs for rugs. Shelves of clothes, boots, sandals. Gilt-edged mirrors. All in black with accents of gold and red.

I moved to the other arch.

This would be mine.

I knew because it was the same, except much more feminine, in apricots with accents of red and gold.

There was a door at the back.

Likely where Tril would be (I hoped, we didn't like to be far from one another).

I turned back to the room.

So he gave me a monkey.

And he gave me a palace.

And he gave me his attention.

And he thought I was beautiful.

I did not know what would be my part in quelling the Beast.

I just was beginning to think that, at the side of the King of Firenze, I would find the courage to do just about anything.

On that thought, I heard the door to the chamber open.

"*Balls*," I whispered, felt the tingle along my back, threw out my arm and gathered my shadow around me, hurrying across the large room as Mars strode in, pulling his hide shirt over his head.

I stutter-stepped at the view of his chest.

He dropped this shirt to the floor, *looked right at me*, stopped abruptly, and said, "Silence?"

Erm.

What?

I noticed the air undulating all around.

My shadow was up.

How did he know I was there?

"Silence," he growled, striding to me, his long legs meaning he was *to me* in a thrice.

His big hands fell on my shoulders and then they moved to cup the sides of my neck as he bent to me.

"Is all well?"

His handsome face with its scars and piercings was filled with concern.

"You can see me?" I whispered.

"Yes, *piccolina*, you're standing right here," he replied, giving my neck a wee squeeze.

I dropped the shadow, but when I did, Mars's brows inched together, and his head twitched as if he'd seen it go but he didn't know what it was.

Only *I* could see it go.

How could *he* see it go?

"Mars," I called, and he focused again on me.

"Do your piercings hurt?" he demanded.

"Erm...no."

"Mama gave you a draught?"

I nodded.

"And one for tonight, so you can sleep without discomfort?" he asked.

I nodded again.

"You must leave the hoops in, Silence," he ordered. "And sleep on your back or your left side so they don't snag the pillows and cause you pain."

And again, I nodded.

"Did your father upset you?" he queried.

I shook my head, now confused.

"No," I answered. "Why would he do that?"

"I just saw him in the hall. He was being vexing."

Oh dear.

Father being vexing to Mars.

"What did he do?" I queried.

"It matters not. Now, what are you doing in my bedchamber?"

Erm...

How to explain this?

"Silence," he prompted.

"I wanted to see," I blurted.

Now it was he who looked confused.

And truly...

How could he make confused look handsome and manly?

"See what?" he inquired.

"Where I would, erm...be sleeping."

"Ah," he murmured, lifting up but not taking his hands from me.

He then studied me with a mixture of tenderness, concern and something I didn't understand.

To stop him from doing that as it was making me feel strange, I noted, "You haven't mentioned what you think about my piercings."

"They are beautiful," he declared, shifting a hand to cup my jaw so he could reach out with a thumb to gently touch the hoop at my lip. "And they will be even more beautiful threaded with my chain."

I hoped he thought so.

"You were right. It didn't hurt. Just a tinge," I told him.

"Mm," he hummed in a way I felt in my belly.

"The ceremony almost made me weep," I shared.

At that, he looked surprised, then everything left his expression.

That was everything, except the tenderness.

"This heartens me," he said softly.

"And Piccola is just wonderful," I went on.

"Piccola?"

"My wee monkey."

His eyes went soft as did his mouth.

And that was even more handsome.

It might be the handsomest of all.

"You're pleased?" he asked.

I nodded but admitted, "I didn't get you anything."

"You gave me this." He touched his thumb to my hoop again.

"Yes, I know. But for our wedding."

His brow went up. "The bride gives her husband a gift at the wedding in your realm?"

"No, I mean, yes. They both do. Bride and groom."

"How odd," he murmured.

I brightened.

"So you haven't gotten me anything so I don't have to rush to a bazaar tomorrow to find something special for you?"

He bent to me again, putting his face in mine. "My Silence, shall we just say that we've already exchanged our gifts? You will take my chain. And I have given you Piccola."

"I think that would be...that would be..." I couldn't catch a thought with his face that close, his body that close, his hands on me...*in his bedchamber*.

"It would be...?" he prompted when I got lost in how black his eyes were.

They were like liquid.

"Good," I forced out.

"Mm," he hummed again, lifted up, touched his lips to my forehead, I felt the tickle of his beard, his soft lips, and I froze.

True kissed my forehead.

On the rare occasion I did something about which my father approved (this was a grand total of two times in my life), my father kissed my forehead.

When I was younger and shorter, my mother kissed my forehead.

I didn't like Mars kissing my forehead.

"I shall walk you to your bedchamber," he announced.

I didn't want to go to my bedchamber.

I wanted to...

I didn't know.

"How did my father vex you?" I asked the skin of his chest.

His hand at my jaw slid down to cup my neck again, but his thumb still moved, this time to stroke my jaw.

"It doesn't matter," he murmured.

My eyes dropped to his stomach, and I saw the boxes there.

How did he get those?

I could not say I'd seen many men's chests.

But I'd never seen those.

"I don't like my father vexing you," I mumbled.

"As it wasn't you who vexed me, I'll share again, *mia bellezza*, it doesn't matter.

His beauty.

And he was going to be my beauty.

Without me willing it to do so, mesmerized in some way by his flesh, I lifted a hand and touched it to one of the dents in his belly.

He sucked in breath.

I didn't notice.

"But I do like your bedchamber," I muttered.

"I'm glad," he said in a voice that sounded strange—deeper, thick.

I slid the tip of my finger down the center groove, which was the deepest.

"Silence," he whispered.

"How do you get your belly to look like this?" I whispered back, sweeping my finger along a side dip under a swell.

"Silence."

That wasn't thick

It was hoarse.

I tipped my head back at the sound.

And with one look at him, my body caught fire.

"Mars," I breathed.

"I would kiss you," he murmured, staring fixedly at my mouth.

"I would like you to kiss me," I whispered back, veering inexorably toward his body.

He stopped me by putting his finger under my chin, tipping my head back farther, dipping his down, and touching his lips to mine.

He then retreated.

As other suitors retreated who stole a kiss.

A peck on the mouth.

Then gone.

"Oh," I mumbled.

"Oh?" he asked.

I looked into his eyes. "I um, well, yes. Thank you. That was nice."

"*Nice?*"

Oh dear.

He didn't look happy.

"Do you play games?" he queried.

My brow furrowed, and I answered. "No."

His eyes moved over my face a moment before he asked another question.

"Do you truly want my kiss?"

Taking in his expression, I wasn't so certain.

"Come here, *piccolina*," he ordered.

"I'm here, Mars."

He bent low, wrapped an arm around my waist, and drew me against his body.

"*Oh*," I breathed.

"Yes," he agreed. "*Oh*."

He felt hard against me.

Not only his body (which was hard) but a certain part of his body (which was *hard* and pressing into me).

"This is what your touch does to me, Silence," he said.

"All right," I whispered.

"Does it frighten you?" he asked.

"Yes," I admitted quietly.

"I will fix that."

I didn't know if that was possible.

"All right," I repeated.

"I'm going to kiss you now. A kiss that is not...*nice*."

Eep!

"All right."

He pulled me up to my toes as his hand at my neck tilted my head far, *far* back with a thumb at the hinge of my jaw.

And his head came down.

He pressed his lips to mine and he did this firmly.

His lips were strong, yet soft. I liked the feel of them. The prickle of his beard. The smell of him all around me. The touch of his tall, powerful body against mine. The heat of his skin. Even the sting at my piercing.

I relaxed into him and lifted my arms to put my hands on his shoulders.

He touched the tip of his tongue to my lips.

My body jerked, and my head came back.

His hand sifted up into my hair to cup the back of my head and hold me steady.

And his lips came back to mine.

"Open your mouth for me," he murmured against them.

"W-why?" I asked nervously.

"Because you will take my tongue."

I would?

Was that what he meant days before when he caught me to tell me he did not like me running from him?

I would take his tongue in my mouth?

"No, my Silence," he whispered, reading my thoughts. "You will take my tongue in your mouth and you will also take other parts of me there."

His arm around me fit me tighter to him, namely a certain part of him, making his point, and I felt my lips part as I stared into his eyes.

"You do not mean this parting for me," he muttered, his gaze again at my lips. "But I will take it."

He then angled his head, his lips pressed to mine, and his tongue swept inside.

Oh, oh, oh...

But he tasted...

Heavenly.

I whimpered and melted into him, arching my back, drifting my fingers up and into his thick hair.

He growled down my throat, slanted my head farther, leaned deeper forward, bending me over his arm, taking me to the tips of my toes, and he tangled his tongue with mine.

His was...

Studded.

He was pierced there too.

I moaned and pressed into him.

His hand fisted lightly in my hair, he drew his tongue under mine and then sucked mine into his mouth.

Oh *my.*

My belly dropped, my legs were trembling, and something was happening between them.

Something tingly and shivery and warm and *lovely.*

Like my magic.

But *better.*

So much *better.*

He suckled on me and then his tongue thrust mine out so it could invade my mouth and I suckled on his.

And as I did that, my hands roamed. His sloped neck. His muscled shoulders. His thick arms.

So hot.

So sleek.

So hard.

Everywhere.

His hand left my hair and clamped on my behind, pushing up, molding me firmly to his hips.

And that was even *better.*

"*Mars,*" I breathed into his mouth.

"*Gods,*" he breathed back, tracing his lips along my cheek and shoving his face in my neck.

"Mars?" I called shakily.

His hand at my bottom slid to my hip, over my waist, in and up my spine before it curled around the back of my neck.

But he still held me to him.

However.

"Did I do something wrong?" I asked.

"No," he groaned. "Fuck no."

"All right then…" I swallowed. "Why are we no longer kissing?"

His big body spasmed with a harsh laugh before he lifted his head and looked down at me with eyes saturated with humor and desire (I knew what it was now, *faith*, but I knew) and sweetness.

"We're no longer kissing, my bride of the silver soul and the candied mouth, because if we do not stop now, there will be no wedding as I'll lock us in these rooms for the next two weeks."

"Oh," I whispered.

He grinned. "Yes, my Silence, *oh*."

"It is not...unheard of...in my land...for a woman...though, I have never...uh—"

"Calm, Silence. I know."

He knew

He knew I was virgin?

How did he know?

He continued speaking.

"And this is why we will take some time, even if we don't have much of it, to get to know one another in that way. Tomorrow night, after dinner, you will come to my rooms and I will share a little more with you so you'll be better prepared for the next night when we will share everything."

"More kissing?" I asked.

His lips twitched. "Yes, amongst other things."

I smiled up at him. "I'd like that."

He smiled down at me. "You did not hide that, *mia bellezza*."

My smile fled. "Was I brazen?" How could I ask that? I was completely brazen. "Oh no!" I cried. "I was brazen."

He threw his head back and roared with laughter, holding me to him as he did, even pulling me closer.

He tipped his head down again and through his laughter said, "You were brazen, yes. And I liked it. Very much so."

I felt heat hit my cheeks and murmured, "Oh."

"And this 'oh' I feel in parts of me I cannot wait to have in her mouth," he murmured back, his gaze roaming all over my face (but mostly, it must be said, my lips and cheeks).

"I think I should probably go to my bedchamber now," I told him, belatedly prudently.

"I think this is wise," he replied, his black eyes dancing.

But he did not let me go.

He bent again to me, pressed his lips hard to mine, then straightened away, only then to release me (which I did not like).

He took my hand (which I did like).

And then he walked us toward the bathing room.

We strolled past his leather shirt on the floor and it was on the tip of my tongue to suggest he don it before walking me all the way down his very long hall to my rooms at the other end.

I did not do that.

This was his home.

His palace.

And it was now my home.

My palace.

And he should be just as he wanted to be in his home.

As he was showing me it was all right just to be...*me*.

"Where is Piccola?" he asked after we entered the hall.

"Tril has her. I'm going to teach her to sleep on the pillow beside mine at night."

"My Silence, as you'll be sleeping on the pillow beside *mine*, I think we should have a discussion about this, no?"

I'd be sleeping on the pillow beside his.

This gave me another tingle.

"I hadn't thought of that," I mumbled.

He chuckled and said, "I'm very glad you like her."

I looked up at him as we strolled, hand in hand. "I *love* her."

He smiled warmly down at me and gave my hand a squeeze.

"Though I don't like her in a cage," I shared.

"She is very clever, like her mama. She will learn soon to stay close to you."

At that, timidly, I gave *his* hand a squeeze.

I didn't need to be timid.

He again gave me another warm smile.

We made the door to my rooms, but before I could reach to the handle, he drew me into his arms.

"Now we bid goodnight," he declared.

I tried not to pout.

I must have failed for he roared with laughter again.

I grinned up at him as he did.

When he sobered, he tipped his chin down to me.

"Tomorrow will be a busy day, but I will not miss dinner with you again," he promised.

"I'm glad," I told him.

"And we will have our time after dinner."

I pressed my lips together as that gave me a shiver.

I released them to say, "I look forward to that."

His fingers slid along my hairline as he said gently, "And the next night, we'll be wed."

"I look forward to that too," I whispered.

He gave me another smile, this one soft and sweet, before he bent again and touched his lips to mine.

"Until the morrow, my Silence," he murmured against them.

"Until then, my king."

I received yet another smile, this one from his eyes, before he straightened and jerked his bearded chin to my door.

I opened it and rushed inside, beginning to shut it behind me with but a small grin up at my king (who was gazing indulgently down at me) as I closed him away from me.

Tril immediately came out of her room once the latch clicked.

"Was that the king I heard?" she asked.

"Yes," I answered dreamily.

She studied my face.

Then she decreed, "He kissed you."

"Yes," I repeated, even more dreamily.

I had a mind to skip and twirl to the bed.

Instead I floated there, turned to it, and plopped backward on it.

I felt it depress and then I saw Tril's face above mine.

She was frowning at my nostril. "Does that gold hurt?"

I looked into her eyes.

"No. It feels like heaven."

Her gaze came to mine.

And it was then, my Tril smiled at me.

27

THE CARDS

Princess Elena
Guest Suite, Second Floor, East Corridor, Catrame Palace, Fire City
Firenze

When the sun was a sliver on the horizon, just touching the sky with the new day, I left my rooms.

I did this after donning my purple body stocking with the thin straps and high cuts at the hips over which I added my lavender tunic with the coral trim that had some gilding at the V-neck and around the hem.

This I tied with my gold belt.

I also took up my rug and cards.

I walked on bare feet through the palace into the still-dark but ever-lightening gardens on a course to the spot on the east side that I'd spied the day before.

I stopped in the small clearing that had the fountain affixed to the garden wall that was a cascade of staggered, carved, rusted stone bowls fed one after the other from the head of a snake at the top.

The snake's mouth was open, fangs bared, water flowing through and down into the bowls, to finally plunge into a small pool on the ground.

I set my cards aside, flipped out the rug and sat cross-legged on it, facing the fountain.

I was not surprised, even with the peaceful falling of the water, when I could not clear my mind in order to find some contentment.

I was tense, not sleeping well, and my head was a jumble of thoughts and worries.

Mother had rested the morning before, rather than joining the others at the diplomatic table.

This was good for she looked paler, was tiring faster, and not eating well.

And her mouth was beginning to appear like it was pinched with pain.

This was a worry.

As it had been a worry for some time.

But it was getting to be *more* of a worry.

However, after the piercing ceremony, she'd been called into the meeting rooms with the others and she was in them well into the night.

Too much for her.

All of this was too much for her.

And we'd be traveling again soon, with Silence and Mars only having a few days of nuptial bliss to enjoy in Firenze (and to my surprise, but tentative delight for Silence, this seemed as if it would be the case) before we would again be on our horses, bound for Wodell.

My mother needed to sit still, conduct some rituals and allow some healing practices.

She was not doing this.

This was a worry too.

Then there was Serena, who had been so vile to Cassius and myself it was beyond her normal level of vile.

I did not understand that.

This was also a worry.

Then, of course, there was Dora.

The man who killed her mother was in that very palace.

I had no intention of telling my girl this was the case. There was no need to speak of it.

Ever.

But with Serena being the way Serena was being, I might be forced to do just that.

Better it come from me than however Serena might connive to impart that information.

Then there was Cassius...

I did not wish to think about Cassius.

Though he had been busy at the diplomatic table as well, even through dinner the night before, so I did not have to engage with him yesterday nor introduce him to Dora as he'd threatened at the betrothal dinner.

But today was another day and I had to find the inner equanimity to handle whatever came of it.

Deciding against continuing to attempt to meditate, I undid my belt and set it aside before pulling off my tunic.

I then straightened my spine further and dropped my chin in my neck, folding one hand over the other at the back of my head to deepen the stretch. The same when I dropped my head to each side.

I then lifted an arm up, fell sideways so my opposite forearm was against my rug, and I reached over my head.

And the other side.

After that, I did a few stretches in quick succession—seated, standing, and twisting—to warm my body before I did them again, settling in them for longer this time. I also added more in order to lengthen my muscles and ease the tension out of my spine, the backs of my legs, the fronts of my thighs, my shoulders, my arms and more of my neck.

With this accomplished (feeling invigorated, but no less worried), I sat cross-legged again, pulled on my tunic, retied my belt and reached to my cards.

I did this with trepidation.

Since I'd turned it, my morning card had not again been the Unicorn.

But what I'd been getting, even with a disordered mind, it could not be denied that the cards were falling appropriately.

The card Besom from the hushed suit (of course, I had been traveling and I was doing it for festivals and ceremonies, which was the indication of Besom, or the broom).

The card Warrior from the middling suit (which made sense, as I needed strength, to brace and be prepared for what came next).

The hushed card of the Wand (obviously, as I needed much magic for the parade).

Another hushed card of the Pentacle (though I could fathom that card, I still found it difficult to meditate, though, through necessity, I had conducted many rituals to draw my magic within).

Further hushed cards, the Staff (not a surprise, I knew I needed to have a mind to the protection of myself and my own) and the Sword (one could say strife surely had entered my life, in the form of an enemy prince as well as my sister).

But I also often got the middling cards of Eros (and that made me anxious, for it foretold of romantic liaison, sexual need, and the instruction to seek a lover, and this, like the Unicorn, was a card I'd never turned before), the Lovers (which I did not understand for it signified union, balance and harmony), and the Dragon (this was understood, fire, endings, power—*definitely* understood).

And I had turned two high cards.

The Star, which signified hope and dreams, though I took it as a need to do a dream reading. However, not sleeping well, I was not having dreams.

And the Siren.

An omen card.

One of only two in the deck and these you never wished to turn.

I had also never turned it.

Danger.

Betrayal.

Falsity.

I moved the cards in my hands with all this on my mind, these weeks past no longer trying to clear it to give a faithful path from my inner self to the cards for the correct reading, as I used to do, for in these times this was an impossibility.

Now I simply pulled a card in any moment when my mind was struck open, even if just for a second.

Which was what I did.

I set the deck aside.

Then I flipped the card I selected, allowing it to fall on the rug before me.

And my heart stopped beating.

The Banshee.

The other omen card.

Death of a loved one, one you hold dear, or one in your heart.

Colossal change in life as you know it.

I had never turned that either.

"Good goddess," I murmured, staring at it.

This couldn't be.

Because it could not be borne.

"Mother," I whispered.

I heard his boots on the mosaics and I knew it was he.

Quickly, I flipped the Banshee but then folded my hands together and left them hanging in my lap.

Perhaps he would think I was meditating and leave me to it.

The sounds of his heels on tiles came ever closer.

Until they stopped right behind me.

His deep voice rumbled at me.

"When you are my princess, you must teach these positions to my warriors. I see how they would increase strength, flexibility and balance," he announced.

He'd seen me stretch.

How?

Dear goddess, he had to have rooms facing the gardens.

Perhaps this wasn't as private a spot as I had thought.

"I'm meditating, go away," I told him.

"You're reading cards," he told me.

Drat it all!

I should have shoved the cards under my bottom.

"I'm meditating over my reading," I lied.

"You're lying in an effort not to speak to me."

I ground my teeth.

I felt him get closer but didn't hear his feet hit the tiles in order to round the rug to get in front of me.

I would find that this was because he'd come to stand on my rug.

And he did this moments before he crouched beside me, at my back, but to my side, meaning his long, thick thighs were straddling me so close, his leathers nearly brushed the skin of my arm.

Which made my arm, in a curious (but not unpleasant in the slightest) way, tingle.

This meant his deep voice was closer too.

"What is your reading?" he asked quietly.

"It's private."

Being what I was coming to learn was Cassius Laird, regardless of my words, he reached an arm out in front of me toward the card that lay before me.

I reached out too.

In order to slap his hand.

He chuckled.

Chuckled!

Goddess deliver me.

Though he withdrew his hand.

"Would you like to do my reading?" he asked.

"Absolutely not."

"I'd like you to do my reading."

"There is no need. I can tell you which card you'd select before you selected it."

"And what card would I select?" he queried.

"The Simpleton."

He chuckled again.

I sighed.

"What does that mean, or do I need ask?" he inquired.

"It means recklessness. Thoughtlessness. Impulsiveness. Inconsideration."

"All that?"

"Also gullibility and imprudence."

"Hmm," he murmured. "Let us see."

At that, for the first time since he arrived, I moved my head to see he was still crouched beside me but now he was reaching to my cards.

"Do not touch those," I demanded precisely when he picked them up with his long fingers.

His hand, I saw, was veined and visibly calloused.

No courtly prince was he.

"Put them down," I ordered.

Even though they were large, he shuffled the cards expertly one handed, not a man, clearly, who was a stranger to the handling of cards.

I was sure he engaged in games of chance regularly.

I just hoped he lost.

"How's this?" he asked, flicked an expert thumb on the top of the deck and thus a card flew out, turning over in midair, to land on top of the one I'd drawn.

The image depicted a majestic lion with a full mane, open mouth, dragon's wings and a scorpion's tail.

It was the manticore.

But of course.

"He looks fierce," Cassius noted.

"Manticore," I forced out.

"And he means?" Cassius asked.

I could concoct something. Something dire. Or awkward.

I did not.

"Power. Battle. War." I hesitated. "Victory."

I was staring at the card, but I would swear I *felt* him smile.

He sent another flying and it fell before me.

"You only get one," I snapped, twisting my head to look at him.

He was very close.

"Do I?" he murmured, his eyes wandering my face.

The way they did that made me uneasy.

Therefore, I gave my attention to the card he'd turned.

It was mostly blues, silvers, grays and black.

A warrior in intricate battle armor with blue stones and accents, standing in front of a wide, imposing, craggy black castle set in a black cliff. There was a barren tree to his right, and in it was a crow, a being that had its own card, an indication of second sight, the need for reflection, magic and mystery.

The warrior's head was bowed, his steel-gauntleted hands at rest at his sides—but the breadth of his shoulders, the trimness of his waist, the manner of his bearing—his strength could not be denied and there was no question about it, even with head bowed, this was not a pose of defeat.

In other words, it was the Warrior card.

"And he is fierce too," Cassius whispered in a way I felt a thrill across the skin of my neck.

"The Warrior," I grunted, and before he could ask, I explained, "Strength. Preparation."

"Hmm," he murmured and tossed down another card.

The hilt and blade of a magnificent bejeweled sword out of which gold, yellow and orange rays shown.

"The Sword," I said. "It means strife."

"Well, that is no surprise," he replied and threw another card.

Goodness.

"Cassius," I said softly.

"What is that, Elena?" he asked.

It was a high card.

A full moon over a dark night on a shadowed landscape through which a river of red meandered through.

Blood.

"It is a high card," I told him. "Blood. Fertility." I swallowed and finished, "Family."

"Ah," he murmured, and if I would allow myself to admit it (which I did not), it was kind that he did not linger on that before he threw another card.

I closed my eyes.

His voice was silk in my ear. "And what is that, my princess?"

I opened my eyes.

On the card was a man floating in the air. He wore white gauntlets from wrists up to his shoulders and they sprung out from there, like wings. Armor at his thighs and over his groin. The rest of him, outside his white, armored boots, was bare. An elaborate bow and arrow were tattooed over his heart. And he held an extravagant white bow in one hand, arrow in the other.

And under him, on the earth, was a woman upright but on her knees, which were spread wide. She was nude. She was fair. And a strapping man with black hair was on his knees behind her, his head bent to her neck, his arms about her, one hand cupping her sex, one hand cradling a bare breast.

His face was hidden in her neck.

But her face bore an expression of ecstasy.

"Eros," I whispered.

"A god of the ancients," Cassius whispered back. "I don't need a reading, Elena. That speaks for itself."

"Are you finished?" I queried.

He was not for he threw another card.

I could not stop my intake of breath.

"Pure beauty," he murmured.

It was.

The Unicorn.

"And she means?" Cassius inquired.

"Joy," I said softly. "Serenity. Fulfillment. Change."

He said nothing to that, but he didn't need to. I felt emotion coming from him, I just could not say what it was.

"Can we be done now?" I asked.

Apparently, we couldn't for although he set the deck aside, he reached forward, took hold of the ones that had fallen, flipping them so mine was facing up.

A card drawn of purples and blacks, whites and charged blues. A landscape of devastation and destruction behind a woman in a long, wide, black skirt with an ornate purple apron at the front, all of which flowed in a threatening way and was decorated with blue lightning. She had black gauntlets on her forearms with gloves over her hands, her elbows pulled back, her fingers formed into claws.

Her bright white hair flowing up and out, she was leaned forward, her eyes spiteful, her mouth opened wide, her expression dreadful in its fury.

The Banshee.

"Bloody hell, what is that?" Cassius asked.

"An omen. The Banshee. Death of someone you care about. The shifting of the whole of your life as you know it," I said quietly. I turned to him again. "Can we stop now?"

He turned his gaze to me.

"I sent Nero away."

I blinked.

"It is but a temporary fix to a troubling problem," he continued. "But you and I need time. Theodora needs time with us. There is much happening. Much change." His sky-blue gaze moved to the card before coming again to me. "If she comes to know me, my men, trust will form. They're good men, Elena. Fathers all to my own daughter. They show Aelia great affection and love. They will do the same for your Theodora."

"This is a tidy plan, Cassius. But first, that trust will evaporate if it becomes known to her who Nero is, and it wasn't shared with her before she came to care about your men, and possibly him. But I have thought on this and I would not like her to know at all. However, my fear is, Serena will take that option away from me."

"I'll handle Serena."

I stared into his eyes before asking, "And how will you do that?"

"Leave it to me," he stated.

I did not want him there at all, definitely not that close, most definitely not reading his cards (which were telling *and* embarrassing) and *most* definitely not conversing.

However, when he made a move to shift away, I caught onto the leather of his shirt, gripping it in a fist.

"How will you do that?" I demanded.

"Your sister is being handled."

Presently?

My eyes narrowed.

"How?"

"It might be best you not know."

"I'll be the judge of that," I told him.

He looked amused (and I wished he didn't for he wore it well). "You cannot be the judge if you know and then wished you didn't."

"Do you intend to harm her?" I asked.

His face softened (and I wished it wouldn't do that either because he wore that better). "Bodily? No. Her pride? I'm certain."

Oh my goddess.

"You intend to humiliate her?" I whispered.

"Yes, though she will be the only one who will know. She and Mars and the man who is pleasuring her in a way she'll become addicted to him. And, of course, now you."

I blinked.

"You have my vow there will be no harm, except to her, which, you must agree, Elena, she deserves. No one ever needed to know Nero's role in Tiana's demise. Anyone who knew such as that would have died with that knowledge. Serena did not. She used it for no reason other than spite and to cause discord. To that end, for Theodora's protection, and yours, she will do as he says while he has her and you and Theodora will be safe from him."

"Controlled by *a man*?" I queried.

"If she liked sex with a woman, we would have sent one in. As reported by the servants who attended her in camp, she didn't mind women present when she engaged in her version of hedonism, but she didn't take any. So, for that purpose only, necessarily, it is a man."

"You intend to...make a sexual slave of my sister?"

"Yes."

"*My* sister? The one who shared her brand of sociability with us the other night. Princess Serena of the Nadirii."

His lips quirked before he repeated, "Yes."

"You do know this is impossible," I shared.

"I don't know this, as he's had her once, the night before last, and since, she's approached him five times, and sent two notes demanding he attend her."

"By the goddess," I whispered, my vision going vague in shock.

"Yes," he agreed, his voice richer with amusement in a way it made me focus on him to see he was smiling.

"*Seven* requests in but a day?" I queried.

"There is a good possibility he will wake this morn, if he hasn't already, to her pounding on his door."

I stared into the most beautiful eyes I'd ever seen, not just the color, which was transcendent, but the shape as well as the thickness and length of his dark lashes.

And then I clutched his shirt tighter as my head fell back and I burst with laughter.

Still doing it, I righted my head, let go of his shirt and grabbed his muscled neck momentarily for balance in order that I didn't topple over with hilarity. Once I managed that, I released it to press my hand into his chest over his heart, all the while talking.

Or stammering.

But actually, babbling.

"I shouldn't...it's unkind...she's my sister...my loyalty should lie with…but I can't help myself." I drew in a big breath and let it out, still laughing. "She can be very irksome. And I was most angry with her when she engaged in these very *loud* hedonistic activities at the camp when Dora could hear. And Dora was upset by them. And then, before the parade…"

I trailed off.

Focused again on his eyes.

And gulped.

I was taught to fear nothing but my own missteps, which, if I used my mind prior to making them, I could circumvent or at the very least learn never to make them again.

But I feared what I saw right then.

Even as I was drawn to it.

Inescapably.

His eyes were no longer sky-blue.

They were midnight.

And at their epicenter, instead of a black pupil, they *glittered* like *stars*.

And when he spoke, his voice was…

Animal.

"She engaged…in these activities…close to Theodora?"

"Y-yes," I whispered.

"And Theodora heard."

I felt his heart thumping a strong tattoo under my hand and I pressed there, what I hoped was soothingly.

"I had words with her," I promised. "With both of them. And Dora is fine now. She has me, but she also has much support. My mother is overtly fond of her. Melisse dotes on her. Hera and Jasmine are like adoring aunties."

When his eyes did not change, I leaned closer and kept speaking.

"Cassius, she's a strong girl. She's smart. So very bright. And she knows she's loved. She's all right."

"She knows she's loved."

"Very much so."

"Not of your blood."

At his words, I ceased speaking.

Cassius's midnight-starred eyes dropped to my mouth.

I would reflect on it, at length, after it was over.

But even when I did, I knew I would never be able to ascertain if it was he who took my mouth.

Or me who took his.

For it seemed in one moment, our mouths were several inches from the other's, with me cross-legged and him crouching at my side.

And the next, our mouths were locked, his tongue was inside mine, demanding, so demanding as to be *commanding*, and I was pushing up toward him, my hand at his heart sliding up to the back of his neck, my other hand cupping the back of his head to hold him to me.

The next I was on my back with his weight heavy on me, his hands spreading heat all over my body.

With a need that was undeniable, a need to discover *his* heat, I tore his leather shirt free of his trousers and shoved my hands inside, feeling the fiery, taut silk of his back, digging my nails in.

He growled down my throat.

Taking it, I moaned down his.

His hand closed on my breast over my tunic, his thumb dragging hard against my stiffened nipple, forcing me to tear my mouth free and gasp at the pleasure, my neck arching.

I then felt the enchanting prickle of his beard, his firm lips at my throat, along my neck, as he dragged his thumb back.

I dipped my chin and said like a plea, "*Cassius.*"

He heeded my plea, lifting his head and taking my mouth again.

I dragged my nails up his back.

His hand left my breast and ducked under my tunic.

I felt his fingers flutter over the heat of me and my entire length trembled beneath him.

He broke the kiss and groaned, "Soaked," against my lips before he took my mouth again, his tongue demanding, mine acquiescing.

His fingers dipped into the gusset of my body stocking, dragged over my clit, and that felt so exquisite, I moaned against his tongue, bucking up.

He rubbed.

I rocked against his finger.

My stomach tightened.

My womb pulsed.

My nails tunneled into his back.

And eventually I broke our lips, my body bowing up into his.

"Elena," he murmured.

My lips parted, my eyes closed, my arms wrapped around him to hold on as I melted into an explosion of stars and drifted in the midnight I'd seen in his eyes.

When I recovered from this splendor, I no longer bore his weight.

He'd fallen off to my side and his hand was not between my legs. Instead, it was an arm around me, it had turned me to him, and he was holding me close to his length.

His other arm was pillowing my head, but cocked, so it could also hold my face to his throat.

I blinked at its corded column.

By the mercy of the goddess, what had I just done?

I tensed and whispered a ragged, "I must go."

He tensed, tossed a heavy leg over both of mine and returned gruffly, "You must stay."

"That should not have happened," I told his throat.

"Perhaps not in the garden where those in the palace can see us, but I hid you so there was naught to see but a couple embracing. Other than that, it should have happened because it was eventually going to happen. Definitely."

The goddess showed no mercy because I hadn't thought of that.

People seeing.

Bloody *hell*.

I noticed belatedly my arms were around him as well. I pulled them between us and flattened my hands against his chest.

"I must go."

"Elena."

"I must see to Theodora."

His tone changed to coaxing. "Do you not think, my warrior, that this is good?"

"No."

"I enjoyed that greatly," he declared.

I went still and stared at his throat.

"And you could talk a millennium and not convince me you didn't enjoy it...even more than me."

By the goddess, this was *mortifying*.

"I would like to go."

"There are other things I will do to you that you'll enjoy even more."

That gave me pause for that was an impossibility.

"Yes, Elena," he murmured into my hair, and on a squeeze of his arms, finished, "*Much* more."

"That was embarrassing," I blurted.

"I cannot imagine why. You were glorious."

I was?

I did not ask him to reiterate that or explain it.

But before I could say anything, he spoke again, fortunately changing the subject, unfortunately changing it to something pricklier.

"Shall we go see to Theodora together?"

"No."

"She must meet me, Elena, and I'll be in meetings for the rest of the day."

"She's not at her best when she wakes up," I shared.

His arm at the back of my head relaxed but that was all he released of his hold on me.

At least I could tip my head back to look at him, a head which was still pillowed by his bulging upper arm.

It was not cushiony.

But it still was comfortable.

Bloody hell.

When I looked up, I saw he was looking down.

His eyes were again sky-blue.

I could not say if I preferred them that way or as midnight.

That said, the midnight was alarming, but not when one knew it came forth when he was feeling deep.

And he was feeling deep that Dora had been upset.

A girl he had not yet met.

"She would sleep the day away if she could," I informed him.

"Children do this," he shared. "A physician in my realm says it's because they grow so rapidly. Their bodies are working hard. Therefore, they need sleep."

"That makes sense," I muttered.

"I still do not allow Aelia to sleep the day away."

"As you shouldn't."

His eyes moved over my face and his voice grew quiet when he asked, "Have we reached an accord, you and I?"

One could say we had.

Though we hadn't.

"Partially," I allowed.

"I would very much like to meet your daughter, Elena," he whispered.

Oh goddess.

There was nothing for it and not just the part where there really wasn't.

The part where he clearly wished to meet her in order to know her.

"When you're not engaged with meetings," I decided. "And we're not engaged with attending royal weddings. When you have time for her and I have time to see to her and assess how she feels about it after you do."

"The day after the wedding. Mars will be occupied. No meetings will happen."

I considered this.

He gave me a shake.

"Elena? Do we have another bargain?"

I couldn't escape it.

Nor could I protect Dora from it.

Though, with the way he reacted simply to her as a child hearing my sister doing adult things, I was beginning to wonder if I needed to.

"We have a bargain," I agreed.

"Good," he murmured, bent, brushed his lips along one of my eyebrows (which felt warming).

After that, he moved us both, adjusting me to my bottom on my rug before he took his feet.

He stared down at me. "I hope we can dine together, but matters are weighty, so that might not be possible."

Matters were weighty?

How could matters be weighty?

The Beast was rising.

That was weighty, the weightiest, but everyone knew about that.

We were all coming together to quell the Beast.

Alliances were forming because of it.

History was being made.

How was that weighty in a way that he'd miss dinner?

Again.

Not that I pined for him last night. Though his absence was noted, as were all the princes and kings.

Oh, who was I fooling?

I'd just climaxed for him on a rug in a palace garden. My first climax that wasn't given to me by, well...*me*.

It wasn't pining, but it was...something.

He broke into my thoughts and when he did, I felt my cheeks heating.

"At the very least, I'll see you as I escort you to the wedding. Though I should hope to see you before."

I nodded up to him.

"Enjoy your day, my princess."

"Thanks," I muttered.

His eyes grinned even if his mouth didn't (he'd noted my cheeks had warmed) and he turned to walk away.

He'd taken three steps when I called, "Cassius."

He turned back to me, his brows raised.

"Don't be too hard on Serena."

He tipped his head to the side, considered me a moment, then replied, "We shall see."

And with that, my prince walked away.

28

THE COURTSHIP

Queen Ha-Lah Nereus

Guest Suite, Second Floor, East Corridor, Catrame Palace, Fire City

Firenze

I sat cross-legged on the bed as my husband moved around the room.

I was annoyed.

But I did not share this with him in any way for he was talking and what he was saying should not make me annoyed, but instead concerned, relieved, and in part, joyous.

The problem was, my husband had started courting me.

And that was all well and good.

In fact, it was extraordinary.

Not to mention the way he was going about it was very sweet.

But now we were getting along.

Communicating.

A great deal.

He knew all about the fishing village from where I came.

How my mother caught a chill when I was thirteen and had died alarmingly quickly.

How my father was a seaman which meant he was away most of the time thus I was raised by my auntie, his sister, a woman I loved and considered my second mother.

How my father never really recovered from the loss of his beloved wife, who I looked much like, and thus he didn't often spend time with me even if he was ashore.

I'd also told him how my grandfather was a smuggler, his territory: The Mystics, and sometimes the Northlands. He'd died to these activities, somewhere in The Mystics. One of his sailors finding his way home years later to tell the tale.

And I'd told him how my grandmother was like my mother, a great beauty. So much so, my grandfather had hidden her away and taken her on his ship before he wed her, so she would not come to the attention of the king.

Aramus knew my auntie made very good fishing nets.

He further knew I preferred coffee to tea in the morning. Ale to wine, if I wasn't eating, for then I preferred wine.

And that I still had two crates of smuggled rum my grandfather had left behind. And, outside my clothes and some other personal belongings, because my grandmother had guarded these because they were of her beloved husband, and my mother had guarded them because they were of her beloved father, these were the only things I brought to his castle for now I guarded them too.

We had also discussed at length what was happening between Cassius and Elena. Mars and Silence. And what didn't seem to be happening between True and Farah (even though it did, just in a friendly fashion—not exactly a love match were those two).

I had shared with him in some detail the piercing ceremony.

Indeed, my husband could (and did) lie for hours beside me, asking me questions and listening to me speak.

What he did *not* do was touch me, hold me, embrace me or sirens-damned *kiss me*.

Who ever heard of a courtship that didn't include kisses?

Even holding hands.

Not me.

And I was finding I wasn't fond of it.

But last night, he'd come to our rooms with tales that Cassius had instigated an unexpected, unintended bloodless coup at the diplomatic table of the King of Firenze, so they'd spent the entire afternoon and well into the evening negotiating this.

They'd even called in two Go'Doan, both of whom I'd met at the betrothal dinner (along with the one called G'Seph).

G'Jell and G'Liam were seasoned in the art of diplomacy, with Aramus sharing that the younger, Liam, was an adept negotiator. Though, he said it was True who seemed to be most capable of containing Gallienus's kingly indignation.

But like all Go'Doan, Aramus did not trust Liam.

This was because he'd been getting appeals from the Go'Doan with irritating frequency to allow them into Mar-el in order for them to build temples (to the Go'Doan gods, of course), schools to teach our children and hospitals where they would practice, as well as instruct in their ways of advanced healing to our people.

But all knew they also worked to spread the faith in their gods and the Mar-el had staunch devotion to our gods and goddesses of the seas and the storms and they would not like this.

So Aramus had refused.

Now, he would spend the day, from but ten minutes from then until probably when I was abed again, dealing with a defiant, but beaten, King Gallienus, his new regent—a prince who had no wish to be that, or indeed be a king—and the future of Airen and how to prevent it from descending into civil war.

In the meantime, before we left Firenze, my husband would sign a proclamation (or six of them, one for each realm, as well as one to be chronicled in Go'Doan, to hold in order to hold him to his promise, not that he wouldn't keep it) to decrease the number of years served for those in service from fifteen to five.

This was the part that made me joyous, for obvious reasons.

Of course, everyone knew not to sail Mar-el waters without Mar-el permission. They also knew, if you did, what might befall you.

However.

I was joyous (and this was also why I felt relief) because my husband made this concession at the diplomatic table and it was a grand one. A noble one. It was not only honorable, it showed forward thinking and the ability to compromise.

As well as, not least importantly, humanity.

And obviously, if he were to listen and act on the things that were important to me, he'd need all of this.

I was also concerned for I did not know how our people would respond to the change he intended to make.

Obviously, the bounden, and those who were not wealthy enough to keep them or were not pirates, and thus they looked down on this practice (quite vigorously), would condone it heartily.

However, the wealthy landowners and pirates, likely not.

That said, when his great-great grandfather had made even more sweeping changes, although there was a period of unrest, it was quickly quashed for the number of those who opposed bondage and how those in it were treated was high, and eventually the landowners saw the wisdom of not rousing them.

But also, many of the bounden continued to be in service to them, rather than sailing ships to home (albeit paid service, and there was a stricture from the king on what they could get paid, so it was fair and equitable for their toil).

Others had simply chosen to stay, enlist in service on ships, open businesses, taverns and restaurants, wed amongst themselves or the Mar-el, for Mar-el was a land of great beauty, the seas held great bounty, and for the most part we were a jovial, fun-loving, friendly people.

"We won't file and herald the proclamation until we're home," Aramus was saying, dressing and wolfing down the breakfast that a servant boy had brought up. "Though I'm sending men. They'll go to the ships. Take one. Sail home. Put pieces in place to control those landowners who might cause problems."

"The King's Will be done," I intoned what every child learned, and what every adult practiced.

And the King's Will was done, as proclaimed by Triton, our god of the sea, and Medusa, our goddess of the same, for legend told both of them had coronated our very first king and thus the king reigned at the will of the gods.

And no one did anything to anger Triton and Medusa.

"Yes, my queen. Do you think there will be issues with this?" he asked, and my head jerked at the question.

"Pardon?" I asked in return.

He stopped lifting a triangle of toast spread with marmalade to his mouth and looked at me.

"I am sea captain and king. I'm on my ship more than in my castle. And when I'm ashore, I'm in my castle with my advisors more than being with my people. You're from a small village. It is my understanding from reports of your activities when I'm away, you often roam the city, attend ill in the hospitals, visit children in schools. In other words, you are often among the people. You've spoken of their thoughts and concerns before. What do you think will come of this?"

He was asking...

Me?

"Um...well..."

I trailed off.

He shoved the toast in his mouth and started slathering marmalade on another triangle, talking with his mouth full.

"I am hoping they find these concessions appropriate. Not simply because all know we are the last to practice servitude. But also, because it's well known around Mar-el that our people think of the practices of the Airenzian toward women range from feeling it's absurd to abhorrent. That said, I'm uncertain if my people care enough that the Airenzian women are freed of their burdens, for they last a lifetime and are much more monstrous than those in our lands in bondage. But as you mentioned, it's of concern, our continued distance from those on the mainland."

As I'd mentioned?

He'd listened to me?

"But I'd already negotiated opened trade of merchants with Firenze and allowed the Firenz passage of their merchant ships not only to us, but to the Northlands, Southlands and The Mystics," he announced.

My mouth dropped open.

He had?

He had not mentioned that last night.

He continued speaking.

"In a small quantity. I arranged the same to mitigate some of

Gallienus's anger, and perhaps cushion the blow to his aristocracy. And it will be known Cassius negotiated it, so his regency will be better taken. The Dellish king seems uninterested. But I've spoken to True in private and if his king can pull his finger out, I'll do the same for Wodell. More goods going both ways, more coin spent both ways. Enough to take minds from things that might cause unrest."

"Are you going to…" I cleared my throat. "Going to disallow the pirates from taking more bounden?" I asked.

"I won't tell seamen what to do," he grunted.

Of course not.

He was a seaman.

"Is this going to go well for Cassius?" I queried.

He shoved half of his second triangle of toast into his mouth, bit off a chunk, dropped the remains to the tray and looked to me, chewing.

He swallowed.

Then he said, "No."

"This means we'll be at war with another land for another land's problems, my king," I said softly.

"I promised my armada," he replied.

"I know."

"You don't think it's a good idea," he remarked, regarding me closely.

"The Beast rises," I reminded him.

"My guess is, we have time, considering the tremors have ceased."

I did not guess the same.

Who knew what those who called to it were up to?

"This will be quite a bit for our people to understand and become accustomed to," I told him. "But your great-great grandfather also made what was then sweeping change. It is not unprecedented. It was also not so long ago. And we may not have much to do with the mainland, but we get news from it. Therefore, we know Ares, as well as Mars, have done much the same in their land. There was conflict, and violence in all that. But both nations became stronger for it."

He dipped his chin.

"And they will be glad of opened trade." I smiled at him. "Even in small quantities."

"Good," he grunted, shoving his shirt with its full, billowy sleeves more firmly under the sash around his waist before he reached to his double-breasted waistcoat, flung it behind his shoulders and shrugged it on.

He'd buttoned the four buttons from the bottom (buttons that went all the way to the base of his throat, but he rarely wore it closed all that way) before he grabbed his wide, studded belt, pulling it over the sash around his waist while he returned his attention to me.

"You bond with these women," he remarked, buckling his belt.

I nodded. "Oh yes. Silence is very sweet. Farah is quieter and more restrained around Elena, for she knows True's feelings for the Nadirii. But Elena is putting her mind at rest about that. And Elena is very good-humored, when you aren't discussing Cassius that is."

"Cassius will win her," Aramus stated confidently.

Maybe.

However, I tired of discussing everyone else.

Every*thing* else.

But us.

"I'm sure," I murmured and carried on, "Elpis is lovely, as is Ophelia, in a more detached way. Elena's lieutenants are chalk and cheese, Hera very intelligent and serious, Jasmine very funny. Sofia makes me melancholy. She feels much guilt for acts she did not do, and she misses her friend greatly even when, often, they are in the same room. I cannot imagine any of them wishing me harm."

"You'll still have a guard in the palace."

I nodded again while containing a sigh.

"You spoke not of Mercy and Vanka," he mentioned.

I looked into his eyes. "Vanka is quiet so I don't know what to think of her as I get the sense she doesn't know what to think of just about everything. I'm also uncertain what I feel for Mercy. She is watchful and seems...cold. Specifically to the Firenz. Most specifically to Farah."

He bobbed his head once, decidedly.

"Your guard will remain. The Dellish king is weak and most of this is around the fact he is not very clever. So much not, for him to remain on his throne without a revolt, someone is pulling his strings. And I'm not certain his counsellor is his sole puppet master. I just have the sense that he does not listen to his son, which is the only Dellish I've met thus far he should lend his ear to."

"You seem to have grown an affinity to that particular Dellish."

"True is genuine. He's intelligent. He's frustrated with his father, which is unsurprising. He seems to have the good of all at heart. And he's tactful. What I read from him, if any of this is false, I'd give up my fastest ship."

"So True is true to his name."

He grinned at me. "It would seem."

I allowed his grin to wash through me.

My husband was handsome.

He looked fine in his clothes of Mar-el, the garments of a pirate.

He was also all the way across the room.

"I must go, Ha-Lah."

"Of course," I murmured.

He started to the door, hesitated, and stopped, turning back to me.

My heart skipped a beat.

"And what do you do today?" he asked.

At that, my heart dropped.

I, of course, liked it that he cared to ask. He had not cared before (though maybe he had, considering his remark about getting reports on my activities when he was away, he'd just never asked me).

So this was progress.

Good progress.

Just not the kind I was yearning for.

But my mouth answered.

"Silence has changed her mind about her wedding gown. She brought one. But she won't wear it. They started sewing her new one yesterday. They finish the fittings today. I attend her." I finished with a mumble, "We'll probably go swimming in the afternoon. She's going to borrow a body stocking from Jasmine. She's excited to swim. She couldn't yesterday."

"This does not please you?" he asked.

"It'll be fine," I answered.

"I could ask Mars to open his library to you," he suggested.

"I'd prefer Silence's company. Farah often joins her. We will get to know each other better."

"As I'm sending men to the ships, if you'd like to write letters to your aunt, your father, they will carry them to your family," he offered.

That was lovely.

Though, writing a letter to my auntie and papa would likely take only half an hour, not fill up a day with delight

And he was still across the room.

"I shall do that," I told him.

He continued to regard me for a moment (from across the room) before he again spoke.

"If you'll be all right..." This statement seemed to end unfinished.

I sat on the bed.

He stood across the room from me.

Come to me and kiss me, I thought.

Kiss me.

Kissmekissmekissme.

"I hope to see you at dinner, or if we break for luncheon," he stated.

He wasn't going to kiss me.

"I hope that too, Aramus," I replied.

"Until later, my queen."

"But of course, my king."

He left the room.

I stared at the door he closed.

I wondered which guard I'd have that day, not really much caring.

My wedding to my king had been a spectacle. A lavish gown. A lavish ceremony. A lavish parade. A lavish feast.

During all this, we probably said twenty words to each other and sadly, fifteen of them for me were, "I take this man as my husband and my king and his Will be done."

We'd then had a colossal argument directly in front of our marital bed, which I slept in alone after he slammed out of the room to drink rum, get loud, and eventually sleep elsewhere.

We had, as prescribed, met only the day before. In the sanctuary of Leuthea, the sacred sea goddess of distressed sailors.

There we knelt at the altar, giving our thoughts to her and not saying a word to each other.

For two hours.

But I'd felt his eyes on me.

And I had found my times to study him.

It was the way of things, for the King of Mar-el to wed his queen in this manner.

And now, months later, I was getting the courtship I should have had back then.

But although often endearing...

It was seeming my husband was no bloody good at it.

I sighed, got off the bed, and moved to the bathing room.

It would hearten me to be in the water.

I would not transform, as it wasn't seawater, but it would feel nice and restore me.

And then I would face my day without my husband, and my night with him but still without him.

On this thought I decided I would give him some time.

He was a man, a very manly man, and perhaps would not take well to such overtures from his wife.

Very manly men preferred to make such overtures themselves.

But tomorrow, Silence would wed Mars, and from their demeanor when they were in each other's presence, they would be down the hall doing what my husband of over seven months and I had not yet done.

We'd wasted enough time not communicating properly.

And there were a variety of ways to communicate.

That piercing ceremony taught me well.

Aramus would have my ear, my mind and my honesty.

He was also going to have my body.

Even if I had to throw it at him.

29

THE KINDNESS

G'Drey
Streets of Fire City
FIRENZE

G'Drey walked (with difficulty) through the city toward the school where he taught.

As his pretense (for his real purpose in this realm was not thus), in a Go'Doan school he had charge of fifty-six Firenz children aged eight, nine and ten.

He taught them Triton history, some maths, reading, the language of the Vale, and how to draw and paint.

And he had found, to his surprise, he enjoyed doing this.

It had not started easily. He was an untried teacher and they had been annoyingly rambunctious and not mindful.

However, some days in, irritated beyond measure, he had been stern.

And somehow, from there, order had ensued (though, with the older ones, he'd had to be stern on other occasions, but for the most part, after their talkings-to, they'd minded).

And when one was proud of his or her painting or assumed a bright look on their face after they conquered the difficult conjugation of a Valerian word, Drey felt something curious in his chest which was not unpleasant.

He had never much thought of children, and to the truth—his thoughts on his warrior, when he would call upon Drey, his chosen one back home, The Rising and the role he played in that—he didn't very much think of them now.

Unless he was with his students.

When he was, he thought, their innocence, excitement over foolish things or their implicit trust in him (which was foolish as well, though they did not know that) was rather, he had to admit, engaging.

This had made Drey seek an audience with G'Liam, who had come from Go'Doan with Jell to attend the ceremonies and be on hand for any diplomatic discussions that might need their skills.

Liam also oversaw the schools across the realms, doing this mostly by post and bird, but sometimes with visits.

Drey had informed Liam that his class was first, too large, and second, the spread of ages too long.

He'd then suggested the ten-year-olds be moved to their own class for they were advanced in studies and easily became bored as Drey looked after and instructed the younger children.

And Drey had learned quickly a bored child was not a child you wished to be around.

After he'd shared this, Liam had examined him at some length.

This he did before saying, "I am heartened you take such interest in your pupils. And in such a short time spent with them. It says much about you. And you speak sense. I will think on this."

Drey had felt an odd sense of pride at this for Liam was known as a lofty personage and he was respected by most, even those priests of The Rising.

But G'Drey had only ever seen Liam in passing in Go'Doan, though he obviously knew of him, as most did.

This was because Liam was very young for his level of responsibility.

He also had an unusual pastime of examining bodies, those being cadavers, in an effort to understand how they worked. How wounds or illnesses affected them and how to identify ailments that struck those with causes unseen, using what he found in the bodies, matching them to symptoms reported before death.

He also had a pastime of concocting potions and elixirs from herbs and minerals and testing them on injuries, lesions and in treatments of diseases.

Further, like Jell, Liam spent most of his time worshiping Go'Vicee, the god of service. Not the gods of obedience and faithfulness, Go'Bedi and Go'Chas, as most other priests did.

However, Drey had heard that Liam had given a rousing lecture to the order of the high priests that had caused much discussion throughout Go'Doan about how Go'Chas was truly about chastity, and not faithfulness to the gods.

He argued that Go'Chas wished fidelity amongst mates and abstinence of those unmarried, and not stalwart faith in religion, as most felt was the case.

And thus (Drey had heard), Liam had asserted they must abandon their baser uses of the Go'Ella and only take wives or bind themselves to husbands.

By the by, although no one asked him, Drey thought he was wrong in that.

And he was not alone, for the furor his words caused had lasted some time.

Though, Drey had heard before he left the domed city, there was rising support for this theory.

Last, Drey knew Liam, nor Jell, were of The Rising.

They had not been to any of the meetings. And his lover never spoke of them.

Though Drey could not say he hadn't been impressed with Liam after speaking with him.

It was Drey's first day back after his time in the catacombs.

He had been fortunate (though he didn't really think on it that way, but in the most base of purpose, it was true) that Seph had ordered spirits to cleanse his wounds (which did not feel nice, especially having them poured on when he was still strapped to that slab, his entire body feeling frozen in place, he'd been there so long).

G'Seph had also ordered salves to be applied. Salves Drey knew (because he felt it) took away some of the pain and hastened healing.

Seph had also given him a crock of this salve to administer to himself.

But he had taken away Drey's acolytes and ordered that Drey go without them until he was healed.

They were not to see his injuries.

They would not know of The Rising and his punishment.

Now he faced a day back in his classroom, another command from Seph.

For others had been told Drey had caught a chill (how anyone could do that in this hot land, he could not fathom, but Seph was talented in donning his false face). This was why he had been abed and at rest.

But now he had to carry on so others would not ask to see to him or wonder about his state.

He had no idea how he was going to teach with the pain. The salve helped, but it helped better when he was abed and not standing. It would take at least a week before he was fully scabbed over and able to move around without great pain, even with the salve.

He could absolutely not sit.

Therefore, he'd have to stand.

All day.

In pain.

As he had to walk to his school.

In pain.

And thus his reprimand endured long after it had been dealt.

Since receiving his "punishment" he had thought much on his predicament.

In fact, that was all he'd thought on.

At first, he had considered sending bird or letter (the latter of which would take a long time, and he wished his vengeance to be much more swift) to Fenn, his lover, explaining what had befallen him.

His chosen one might be angry he had played with a Firenz warrior (or let that warrior play with him).

But he would be angrier that Drey had been abused.

G'Drey had also thought much on the severity of his punishment for a transgression he did not see as a transgression.

Go'Doan regularly took lovers. Most availed themselves of their acolytes. Others took lovers amongst their fellow priests. And others often and openly found their assignations amongst the lands where they were stationed.

Men.

Women.

Both.

He could not begin to imagine how allowing himself to be used by a warrior, his wife and their playmate could put the plot at risk.

And if it did, Seph could have simply asked him for an aside and told him.

Not delivered a head blow, whipped him bloody, humiliated him, and left him tied to a slab for *hours*.

He was a soldier of The Rising.

He was at one with the Go'Doan utilizing their carefully gathered recruits, specifically in Wodell, but also Firenze, and their equally carefully gathered weapons to rise up and take control of those lands in order to conquer Airen, enslave the Nadirii, and force all to worship the true gods.

Not to mention, pay homage, in word and coin, to the temples in the city-state of Go'Doan.

But he was not at one with *this*.

On this angry thought, he was torn from his path, pulled down an alley, and his head was covered with a hood.

In the sudden darkness, he opened his mouth to cry out, but before he could, he heard, "You make but a noise, you'll regret it."

His warrior.

He shut his mouth and felt what seemed like a large, heavy blanket enshroud him. He was then lifted over a shoulder, walked a short distance, and thrown belly down on a horse.

He could not stop himself from crying out at that, for the pain in his backside was such he could not quell it.

Not to mention the pain in his gut, where the saddle horn dug in.

"*Debole*," the warrior grunted in disgust, and Drey felt him swing up on the horse.

He was not weak.

And he tired of being used.

And abused.

He worshipped Fenn more than any of his gods.

But he was wondering if that devotion was worth any of *this*.

They rode, too hard and too fast. Along their short journey the pain becoming excruciating, Drey knew they were going to the warrior's house.

He also knew the warrior took him to the back for he smelled the honeysuckle that grew splendiferously at the side, before he reined in, dismounted, dragged Drey unceremoniously from his steed and carried him inside.

The Firenz walked and Drey knew he was taking him to the man's bedchamber (for he had walked this himself numerous times) before he was tossed like a sack of nothing to the tiled floor.

G'Drey bit back his cry of pain at that, but it was of such strength, it might not have come out as a cry, but it came as a strong whimper.

The hood was torn off and Drey shook his hair out of his face as he tossed the blanket from his person and stared mutinously up at the man.

"I sent a missive," the man said. "Yesterday. And when you are called, you come."

His wife was standing at his side, but Drey didn't look at her.

"I got no missive," he retorted.

"Do not lie," the warrior warned.

Drey leaned forward and spat, "I got...*no*...missive."

And it was likely he did not because it had been confiscated by Seph.

He did not share that with the warrior.

His (current) tormentor opened his mouth to speak, but the wife spoke first.

"*Sanguina*," she whispered.

He bleeds, she said.

The warrior looked, and before Drey could blink, he was on his stomach on the bed and his robes were thrown up over his arse.

He heard her shocked gasp.

And the warrior's surprised grunt.

But it was her who spoke.

"Who did this to you?" she asked in his language.

G'Drey started to struggle to get up. "It is not your concern."

He could not get up for the warrior held him down with a hand in the middle of his back.

G'Drey felt the bed depress at his side and another touch, a lighter one, which pulled his hair from his face.

G'Drey stilled.

Except for his chosen one, and even his chosen one could not stroke as lightly, he'd never been touched in that manner in his life.

The wife was on the bed with him.

"Who did this to you, *mio piccolo buco*?" she whispered.

G'Drey stared at the silks.

She had called him *my little hole*.

And the manner she referred to him thus made something in his stomach loosen.

Therefore, his tone was much changed when he lifted his eyes to her and replied, "I cannot say."

She turned her head to the side and tipped it back.

"Where did you find him?" she asked her husband.

"On his way to his school," her husband answered.

"Riding?" she inquired, sounding horrified.

"Walking," the warrior told her.

"That is not much better," she snapped.

And in the manner she did, something loosened further in his stomach.

"Release him," she demanded.

"*Amore*," the warrior murmured.

"Release him. You might be causing him pain," she ordered.

The hand went out of his back.

Drey rolled to his side, gritting his teeth as his injury again made itself known.

"Do not move, priest," she said in a gentle tone. "Why are you not abed?"

"I cannot speak of these things," he told her.

"You should be resting," she replied.

He shook his head.

"You must know you should be resting," she pressed.

"I am not...allowed," he admitted.

Her brown eyes studied him before her mouth grew tight and she looked up to her warrior.

"We will keep him here," she decided, and Drey's eyes grew wide as his mouth opened to protest. However, she was not finished, "I will tend him, and you will send a missive to his temple that they are warned of an investigation into this matter."

Drey spoke at that, doing it to exclaim, "*No!*"

She turned to him and raised her elegant, arched brows. "Why no, *piccolo buco?*"

"You cannot," he said.

"Why can we not?" she pushed.

"You simply cannot," he returned.

She seemed to consider this.

Then her gaze moved down his body before coming back to his face.

And her tone was again gentle when she queried, "You enjoy your times with us, no?"

"Yes," he gritted.

"And we know this, or we would not use you as we do," she shared.

He clenched his teeth.

"You give us much pleasure," she whispered.

At that, his jaw went slack.

"This has meaning to us. You must know this," she said. "A Firenz does not take to his or her bed someone who has no meaning. If you had no meaning, my husband would take your arse against a wall in the back room of an *osteria* or in an alley while I watched. We would not see to your pleasure. And he would walk away with his seed dripping from you without giving you another thought."

Drey had...

Meaning to them?

"The mated ones of Firenz take others to their beds but only at the request of their mate, to the desires of them both, and with the presence of their mate," she explained. "They do not, however, give their mouths to another but their own. Thus he, nor I, will ever suckle you or kiss you."

"I did not know this," he muttered.

He did, in a fashion.

Though he didn't understand the whys of it.

She gave him a small smile and it was...

Appealing.

"Now you do," she said quietly. "So now, I would hope, at the very least, if you cannot tell us what befell you, and that is yours to give, we will not press, you allow us to tend to you."

He shook his head. "I am instructed to attend my pupils at school."

"And not attend us," the warrior entered the conversation, and Drey looked up to him.

His face was as fierce as ever, but there was disquiet in his eyes and anger about his mouth.

Anger.

About what befell Drey.

And the warrior knew where his missive had gone astray.

Even in his surprise, Drey nodded up to him.

"It is not known the Go'Doan do such to their own," the warrior stated.

"It is not...it is for the worst..." He had to lie to them, and for some inexplicable reason, he was having difficulty doing this. "It is for the worst of transgressions."

"I have had other Go'Doan arse," the warrior declared. "My wife likes the white robes, the paleness of your skin and the contrast against my shaft penetrating it."

How, he did not know, but he was growing hard.

"Though we have never used any, Go'Doan or no, as we have used you and how we use you is something we've both desired for some time," he continued.

Why did that make him feel...

Special?

"But none of them have been mistreated as such," the warrior carried on, jerking his bearded chin toward Drey.

G'Drey fought biting his lip.

"Further, they cannot know how we use you, so it cannot be that," the warrior said. "Unless you told them."

"I did not tell them," he said quietly.

The warrior jerked up his head. "So this transgression, tell me one thing, whatever it is, is it one you are guilty of?"

Drey would absolutely not admit to that.

"No," he declared forcibly.

The warrior's face turned to stone.

At seeing that, Drey could not stop biting his lip.

It was then the warrior's voice went gentle, though it appeared he accomplished this with some difficulty, and Drey definitely felt that in his cock, even in his abused arse, but also elsewhere.

"Allow my wife to show you kindness," he urged. "I will handle the Go'Doan. You will be given a leave of absence. No one will know the true reason why or where you are. But you will be safe to be here with us."

He should not.

He knew it.

That lesson had been learned.

But he did it regardless.

And he did not know the why of this either.

"I will allow this."

The instant he said the words, the warrior turned to his wife. "Call for Persephone. She will suckle him. A climax will relax him. Then he can be cleansed and salved and given a sleeping draught."

Drey knew none of their names. They'd never spoken them. Even in the heat of passion.

Though he now knew their playmate was called Persephone.

"Not Persephone," Drey blurted.

The warrior looked to him but a moment before he returned his attention to his wife.

"Saturn," he grunted and then he looked again to Drey. "He is a soldier. Young. Strapping. We use him when my wife wishes to watch others at play or me at work up a warrior's arse. He likes hole and cunt and taking cock. He will gladly suckle you, *amico*. And once you heal, when you need a shaft up your arse with a milking hand to your cock, he will give that to you too."

"My name is G'Drey," he whispered.

"It is not," the warrior returned. "What is your true name?"

Drey was still whispering when he said a name he hadn't said, or heard, or thought, in years, "Tedrey. I am Tedrey Swensson of the Dellish."

The warrior nodded. "And I am Lorenz Chronis, and this is my beloved, Nyx, as you know, of the Firenz. And you are now not only of our bed, but of our house, which means under my protection. And that means no one will harm you again."

And with that, the warrior stormed out.

Drey watched him do this, witnessing the stiffness of his gait, which meant his control of his fury.

He was furious.

For Drey.

"You'll find he's overprotective, *caro*," the wife, Nyx, shared. "Though this sometimes causes problems, most of the time, it's quite charming."

He looked to her.

"I have concerns," he admitted, his voice beginning to tremble.

She lifted a hand and laid it light on the side of his face, her eyes warming.

"Think naught of them, *mio piccolo buco*. Lorenz is crafty, and he is thorough. You are safe. You will be looked after." She smiled a lovely smile. "And you are now truly ours, so we will both take care of you."

She dropped her hand, and oddly, Drey missed it when she did.

She then scooted off the bed and looked down at him sternly.

"Rest here for now. Do not shift your robes over you, for they will aggravate the gashes. I shall call for Saturn. Ask him to attend you. Request he bring Faunus. While they make their way to us, I will see to your wounds. I have a special salve that is numbing. It should offer you some relief."

She suddenly grinned a grin he was used to, but he had never liked.

Until now.

"Saturn will be much aroused, suckling you, and thus will need his own cock, likely at the back. I'll get leave from Lorenz. He would not normally grant it for me, but in your state, I feel he'll be generous. Thus, after Saturn is done swallowing your seed, we will together watch them at play while the sleeping draught works within you. That will be sure to give you good dreams."

They would watch them *together*?

Like...

Friends?

She leaned his way with a wicked look in her eyes which he also found quite appealing.

"Faunus is most rough, *caro*, and Saturn is nearly as big as my husband. Quite the sight to behold as he very much enjoys a strong, thorough fucking. And when he gushes, his seed," she rolled her eyes in ecstasy, rolling them back only for him to see they were dancing, "so much, you will think he won't ever stop climaxing. Or this is what you will hope. If you wish, if it won't cause you pain, we will make him do it in your mouth."

"I wish," Drey whispered fervently.

Oh, did he wish.

He didn't care if it caused pain.

She gave him an indulgent smile.

"And so he shall. Thus they will be sweet dreams indeed, my Tedrey."

With that, she swept out.

And G'Drey lay atop their soft bed, on their smooth silks, no pain at his arse for he was not moving, and he stared at the door she'd walked through realizing he'd just been claimed by a Firenz husband and his wife.

He was theirs.

To use.

To amuse.

To protect.

And to care for.

He had never had thus in his life.

Not even, really, from his chosen one for Drey was there and definitely unprotected.

Therefore, for the first time since his father beat the ability out of him when he had caught his son taking farm boy cock in the stables, this before sending him away with orders never to return, Drey began weeping.

IT WOULD BE some time later, on his back, his arse on soft cushions, his head too, his mouth filled with a thick cock, his own shaft was hard again after a previous climax and now taking another ardent sucking.

And his eyes were watching an enormous shaft thrusting roughly between two sculpted cheeks of a brown-skinned arse.

He tried, but found he could hold back no longer.

Thus, Drey reluctantly shut his eyes as he shot his seed into a hot mouth that gulped it down.

His climax finished, his cock released, he then felt the fierce grunts against his balls of the warrior he was sucking as he had been on all fours but was now kneeling with arse offered high and resting his bearded cheek against Drey's thigh.

This before Drey's sac was captured in a wet, warm hold, drawn upon by his warrior's mouth, and he groaned long and splendidly around it as Drey gladly swallowed down some, more, more and even *more* of the salty, hot seed flooding his throat.

He suddenly felt his sac released and a chest pressed at his belly as the warrior over him arched his big body and bellowed, *"Fuck!"* just as the warrior above Drey embedded himself inside and roared his own climax.

Astonishing.

He had never had thus.

And he hoped to have it again.

Though perhaps with him the one on his knees.

G'Drey continued to suck the shaft in his mouth.

As he did, Saturn hummed while alternately licking Drey's softening cock and spent balls and taking a gentle thrusting.

Faunus eventually pulled from him and Saturn withdrew his cock from between Drey's lips and pushed up to his knees above Drey.

Watching that muscled arse taking cock had been better.

Though simply seeing its magnificence hovering above him was not something about which Drey would complain.

"Would you like to lick Faunus from him?" he heard Nyx offer.

Drey felt a stirring at this offer, but sadly, in his state, two climaxes and after taking a sleeping draught, he could not.

"Most drowsy," he muttered.

"Pity," Saturn's deep voice murmured amusedly.

He then swung his mighty leg over Drey's head, shifted in bed, lent over Drey and cupped his shaft and sac in a large, but gentle, hand.

"Rest well and heal quickly, priest. You owe me," Saturn teased, even if the look in his eyes said he meant his words.

G'Drey stared up at his striking features and gave him a sleepy smile. "All right."

After delivering a wolfish smile in return, Saturn's face disappeared, as did, regrettably, his hand, and Faunus's attractive visage took its place.

"You don't owe me shite, I'm still fucking you," he said with a playful grin on his full lips.

Drey mind filled with visions of Faunus's enormous cock.

"All right," he replied.

"Most handsome," Faunus murmured, his gaze moving over Drey's face, and Drey blinked at him. "I could keep you full of me for days. You'll be beautiful shooting before me with me moving deep inside."

And Drey's stomach loosened more.

Even his lover had not spoken to him such admiring, affectionate words.

"I'll be glad to give you that," he murmured hazily as the draught continued to work its magic.

"I will be glad to take it," Faunus murmured in return. "Until then," he said before he touched his mouth to Drey's (*touched his mouth*). The playful had returned when he pulled back and finished, "Or until we feel the need to use Saturn again. I'll give that, perhaps, a day," and with that and a cheerful wink, he moved away.

Only for Nyx to be there.

"Roll, *mio buco*," she ordered quietly. "It is time for you to rest."

As bid, beyond replete, Drey rolled to his front.

She carefully pulled the silks of the bed to his shoulders (a bed in another bedchamber which was quite lovely where she'd led him earlier before seeing to his backside with tender hands).

She then sat next to him and stroked his hair.

"Sleep, Tedrey," she cooed.

"Yes," he mumbled.

"You are safe," she said, still stroking his hair.

"Yes," he repeated.

"You are home, *caro*," she whispered.

Drey closed his eyes and fell asleep.

But as he did, another tear swept over the bridge of his nose.

For he felt just that.

For the first time in his life.

Tedrey was home.

~

Nyx Chronis

Guest Bedchamber, Manor of Lorenz, Captain of the Trusted, Fire City
Firenze

Nyx watched the tear fall.

And she remembered his reddened eyes when she'd returned to him earlier after sending a servant for Saturn and Faunus.

She also remembered the way he'd averted his face so she would not see his wet cheeks.

She had been told of this priest, his use to her, and his different use for her husband.

She had not cared much for entering in such deception, but she would do anything for her Lorenz and for her realm.

Further, he was most enjoyable.

But now, her chest burned.

Her head felt too full.

And she knew her husband's did the same.

Even feeling thus, she stroked her plaything's silky, golden hair, beheld his face, soft and handsome in sleep, and only when she knew his sleep was deep, did she get off the bed and move from the room.

Her husband was busy at the palace.

But he would come at her call.

Then he would take her violently so she could expend some of her wrath (and titillation at what she'd just witnessed).

After that, he would listen to her words.

And she felt certain he would agree.

Persephone had her own pursuits.

As did Saturn and Faunus.

But this one would give up his white robes.

Because this one, they'd be keeping.

30
THE SNOOP

Lady Silence Mattson

Second Floor, East Corridor, Catrame Palace, Fire City
FIRENZE

I rushed down the corridor, clutching my dressing gown around me over Jasmine's body stocking.

The fitting was complete for my wedding gown and I was delighted with the results. There were some last touches, but Mars's servants were clearly honored to help Tril with such an important project for their beloved king and future queen. They had the rest of the day and most of the morrow, and there were many of them, thus I knew it would be completed in time.

And it would be perfect.

I could not wait to see its final incarnation.

More, considering his reaction to my red dress, I could not wait to be wearing it when Mars saw it.

For now, I could not wait for something else.

This being bathing in the pool in the garden with Farah and Ha-Lah.

Elena, Hera and Jasmine said they'd meet us there later. And my future mother-in-law said she would try to join us, but with the wedding preparations and all the guests that were arriving, she was quite busy, so this might be unlikely.

Sofia had begged off, saying that she wished to give us younger girls time together without an old fuddy-duddy around (though she didn't use the word "fuddy-duddy").

I didn't agree with this. She was welcome with us anytime. But with her manner, which was growing more morose as time went by and Elpis remained remote, I did not say anything.

I could do naught about that.

But it made me sad.

I had my wedding gown on my mind, Mars's reaction to it, my impending nuptials on the whole and a lovely afternoon in the pool under the sun with my new friends as I dashed down the corridor, so I was not thinking of aught else when, outside my king and queen's bedchamber, I heard:

"It cannot be countenanced. Your son commits *treason*."

And this was said by Carrington, my uncle's counsellor.

Hearing these words, words I assumed were said about True, words that could in no way be correct, in extreme shock and complete dismay, I instantly drew my shadow over me and moved to the wall so no one who might be coming or going would run into me.

It was then I realized what I'd done, right in the middle of the corridor, and my gaze darted to the end, where there was often a servant boy (or two) to attend to the guests of the palace.

And guests at the palace were growing in number. Those personages of import in Firenze were arriving to attend the marriage ceremony of the king, something which would happen tomorrow, early evening. They would also present their wedding gifts to their king (and me, their future queen) tomorrow morning.

Indeed, we were to dine with some of them that night.

Which I hoped meant Mars would not be in meetings. Something like that would be much easier to do at his side.

There was a boy there, though he was bent over, tying the strap on his sandal, so he did not see me shadow myself.

I glanced to the other end of the hall and saw no servant.

I heaved a sigh of relief but choked on it when Carrington carried on, "If Cassius is allowed to usurp his father's throne, do not think, my king, that True won't get the same ideas."

Cassius usurped Gallienus's throne?

When did that happen?

How did that happen?

I kept my gaze on the servant as he straightened, pleased to see he was looking down the corridor, but it was clear he didn't see me.

My shadow was not faulty as it had been last night.

Perhaps it was my agitation at getting caught in Mars's rooms that had led to it abandoning me.

"Our prince has already promised the use of *your* armies in this lunacy Cassius is instigating," Carrington went on.

Lunacy?

What lunacy could Cassius possibly be instigating?

He did not seem a "lunacy" type of fellow.

"And he did this without your consent. Without even discussing it with you. And that is treason," Carrington finished.

"It's hardly treason," I heard Aunt Mercy murmur. "Perhaps misguided as he was swept up in the discourse. But not treason."

"I think promising your *king's* armies to another country to get involved in what is guaranteed to be a civil war is something quite a bit of a departure from simply *misguided*," Carrington spat.

"Mind your tongue to my wife," Uncle Wilmer ordered in a sharp voice I'd never heard him use.

But in defense of his wife, I liked it.

Or, actually, I liked him demonstrating he had any backbone at all.

"I'm afraid I'm not myself, Your Grace, such is my state of concern about what is happening," Carrington retorted acidly.

There was a brief moment of silence before Uncle Wilmer returned on what sounded like a sigh, "I'll have a word with True."

"How will that be? They're drawing up the proclamations now and you've already agreed to sign them," Carrington rejoined.

"Perhaps this civil war won't come about," Wilmer suggested.

I heard Carrington's scoffing chuff of expelled air.

"Do you think for one second that the gentry of Airen will stand for their new *regent* demanding they disband their militias? Not to mention the males of that nation will surely have something to say about giving women right to own property. Eradicating limits on their education and professions. Setting minimal remuneration for their labor at amounts much higher than what they're currently receiving. And worst of all, offering them the privilege of assembly," Carrington remarked with disgust.

Cassius intended to do all of that?

And he'd assumed rule, become regent, in order to do it?

Oh my...*faith*.

"My husband has kept neutral on these gender issues in the past, Carrington, but we've always been allied with Airen," Aunt Mercy noted. "Our people will find it no surprise we've tendered our support for the wishes of their sovereigns."

"We have indeed. Neutral to *Gallienus's* rule," Carrington rejoined. "To that end, any time one of their females entered our lands for refuge and they demand her return, we grant it. In other words, this is not neutral. This is an about face."

"And there are many in Wodell who do not like that this is the *king's* policy," Aunt Mercy returned, emphasizing the word *"king's"* in a manner that stated it wasn't the king's policy at all.

And I knew this to be accurate. True had told me. Returning refugee women to Airen was a thorny subject between my country's king and his son. True without fail advised his father to grant asylum. Carrington advised it would not be good to anger King Gallienus or the members of his gentry who had command of standing armies.

"Enough they're willing to allow their sons to die for it?" Carrington fired back.

"I do not know," Mercy retorted. "Though it would be *my son* in service to *his realm* and *his king* who leads the king's armies and knows the minds of the king's men, and I would wonder which they would prefer. Riding in aid of a new ruler making just changes in his realm or riding to a folly in order to increase their king's chest."

"Mercy," Uncle Wilmer muttered warningly.

"I am sorry, my husband," she declared like she was not. "But I will not sit silent and allow anyone to call my son a traitor."

"Your king's chest is also yours, my queen, and it grows low," Carrington spoke as if my aunt had not.

"And why is that, Carrington?" she asked quietly.

Why it was, I knew, was because of the campaigns against Firenze.

There was silence, and while I waited on tenterhooks, my heart beating madly, it jumped, as did my entire body, when I heard a door open down the hall.

I turned that way.

And my mouth dropped open.

Serena of the Nadirii was rushing down the hall.

And she was wearing the garments of a female Firenz.

An orange brassiere festooned in yellow, red and salmon beading, sheer orange skirts that showed her legs with an elaborately bedazzled waistband that went over her hips and fell in dangles and fringes of beads.

She was not hurrying.

She was *scurrying*, her eyes darting this way and that, as if she feared someone would see her (and fortunately, as she did this, she did not see *me*).

And I would imagine she did for I *never* would imagine I would be seeing her in such clothing.

What on earth?

Had the world turned upside down?

"We can salvage this situation, Your Grace," Carrington was speaking again, sounding like he'd calmed himself.

Serena scooted around the corner to the stairs and I lost sight of her.

But I would have returned my attention to what was happening in my king and queen's chamber regardless of Serena's shenanigans.

For I, like my aunt, did not take kindly to anyone calling my cousin traitor.

"Aramus has promised his armada to Cassius's crusade," Carrington continued. "Ophelia would not make a binding vow at this time to offer Nadirii arms, but as you know, if what Cassius intends to do is instigated, she'll obviously offer support, and if it should become necessary, her warriors' bows and staffs. Most importantly, *Firenze* has promised their horses to Cassius's crusade."

With True's offer of the Dellish army, this meant the entirety of Triton would stand in support of Cassius.

That made me feel warm inside.

Especially as Mars had offered his as well.

"However," Carrington went on, "when Airen descends into chaos, as it will, and the Mar-el armada sails to its shores, the Nadirii warriors align behind their princess, who will be princess to the Airenzian usurper, and Firenz horses ride in aid, *we* will send our armies to Firenze. With the warriors of Firenze occupied on their northeastern border, indeed *everyone* occupied elsewhere, *we* will retake our southwestern border that Firenze stole from us with ease. And once we do, we will *continue south*."

I gasped then bit the inside of my cheeks and again studied the servant.

But he was well down the hall and he did not have as good of hearing as I did, so he made no sign he heard me.

"You're saying break the promise King Wilmer made to all the realms in order to secure a ruby mine and a saffron field?" Aunt Mercy asked in derision.

"The promise Prince True made," Carrington corrected.

"It will not be True's name on the parchment, Carrington," Aunt Mercy retorted.

"Then yes. Rubies. Saffron. And riches *south*," Carrington stated confidently.

"Do you not think Mars will send his warriors west the minute he hears of this?" my uncle asked.

"Yes. I do. But when he does, if what I have planned comes to fruition, it will be too late," Carrington answered. "Thus, at your leave, I'll dispatch a raven and send a rider on its tailfeathers. We'll begin recruiting immediately. Add to our numbers now. Begin training. Prepare for our campaign. We'll overwhelm them with our force this time. And as we have months to plan, we will be ready."

"And use what, precisely, to pay these new soldiers, Carrington? The dust in our king's chests?" Aunt Mercy asked.

"Those chests they will know will be far richer once we re-secure what's rightfully ours," Carrington sniffed.

"So we promise them pay, just...later?" Aunt Mercy scoffed. "Should any be foolish enough to agree to that, how do we arm them, provide armor, and, say, *food*?"

"There are those in our fertile lands who would offer us loans," Carrington suggested.

"Ah yes, be in debt to our aristocracy and merchants. On a quest that will again prove fruitless, so we'll have to tax our citizens in order to pay their beaten, downtrodden sons and repay our debts. This is an excellent idea," Aunt Mercy murmured.

"When you're dripping riches and furs, I've no doubt you'll have more assurance in my plan," Carrington returned.

I wasn't sure she would. Aunt Mercy wasn't a riches and furs type of female.

She made that clear to Carrington.

"I'm sure you're aware that that tract of land you so desire, Carrington, was of Firenze first, five centuries ago. We wrested it from them. They wrested it back, *seven generations ago*. Do you not think it's time to forget this and focus on Wodell's strengths as well as negotiate trade and safe sea passage with Mar-el while we have their king here and at the diplomatic table for the first time in recorded history?"

"What I *know* is the Dellish want their wealth back," Carrington replied.

"I do not agree," Aunt Mercy returned.

"Stop it," my uncle demanded wearily. "The both of you. You're giving me a blinding headache."

"You need to think on this, my king," Carrington urged. "With urgency."

"I've done nothing but think for days," Uncle Wilmer complained.

"We must move swiftly. I must send a bird as soon as—"

My uncle interrupted his advisor. "I will think on it, Carrington. Enough. We'll speak later this afternoon."

"Your Grace—"

"Later this afternoon."

There was silence, then a heavy sigh, murmured farewells, and I drew in my belly for no purpose as the door to the bedchamber opened and I saw Carrington skulk out.

He closed the door behind him and stormed to the stairs.

I then listened for some time before Aunt Mercy spoke.

"Your son is no traitor, Wilmer."

"True shouldn't have promised my armies without speaking to me."

"Your son is *no* traitor."

I pressed my lips tightly together at the tone in which Aunt Mercy reiterated her assertion.

Though I had to agree with her. In all his frustrations, True had many opportunities to break from his father, his king.

He never did.

And now, when all the realms were aligning for positive change, it seemed foolhardy to me that Wodell would choose to do something that would only serve to upset perhaps all the realms.

But definitely the most wealthy and powerful one on the mainland.

"I urge you to speak to your son, my husband, and *listen to him* before you speak to Carrington again," my aunt stated.

"I need a moment to close my eyes and clear my head," Uncle Wilmer murmured.

"Promise me you'll do as I ask first," Aunt Mercy pressed.

"Just half an hour."

"Wilmer."

I jumped when Uncle Wilmer snapped, "Half an hour, woman!"

There was a moment of silence before Aunt Mercy said softly, "Of course, husband."

It didn't take long before I saw her sweep out.

And I pressed my lips together even harder at witnessing the cold fury on her face when she did.

I did not know my aunt very well.

I had been in her presence many times.

She was simply not a knowable person.

Hurriedly, I dashed back to my door, opened it, dropped the shadow and walked out, as if I'd been in there the whole time.

I smiled at the servant boy who was studying me quizzically, for he probably saw me starting down the corridor some minutes before and was surprised to see me back.

I could have no mind to this.

I needed to speak with someone.

I just didn't know who.

Though I knew my father was not an option, nor my mother.

However, the thought occurred to me I knew someone who was wise and who also had the best interests of Wodell *and* Firenze at heart and who also had experience of the volatility of politics.

Therefore, I went directly to the door of Farah's bedchamber, hoping she was still within, for I did not wish to speak to her in front of Queen Ha-Lah.

I knocked and was heartened when, in moments, the door opened.

But it was not Farah.

It was Sofia.

"I'm sorry to disturb you. I was looking for Farah. We're going to bathe," I said on a smile I could feel was trembling. "Is she in?"

Sofia, wise in many ways as well, did not miss my trembling smile, thus didn't answer my question.

She asked her own.

"Is all well, young Silence?"

"Yes. I just thought we could walk together to the bath."

"I've no idea if she's gone yet, child. You should try her chamber," she suggested.

I was confused. "Is this not Farah's chamber?"

Something occurred to her and she nodded. "It was. I apologize. Your fitting this morning, you probably didn't notice. When the queen moved, as my other chamber was...closer to hers, we decided this morning to...um..."

I didn't make her finish.

"Of course, you switched. I didn't know that. I apologize as well. I'll go there to find your daughter."

Sofia nodded again before she tipped her head to the side. "You seemed troubled, my future queen. Is there something I can help you with?"

I shook my head and somewhat fibbed, "No. All is well. Just, perhaps, a little anxious that the king will still be in meetings at dinner."

Sofia's face got soft and she reached out to touch my hand briefly.

"You will charm them, with or without our great king, Silence. This is because you are most charming, *cara*. So please, do not worry."

She really was so lovely.

"Thank you, Sofia," I whispered.

"Run along. Find Farah. Relax in the baths. And I'll see you at dinner and while doing it, watch you charm all of Firenze."

I gave her a smile that was a great deal brighter as she shut the door.

I then rushed down the hall to Sofia's former bedchamber, which was indeed closer to Queen Elpis's that was now at that end, rather than the other.

At my knock, when no one answered, I realized I had a conundrum and it was one I would have to work out on my own.

But really, I needn't worry.

I knew exactly what to do.

Thus, I changed direction, rushed down the corridor, lifted my dressing gown and raced down the stairs. I turned right, a direction I rarely went, for this was where the formal rooms in which the king did business were located, and except in the beginning, Mars was never formal with me.

As it had been for days, it was rife with men.

Mars's Trusted.

True's personal guard.

The same of Wilmer, Gallienus, Cassius and Aramus.

I went right to Alfie, True's closest lieutenant.

His attention had shifted to me the moment I hit the hall, as had Kyril's and Guard's, Mars's men.

"Countess," Alfie murmured when I arrived at him.

"Sir Alfie," I murmured back. "Is our prince still behind those doors?" I asked, glancing at the closed doors to the meeting room where they were having their diplomatic discussions.

"He is, milady."

"I would speak to him, please," I requested.

He was openly surprised and thus spoke carefully. "Talks are such they shouldn't be interrupted."

"I understand." And I certainly did with all the goings-on I'd over-heard. "But this is important." I paused in hopes of adding the signifi-cance I needed to my emphasis. "*Very* important."

I felt a presence beside me, turned my head and saw Kyril there.

"I will get my king," Kyril stated instantly.

"She asks for her prince," Alfie replied.

"She has no prince. She has a king," Kyril announced implacably.

Oh dear.

"I wish to speak to my cousin, Kyril," I told him.

"And you shall. As well as your king," Kyril told me.

Balls!

Kyril turned on his sandal and stalked to the double doors.

Alfie threw me a certain kind of look and followed on his heels.

I fought wringing my hands for this was not going well.

I could tell True. True needed to know.

I couldn't tell Mars what I'd overheard.

Though, it must be said, he needed to know too.

It would seem I had no choice. I either had to keep it to myself, wait to get True alone and tell him later, fabricating some other reason I urgently had to speak to my cousin, thus interrupting political discussions of grave important.

Or I'd have to share with True *and* Mars.

For both were right then stalking my way.

Well, True wasn't stalking. He was striding with purpose.

Mars, however, was definitely stalking.

"Is all well?" my intended demanded when he was four feet from me.

"I...well, I..." I looked to him, to True, to him.

They both arrived at me, stopping very close, tipping their chins down to stare at me.

And in that moment, I remembered Sofia.

She had not known what her husband intended to do.

And from the words of the piercing ceremony, I wondered if she had, what she would have done.

That ceremony stated your first allegiance was to your husband, not your realm.

But if she knew her husband would personally murder her king...

If he'd told her this, he would have put her in an unbearable position.

And I was in somewhat the same position right then.

Except I knew the kind of man my cousin was.

I also knew that I would, the very next evening, be the Firenz queen.

I had alliances to both sides.

And one of them was to my (very soon-to-be) husband.

So I understood what I had to do.

"Can we speak privately?" I requested.

Mars took my hand immediately, and I rushed with him as he strode down the hall to a door. He opened it and pulled me inside.

True followed and closed it behind him.

It was his receiving room swathed in bold silks and furnished with cushions and divans.

I very much liked that room, a room I would in future use to do my own receiving with and without my king.

Then again, I liked all about the palace that would be mine.

This heartened me, this reminder of who I was and who I would be in this palace.

On that thought, I straightened my shoulders and lifted my gaze to my king and my prince.

"Silence, *mia piccola*, there are matters of—" Mars started.

Before I lost my courage, I interrupted him.

"I overheard Carrington speaking to King Wilmer. In the king's chambers. At what I heard, I listened, and it was shocking. And concerning. So much so, you...you..." I lifted my chin. "You both need to know."

"Silence," True murmured, clearly feeling his own shock.

And worry.

"Carrington called you a traitor," I told True and watched my beloved cousin's eyes flare in an odd way I'd never seen.

It made them seem impossibly more green.

And it was impossible because they were already *very* green but now they seemed *alive* with green, like a burgeoning leaf unfurling at a fantastical rate.

Matters were of such import, I tore my gaze from that wonder and looked to Mars.

"And he has advised King Wilmer to renege on our promise to aid Cassius in his endeavors, and instead, when all ride and sail to Airen's aid, he will invade Firenze on their northwestern border."

Mars looked to True.

True turned to Mars.

"The king is thinking on this," I added, and both men looked to me. "Aunt Mercy was there, and she strongly advised against it. However, you should...I felt you both should..." I swallowed. "You should both know."

There was a worrying moment when they were silent.

True spoke first.

"You did right, and you did well, Silence," he said gently. "Now think not of it. We know but they will not know how we do."

"They absolutely will not," Mars growled.

"But we will handle it from here," True went on. His gaze moved over me. "You seem to be prepared for something enjoyable. Go forth and do that, my cousin. And do it knowing the decision that had to be weighty was made correctly."

I nodded to him.

True again looked to Mars.

"Return. I'll be one moment, and I'll join you," Mars said to my cousin.

True nodded to Mars, looked to me, seemed to hesitate, and I knew he intended to touch me, probably to kiss my forehead, but he realized he could not with Mars there.

I'd have to discuss this with my intended. I missed the affection of my True.

I couldn't say he was overtly demonstrative, but when he was, it was warm and genuine and some of the only type of that I received.

"Thank you, Silence," he whispered with grave feeling.

My shoulders slumped in relief.

I *had* done the right thing.

"You are welcome, my cousin," I whispered back.

He inclined his head, turned, and walked out of the room.

I lifted my gaze to my betrothed.

"He is correct. You did rightly, my little monkey," he declared.

I smiled up at him. It was again trembling, this time with relief, but as I did it, it grew stronger.

"You were incredibly foolish as well, and I'll have your vow right now never to do it again," Mars commanded.

My smile died, and I blinked.

"I'm...sorry?"

"Eavesdropping on the conversation of a king?" he asked.

Begorrah.

"Mars—"

"I was wrong. This was not foolish. It was reckless. And perilous. And you'll not do it again, Silence," he somewhat repeated.

It was not perilous (precisely).

He didn't know about my shadow.

No one did.

And it was true, very true, I was coming to care about him (a great deal).

But I was not near ready to share that (and all it could mean).

"No one saw me," I assured.

"It matters not," he returned.

"But Carrington called True a traitor," I shared. "I know my cousin, Mars. He's no traitor. And he was suggesting riding against what will be *my* country. Or, erm...my *other* one. What was I to do?"

"Not listen," he retorted, got close, cupped my jaw in both hands and bent low to put his face in mine. "You must heed this, *piccolina*. It would take philosophers much wiser than me to determine whether it is the greedy man, or the desperate, who is more dangerous. This advisor, from what True has told me, what I've witnessed, there is something off about him. He has king nor country in his heart when he offers his counsel. He wishes something for himself or has promised something to someone who would be more dangerous than his own king if he were not to deliver."

Mars's face came even closer before he went on.

"And listen to this, my wee monkey," he said softly. "If my lands and my peoples were attacked, I would defend them with my last breath. But if anyone did anything to my queen, I would blaze a fire of vengeance that would never be forgotten in all of history. The mighty forests and the fertile fields of all of Wodell would be ash. So I beg of you, please, do not give man nor woman reason to make me do this."

He'd do that for his queen?

For *me*?

If he'd do that for me, already, I should tell him about my shadow.

He needed to know.

And he would be my husband, so he *should* know.

I looked into his eyes and decided I'd do that.

Later.

But for now...

"I promise, Mars."

He nodded, moved even closer, touched his mouth to mine and then pulled away, his hands sliding to my neck as he lifted his head but kept gazing down at me.

"It would seem I'll be having dinner with my bride and my guests tonight," he announced.

That made me smile up at him fully.

"You're off to bathe?" he asked.

I nodded.

"Mm," he said, his gaze moving down my body.

"I wear Jasmine's body stocking," I told him, feeling my cheeks pink.

"Mm," he hummed again, his eyes moving back up to mine, and when they arrived, there was a darkness to them that was marvelous and frightening.

"I should go. I believe Farah is waiting for me," I told him. "And likely Queen Ha-Lah too."

"Then yes, you should. But before, I'll have your mouth."

That was marvelous and frightening as well, and I stood frozen, staring up at him wondering which one would prevail as he bent and took my mouth in a hard kiss, touching his tongue to my lips.

I opened them.

His tongue slipped inside.

All right.

It was just marvelous.

I melted into him, wrapping my arms around him as our tongues danced and Mars held my head at the back, and with an arm about me, pulled me deeper into his frame.

He broke our kiss all too soon, lifted away and kissed my nose.

"Until dinner, my Silence, and after," he murmured.

After.

More kissing.

Again, *marvelous.*

"Yes," I whispered.

His gaze went soft, he tucked my hand in his elbow and led me out of the room.

He handed me to Kyril with the order, "Escort her to the garden bath."

Kyril took my hand as Mars offered it and then I was tucked at his elbow.

I looked back to see Lorenz approach Mars before he went into the meeting room.

"You meet Farah?" Kyril asked, and I turned to face where we were heading.

"Yes. And Ha-Lah. And perhaps later, Elena, Hera and Jasmine."

"Ah, to be at the baths with the loveliest females in the palace instead of loitering in the halls, doing nothing," Kyril murmured teasingly.

I took a chance, what with my newfound friends, being in a place where it seemed everyone liked me.

And the chance I took was to tease him in return.

"Just to say, if you were to wish to offer Jasmine a private session, I do not know her well, but what I know, she would not be averse to this."

"And which is she?"

"Elena's lieutenant with the brown hair."

"An introduction is in order at dinner," he proclaimed instantly, and I giggled.

"I'll see to that."

"Much obliged, my future queen," he replied, grinning down at me.

He then led me to the pool with the same kind of teasing, sweet banter the whole way.

It was lovely.

He was lovely.

And if anyone harmed me, my future husband would burn down an entire country.

I should find this frightening.

I did not.

I found it utterly *marvelous*.

~

King Mars Laches
First Floor, West Corridor, State Wing, Catrame Palace, Fire City
FIRENZE

"HAVE you heard of this happening before, Mars?" Lorenz asked him.

"Never," Mars murmured, staring at a space over his general's shoulder.

"I've not either."

Mars looked to his man. "This is not a ruse? Something to earn your pity? Lower your defenses?"

"The state of his wounds, I cannot believe it to be," Lorenz replied. "I've seen the results of a lash. I've wielded a lash. I've never seen anything the like. He had to be in agony."

This made no sense.

"The Go'Doan do not punish their priests as such. It is usually counseling, and if the transgressions carry on and are insurmountable or untenable, expulsion. Corporal punishment is abhorred by that religion."

"This is also my understanding," Lorenz agreed. "Though he said it was as such for the worst of transgressions. But in all he said, that was the only time I knew he was lying."

"Then you cannot trust him," Mars remarked. "You play him, even if this is extreme, he may have understood your intent and be playing you."

"I won't trust him, for the now, but you must know, Nyx does. She wants to keep him."

Mars lifted a brow.

Nyx was less trusting than Lorenz. She suffered no fools. And the burning walls around Fire City would blink out before she was taken in by a deception.

"She felt his arrogance at the Tebes was immaturity and bravado," Lorenz explained. "She's had a soft spot for him since. She is the one who sensed he would enjoy the play we introduced. And he does. But today..." He shook his head. "Mars, I cannot stand here and tell you the man with those injuries, the manner in which he responded to a kindness that anyone would pay him in his state, is playing at anything."

"Do not let your guard down," Mars warned.

"Agreed," Lorenz stated. "But my king, one thing seemed clear. Someone in the Go'Doan did this to him. Therefore, something is afoot. Or someone is going rogue."

"And he might be a part of it," Mars noted.

"My beloved will not wish to deceive him. She's taken him under her wing."

Mars sighed.

And if Nyx gave you her loyalty, she'd die to it.

"And you?" Mars asked and watched his warrior's face get hard.

"You did not see what I saw. You did not feel his fear when Nyx demanded an investigation. He is in my home, sleeping off a draught after a session with Saturn and Faunus. And this is where Nyx intends him to stay, and I as well for I cannot imagine anyone with a good heart sending him back to face a repeat. Or worse. And this has naught to do with my wife and I enjoying his arse. At what I saw today, something calls to me about the man. I think there's something to him and I think, if he's given what he appears never to have had, it would be he who returns our kindness. I just don't know how that would come to be."

This meant more to Mars than even Nyx's instincts.

"And Saturn and Faunus?" Mars asked. "Have you spoken to them?"

"I have not, but Nyx reports Faunus, especially, took to him."

Faunus, like Saturn, was a whore. He'd fuck anything. If he was not so good with a broadsword, he'd be a popular attraction in the Heden District of Fire City.

But he tended to veer toward hole and it wasn't unknown for him to take a lover for a time if something struck his fancy.

He also desired to be a Trusted.

As did Saturn.

And perhaps this was a way for them to begin to earn their place amongst that elite.

"I want him continued to be played," Mars decided. "Draw in Faunus and Saturn."

"Nyx will not like it," Lorenz warned him.

"It is a command of her king. But if he is what you sense he is, or if he is not, in the end, either way, it'll be as it should be."

Lorenz lifted his chin and moved away.

Mars drew breath into his nose.

He did not wish to deal with unknown machinations of the Go'Doan when he had the weakness of the Dellish king and the pomposity of the Airenzian one to handle.

But mostly what he truly wished was to think of nothing but the woman who would soon be his wife and where he would take her teachings in his bedchamber that night.

But his father would juggle all of that, with seventeen more dire problems, and still smile and kiss his wife like nothing was amiss when he sat beside her at dinner.

This would be the king Mars would be.

And it would be the husband he would be.

So this was what he set about doing.

31
THE CHOICE

Queen Mercy Axelsson
Catrame Palace Lofts, Northeastern-Most Corner, Catrame Palace Grounds,
Fire City
FIRENZE

The raven flew, and Mercy instantly turned her head and nodded.

The tall man beside her lifted the small green flag and waved it before he quickly withdrew it.

And thus the man on a horse two hundred yards away went galloping.

This meaning the raven would be shot from the sky before it left the Fire City, the rider then would lay in wait for the messenger on his mount which was sure to follow.

Lamentable.

Ravens were noble, wise and full of magic. If she were queen in more than name only, she would make harming a raven a punishable offense.

However, she must do what had to be done.

And Mercy did that.

She waited.

The man at her side waited.

And the men on horses in the distance waited.

But so sure was he that he had immunity to do anything, Carrington dashed down from the raven lofts, and without a glance around, made his way back to the palace.

"Wait here. If a man loyal to Carrington arrives to dispatch another bird, send the signal. And have Carrington closely watched. I want reports on all his closest associations with my husband's men. And I'll have all his communications, Bram. However he should send them. The instant you can get them. I don't care if it's delivered to me during a royal wedding."

"Yes, my queen," Bram murmured.

She moved from her secluded position back toward the palace.

It really didn't matter what the message was that Carrington sent. Even if it was treason, her husband might not care. Carrington seemed to have the disturbing skill of being able to talk his way out of anything.

And Wilmer would wish to know why Mercy was using his men (or True's men, she could not trust Wilmer's men were actually Wilmer's) to shoot his closest advisor's birds from the sky.

However, matters were progressing at an alarming rate, and for Wodell, her beloved husband, and her beloved son, they weren't heading in the right direction.

It may be she'd have to make a choice.

Her king.

Or her son.

It was no choice really.

She loved her husband. She very much did.

But he was weak.

She tired of standing behind a man who was weak.

Being his wife, it meant a lifetime of holding him up.

And she intended to see her son seated on the throne of Wodell.

Even if she died doing it.

No, there was no choice.

Mercy picked True.

32
THE OFFER

Princess Elena
Grand Stairwell, Catrame Palace, Fire City
FIRENZE

"I'll have your ear, if I may, Your Grace."

I turned to see the Go'Doan calling to me.

What was his name?

G'Liam.

I stopped where I was on the landing and dipped my chin.

"Of course, Liam, how may I assist you?"

"Do you have a moment to speak privately?"

I studied his face.

It was bland.

Giving away nothing.

But one did not waste the opportunity of getting at least something from a Go'Doan.

Or I didn't as I found fascinating each tidbit of the puzzle that was them.

"Perhaps one of King Mars's informal rooms," I murmured.

He stepped to the side and lifted an arm, the long alabaster sleeve of his robe falling nearly to his knee.

And he was tall.

He was also handsome. Fair. Prominent features that were manly, but not aggressive. Hazel eyes with spiky lashes.

The Go'Ella acolytes probably lined up by the score to be selected by him.

This thought made my stomach curl with a certain kind of sick.

I nevertheless preceded him, making my way back down the stairs, and looked right at the bottom when I didn't wish to look right.

I just couldn't stop myself.

And of course, although the last days I rarely saw him, Cassius was standing outside the meeting rooms, appearing most perturbed, one of his men at his side, King Aramus at his other, all of them listening to True, who had Alfie next to him.

And of course, Cassius's gaze came to me as if he could sense my very presence near his.

His eyes took me in then instantly narrowed on the Go'Doan.

"This way, princess?" Liam suggested.

I turned away from the prince and nodded to the priest.

We pivoted to the eastern corridor, walked down the hall and went into a room with an open door that was empty.

Liam closed the door behind us.

"Is all well, G'Liam?" I asked, walking deeper into the room.

"I do not think so," he answered, coming toward me, and with that as his only preamble, he announced, "For your mother is gravely ill."

My stomach pitched as my blood ran cold, but despite this, I hoped my expression was as bland as his had been on the stairwell.

And I was pleased to hear my voice was neutral and steady when I replied.

"She is well, Liam. Whyever would you suggest differently?"

"She is ill, Princess Elena, and I'm sorry to say, but from what I've learned of her condition, she will not recover."

Oh my goddess.

A pain pierced my chest.

But I could not think on that injury.

I didn't know how he knew she was ill or what he knew about her "condition" as I didn't even know of her condition.

I just knew that unless she talked about it with one of her lieutenants, she didn't talk about it at all.

And it would be safe to assume, especially in a time like this, she didn't want anyone to know about it.

You were only as strong as your leader.

Melisse didn't teach me that.

My mother did.

For these reasons, I added heat to my tone when I demanded, "Why would you say such things?"

"Because I have studied this, as did my mentor before I entered the Go'Doan. We have potions. To help with the pain. To aid in keeping the appetite healthy. Both we believe will not only help lift fatigue but also prolong life with a quality that is...tolerable."

Tolerable.

"Again, I will stress my mother is not ill. But regardless, generally, and I hope you take no offense, Liam, but Nadirii treat Nadirii," I reminded him.

He spoke like I did not.

"I cannot say I'm making great advancements. It would take many more who had an interest in this study, more subjects to study, and it would be important to oversee the effects of treatments for a longer period of time. What I will tell you is what I've noticed so far is promising."

I was saved from replying when the door opened, and Prince Cassius strode in.

I studied him as he did.

Really, did he have to be that tall?

And did he have to fill out his leathers like that?

Also, did he have to button his leather shirt up to his throat so the ink slithered out on the left side of his neck only to disappear into his beard and then slink up his cheek and around his eye?

And could he at least have a patchy beard? Not a full, thick, manly one you wanted to catch in your fingers and tug.

Last, couldn't he be just a bit awkward? Witnessing his confident, long-legged soldier's stride as he made his way to us was most annoying.

I would soon not be annoyed.

I would be stunned immobile when he did not simply arrive at our small huddle and stop.

He arrived *at my side*, slid an arm around my waist, his fingers curling at my hip, and he pulled me into *his* side so roughly, my head bounced on my neck.

"Is all well, my princess?" he growled in a manner in which he already knew the answer to that question, it was not well, he very much didn't like that, and he intended to rip someone's head from their shoulders because of it.

"It's perfectly fine," I told him.

He scowled down at me.

And really.

Did he have to bloody *scowl* so magnificently?

"I'll leave you two to have some time together. There is not much of it these days," Liam offered, his eyes on me. "But I'll have some vials sent up to your rooms with instructions on how to use them and things to look for, should some adverse effects start happening. It's not usual, but it's good to know just in case."

"That's not necessary," I said sharply.

"What's not necessary?" Cassius asked, still growly. "And what vials?"

This was, I assumed, precisely why my mother didn't want people talking about, and certainly not knowing about, her predicament.

Because once talk started, it had a tendency to spread.

"I'll send them regardless," Liam told me. "Should you change your mind."

"What vials?" Cassius repeated.

But G'Liam was bowing to me, to the prince, then he turned and walked from the room.

When the door closed behind him, it was me who was turned, and as I was learning that Cassius was wont to do, this was not of my volition.

But I didn't have it in me to protest when the front of me was pressed to the front of him.

I tipped my head back.

"What vials, Elena?" he demanded.

"It's nothing. It doesn't matter. If he even sends them, I'll be disposing of them."

"If it doesn't matter, then you shouldn't have any issue with telling me what they are."

"It *doesn't* matter so it isn't worth wasting time talking about it."

"If your husband wishes to know something, you should tell him."

I was losing patience.

"First, Cassius, you are not my husband...yet. But when you are, if you wish to know something I wish to keep to myself, as my husband, you should allow me to do that."

"This does not make a healthy marriage."

He would know. From reports, he'd had a very healthy one.

And it ended in anguish.

Therefore, I gentled my voice when I replied, "I intend to cause no harm when I say that you should be aware and come into it from the very beginning understanding that our marriage will not be like your last."

He replied instantly.

"You are fair, she was red. You are tall and trim, she was petite and plump. You ride like the wind, she was afraid of horses. She found delight in the flight of a sparrow, you'd probably shoot it out of the sky at two hundred feet."

I was deeply offended.

"I would not kill a sparrow," I snapped.

He shook his head once at the same time his arm tightened, and he shook *me*.

"I think you understand my meaning."

I did.

I was still offended.

"I don't even eat meat," I informed him.

His head jerked in surprise. "You don't eat meat?"

"You sat beside me at dinner the other night, Cassius. Did I eat the roast?"

"I thought your appetite was off due to your sister's mischiefs."

"No. Most Nadirii don't eat meat. Though, I will note my sister is one of the ones who does."

"This is preposterous," he declared.

"Why?"

"Because the body needs meat."

"It does not for I've never in my life eaten meat and as you can see I'm just fine."

He seemed to be considering that knowledge at the same time finding it fascinating.

I did not have time for him to be fascinated.

I also did not have time to enjoy watching him *be* fascinated.

I had things to do.

These being dallying in a bath with my lieutenants and my fellow Sisters of the Beast, this while my ill mother was negotiating whatever she was negotiating with four countries we didn't get along with terribly well, one we warred with constantly, and one we barely knew at all.

I did not know Airen to have Firenz-style baths.

And Cassius had asked me to teach his soldiers my stretches.

But I feared a lifetime yawned in front of me where the things I did to fill my days that had meaning and purpose were gone and such as dawdling in baths (or the like) was my future.

Thus, I told him, "You may release me. I'm to meet the others at the baths."

"I know you are not her."

The way he stated that, firm, but pensive, made me focus on his face.

"You need to understand that, Elena. She was lost years ago. I will not pretend I didn't pine for her. I will not pretend that she isn't in my thoughts the many times she comes to me and will in the future. But she is gone. I am not. You are my destiny. My daughter needs a mother. Your ward needs a father. It is how it was meant to be, and we must find a way to move forward in that."

"Do you mind if, perhaps, we take longer than a day to find the manner in which we'll do that?" I requested.

His lips quirked.

"No. I do not mind," he allowed, and then said, "You can have today and tomorrow too."

And *really*.

Did he also have to be amusing?

I glared at him.

His lips quirked again.

They stopped quirking when he asked, "Why was your sister in Firenz garments?"

It was then I stared at him.

"I did not see her," he carried on. "But my man did, and he said she was regaled in the finest of be-spangled, female Firenz attire."

I could not picture this.

I couldn't even fathom it.

"Serena?" I asked breathily.

He nodded. "Undoubtedly. She's rather notable, especially wearing the sheers and brassiere of a Firenz."

Heavens.

"Do you think, your, uh...*person*, is...?"

I didn't finish that query.

His other arm came about me, and he burst with laughter.

And...

Really.

Did he have to look so handsome finding something amusing?

"It seems she received an instruction," he stated through chuckles.

"And thus, she walked through Catrame Palace in garments that surely had her skin burning?"

"I would say, as that was some time ago, about now her skin is defi-nitely burning in one way or another, my warrior."

My skin started burning, that being my cheeks.

I stared at his throat.

Not a good selection.

I decided on his ear.

"Elena," he murmured.

I forced myself to look in his eyes.

"I'll be joining you for dinner."

Why did that make my heart feel light?

"I'll alert the heralds," I quipped.

His eyes danced.

This they did right before his mouth took mine (it was definitely his taking mine that time, not the other way around).

He thrust his tongue inside in a claiming manner that should have outraged me.

It did not.

Instead, I lifted my arms to wrap them around his neck and I tilted my head so he might have more of me.

Cassius took it.

His arms tightened, drawing me up to my toes and deeper into his body, and I drifted a hand over his short hair that brushed toward his forehead, taking that path with my hand, then down, where I did what I wished to do dearly.

I caught hold of his beard at his jaw and tugged.

He nipped my bottom lip with his teeth in response.

I whimpered at the pleasant sting of the bite, my eyes fluttering just enough to take in the heat of his and my mouth was captured again as he ground the hardness of his hips into my belly.

Making him thus, feeling it evident and proud against me, feeling a corresponding flood between my legs, I broke our kiss and whispered, "Cassius."

His beard scraped my skin as he put his lips to my ear.

"After dinner, you attend me in my room," he rumbled.

Oh, by the goddess.

"I can't. I have to look after—"

He fit me more snugly into his hips.

"You found relief this morning, my warrior. I did not," he reminded me.

Oh heavens.

He didn't.

I pulled my head back, he lifted his, and I caught his eyes.

"I'm so sorry," I whispered. "I didn't think. That was selfish of me."

He stared at me, desire retreating, contemplation seeping in.

Finally, he spoke. "It is far from the end of the world, Elena. And when you join me tonight, we will first talk, and after, you must know that we will not do anything you don't wish."

"You seem to be able to make me do a variety of things I don't wish," I mumbled.

"This is because you wish them, my princess," he replied. "You might not *wish* to wish them, but you do."

I couldn't argue that.

I *wished* I could.

But I could not.

"We will be wed in less than three months," he reminded me. "We must find our times to learn of each other."

"What I find is that you're annoying," I blurted.

He raised his brows. "This is because I'm right most the time."

"'Most' is not the correct word. We've known each other but days. It's impossible at this juncture to know if that word has relevancy."

He grinned at me.

And then he did what he was known to do very well on a battlefield. Something that caused my sister no end of complaint.

In our banter, with my lips swollen from his kisses and my body pressed close to his, he perpetrated a sneak attack.

"What vials was that Go'Doan talking about, Elena?"

"Please don't ask me that," I said softly.

He studied me.

"You are right," I relented. "We must share. We must do it openly. But don't ask too much of me too quickly, Cassius. You've been a husband. You've...dallied."

The reflection left his gaze as humor sifted back in.

"I have indeed dallied, my warrior," he murmured.

"I have not."

He grew serious.

I continued to speak.

"My mentor, Melisse, taught me that if you find a raging river you need to cross, you might make it if you take a great bound. However, you are more likely to find yourself falling into the waters, lost to them. But if you took your time and studied the riverbank, eventually, you would find safe passage."

"Your mentor sounds wise."

"This is why she's a mentor."

He gave me a squeeze with his arms, stating, "You'll have what you wish, my princess. I'll give you today, and tomorrow, and the next day as well."

I didn't want to smile at him. I fought it.

But I was almost certain part of it leaked.

Cassius released me with one arm and tucked my hair behind my ear before he fully released me.

He walked to the door but didn't open it.

He turned back to me.

"I will share in my rooms tonight when we have privacy guaranteed. But much is happening that if you don't know of it, you need to. To that end, it would be cataclysmic now much more than it normally would if Serena assumed reign of the Nadirii."

I was suddenly unable to breathe.

His voice grew quieter when he finished, "The Go'Doan, particularly G'Liam, know many ways of healing. I urge you to consider using those vials. As much as this might be loathsome to you, I advise you test them first on an animal. If they're safe, then use them. With what is happening, we all need more time with those having wise, composed heads." His voice went downright low when he concluded, "And I would suspect the one who would need that time most is you."

After delivering that, and with a short bow, he opened the door and walked through it.

I studied it after he closed it behind him, feeling a chill on my skin.

I knew what this chill meant.

My mother was hiding nothing.

~

Princess Serena
Private Play Suite, Dahlia Rooms, Heden District, Fire City
Firenze

THERE WAS a large mirror before her.

Her sheers were on the floor.

The cups of her brassiere were shoved down, pushing up her breasts, their rosy peaks stiffened and jutting with need.

Her wide belt of beads and fringe was about her hips, the bits dangling driving her mad as they consistently brushed her sensitive skin.

The curls between her legs were partly exposed to the eye.

Her arms were high above her, tethered at the wrists with suede straps.

There was a tool thrust inside between her legs that was long and bulbous, coming down to a narrow end with a handle that could be seen. It was filling her so wide, it would stay in place on its own. However, the walls of her cunt were spasming around it uncontrollably.

And he stood beside her, examining her arse like he was a physician vaguely interested in a patient.

Serena watched as he then swung back and landed a sharp swat on her already stinging cheek, the beaded fringe digging in, and her eyes rolled back in her head as her pussy spasmed again.

Another sharp slap and he held on, gripping the abused flesh and bouncing it about.

Then a few lighter strikes that would almost seem affectionate, if she did not open her eyes and see he was more involved with opening the fly on his leathers with his free hand than he was in her.

"Please," she whispered, needing his attention. Needing an admiring eye. An indication she was behaving rightly. That he liked what he saw. That he wanted what she was giving him.

That she was pleasing him.

He took his cock in his left hand and shifted slightly so he could take the handle of the tool inside her in his right.

With that, he fucked her as he stroked himself, turning his gaze to the mirror to watch his ministrations between her legs.

Her stomach tightened, her nub throbbed, her nipples ached.

Goddess, she needed *release*.

His eyes lifted to hers.

"Watch me fuck you," he ordered emotionlessly.

Immediately, Serena looked down, seeing the slick, smooth wood disappear inside her then reappear. And again. Again. Again.

It was mortifying to be used thus.

It was also beautiful.

"*Please,*" she begged.

He thrust it up, left it inside and turned fully to her, shifting hands, left to right as he carried on stroking himself, but now not touching her.

"Do you know my name?" he asked.

She tore her gaze from his magnificent shaft and lifted it to his face.

"I—"

"I told you my name when we met. Do you know it?"

"You are Shen, of the Trusted," she said.

"That is the name the person you asked after me was instructed to give. That is not my true name. The one I gave you when we met."

Oh no.

"I'm sorry," Serena whispered. "Our relations were such, I thought of naught else but what you gave me and everything else slipped my mind."

He released his cock and struck her arse, one cheek, the next, back, again, and again, her breasts bobbing, her disregarded nipples in agony, until the pain drove up her pussy, convulsed at her clit, her head fell back, and he grasped both cheeks and squeezed hard.

She whinnied in sheer *need*.

He released her arse and pulled the tool from inside her, dropped it to the floor and thrust his cock through her crevice, gliding it along the lips of her wet.

She forced her gaze back to the mirror and saw the slick cockhead framed with her curls and the beads.

At the sight, the feel of him, Serena shivered everywhere.

"You lie," he growled in her ear, easing his shaft back and forth between her legs, but not inside.

She did.

She did lie.

She did not remember his name, for when she met him, she did not think it would be worth remembering.

And she didn't know if she wished to continue to lie, and make him angrier, earning what he might deliver, or if she should be honest and admit it.

She wanted to please him.

She *only* wanted to please him.

But she did not know how.

Mercifully, he told her.

"If you're honest, you get a reward."

"I lied," she said instantly.

And then maddeningly, he kept riding her without riding her.

But he also reached around and pulled at her nipples.

Serena's head fell back, hit his shoulder, and she moaned.

Cruelly, he twisted his fingers.

"Watch me work you," he ordered.

It took much, but she made her gaze go back to the mirror.

Still at her breasts, he pulled his shaft back, shifted his hips, and she felt her eyes get wide as he touched a finger to her hole.

Her lips parted as he put pressure there, spreading her, opening her.

She'd never done this.

She didn't because she'd never desired this.

"I will fuck you here," he said in her ear.

"Yes," she whispered without hesitation, willing, *needing* to get anything from him.

His finger disappeared, and he slid between her legs, but this time, he dipped his knees and drove inside her pussy.

"*Yes,*" she hissed, convulsing against him, against her bindings, tipping her hips to get more.

He drove hard and deep, still tormenting her nipples.

"What's my name?" he asked, his hips pounding into the heated cheeks of her backside, stinging pain with each thrust, shafting pleasure in its wake.

She quivered.

"What's my bloody name?" he demanded.

"I-I don't know."

He pulled out.

She gasped and cried, "No!"

He went to where the tethers were looped around a hook on the wall, released them, gave them slack and demanded, "Knees."

Serena dropped at once to her knees.

He re-secured the suede in a manner her arms were still over her head, walked to her front and shoved his cock in her face.

"Worship," he grunted.

She did not like the taste of herself. She'd taken it the time he had her before without thought, but this time, the length of their play, the attention she was receiving, along with the inattention…

He took hold of her hair, yanked her head back, with her arms still straight over her head, pain charged through her shoulders.

"*Worship!*" he barked.

She opened her mouth.

He released her hair, drove between her lips and fucked her face.

She suckled him, hoping to give him what he wanted, earn her reward.

Instead, he used her mouth for so long, she knew he would again flood his seed in her throat and she wanted it inside, but elsewhere.

Just when she'd given up hope, he pulled out, put his hands to her bindings, released them but before she could drop her arms to regain control of them, he jerked both down, twisted them back and then up so they were contorted unnaturally.

She grunted, forced forward into him now, as he held them in one fist, bound them again and then shoved her head down, cheek to the floor.

"Stay," he ordered.

Oh goddess.

He moved.

Back to the hoop, she moaned as he took away all slack, lengthening her arms, pulling them up behind her.

He then moved again, dropped to his knees between her calves, and he penetrated her, driving into her pussy.

Her reward.

"Yes, please, yes, *please*," she whispered.

He thrust, harder and faster, grunting with the effort, smacking her arse as he did, gripping it tight.

She panted, whimpered, taking each thrust, the fringe at her belt coasting across her skin an agony of bliss, she was going to climax just from the pounding.

But he again pulled out, and with a heavy sigh, released his seed all over her arse.

She blew out her breath, holding every inch of her body still, waiting, for she knew all he would need to do was tweak her clit and she'd explode.

He smacked her arse with both his hands and again gripped hard.

"You don't climax until you know my proper name."

With that, he released her bottom and took his feet.

She slid her eyes to the side, gazing up at him in desperation as he tucked his cock into his trousers.

"But—"

Gazing down at her, he put his finger to his lips.

Serena quieted.

He dropped his finger and finished with his fly as he shared, "You speak when spoken to, Your Grace."

She nodded fervently.

"Little mouse," he said softly. "That is what you'll be. Do you under-stand me?"

She did not.

All she knew was she needed to.

She shook her head.

"You are mine, princess. At all times. Even when you aren't with me. You sleep. You eat. You breathe. You wait for me to call on you. When I do, you do precisely what I command you to do. You tell no one of me. You don't call attention to yourself. You connect with others only as much as you have to." He bent slightly at his waist. "And you don't touch yourself. At all. Unless you have my leave." He straightened. "And if you're a good, quiet, obedient little mouse, you'll receive your reward."

"All right," Serena agreed.

"All right, what?"

She squeezed her eyes shut.

"Do not take your eyes from me unless I command it."

She opened her eyes.

"All right, what?" he demanded.

"I'm sorry, sir, I do not know your name."

"You will know it. And you will wait to know it until I give it to you. But in all I'll be to you, the proper way to address me, I am Master."

Oh goddess.

She could not speak that word.

She could not.

But she would.

She had to.

To get what she needed.

"Say it," he ordered.

"Will I get a reward?" she bargained.

He bent deep and bit, "*Say it!*"

"Master," she whispered.

He moved behind her, dropped again to his knees and leaned over. Holding her by her hips, he shoved his face between her thighs, suckled hard at her clit and made her orgasm within five seconds.

Blindingly.

Worth it.

Worth everything.

Completely.

"Thank me, little mouse," he murmured, stroking gently inside with two fingers.

"Thank you," Serena said with feeling.

"I'm sorry?"

She gulped.

And she gave him what he was to her.

"Thank you...Master."

He stood. "You'll be attended."

And then, to her humiliation, leaving her still quivering from her orgasm, kneeling, bound, prostrated, his seed dripping down the backs of her thighs, Serena of the Nadirii waited to be set free.

But really, even if he had just finished using her, she waited to be called to service again.

And hoped she would be.

Soon.

33

THE BUDDING

Prince True Axelsson

The Lantern Room, First Floor, East Corridor, Catrame Palace, Fire City
FIRENZE

True studied his betrothed as she stood at the screened windows, looking out.

She was incredibly lovely.

Lovely in repose. Lovely in reflection. Most lovely when she smiled.

Cassius had won Elena.

He'd done it with a brooding look down at her from the podium at the parade.

True knew this for he had felt her loss in that instant as if she was physically attached to him and had been torn away.

And now he had to hide that grief from a beautiful woman with kind, sad eyes.

A woman who was falling in love with him.

"Are you going to confront him?" she asked the screen.

He'd told her of Carrington and his father.

And Silence.

Mars knew.

And Farah could have no desire but what was best for Firenze, and what would be her kingdom of Wodell, therefore it was not a risk to share the knowledge with her.

Regardless of all of this, he trusted her.

Not because she was falling in love with him.

Because he sensed, above all, she was trustworthy.

"It might expose Silence," he replied.

She turned her head his way.

Yes, she was incredibly lovely.

"If they were speaking in a way that could be overheard, it could have been anyone that reported this to Mars and you. Most especially Mars. There's at least one servant in that corridor at all times."

True trusted Farah.

But he did not share that he had noticed his cousin had an unnatural ability to hear things others could not. So he could not know that just anybody would have overheard this conversation.

What he did know was that his cousin could.

Silence tried to hide it, and she'd been so roundly neglected in her home and by the people around her, he reckoned she succeeded.

But she hadn't hidden it from him.

"I do not wish to risk that, and Mars definitely doesn't."

She smiled a small smile. "He wouldn't. He's much charmed by her."

"My cousin is charming."

The smile that received was not small.

It faded as she turned fully his way and walked to him.

She stopped close enough to reach out and touch.

But she didn't do that.

"May I speak candidly?" she requested.

"In all things," he granted.

Her beautiful almond eyes softened.

"You must negotiate this counsellor out," she said.

"I know this, sweets," he replied. "But he has a hold on my father that is unhealthy. If I even begin to suggest it, he ends our discussion."

"This unhealthy hold," she began. "Do you think he knows something about the king that makes him do his bidding?"

"Blackmail?"

Farah shrugged uncomfortably.

"It would surprise me," he told her.

"But it isn't out of the question."

"There are times, Farah, when Father doesn't take Carrington's counsel. These are whims or when he tires of Carrington's nagging or when I suspect my mother has had his ear. And Carrington doesn't like that much. If he knew something sensitive about my father, my father would just be a puppet."

"Hmm..." she murmured, her gaze drifting off.

"We know his plan and even if he convinces my father and moves forward with it, we leave for Wodell in but days. The journey to Notting Thicket is less than three weeks. He would have little time to bring any fullness to his schemes, and being closer to them unfolding, I could keep an eye, uncover them and assume on my own shoulders whatever would fall when they're exposed."

She turned her attention again to him.

"On your shoulders," she said quietly.

"It is the right thing to do."

"It is the True thing to do."

His name was odd and on more than a rare occasion caused some confusion.

But True was not confused with her current meaning.

"I can take it on my shoulders," she suggested.

True blinked.

Slowly.

"Pardon?" he asked.

"When we get to your capital city, and I will say, a capital city named Notting Thicket is someplace I very much desire to see, in hopes the city is as charming as its name," she said with a grin to start. A grin and words that were designed to deflect his attention from the dangerous absurdity of what she would say next. "I will pretend I heard something, or saw something, and did what Silence did, though no one will know she did it. I would tell my prince...and my king."

She would do nothing of the sort.

"You won't do that, Farah," he stated.

"No one would question it."

"It would make you visible."

"And I'm not visible now?"

True felt a burn hit his throat.

For she was.

Even if those who felt her *very* visible were pretending that she was *in*visible.

Carrington hadn't yet acknowledged her.

But that didn't matter.

His mother, father, Aunt Vanka and Uncle Johan very poorly masked their antipathy to his future wife.

It was beyond rude as to be sickening.

"I'll have a word with my mother, Farah," he said gently.

She shook her head. "No, True. We've spoken of this."

They had.

They'd discovered there was very little on which they didn't agree.

Except that.

"She'll be your mother-in-law," he noted.

"It is often the mother-in-law does not like her son being taken away by another woman, no?"

That wasn't it and they both knew it.

"I'll be talking to her, Farah."

"I wish you wouldn't."

"Why?"

"Because the only way to make someone who does not like you for reasons that have nothing to do with you, and only to do with their preconceptions, or, I'm so sorry, True, their ignorance, is to prove them wrong."

He made no response because he didn't have one.

He would not know.

But he suspected she was right.

"It will not help matters and might hinder them if you waded in," she carried on. "Regardless, you have enough to occupy your time. That's the least of your worries."

He had something to say to that.

"My future wife is not the least of my worries, Farah," he retorted. "You need to mark that, sweets. You might not have the regard of my mother or my father, and regrettably, that is true. But you have mine. You are beautiful and kind and sage and my wish is to lift the sadness from your eyes and give you at least peace, but I would strive for happiness."

She gazed up at him, her appealing, puffy lips slightly parted, her eyes like burning topaz.

Yes.

She was falling in love with him.

He felt that look in his groin.

He wanted to taste her and that need grew greater with every moment he shared with her.

He simply would not do it until she knew the man who claimed her mouth, or any part of her, wanted only hers without the loss of the one who fates ripped away fresh on his mind.

He feared she'd get little respect where she was going.

And in truth, outside of Mars, her mother, Silence, Ha-Lah, Elena and her women, she got little respect where she was now.

So she would have his.

In all things.

"I will allow this to carry on, for a time," he told her. "But, Farah, I'll stress it will be for a time. You've done not one thing to earn this rudeness. I will abide it for your sake at your request. But there will come a time I will not. Do we have an understanding?"

She sighed and said, "I suppose."

He grinned at her and replied, "My deepest appreciation."

She cast her eyes to the side briefly in her brand of an eye roll, her lips tipped up at the ends.

"Come," he said, reaching out and taking her hand to tuck it in his elbow. "We must prepare for dinner. As meetings have concluded, Queen Elpis has decided to do the presentations this evening, rather than tomorrow. We have less time to get ready."

He led her to and through the door.

The corridor was busy.

"There is much happening," she said under her breath. "And oddly, I fear it more than the rising of the Beast."

"It will all work out in the end," he assured.

She looked up at him just as he turned them to the stairs.

And she trusted him fully in return, gazing at him as he guided her to the stairs, taking his lead without looking where her feet were falling.

There was something gravely affecting in that.

So much, it also made his throat burn.

"How could you know?" she queried.

He folded his hand over hers at his elbow.

"Because in the end, the Beast is rising. No one will think of trade and proclamations and wars and regents. When we defeat him, there will be naught but relief that those who are still breathing are indeed breathing. The rest will fit in place as it should. Good and just."

They made it to the top landing as she murmured, "This is very true."

True led her to her door and bent to kiss her cheek.

"Send a servant when you're ready to be escorted down," he ordered after he straightened, though he didn't need to. Since meeting her, if he was at dinner, he'd done the same. "I'll attend you."

She gave him her look of shining topaz, budding love glowing in her eyes.

And yes.

She was so very lovely.

She was also his.

And he was hers.

And he wished nothing in that moment but to want to be hers.

Eventually.

34
THE PRESENTATIONS

Lady Silence Mattson
The Throne Room, First Floor, West Corridor, State Wing, Catrame Palace,
Fire City
FIRENZE

I sat on a stack of cushions next to Mars's throne.

The stack was nearly as high as his seat.

But it was no chair.

And had no back.

It was difficult to be perched on cushions, unable to recline. I knew this because this was how I had to sit, on my stack of cushions, throughout the parade.

Though this time, Mars noticed this with a narrowing of eyes practically the second I rested my behind on them, and after but moments of me sitting as such, he solved this problem by pulling me to the side so I could lean against the arm of his chair.

This also allowed him access to the back of my exposed neck, something he took advantage of, stroking it lightly with his finger.

This felt nice, at first.

This was then noticed by his people.

Everything was noticed by his people.

And the way they noticed Mars touching me was not something they appeared to like.

So even though he kept doing it, and it was lovely, it sadly didn't feel as nice.

I'd been told of the presentations, though I thought I had until the next afternoon to prepare for them.

But Elpis wanted it done prior to having dinner that night as well as to clear the schedule to have more time to prepare for the big event the next day. When the discussions at the diplomatic table ended early that afternoon, she had her chance, and took it.

So there I was, wearing the Dellish wedding gown Tril painstakingly crafted along our journey from the exquisite fabric we'd been lucky to find when we went into town to urgently pull together my trousseau.

I was glad of the chance to wear it for an important occasion for Tril's sake. All that hard work would be sad to waste.

And I was glad to wear it because it was important I put forward my best for this ceremony, not only to represent Mars, but Wodell.

At least these were my thoughts, in the beginning.

Yards and yards of diaphanous material in a pink so pale, it was almost white. There was embroidery so delicate throughout, it looked almost like lace. This grew heavier down at the scalloped hem. An also scalloped, demure V-neckline and graceful, full sleeves that gathered tight at the wrists with a satin ribbon and flared out to a dramatic ruffle of embroidery.

My hair was up in soft curls threaded with a slender pale-pink satin ribbon.

And I wore my marital chain hoops.

The wide skirt of the gown with that embroidery looked lovely arranged in a fall around my cushions and swathing the floor of the thronal podium.

But I knew, very early in the ceremony, that there would be no flower petal throwing or coin tossing with this lot.

The Firenz men who moved into that room to make their presentations to the king did not like me.

And I was not certain they liked the other things they saw either.

Even with Queen Ha-Lah, Farah, Elena, Serena, Sofia, Queen Mercy, my mother and father, Jell, Liam, Seph and Queen Elpis sitting in chairs at the side, a few members of personal guards milling about, the throne room was so large, it was not near full.

But the thronal podium was crowded.

Aramus sat on a grand chair to Mars's right.

Wilmer sat to Aramus's right with True standing to the back, right of his father's chair.

Ophelia sat in a chair to Mars's left.

But Cassius sat to Ophelia's left with Gallienus, looking mutinous, in a chair that was set to Cassius's left, but it was set five inches back.

Those five inches were important.

And the men who filed into the room did not miss it.

I just couldn't work out how they were reacting to it.

Lorenz, Mars's captain, stood in front of us but a bit off to the side, and he heralded every new man who entered, saying his name and his clan.

He would then order, "In celebration of their marriage, make your presentation to your king and your future queen, Silence, Countess of the Arbor."

I noted that he mentioned my title, but he did not mention I was Dellish.

However, I knew this was not missed and not simply because it was already known.

Each man then laid a small chest or a pouch on the steps in front of Mars. After it was lain, with no ado, they bowed at the waist deeply, then walked out without a word spoken.

The men were known as barons and they were the heads of the various clans throughout Firenze.

There were seventeen of them.

I saw only two of them were elderly, most of them I approximated at around my father's age, and just three of them were Mars's age (which I had learned, that very day, was thirty-two).

Elpis warned me they did not all get along (a'tall).

Or support Mars as sovereign.

They were followed by the heads of the nomadic tribes which

roamed Firenze. They were referred to as chieftains. All of these men were either my father's age or older.

There were six of them.

They reportedly didn't get along either.

Or all support Mars.

For the barons, the presentations were anything from small chests of gold coins, diminutive chests of Firenz emeralds, amethysts, or topaz, or a pouch of Firenz rubies.

Altogether, or even separately, it was an extraordinary offering.

When the chieftains of the tribes came through, the presentations changed.

Chests of silver coins. Ceremonial daggers. And one tossed down two large hides of dense but short-haired fur from some animal I wished I'd seen before its hide was taken (and wished the hide wasn't taken—I had to admit, I could enjoy a thick fur on a cold Dellish night, but it still gave me a sorry feeling, so I tended to seek a blanket instead).

I did see some vague surprise, and even slight approval, that I wore my marital hoops.

But there was nothing but censure for my lovely gown.

As lovely as it was, it had been a mistake.

The Firenz knew of Dellish fashion and our bent to cover bodies.

The red gown I'd worn for the parade had been a success for it indicated my desire to adapt to my new country, to be a Firenz queen to my new king.

This one said the opposite.

It was odd, how something so inconsequential, for a woman especially, said so much.

His people probably wouldn't care in the slightest what Mars wore. Or True, Aramus, Cassius.

But me, somehow, I spoke volumes putting on a gown of which they disapproved.

This upset me.

Though it was also a lesson I learned well.

And I was glad I'd decided on a different wedding gown.

Perhaps I'd win a few of them the next evening.

Regardless of my misgivings, Mars had taught me a different lesson on our first meeting, and Elpis had reiterated it when she explained what would happen at this ceremony.

And my small part in it.

"You will be queen, Silence," she'd said, holding my hand and looking into my eyes. "Of Firenze. The throne is only as powerful as the man who sits it, his strength, his courage, his intelligence. And that includes the woman he chooses to sit by his side."

She squeezed my hand, got closer and finished.

"You meet eyes, *every* eye, Silence. These will be your people, but they will also be your subjects. You do not bow to them in *any* way. They bow to you. And that is all."

I'd nodded.

But in the moment, I found it difficult to meet the dark eyes and dark stares of the tall, formidable men standing before me.

Though I did it.

After the presentations were done, Mars took my hand as he had Farah's those days before when I'd first laid eyes on him, and he pulled me from the cushions.

He then tucked my hand to the side of his chest. I lifted my skirts with my free hand.

And we stepped down the three steps that led to the podium.

And as Ha-Lah met Aramus behind us, Farah met True, Elena met Cassius, and with Elpis at the lead after them, the others filed out in order of importance after the betrothed (Queen Ophelia, King Wilmer and Aunt Mercy, King Gallienus, Sofia, Serena, my mother and father, etc.) we headed into the hall for the short trek to the formal dining room.

"That wasn't so bad, no?" Mars murmured, clearly reading my mood.

"I wore the wrong gown," I murmured in return, very much not looking forward to sitting at the head of the room with all the other intendeds, being the center of attention.

Though it was more.

I felt something curious forming in the pit of my belly and I sensed it didn't have anything to do with what had happened during the presentations or what would happen next.

"Your gown is lovely," he replied.

He'd said my other gown was "becoming," and although one could argue the semantics of each word, one could not argue the tone in which he'd said them.

Yes, I was glad I designed a new wedding gown.

"You did well in there," he said, putting some pressure on my hand at his chest in a way that made me walk closer to him. "I am, as ever, proud of you, little monkey."

That made me feel better.

Under the eyes of many, we walked into the dining room. The barons and chieftains had been met by their wives, older children (as in my age) and lieutenants. There were other important personages about as well, and this meant the room was ten times as full as it had been the night of the betrothal dinner.

And I felt all eyes on me.

Mars guided me up the step where our long table was, and I was relieved to see the couples' seats this time were not separated. I would be sitting right next to Aramus, which meant closer to Ha-Lah, and this heartened me.

My wineglass was filled almost the second Mars finished pushing in my chair after I was seated.

I turned my eyes from my glass to the crowd that was also being served wine from servant boys who held trays laden with glasses. They were milling about, looking for their assigned seats, but also not surreptitiously watching me.

It was the first time, in this elegant room with its circular tables inlaid on top with tiny, square mother-of-pearl tiles that had mirrored trays filled with lit, red candles, tall poofs of exquisite red roses bunched close together in vases, and large silver chargers and gleaming silverware at each place setting, that I realized that Firenze was not the Firenze of Catrame Palace and the cosmopolitan Fire City.

It was the Firenze we'd traveled through to get there.

It was the Firenze of tales told through Triton.

The lines of camels, horses and people of the nomadic tribes trekking over the dunes.

The tent cities mixed with adobe buildings and open store fronts filled with lanterns, bright pots, bushels of grains, baskets of spices, fruits or vegetables, woven rugs, wicker wares (and the like), bustling with people.

It was tall, large, pierced, fierce men who wore leather kilts or short sarongs with thick belts at their waists which carried ornamented daggers. These were worn with fine shirts and mantles at their shoulders that went down to the backs of their knees.

And it was exotic, beautiful, lush women wearing bead and sequin and jewel-encrusted finery and sheers that exposed more than they covered, gold chains or elaborate pins or lavish flowers in their hair, dripping in jewelry and pierced magnificently, with large, dark eyes that spoke more than words could say.

It was a land that clashed with violent conflict amongst themselves.

A land that but decades ago was considered savage.

It was not mine.

It was not of me.

And I was being told, if not through deed, but instead by look, I did not belong there.

Definitely not at the side of their king.

I took a sip of wine on this troubling thought, my mind consumed with what I could do to change theirs.

My wedding gown was fabulous.

But it wouldn't win the love of an entire country.

Further, I had little time. I would be wed the next day. Mars and I had but a few days together (and I had a feeling that time would be busy, something I didn't think about or it would be unnerving as well as stimulating, neither of which I could focus on in the now).

This would be only two days before we were away on the long journey to Wodell to see Farah and True wed. Only for us to travel to Airen after that.

And who knew what could happen in the months their king and new queen, one not all supported, the other they didn't approve of, were away.

My mind was so consumed with these thoughts, when the curious feeling in the pit of my belly changed with no warning to something more extreme, I gasped.

"Silence?" Mars, hearing my gasp, called my name.

I put my wine down, composed my expression, and looked up to him.

"Are you all right?" he asked.

"Yes. I just thought of something I need to be sure to remember for the morrow," I lied.

He studied my face.

I hated lying but I didn't need to get into a discussion about suddenly feeling like something was burning through my stomach with Mars, who would be concerned, possibly in the extreme, maybe whisking me away to see to me, when I could absolutely not be whisked away in front of his people.

I certainly would not win this lot by being faint and queasy, unable to sit through even a dinner under their notice.

"Should I send a servant to share with your woman what you don't wish to forget?" Mars offered.

And that was my intended.

I might have a much bigger challenge on my hands for my future than I let the thrill of discovery of a fabulous palace, an exciting city and a handsome man I'd come to care about strongly in a short period of time blind me to the fullness of it.

But at least I had Mars.

So I gave him a smile. "It is such I won't again forget, Mars."

"Good," he murmured, leaned to me, touched his mouth to mine, and I allowed it because I liked the feel, his closeness, the spicy scent he had that night and the tickle of his beard.

I was smiling again, wider this time, when he pulled away.

His eyes twinkled as he took it in, and he turned to his wine.

I reached to mine as well, just when the burning came back.

Stronger this time.

But also, this time, I felt something else.

I turned my head left and saw Farah leaning forward, her gaze on me.

Nearly the instant I saw her, Ha-Lah leaned forward.

She looked to Farah, then to me.

After she caught my eyes, Ha-Lah looked beyond me.

I turned my head that way and Elena was leaned forward, her attention moving between all of us.

My heart squeezed so hard, I felt the blood racing from it all through me.

Because I knew it.

I knew exactly what I was feeling.

We were feeling.

We were Sisters of the Beast.

And the Beast was rising.

35

THE BEGINNING OF EVERYTHING

Lady Silence Mattson

Second Landing, Grand Stairwell, Catrame Palace, Fire City
FIRENZE

"Your rooms are *this way*, Silence," my father called sharply as Mars guided me right after we reached the landing, toward the west corridor, not left, toward my rooms.

I turned to glance over my shoulder at him.

Mars did as well.

"That they are," Mars replied, even if my father was speaking to me. "Goodnight, Johan," he finished pointedly.

"Goodnight, Papa. Mama," I called.

My mother, standing at my father's side, looked worried.

Father looked infuriated.

Neither bid us goodnight.

Mars turned to face forward and continued calmly to lead me that way.

I was not calm.

Dinner went without incident, and during it, Mars had stood and made a short toast to his barons and tribal leaders. He'd thanked them for their gifts, then promptly proclaimed they would, immediately after our wedding, be transferred to the treasury of Firenze to be used for the further advancement of the country. Or, in the case of ceremonial daggers (and such), they would be displayed at the Royal Museum in Fire City.

This caused a stir.

But Mars ignored it, turned to me, and finished the toast with, "And to my bride. My destiny. My future. May tomorrow come quickly." He then smiled a wolfish smile that could not be misconstrued he was speaking about the dinner, "But first, we will enjoy tonight."

I could not fight my blush.

This only made Mars smile bigger.

And that was one of only three times I felt anything remotely like approval from his people.

One was my wedding hoops, of course.

The other was when dinner was done and Piccola was brought to me.

Since I was given her, we found our times to play and I made sure Tril allowed me to feed her, for I wished her to know who her mama was.

I couldn't say she was as yet used to me.

But in that crowded room, she clung close to my finger or my neck, and I was glad of her presence, not to mention her providing distraction.

And apparently, even if hides were tossed on thronal steps, my maternal instincts to a monkey were looked upon favorably.

She was still with me, clutching the scallops at the side of my neckline while I stroked her tiny back as we walked to Mars's rooms.

She wouldn't be with me very much longer, for as we drew closer to his chambers, Mars called out, "Take Piccola from your future queen."

The lingering servant boy rushed to me as I disengaged my pet from my gown.

Mars stopped us, and I brought her up to my face.

Her face was teeny-tiny.

But her black eyes were *so smart*.

"Until breakfast, my wee one," I murmured and brushed her against my cheek.

She made a chirrup in response before I handed her off.

The boy headed the other way and Mars instantly started us moving again.

And thus, I instantly had something new to worry about.

I did not tell him about the feeling in my belly that I knew I shared with the others.

It came.

It was strong.

But once we all recognized it amongst each other, it was gone.

I'd watched and noted that none of the others shared with their betrotheds either.

Thus, I decided I would call us all together early on the morrow to discuss it before I discussed it in full with Mars, sharing with him as well what the others thought.

Now I had what lay next to consider.

Mars moved us into his chambers, shutting the door behind us, and I immediately noticed that they were much changed.

Low lamps at each corner of the pool were lit, but the chandelier above it and the lanterns on tables were not, as they had been when I was there the night before.

Also, a soft glow came from the sitting room-cum-study, but it was not beckoning, as it had been before. It was dim and signified retiring, not working, reading or communing.

But Mars had no interest in either room.

I knew this as he guided me straight to his bedchamber.

He moved the sheers aside for us both and led us in, declaring, "You shouldn't worry."

There were so many things to worry about, I didn't know to which he was referring.

"About what?" I queried as he let me go when we were fully in the room.

He put his hands to the black, sleeveless, long-tailed jacket that was over the black silk shirt he wore.

He shrugged it off.

My mouth got dry.

"The clans and the tribes," he answered. "And what they think of you."

He then turned and moved toward the archway to his dressing room.

I stood rooted to where he left me.

Unable to move, I was fortunately not unable to speak.

"Why do you say that?"

He'd not disappeared behind the sheers that covered the archway, I could see his shadow moving in the dimly-lit space.

And thus, I watched as he tossed his jacket to the daybed.

"Because they don't think much of me."

"Your mama shared they did not all support you."

"Not all," he agreed, as I watched his hands move to the buttons of his shirt. "Only three."

This surprised me.

"Three?"

"Three. My direct clan. The royal clan my father's side was born of. Also, my maternal clan. The one my mother is descended from. And last, Sofia's clan."

I had noticed that last for certain.

That night, Sofia and Farah finally were shown some support. At least from one quarter. A clan headed by a man my father's age who, along with his wife, and what Mars had shared were his son and daughter, looked on Farah kindly as she sat at the head table. They sat with Sofia, drawing her into discussion warmly.

I had been wrong earlier, I'd felt approval one other time.

Coming from Sofia's table, her clan, after they noticed that I engaged in a friendly way with Farah.

"I was glad to see Sofia amongst her own," I told him.

"Indeed," he replied, shrugging off his shirt and tossing it aside. "Particularly since they're a powerful clan. Outside my direct line, the most powerful in the realm."

His hands then went to his trousers.

Oh my *faith*.

I turned away.

"Why was the...um, announcement you'd be giving the offerings to your country such a surprise?" I asked.

"Such has never been done."

This I didn't find surprising, for if Wilmer was younger and just wedding Mercy, I knew he would not hesitate to put such in his own chest.

"They must surely be glad for the advancements," I noted, staring at his bed, which probably was not a good place to set my eyes.

Therefore, I moved them to the short, mirrored dresser by his bed.

Better.

"The nomads don't care. They roam. Educate their own. Worship on their rugs under the sun. Practice their own healing techniques. Fight their own fights. When there is war for Firenze, it is rare they send their men."

"Ah," I mumbled loudly when he didn't continue speaking.

"The clans, they vacillate depending on where I decide to focus currency. If it's the betterment of their schools and hospitals, building temples and monuments in their towns and cities, which means their people are laboring and receiving the crowns' coin, they are happy. They do not understand the creation of straight, easily traversed roads or irrigation of rivers, which is something my father started, and I continue. But if it is their people remunerated for it, they do not complain. But if it is that of others…"

He did not finish, but I understood.

"They keep a close eye and protest favoritism frequently," Mars concluded.

"Do you play favorites?" I asked, only for something to say because I couldn't imagine he did.

His voice was getting closer when he replied as I expected, "No."

I turned to his voice.

He was in his silky panel pants, this pair a deep burgundy.

Chest bare.

Piercings shining in the much more lit (but still less lit than the time I'd been there before) room.

All right, maybe I wasn't ready to learn more of what marriage would mean between Mars and me.

It would seem I didn't have a choice.

For he came direct to me, took my hand, and walking slowly, he led me to the bed.

I gulped down saliva from a suddenly full mouth.

At the top of the steps, he turned, sat on the edge of his bed, opened his long legs and guided me to standing in between.

He then took up my other hand, and holding both, tipped his head back to look up at me.

"You are nervous," he whispered.

I stared into dark eyes that were soft with tenderness and empathy.

And I felt the tension ease from my shoulders.

"A little," I whispered in return.

"We will kiss more, my bride. And that is all if that is all you're ready for." He pulled me the tiniest bit closer. "And know this, Silence, for I refer to tonight and tomorrow and for as long as you need to get used to this intimacy we will share. I am ready. I desire you. I want to know your taste. Your mysteries. But if you are not, that means *we* are not. Is this something you understand?"

It was.

It was something I understood.

And something I found incredibly generous.

And beautiful.

"Yes," I answered.

"Then kiss me, Silence, and guide our way tonight."

Could I kiss him?

He let my hands go and sat there, his eyes steady on me, our time together brief, just a snatch in what I hoped would be a lifetime of knowing each other.

But he had shown me nothing but interest, respect, kindness, protectiveness, gentleness and desire.

Thus, I bent forward, resting my hands on his broad shoulders, feeling the heat of his body, the power of his muscles, and dropped my lips to his.

Mars allowed this.

But he did not take hold on my body.

He did not press anything from me.

That was when I touched the tip of my tongue to his lips.

They opened.

I slid inside.

He tasted warm and musky and delicious.

He also made a low noise I felt in regions south of my belly.

So I pressed my lips harder to his, tilting my head, sliding my hand up into his hair at the back.

He put both hands to my hips.

I liked their weight. Their warmth. The steadying feel of them.

I didn't know how, but nevertheless, I made an attempt to coax his tongue into my mouth.

Mars didn't make me work at it.

He gave it to me.

I sucked it deeper.

And gods, but I loved that stud in his tongue.

A lower, rougher noise rumbled into my mouth as his tongue played with mine.

I gave him more of my weight in my hand at his shoulder, this resulting in his hands sliding to the small of my back, one gliding up my spine.

I liked his touch.

So much, I trembled. And it was a trembling that felt marvelous to me.

I bent my elbow and gave him more weight.

Mars fell back, wrapping his arms around me, so I fell with him, to land on his chest.

Oh.

All that hard man beneath me.

So, so...

Lovely.

I lifted my lips from his and whispered, "Mars."

He rolled me so I was on my back and he was partially on me.

Oh.

My.

So lovely, that hard man *on* me.

"Mars," I breathed.

And he kissed me.

It was deeper, sweeter, his hands roaming my sides, my hips, my ribs.

I pressed up into him, trying to share I wanted more.

He in turn pressed into me and I felt it. Something I might fear, but in that moment, with him as he was, us as we were, I did not.

It made me feel powerful and beautiful and womanly.

So I met the hardness at his hips with my body, arching into it.

"Silence," he growled against my lips.

"Mars," I whispered against his.

We were looking into each other's eyes.

I noticed some unusual red in his that had to be a reflection from a lantern before whatever question he was asking was answered and I took more of his weight.

I also got his mouth back.

His tongue.

And this was no longer a gentle, exploratory dance.

There was hunger.

I knew what it was instantly.

And it was utterly *enchanting*.

I met it with mouth and touch, our tongues dueling, my hands wandering the skin of his back, tracking the slopes, riding the dips, not discovering, *claiming*.

He rolled off, pulling me up, righting us in bed, falling to his back and drawing me over him.

And there was *so much* of him.

I'd had his mouth.

I wanted more.

I dipped my head and took his flat, brown nipple.

"*Fuck*," he grunted.

Oh no.

I'd done something wrong.

My head shot up.

His hands came under my arms and yanked me up before he took my mouth again, his fingers diving into my hair. I could feel the pins loosen, the curls falling, the ribbon sliding out, but only vaguely.

My betrothed was not hungry.

Now he was *starving*.

And feeling that from him, knowing I made him that way, he took me there with him.

I explored his neck.

He explored mine.

My hands were urgent on him.

His hands were urgent on the buttons on the back of my gown.

His lips at my ear, he groused, "How many of these bloody things are there?"

"Too many," I breathed.

And there were.

Way too many.

My skin felt hot, burning.

The dress had to go.

He sat up and I came up with him, straddling his hips, my knees fighting material.

He tugged at my skirts.

I did too.

"Fucking *acres*," he grumbled.

I almost giggled.

I didn't giggle.

My skin was far too hot.

I needed that dress *off me*.

And Mars *on me*.

Immediately.

Eventually I pulled it away at the neckline and lifted it up.

Mars helped me, pulling it higher.

I raised my arms and he gathered the folds, freed me of it, tossed it aside...

And I sat astride him in nothing but my white lace corset and panties.

Suddenly, I needed my dress back.

Until Mars's eyes fell to my body.

That red came back, and I felt my brows titch together at the sight before I was thinking nothing.

I was on my back and Mars was at my side, drawing my panties down my legs.

"Mars," I called tremblingly.

He looked from my legs to my face.

And his eyes were *afire*.

"I promise," he stated gutturally.

I didn't know what he promised.

I just knew he meant it.

I nodded.

He shifted down, rolled over one of my legs, moving the other aside, then he...he...

Gently pressed them apart, dropped his head...

And he *fed from me*.

The touch of his mouth was such beauty, the stroke of that studded tongue sheer bliss, my back bowed, my toes curled, I cried out, unable to contain the pleasure I was experiencing.

Mars tossed my legs over his shoulders, spanned my hips in his big hands, and bore down on me.

"Oh, by the gods," I breathed, raking my nails through his hair against his scalp, holding the gloriousness of what he was doing to me, "Oh gods, Mars. Don't stop. Please, don't stop."

But then, it happened.

I dug my heels into his back as I fought the greatness of the sensations that seemed both awesome and threatening.

"Please. You need to..." I began, but before I could complete that with *stop*, it overtook me.

Engulfed me.

I bucked under him as fire consumed me, my body, my sex, my vision, my mind. I was writhing in an inferno of pleasure and ecstasy.

No.

Not consumed.

I was feeding from the flames.

I did not know such existed. I did not know this was something to be had.

What I knew then was that I adored it with every part of me, now that I'd had it.

Vaguely, when I started simply drifting in their heat, I felt Mars lapping at me gently.

This before he moved up my body, kissing my belly. My midriff. My chest. The base of my throat.

And then his weight was on me, warming, heavy, but not over-whelming, and his beard tickled my neck as his mouth moved there.

Should I be embarrassed about what just happened?

If I should, at that moment, I did not have it in me.

Mars kissed below my ear where his hoop at the lobe pierced me.

And his voice was lovely and gruff when he said, "I think we'll stop there for tonight."

I was glad of this because I was not certain I could move.

I was wrong.

When he ordered, "Put your arms around me, Silence," I did as told. And when he continued, "Wrap your legs around mine," I did that too.

He was wise.

This was better.

So much better.

His mouth moved on my neck, his fingers coasted on my bare hip, and I could tell he was holding some of his weight in his other forearm. I knew that because, with the way he was touching me, the way he wanted me wrapped around him, if he could use that hand to touch me more, he would do it.

I felt little under him.

Tiny.

But knowing how much he enjoyed the feel of me, I also felt precious.

"No," he whispered to my throat on his way around to the other side of my neck. "It does not matter if the clans and tribes like you."

He lifted his head and I gazed up at his handsome face dazedly.

"Because I like you," he finished.

"I like you too," I mumbled.

He grinned. "You demonstrated that."

"I'm afraid I'm brazen," I admitted.

His big body moved on mine for a time before his chuckle was audible.

"I'm not afraid, *piccolina.* This makes me happy."

"Well, it would," I muttered.

He just smiled down at me affectionately.

I kept muttering for I had the ability to do no more. "Your weight feels nice."

"This is good, you'll be feeling it a great deal."

I shivered.

His smile got bigger.

"And you are very warm," I told him.

"This is all well for you, my Silence. Our days are hot, our nights are cold."

"I've noticed that."

"Silence?"

"Yes?"

He took his hand from my hip so he could use his thumb to brush across my cheekbone.

And then he said, "Thank you."

That was what he said.

I felt like I would cry.

His head came toward mine, but when I thought he'd kiss me (and it must be said, I very much wanted him to kiss me), he slid his bristly cheek down my smooth one and continued in my ear, "Your trust means much to me. I treasure it. More than any chest of gold or pouch of jewels. Your pleasure, so freely offered, means much to me too, and I treasure it as well. Not as much as your trust, but it's important you know it means a great deal to me."

Yes, I definitely could cry.

"Mars," I whispered.

"We will choose wisely when we bring others to our bed."

I blinked at the dark overhang.

"But at first, for a time, I will only have you before I take another. And you will only have me before I allow another to have you."

Others?

To have him?

And me?

Oh gods.

The Firenz way of marriage.

No.

"Now," he stated, lifted his head, touched his mouth to mine, then angled up, taking me with him, "it is time to get you to your own bed before I get further ideas."

He pulled me off his bed, toward where he tossed my gown.

And I moved with him.

Automatically.

He snatched up my panties and handed them to me.

I suddenly felt entirely exposed and quickly bent to step into them.

When I straightened after smoothing them over my hips, I saw he was wrestling with the "acres" of material of my gown.

"Mars, um...the others," I began.

He turned to me with the skirts of my gown bunched in a way he could pull it over my head.

Which was what he did, forcing me to struggle my arms through the dress to get to the top opening.

It would seem he had practice doing such as that.

My belly twisted.

He performed this task while speaking.

"I will take arse for you, if that's what you desire to see. Though it is not normally my choice. I am like Lorenz. If it tantalizes you, it will do the same for me. Though the Trusted, you should know, Silence, are not available to you, except Basil, if he is to your wanting, for he will not take you, only me. But if there is a warrior of mine..."

He trailed off, turning me after I shoved my hands through the sleeves, and he began to close the buttons at my back.

I was staring at the lit lamp on the dresser on that side of his bed, my gaze drifting, noticing in the peach of the walls there was a slightly darker motif that was barely discernible.

It looked like cherry blossoms.

Or blossoms of something.

When done with my buttons, he turned me again and framed my neck in his hands.

"Do you understand this?" he asked, staring down at me.

I did not.

Not any of it.

"Yes," I murmured.

He smiled and noted, "I must remember this stupor you fall into after climaxing. It is very endearing, but should I not finish with you, the wait would be excruciating."

Climax.

So that was what it was called.

Apropos.

Truly.

"I will endeavor to...next time...recover much more quickly," I stated, sounding stilted and not myself.

He bent, touched his lips to mine, then to my nose, my forehead, before he moved away a spare inch, again smiling at me.

"Don't. If I can move you so deeply that you behave like an undead, I will then go out and slay a dragon."

"Slay a dragon?"

His gaze warmed (or further warmed). "Your pleasure empowers me, *piccolina*."

That was nice.

Not as nice as it should have been.

But it was nice.

"I will walk you to your room, my monkey," he offered. "I would do it regardless, but you might lose your way in this state."

This should have been amusing.

I did not laugh.

"Your slippers, Silence," he remarked.

I blinked up at him.

He twisted at the waist and reached into the bed, rescuing my slippers that had fallen off.

He then dropped to a knee in front of me, and I lifted my skirts and offered my feet one by one as he slipped them on.

I watched the bigness of him, the power of him, all of it bowed to me and did it again thinking I might weep.

But once he had my feet shod, he did just as he said he would, straightening, tucking my hand against his chest and starting us across the room.

"Basil?" I forced out.

"Yes. He only takes men."

"I know, but he's your lieutenant."

"Yes, and they have all had each other. It's part of the ceremony to become a Trusted. The bonds formed through such intimacy and knowing of the other, it's crucial to that brotherhood. All my warriors engage this way. Freely. And it's encouraged they do. But I would not want one of my men to look on you with desire. This would not promote bonding. And Basil would not do that."

They have all had each other.

And Mars would have Basil with me there, if I desired it.

And he would have other women, if he desired it.

Other women, not me.

Other women he'd put his mouth between their legs giving them what he just gave me.

Women who were not me.

And put other things between their legs.

Legs that were not mine.

"Silence?" he called, and when he did, I realized we were well down the hall.

I looked up at him.

His expression grew gentle, and with us still walking, he bent and kissed the top of my head.

When he straightened, he murmured, "My bride has had a full night. I must get her to bed so she will be ready for her next."

It was true.

I'd had a full night.

But right then, I had a full head.

I was in Firenze.

I would be their queen.

Which was their king's wife.

This was what they did.

I'd heard this whispered about and I remembered my mother saying they were not faithful to their spouses.

But I had forgotten.

And at the piercing ceremony, it was spoken of the intimacy of listening to, thinking of, being honest with your husband.

Nothing, however, was mentioned about the body. These intimacies were solely of the heart and mind.

That was all.

I hadn't thought about it then.

I was thinking about it now.

At my door, Mars took me in his arms and kissed me deeply, and for a glorious moment, I forgot what I'd just remembered.

I remembered again when he broke away and said, "I'll see you at breakfast, *amore*."

"Yes," I replied.

"Goodnight, my Silence."

"Goodnight, Mars." Oh dear. What was etiquette? There had to be some etiquette after someone gave you a climax. "And thank you too," I tried.

That got another big smile and dancing eyes before he replied, "Anytime," his lips again came to mine, and he growled, "as often as you like, *mio ardente.*"

He brushed our lips, lifted away, opened my door, and scooted me through himself with a hand at my behind.

Like the night before, he was gazing down at me indulgently as I closed the door on him.

When I had it closed, I rested my forehead against it.

I felt Tril coming toward me.

"Silence, are you all right? Did things go well with your groom?"

"I would...like to prepare for bed on my own tonight, Tril," I said quietly to the door.

I felt her hand light on my back.

"Oh no, my girl," she whispered, sounding distraught. "Did he hurt you?"

"No, it was beautiful."

"Your hair is disheveled. Did he—?"

"Please, Tril," I begged.

"I don't—"

I turned my head to her. "Can you unbutton me? And then I need to be at my thoughts."

Her face screwed up. "Did he scare you?"

"No."

"Silence, love, talk to me."

I shook my head. "I just really need to think. Tonight was quite a bit. This country is not a'tall like our own, Tril. And tonight, that was made very clear to me."

She examined my face, fortunately found what she needed to find, then nodded.

"I shall help you with your buttons. Come to the dressing room. Let's get you sorted. And then, if you should need me, as ever, I am right next door."

I loved my Tril.

She took my hand and we walked together to the dressing room.

And just like Tril, she gave me what I needed, unbuttoning my gown and leaving me.

I saw to my toilette, donned a nightgown, and entered my room, seeing that Tril had left only the lamps by my bed to blow out.

I did this one by one, then stretched out under the silks, staring at the dark ceiling.

I had nothing to give.

I came with a dowry Mars did not need for he had gold and silver and jewels and hides laid at his feet.

I had no palace.

I had no title he would want.

I certainly had no kingdom.

I was but a girl with a little bit of magic that prophecy foretold might do something extraordinary.

At the side of her king.

It wasn't even just *me* who would do it.

But me being a part of Mars, and a part of six others.

I was not nothing.

I was also not anything.

I had never been anything.

Not really.

No friends.

Few suitors.

Even my father only found use for me after twenty-three years when a curse seemed to be brewing under the earth.

And Mars had told me that he would like only me for a time.

And then he wanted others.

And he would have them because he was Firenz. He was king. This was his country, his world, his way.

I would have to watch him with other women, touching them as he touched me, kissing them as he kissed me, putting his mouth where he'd given me so much that night.

The world was indeed upside down.

The Beast rising.

Cassius's regency.

Carrington's conniving.

A Nadirii to be wed to an Airenzian.

Two Dellish to be wed to Firenz.

But through that, I had Mars.

And going forth, I would still have him.

But he wouldn't be mine.

I had come to Firenze with nothing that was mine.

And, even wed to a powerful king, I would go forward with nothing that was *mine*.

On that thought, the tears started falling.

And with them still rolling down my temples, I turned to my side, curled into myself, let them flow, and fell asleep with only their company.

ALL MY LIFE, I did not sleep well even in my bed in the Arbor.

Though, after the first days there, I had slept well in my bed in Catrame Palace.

Therefore, I did not know what woke me that night. Feeling distressed. Unsettled. Restless after weeping.

I was just glad I did.

Even if it changed everything.

Everything about me.

Everything about *everything*.

But my only other choice of outcome that night was not to be abided.

It was the whisper of the screen at the window being set down that I heard.

But it was the feel of the air that made me freeze.

This before I shouted shrilly, *"Tril! Get help!"*

I then rolled off the bed in the opposite direction to where I heard the noise (which was sadly farther away from the door).

I landed on my knees, my hand at the same time reaching to the dresser beside the bed where I kept a small dagger True had given me.

It had a beautifully veined malachite in the hilt.

And True had told me never to be without it.

I didn't carry it on my person.

But I always kept it close, mostly, until that moment, simply because it had been a gift from True.

"Get help, Tril!" I yelled, hoping to all the gods she heard me, starting to open the drawer.

I didn't get my hand on the dagger.

A man was on me.

I screamed as he threw me to my back, straddled me, his hands closing around my neck.

It was then I choked, clawed at his arms, kicked out my feet, bucked my hips, my mouth wide open, trying to pull in breath.

I tried to twist, to turn, vaguely hearing feet hit floor.

Coming in the window.

Not just him.

Others.

I opened and closed my mouth, fighting for breath and fighting to scream.

And I heard the loud, welcome clang of steel hitting steel.

Tril got help.

Oh, I loved my Tril.

The room filled with coral light, like a starburst, before it started fading, and the sounds of a swordfight renewed my strength.

And as another starburst filled the air, more sounds of steel clashing rang through it, I focused all my concentration on getting those hands from my neck, when suddenly, I felt a thrill up my spine.

One I didn't call.

And the man straddling me grunted in surprise before he released me.

I drew in a much-needed, burning breath.

The man above me was lifting his hands in the front of him.

This right before they burst into flame.

I would have stared in shock.

But this was a scant second before his head left his shoulders.

Blood sprayed over me before the heavy weight of his headless body fell on me.

It was almost instantly shoved off, I had a hand wrenching my upper arm, pulling me up, and I heard Elena shouting, "Run, Silence, *run!*"

In another coral starburst, she let me go, but I stood frozen at all that was happening. Thus, I saw her engage with a man taller and larger than her, he was dressed in all black, a mask covered his head and face, all but his eyes, their swords slicing through the air, and connecting.

And another starburst showed Serena at the end of the bed, engaged with two men wearing black.

As well as Ophelia inside the door, seemingly holding four back.

Aramus rushed past Ophelia, a long saber in one hand, a curved blade that looked like a handheld sickle in the other. He arrived slashing with one and stabbing with the other at anything moving that wore black.

And the room was filled with men wearing black.

With more coming in the window.

The one Elena was fighting fell to the ground at my feet and she screamed, *"Silence, run!"* as she leaped on the bed, dashed across it, jumped off and engaged a villain on the other side.

It was then, True stormed in with broadsword swinging.

Which was when I turned to my dresser, yanked open the drawer, pulled out the dagger, and as Elena had done, I leaped on the bed (likely not as gracefully), nearly fell over running across it...

I then stabbed the man she was fighting in the shoulder, yanked it out, stabbed again and again, quickly.

He bellowed, turned, a beefy arm struck me, and I slammed into the headstead, cracking my skull against the wall.

Elena took that opportunity to gut him.

Another coral flash filled the room, and vaguely I realized how clever that was as I was temporarily blinded with it, just as anyone but the Nadirii surely were. It gave them a view of the room at the same time crippling their opponents, if momentarily, still effectively.

I saw in the waning flash the man Elena gutted slumping forward.

Another kill for the Nadirii.

Oh gods.

However, he did this as a man who'd just come through the window at Elena's back began to raise his broadsword two-handed toward the ceiling.

I opened my mouth to scream a warning...

But an animal roar exploded through the room as the very air lit with the stars of a clear sky in midnight.

Cassius had entered the fray, fighting toward Elena.

But thank the gods, True was already there.

He caught the downward swing aimed at the Nadirii.

She whirled, and as True held the villain's sword high with his own, she jerked her arm back and speared the rogue through the stomach, drawing up.

In that moment, I let out a screech as I was torn from the bed, an arm around my throat from the back, that arm dragging me rearward.

I lifted my dagger over my shoulder and brought it down, again experiencing the sickening feeling as it stabbed through the flesh of his shoulder.

He dropped me, and I was unprepared, so when my weight hit my ankles, they gave way and I fell to my knees.

Steel clashed.

Men and Nadirii grunted.

Coral flashed in the air.

The stars sparkled midnight as the edges of the room started to creep with trails of a peculiar green, like vines unfurling, and I was sure to be going mad as we were nowhere near water, but I could swear I heard waves crashing.

The man had bent to me, and I dropped to a hand to evade him, stabbing him in his calf.

He howled, caught my hair, pulled me up, and I cried out again, this time in pain as he started dragging me toward a screened window just as the screen burst forth and another man wearing black surged through.

"Silence!" True shouted.

I did the only thing I could do.

I struck out at everything with my dagger, catching flesh, but not nearly enough.

He was almost to the window, lifting me by my hair as if to throw me out.

This was when the green disappeared.

The stars blinked out.

The coral starbursts ceased.

The sound of crashing waves ended.

And the room lit brightly.

It lit blood red with what appeared to be eruptions of licks of flame.

Licks of flame that erupted *in midair*.

This happened right before a loud, thunderous snarl rent the air.

The man who had me froze.

It seemed the whole world froze.

And then Mars was there. His big body two-fisting a gigantic sword, he twisted at the waist and let fly, cutting the man who had me *in half*.

In.

Half.

Torso plummeting one way, hips and legs falling the other, obviously his grip on my hair released, and thus, Mars caught me under my arm and swung me so I was on his back.

I curled around, arms at his neck, legs at his hips, holding so tight, I dropped my dagger, thinking his intent was to take me away from this madness.

But with mighty swings of his sword in the crimson light, he cut through everything wearing black.

Everything.

I heard an enraged female cry and turned my head in its direction, fearing Elena, Serena or Ophelia had been harmed, only to see Cassius had hold of Elena at his front. He was fighting his way to the door as well as fighting her, for she was struggling like a hellcat to get out of his hold.

He made it to the door and she emitted an outraged scream as, with a mighty heave, he threw her out.

Bodily.

I saw no more as Mars swung around, carving through flesh—arms, thighs, middles, necks, men dropping in pieces, littering the floor.

He just climbed over them to get to the next one.

And the next.

I shoved my face in his neck.

He kept killing.

The nauseating thuds stopped, the grunts of effort, the ones of pain, the clangs of steel, and I realized Mars's chest was heaving under my arms, but he'd stopped moving.

I lifted my head.

We were in the hall.

All of us.

Elena and Cassius.

A covered-in-blood Ophelia with an equally blood-soaked Serena standing not close but not far from her mother.

True, also covered in blood (as were Elena and Cassius, by the way), stood with Farah, who did not mind the blood. Her front was pressed to True's side, both her arms around him.

Aramus was in the same state, Ha-Lah to his front, pressing herself there tightly, her arms about his waist, his about her shoulders.

Chu, Kyril, several of Cassius's and Aramus's men, as well as True's lieutenants Wallace, Luther and Florian. All held bloody swords or daggers.

And down the hall I saw some of the barons and chieftains, also holding swords, some of their blades blood-stained.

Tril was pressed to the wall opposite, wearing her nightgown, both her hands covering her mouth as if she was trying not to be sick.

Or holding back a scream.

Queen Elpis was approaching on a rush from the end of the hall, Guard, who I suspected had been holding her back, followed her.

King Wilmer's head was peeking out his door, but Aunt Mercy was standing in the hallway.

My father was out, my mother was still within, and I couldn't see her.

Carrington as well was only sticking his head out his chamber door.

Men wearing black lay where they died on the ground, though they were but a small trail that went along the hall. Maybe a couple dozen.

A few more.

Two dozen dead men.

Or a few more.

I looked back to my room.

The floor was covered in bodies (and parts of them).

The red hue was gone.

I was going to be sick.

Or scream.

My arms loosened.

Until Mars growled, "Do not *fucking* let go."

I thought it prudent to hold tight.

"Get Lorenz," he ordered curtly.

Chu turned and sprinted down the hall.

"They came through the windows?" he asked Kyril.

"I'll get a report," Kyril answered, turned and ran down the hall.

"If there are more, I want one of them alive!" Mars shouted after him.

Kyril just lifted a hand to indicate he'd heard and disappeared around the corner to the stairs.

"If this is you, I'll watch you walk to the pit, and so will your queen *and* mine," Mars went on, his voice terrible in its quiet fury.

I looked to his profile to see his eyes aimed at my uncle.

"I would never." My uncle, realizing the threat was over, stepped into the hall.

"Yes, you would, and if you wouldn't, your counsellor would," Mars ground out.

Uncle Wilmer's face got red.

"Slander!" Carrington shouted, also stepping into the hall.

"We shall see," Mars bit out.

"Can I let go?" I asked softly.

"Fucking *no*," Mars answered, not even turning his head to look at me.

I held on.

"Where's Sofia?" Elpis asked.

I went still.

Mars went solid.

Farah let True go and raced down the hall.

"Farah!" True shouted, racing after her.

She got there before True, threw open the door...

And let out a blood-chilling scream that set my veins in ice.

She then started to dash in only for True to catch her about the waist and pull her back.

It was then Mars moved, pulling me from his back, tossing me toward Luther, who caught me, and he did this lifting a finger in True's man's face and warning, "Harm comes to her, you die."

He then stalked True and Farah's way.

Finally, my feet were again to the ground.

Though they were to the ground about a foot away from where a dead man lay.

"Close the door," True ordered Cassius, who had arrived next.

I saw Elena peer around Cassius and pale.

"*Close the bloody door!*" True bellowed, having trouble containing a now hysterical Farah.

Mars arrived in time to look in as Cassius stepped in what seemed cautiously, holding Elena back with a strong arm, and closed the door.

"I swear to the bloody goddess, Cassius—" she began, her voice trembling with fury.

"We'll talk later," Cassius grunted.

"We *fucking* will," Elena threatened.

But I was watching Mars.

His head was bowed, his eyes closed.

My heart sunk.

He looked...

Grieved.

Elpis had made it to them, and she had her hands on Farah, trying to help True soothe her, but her attention was on her son.

"Mars?" she asked tremulously as Basil came jogging down the hall.

Mars looked right to him.

"Get a bloody snake charmer," he bit out.

Basil halted, his head jerking in shock, then he walked backward four steps before turning and jogging again, this time the other way.

"A bloody dozen of them!" Mars shouted at his back.

Snakes?

Farah collapsed to the floor.

Elpis went down with her, pulling her in her arms, tears falling down her cheeks, shushing noises coming from her lips.

I pulled at Luther's arms.

"Countess," he murmured.

I looked up at him.

"Farah," I whispered.

He made the correct decision at the expression on my face, took my arm and guided me to her.

I got down on my knees and did my best to pull both her and Elpis into my arms, for they'd collapsed into each other, sobbing.

But I glanced up when Cassius murmured, "Aramus," as Aramus opened the door to Sofia's chamber.

A black snake with emerald eyes slithered toward freedom only to be caught on the tip of Aramus's sickle, picked up but an inch only to fall in two parts from the honed blade.

Where it separated, there was a weak spark of yellow light.

He did the same with another one.

And got the spark.

And another.

With spark.

Magic.

I looked beyond his bulky body.

Only to see the bed covered in slithering, glistening black bodies, unblinking emerald eyes, and Sofia all but buried under them, staring unseeing at the ceiling.

I closed my eyes tight.

"Cassius, don't you go in—" Elena started.

I opened my eyes only to see the door close on Cassius with Elena on this side.

I saw movement and turned my gaze toward it.

Mars was crouching by a body in black, pulling the tight-fitting hood off, lifting the head by its dark hair and staring at the face.

Still holding it, his eyes came to me.

And they were what I thought was a trick of the light earlier.

But it was no trick.

They were twin flames burning into me.

I had never been afraid of him.

Not really.

I knew that then.

Because in that moment, he terrified me.

"You will now, my little monkey," he started, his voice a physical thing, slithering at me threateningly like one of those emerald-eyed snakes, "learn what it truly means to be *a Firenz*."

I held the women sobbing against me, but now I did it trembling.

It was then, I swayed powerfully back, Farah and Elpis swaying with me, Ha-Lah, who was moving toward us, throwing her arms out to catch her balance.

The floor moved more, more, shaking us, the walls, the chandeliers in the ceilings.

The door to Sofia's room burst open and Cassius and Aramus surged out, Aramus slamming it behind him, Cassius's long arms snatching Elena to him as Aramus raced to Ha-Lah.

This while True crouched over Farah, Elpis and me.

But Mars moved to me with long, sure strides, plucking me up, turning me into him, bending and lifting my legs as his knees buckled.

He fell to his rear, curling over me with his body and holding me tight just as plaster disengaged from the ceiling and started raining down on us.

I heard cries, people scurrying, a chandelier down the hall crashing to the floor.

And then it came, low at first, but it grew, built, filling the air around us so full, you were breathing it in.

It was like thunder rumbling up from below, shaking the dirt, the palace, the very *planet* as we were enveloped in low to louder and then to a final deafening, *enraged* roar that was so earsplitting, so terrifying, I forced my hands through the small amount of space between Mars and me and covered my ears.

It did not stop suddenly.

It ran down, decreasing in volume as the quaking around us settled.

Until both at the same time were gone.

That was the worst.

The worst quake *by far*.

And we'd never, not once, heard that roar.

Mars curled up, still holding me close to his chest.

I looked to him.

He was looking at True.

I turned to True, only to catch Farah's wide eyes on me.

They flashed topaz.

"The Beast is almost here," Queen Ophelia whispered.

Oh.

Gods.

The End of Part One
The Rising Series continues with The Plan Commences.

THE RISING SERIES GLOSSARY

Terms, Words, Places

Abhainn Mouth – (AH-been) (n/place): Harbor city in the north of Airen located at the mouth of the Dunleth Abhainn (river).

Abyss (the) – (n/place): Large "bottomless" hole in the rock of a cliff on the coast of Mar-el fifteen miles down the coast from Nautilus, the capital city of Mar-el.

Airen – (Air-EN) (n/place): Country of Airen located in the northeast of the Triton mainland. The northernmost area is barren and craggy and made up of great boulders of black rock. The rest is mountainous or fertile and green, mostly pastureland, forests and rolling hills.

Airenzian – (Air-EN-zee-an) (adj.): Of Airen.

Alabasta – (Al-ah-BASS-tah) (goddess): Of Wodell. Goddess of Wisdom and the Earth. A goddess shared with Lunwyn in The Northlands.

Amphite – (Am-FITE) (n/place): Underwater capital of the Mer. Location of royal palace of King of the Mer.

Ancient Ritual Ground – (n/place): Area in the Lesser Thicket Forest of the country of Wodell where rituals were (are) conducted, including human sacrifice.

Argyll Forest – (n/place): Forest on the western border of Airen, butting The Enchantments, the city-state of Go'Doan and Wodell. The parts of it in Wodell are known as the Lesser Thicket Forest. Location of the Silbury Henge.

Ashesh – (Ash-EHSH) (n): Drug akin to opium. Available throughout Triton. Grown in Firenze.

Angmostros – (Aing-MO-stros) (n/creature): Sea creatures in the shape of enormous eels, some one hundred yards long, with two heads with long necks, very large mouths and very sharp teeth.

Aviast – (Ay-VEE-ast) (n): Keeper of a loft of ravens used for sending messages.

Bayzian – (Bay-ZEE-an) (n): Citizens of Sky Bay, the capital of Airen.

Birchlire Castle – (Birch-LEER) (n/place): Home of the King of Wodell. Located in Notting Thicket.

Bishop Cross – (n/island): Island off the southeast coast of the country of Airen. Temperate, but barren and very remote.

Bloody Boy Cove – (n/place): Deep cove to the north, across the wide bay (and hidden from sight) from Nautilus, in Mar-el.

Body stocking – (n): Worn by the Nadirii under tunics. More like a leotard or bathing suit. Can be tank/spaghetti strap/long-sleeved/strapless at top. Regular cut or high cut at the hips.

Bounden (The) – (n): Those taken into service on Mar-el as punishment for sailing the Triton seas without permission from the Mar-el king.

This punishment is known and anyone who sails the seas risks it if caught doing so. The service of the bounden lasts a specified amount of time and those taken into it are guarded under significant strictures as by law as to their treatment. Once service is done, many of the bounden remain on Mar-el to make their lives there.

Cairngorn Lake – (KAREN-gorn) (n/lake): Very large lake located in the southeast of the country of Airen.

Carleigh Manor – (Car-LAY) (n/place): Royal manor house about thirty-five kilometers south of Sky Bay in the country of Airen.

Catrame Palace – (Cah-TRAME) (n/place): Royal palace of the King of Firenze. Located in Fire City.

Cells – (n): The room or rooms of a Go'Doan priest. In Go'Doan, they are quarters, with more than one room. For new priests or those in Go'Doan temples in other countries, the cell could be one room. However, they are not spartan, ranging from very comfortable (for a Go'Tish, a new priest) to luxurious (for a Go'En, a high priest).

Close – (n): A narrow, dead-end alleyway in a city. Mostly a footpath and not used for carriages or horses, etc. Opposite of "wynd" [see below].

Collected (The) – (n): Old or ancient books gathered and translated by the Go'Doan from all the realms of Triton. These were protected and kept safe in the Narration Hall (main library) of the Dome City.

Crittich Keep – (Crid-ITCH) (n/place): Royal prison and dungeons of Wodell, located in the capital of Notting Thicket. Also contains administration offices of the constabulary, prison and guard system in Wodell, interrogation rooms, cells for those held for questioning, and in the bowels of its depths, ancient torture chambers. Outside the Keep is the Lawn, where executions take place.

Cyrus – (SEAR-us) (n/place): Large merchant town to the northeast of Silbury Henge on the outskirts of the Argyll Forest.

Dahksahna – (Dahk-SAH-nah) (n/title): Means "queen" in Korwahkian, the language of Korwahk in The Southlands.

Dahlia Rooms – (n/place): Sex palace in the Heden District of Fire City in Firenze.

Dax – (n/title): Means "king" in Korwahkian, the language of Korwahk in The Southlands.

Dellish – (Del-ISH) (adj): Of Wodell (akin to English, Spanish, etc.).

Dome City – (n/place): Another name for the city-state of Go'Doan, named as such as it's known for its plentiful gold domes.

Doors (The) – (n/place): A magical gnome settlement in the Great Thicket Forest of Wodell where the gnomes live in the trees, the name referring to the many doors carved into the trunks.

Dune Desert – (n/place): Desert north of the Sheeonee Mountain range in Firenze.

Dunleth Abhainn – (DONE-leth AH-been) (n/river): Long, wide river running from an inlet in the northern shore of the country of Airen, southeast all the way to Cairngorn Lake. At the town of Kilcree Break, the Dunleth forks into Westfork River, which runs southwest to the Argyll Forest. (Abhainn means "river" in Gaelic).

Emerald Oil Asps – (n): Snakes in Firenze. Black with emerald-colored eyes. Highly venomous.

Enchantments (The) – (n/place): Forest in the center of the mainland of Triton with trees made magically tall and stout in order to house the Nadirii Sisterhood in their treehouses. Protected by fierce magic, The Enchantments cannot be breached by anyone other than one of the

Sisterhood or unless given Nadirii permission. Regardless of the intensity of magic that protects it, it is patrolled constantly by Nadirii warriors.

Fire City – (n/place): Capital city of Firenze. Located to the north of the Sheeonee Mountain range that takes up the center of Firenze. Fire City is close to Fire Lake, the largest lake in Firenze.

Fire Lake – (n/lake): Very large lake to the east of Fire City in the country of Firenze formed by runoff of melted snow from the Sheeonee Mountains.

Firenz – (Fir-EHNZ) (adj): Meaning, of the country of Firenze.

Firenze – (Fir-ehn-ZAY) (n/place): Country of Firenze situated across the south of the Triton mainland. The largest country in Triton. Most of the country is desert or sand dunes with the middle of the country having a very large mountain range with high peaks that get great amounts of snow. When this snow melts, it floods Fire Lake, close to Fire City, and leads off into a large number of rivers and tributaries that cut through the desert and dunes with strips of fertile oases.

Firenzii – (Fir-ehn-ZEE) (n): Language of Firenze (much like Italian).

Fotiá Sea – (Foh-SHAH) (n/ocean): Body of water to the south of the continent of Triton.

Fumeria – (Foo-mare-EE-ah) (n): Water pipe. Akin to a marijuana bong but much more elegant and ornate.

Gairn Plain – (n/place): A stretch of plain southeast of Sky Bay and west of the Dunleth Abhainn in the country of Airen.

Go'Doan – (Go'Dōn) (n/place/religion):
  (1) City-state of priests, scholars and healers with temples, archives of the history Triton and a university. Also known as Dome City.
  a. Go'Da (Go'DAH) (n): University in Go'Doan

(2)   Religion in Triton with temples across the continent where people worship:
   a.   Go'Bedi (Go'bed-EE) (god of obedience)
   b.   Go'Vicee (Go'vee-SEE) (god of service)
   c.   Go'Chas (god of faithfulness)

(3) Orders of Go'Doan:
   a.   Go'Fell (order of priests as a whole)
   b.   Go'En (high priests)
   c.   Go'Ar (Advanced priests, often are sent to do missionary work or teach in Go'Doan schools across Triton)
   d.   Go'Tish (new priests/trainee priests)
   e.   Go'Tec (priests who teach/scholars in the city-state)
   f.   Go'Nis ("Keepers of the Records," priests who record history)
   g.   Go'Ella (female acolytes that serve priests and the city-state)

Great Thicket Forest – (n/place): Massive forest in the middle of the country of Wodell, to the east of which is Notting Thicket, the capital city of Wodell.

Great Wohd (River) – (n/river): A very wide, very long river separating from the River Dorian in the north which runs from the Seil Sea. The Great Wohd cuts through the eastern part of Wodell, meeting the River Fae at Notting Thicket, the capital of Wodell, and continuing westerly nearly to the border of Wodell.

Green Sea – (n/ocean): Body of water to the east of the continent of Triton.

Gulliver – (n/place): Town in the south of Wodell located seventy-five miles from the Firenz boarder.

Hawkvale – (n/place): Country in the middle of The Northlands, south of Lunwyn, north of Fleuridia, ruled by King Noctorno and Queen Cora.

Heden District – (HEE-den) (n/place): Red light district of Fire City, Firenze. Where to find prostitutes (male and female), participate in orgies or other sexual games and play, consume smoke or *ashesh* or *koekah* and other forms of decadence.

Highgate – (n/place): Large gate at the top of the cliffs protecting Sky Bay, the capital city of Airen. Situated slightly to the southeast at the highest heights of the mountains that surround the capital city.

Ibex-whales – (EYE-bex whales) (n): Whales of which the bulls have enormous, ridged tusks that look like that of an ibex.

Irons – (n): Used in fireplaces or freestanding in rooms in Airen, Mar-el and Wodell, wood or other burning fuel in them or piled on them to heat them in order to heat a room.

kah rahna fauna – (n): Loosely means "my golden doe" in Korwahkian, the language of Korwahk in The Southlands.

Keel Castle – (n/place): Home of the king of Mar-el. Located in Nautilus, the capital city.

Keeper of The Lights – (group): A group of fairies who oversee and protect the area where The Lights (see: Lights (The)) can be viewed in the Greater Thicket Forest of Wodell.

Keerian Name – (description): The way Lunwynians (people of Lunwyn in the Northlands) describe a given name or as we know it Christian or first name.

Kilcree Break – (Kill-KREE Break) (n/place): Town in the middle of the country of Airen located at the break of the Dunleth Abhainn (river) where the Dunleth continues on to Cairngorn Lake and the Westfork River begins, running toward the Argyll Forest. A gentry seat.

Koekah – (koe-KAH) (n): Drug akin to cocaine. Available throughout Triton. Grown and manufactured in Firenze.

Korwahk – (n/place): Country taking up the northern part of the continent, The Southlands. Ruled by *Dax* (King) Lahn and *Dahksahna* (Queen) Circe of the Golden Dynasty.

Korwahn – (n/place): Capital city of Korwahk in The Southlands.

Lawn (The) – (n/place): Grassy area outside Crittich Keep, the royal prison and dungeons of Wodell, where executions take place. Located in Notting Thicket.

Lesser Thicket Forest – (n/place): Forest on the east border of the country of Wodell, west border of Airen. The parts of it in Airen are known as the Argyll Forest. Within it in Wodell is the Ancient Ritual Ground.

Leuthea – (LOU-thee-ah) (n): Sea goddess of sailors in distress. Worshiped by Mar-el.

Lights (The) (n/place): Atop the highest hill in the center of the Great Thicket Forest of Wodell where, on occasion, the sky illuminates with colored lights (akin to the Northern Lights). The reason for the phenomenon is unknown.

Lotus Den – (n/place): Bar and drug den with rooms for rent for a variety of hedonistic activities in the Heden District of Fire City in Firenze.

Lowgate – (n/place): Large gate in the downslope of the cliffs that protect Sky Bay, the capital city of Airen. Situated to the northwest in the lowest area where the cliffs meets the sea at Twilight Harbor.

Lunwyn – (n/place): Country taking up the northern part of The Northlands. Ruled by Queen Aurora.

Mar-el – (n/place): Country of Mar-el, island nation situated to the northeast of Triton (off the coast of Airen). Made up of dark rock around the shores, beaches, fertile land inland. Most of population works in some form of sea trade.

Marital Chain – (n): Firenz form of a wedding ring. It starts at upper ear, threads down to the lobe, across to the nostril and down to end at a hoop at the side of the mouth. In most cases, if it indicates marriage, it's worn on the right side. It's meant to signify listening to your mate, keeping them in mind, and communicating honestly with them.

McGarrity's Teahouse – (n/place): A brothel in Wodell.

Medusa – (n): Goddess of the sea. Worshipped by Mar-el.

Medusa's Gate – (n): Large, ornate monument to the goddess Medusa in which is the gate to the lane to Keel Castle in Nautilus, the home of the King of Mar-el.

Mer (The) – (n/people): Race of underwater charmed folk, including mermaids and mermales. Their fins split into legs and their gills disappear when they swim close to land so they can "pass" as human and move about on land.

Miet – (n/celebration/holiday): The celebration of the crop yield in Firenze, held as autumn subsides to winter. Celebrations mostly center around planned orgies, but they also include copious intake of liquor, food and drugs.

Mystics (The/the) – (n/place/spiritual practice):
(1) The continent to the west of Triton across the Triton Sea. Referred to with capitalized "The."

(2) Spiritual practice that includes personal reflection, transcendent study and deep training in various physical skills of defense and attack. Referred to with a lowercase "the."

Nadirii – (Nah-DEER-ee) (n): Sisterhood of warriors who live in an enchanted forest (The Enchantments) with no men. The veil around this forest was raised after the women of Airen revolted against their oppressors, magicking them to sleep, slitting their throats and escaping by stealing into the night to the newly established enchanted forest. No one can enter without Nadirii permission.

    (1) "Nadirii" means "oppressed" in the old tongue.

    (2) "Nadirii" means "sisterhood" in the ancient tongue.

Narration Hall – (n/building): Very large library that is very tall as well as built down deep in the earth in the Dome City where the tomes of history are recorded and kept, as well as all other books the Go'Doan have collected.

Nautilus – (n/place): Capital city of Mar-el, located on the southwest coast.

Night Heights – (n/mountain range): Range of mountains to the east of Sky Bay, the capital city of the country of Airen.

Nippenlas – (n/festival/holiday): A festival held midwinter in Wodell for the sole purpose of drawing the citizens out of their homes and to break the monotony of long nights and cold winters.

Northlands (The) – (n/place): One of two continents to the east of Triton across the Green Sea.

Notting Thicket – (n/place): Capital city of the country of Wodell, located to the east of the Great Thicket Forest.

Our Lady the Queen's Orphanage – (n/place): National orphanage in Notting Thicket, Wodell. Under patronage of the Queen of Wodell.

Pennyrium – (Pen-EER-ee-um) (n): A drug a woman can take through dissolving a powder in water in order to protect against conception.

Piercing Ceremony – (event): Done at age thirteen to boys and girls in Firenze, it is the ceremony where the right ear is pierced at the top and lobe, as well as the nostril and the side of the top lip. It is where the marital chain is threaded after a Firenz is wedded. Small hoops are worn in these piercings until a person is married and takes their chain.

Rayloo – (command): A Korwahkian word meaning [as it is in the imperative conjunction] "be quiet."

River Dorian – (n/river): Long, wide river running from Seil Sea through the eastern region of the country of Wodell, through the Lesser Thicket Forest, to the city-state of Go'Doan.

River Fae – (n/river): A river running from mountains to the north of the country of Wodell, through the mid-eastern part of the country to join with the Great Wohd at Notting Thicket, the capital of Wodell.

Royal Service Infirmary – (n/place): National hospital in Notting Thicket, the capital of Wodell, that treats all, but was created and caters to Dellish soldiers.

Seil Sea – (n/ocean): Body of water north of the continent of Triton.

Sheeonee Mountain Range – (SHE-oh-nee) (n/place): Large mountain range that makes up most of the central part of the country of Firenze. Very high peaks that get a great deal of snow. Snow melt feeds Fire Lake (outside Fire City) and five large rivers that run through the country, including the widest that flows north toward Wodell, the Tebes River.

Smoke – (n): Marijuana. Used mostly in Firenze but available throughout Triton.

Silbury Henge – (n/place): Standing stone henge in the forest on the western border of Airen where it meets The Enchantments and the city-state of Go'Doan. Made up of five standing stones and a sacrificial/ritual slab.

Sky Bay – (n/place): Capital city of Airen, located in a northwesternmost bay of Airen, close to the border of Wodell.

Sky Citadel – (n/place): Home of the King of Airen. Located in Sky Bay.

Slán Bailey – (SLAHN) (n/place): Royal prison in Airen, the building of which takes up a full, small island off the coast of Twilight Harbor in Sky Bay.

Soldier's Poison – (ritual): If a soldier is wounded gravely in the service of Airen or Wodell, he can request to be relieved of his life. This request is made of his commanding officer, and that officer can grant or refuse it. The ritual allows for a farewell from any loved one the soldier selects and making peace with his gods, before he's given a fast-acting, pain-less poison of a dense concentration of undiluted *taibac* to take, or if he's unable to drink it himself, it is administered to him by his commanding officer.

Southlands (The) – (n/place): One of two continents to the east of Triton across the Green Sea.

Strait of Medusa – (n/waterway): Narrow body of water that separates Mar-el from Airen.

Sparkles – (n): (When referring to a beverage) Champagne.

Taibac – (TIE-back) (n): Tobacco. Not smoked. Used as a poison to induce cardiac arrest. Can go undetected if poison is administered in small doses for a long time.

Tebes River – (TEH-behz) (n/river): Large river that flows from the Sheeonee Mountain range in Firenze, north toward the country of Wodell.

Temple to Wohden – (WOE-den) (n/place): National cathedral in Notting Thicket, Wodell where parishioners worship the god Wohden, the Dellish god of power and war. Also, where all royals are wed.

Trevor's Gorge – (n/place):
    (1) A gorge south of Notting Thicket in Wodell that runs through a

small, ancient mountain range (thus not high). It was formed by a narrow, but strong tributary that breaks off the Great Wohd River in Wodell.

(2) Also, the name of the large town situated at the west end of the gorge. This town is known for the making of sharp, but rich, goat's cheese that is renown throughout Triton.
    a.   Trevor cheese (n/food): Cheese from this region.

Triton – (n/place):
(1) The continent to the west of the Northlands and Southlands, and to the east of The Mystics. It is surrounded by the Green Sea to the east, the Triton Sea to the west, Seil Sea to the north and Fotiá Sea to the south. It consists of one large land mass about the size of Australia and one large island (Mar-el) to the northeast. Countries include Airen, The Enchantments, Firenze, Mar-el, Wodell and the city-state of the Go'Doan.

(2) (n/god): God of the sea, worshiped by Mar-el.

Triton Sea – (n/ocean): Body of water to the west of the continent of Triton.

Trusted Ones (The) – (n): The elite guard that is commissioned with the safety of the King and Queen of Firenze. Also known as "The Trusted."

Twilight Harbor – (n/place): Wharf/dock in Sky Bay, the capital city of Airen.

Westfork River – (n/river): Short, narrow river in the country of Airen running from a break in the great Dunleth Abhainn at the town of Kilcree Break. The Westfork River runs southwest to the Argyll Forest.

Wodell – (n/place): Country of Wodell situated at the northwest of the Triton mainland. Very fertile and green, consisting of mainly farmland, forests, hills, dells and moors.

Wynd – (pronounced like "to wind your way") (n): A narrow, open-ended alley. Mostly a footpath and not used for carriages or horses, etc. Opposite of "close" [see above].

Zees – (people): A race of wanderers. Mostly in Wodell, but also some would travel around the westernmost border of Airen.

Full glossary, including character lists, tarot meanings, and gods and goddesses can be found on The Rising Series page at KristenAshley.net

KEEP READING FOR MORE OF
THE RISING

The Plan Commences

Once upon a time, in a parallel universe, there existed the continent of Triton...

The prophecy has begun. The Beast has been stirred. And Triton is in turmoil.

Our four warriors and four witches, destined mates, have begun their adventure, knowing the fate of their world is at stake, but not having any idea there are other factions plotting against them.

Now they face political intrigues, religious zealotry, father against son, wife against husband, a mother's plotting, a sister's envy, grief, betrayal and despair as the prophesied journey across the sands of Firenze into the lush green of Wodell.

The lovers are united, but their stories have just begun. They know the battle ahead will be a fierce one they cannot lose.

What they don't know is a diabolical plan has commenced...

And no one is safe.

Keep reading for more of The Plan Commences.

THE PLAN COMMENCES
CHAPTER 1 - THE GRIEVING

Prince True
Guest Suite, Second Floor, East Corridor, Catrame Palace, Fire City
Firenze

"We should give her another sleeping draught," Queen Elpis said fretfully. "The last is clearly not working."

True did not even attempt to hide the censure in his gaze when he looked from the weeping beauty that was in his arms to the Queen of Firenze standing at the side of the foot of Farah's bed.

Elpis was as far from them as she could get at the same time staying close.

Her wont these past days when it came to Farah and her now-dead mother, Sofia.

Elpis's eyes were swollen and bloodshot from her own tears.

Too little.

Too bloody late.

Elpis flinched when she caught his gaze.

"You may leave," True rumbled.

"But, I—" Elpis started.

"You. May. *Leave*," True said lower and slower.

Her head jerked before she lifted her chin and stated, "This is my palace. She is my subject. I am queen and I—"

"For thirteen more hours," he interrupted her to note. "Then my cousin will be the Queen of Firenze and you will be naught but Relict Queen."

She gasped in affront.

True did not give a gods-damn.

"You leave, or my men will remove you," True warned.

"You cannot—"

"Leave, Your Grace, or my men will remove you," True repeated, and Florian made a move toward the queen.

"They have no authority here," she snapped.

"I am their prince, which means I will be their king and Farah will be their queen. Ask your son what authority that gives me," True retorted.

He immediately noted she took his meaning.

Then again, after the attack on the palace that occurred not two hours before had been quashed, Mars—her son, her king—had not allowed Silence, his intended, to climb down from his back where he held her as he battled their assailants.

It was safe, and still Mars kept Silence as close to him as he could without absorbing her, something he could not do, or he would have done that instead.

Yes.

Elpis took his meaning.

Her face softened, and her gaze moved to Farah, who was in his arms, silently crying, her head turned toward True's body, even if she was not holding him in return. Something that alarmed him and something he wished to address with his betrothed.

It was just that he'd do that when the bloody queen left.

"I am glad she has you," Elpis whispered.

"It would have been good if she'd had *you*," True retorted. "If they'd *both* had you."

Pain sharpened her features.

Pain and regret.

But Farah tightened in his arms.

This was upsetting his intended.

Therefore, this had to end.

"Go," he ordered the queen.

Elpis seemed to crumble before his eyes and True wished he didn't care about that either.

But he understood regret.

The woman could not know her friend would take hundreds of bites from poisonous emerald oil asps and die in her bed under a pile of them before they could find their way back to a friendship that had been torn apart by treason and murder.

However, now he didn't have time for Queen Elpis.

He needed to see to his future queen.

Fortunately, Elpis knew the only one who could look after Farah was in her bed holding her.

Thus, she gave up the fight and moved slowly from the chamber.

The door latched shut behind her.

"Leave us," True ordered Florian, Bram and Alfie, the members of his guard who were in the room. The others, Luther and Wallace, were guarding it elsewhere. One, Luther, in the hall. The other, Wallace, outside, under the window.

"True—" Alfie began.

"Leave," True said.

Alfie looked to Farah then to True.

"Magic," he replied quietly.

Indeed.

The asps that had killed Sofia had been very real.

They had also been transported to her bedchamber through magic.

A bedchamber that had been Farah's before her mother and she had switched in order to place Sofia farther away from Elpis's room.

True knew all this.

As did Alfie and his other lieutenants.

But he could have fifty swords in that room.

They wouldn't be able to fight magic.

"I'll want you in here, guarding her after I leave. But now, we need privacy," True told his friend.

"I think—"

"Go, Alfie," True demanded.

Alfie hesitated before he nodded then he jerked his head to Florian and Bram and they walked out of the room.

The Plan Commences is available now.

About the Author

Kristen Ashley is the *New York Times* bestselling author of over eighty romance novels including the *Rock Chick, Colorado Mountain, Dream Man, Chaos, Unfinished Heroes, The 'Burg, Magdalene, Fantasyland, The Three, Ghost and Reincarnation, The Rising, Dream Team, Moonlight and Motor Oil, River Rain, Wild West MC, Misted Pines* and *Honey* series along with several standalone novels. She's a hybrid author, publishing titles both independently and traditionally, her books have been translated in fourteen languages and she's sold over five million books.

Kristen's novel, *Law Man*, won the *RT Book Reviews* Reviewer's Choice Award for best Romantic Suspense, her independently published title *Hold On* was nominated for *RT Book Reviews* best Independent Contemporary Romance and her traditionally published title *Breathe* was nominated for best Contemporary Romance. Kristen's titles *Motorcycle Man, The Will*, and *Ride Steady* (which won the Reader's Choice award from *Romance Reviews*) all made the final rounds for Goodreads Choice Awards in the Romance category.

Kristen, born in Gary and raised in Brownsburg, Indiana, is a fourth-generation graduate of Purdue University. Since, she's lived in Denver, the West Country of England, and she now resides in Phoenix. She worked as a charity executive for eighteen years prior to beginning her independent publishing career. She now writes full-time.

Although romance is her genre, the prevailing themes running through all of Kristen's novels are friendship, family and a strong sister-hood. To this end, and as a way to thank her readers for their support,

Kristen has created the Rock Chick Nation, a series of programs that are designed to give back to her readers and promote a strong female community.

The mission of the Rock Chick Nation is to live your best life, be true to your true self, recognize your beauty, and take your sister's back whether they're at your side as friends and family or if they're thousands of miles away and you don't know who they are.

The programs of the RC Nation include Rock Chick Rendezvous, weekends Kristen organizes full of parties and get-togethers to bring the sisterhood together, Rock Chick Recharges, evenings Kristen arranges for women who have been nominated to receive a special night, and Rock Chick Rewards, an ongoing program that raises funds for nonprofit women's organizations Kristen's readers nominate. Kristen's Rock Chick Rewards have donated hundreds of thousands of dollars to charity and this number continues to rise.

You can read more about Kristen, her titles and the Rock Chick Nation at KristenAshley.net.

facebook.com/kristenashleybooks

twitter.com/KristenAshley68

instagram.com/kristenashleybooks

pinterest.com/KristenAshleyBooks

goodreads.com/kristenashleybooks

bookbub.com/authors/kristen-ashley

A Christmas to Remember

Rough Ride

Wild Like the Wind

Free

Wild Fire

Wild Wind

The Colorado Mountain Series:

The Gamble

Sweet Dreams

Lady Luck

Breathe

Jagged

Kaleidoscope

Bounty

Dream Man Series:

Mystery Man

Wild Man

Law Man

Motorcycle Man

Quiet Man

Dream Team Series:

Dream Maker

Dream Chaser

Dream Bites Cookbook

Dream Spinner

Dream Keeper

The Fantasyland Series:

Wildest Dreams

The Golden Dynasty

Fantastical

Broken Dove

Midnight Soul

Gossamer in the Darkness

Ghosts and Reincarnation Series:

Sommersgate House

Lacybourne Manor

Penmort Castle

Fairytale Come Alive

Lucky Stars

The Honey Series:

The Deep End

The Farthest Edge

The Greatest Risk

The Magdalene Series:

The Will

Soaring

The Time in Between

Mathilda, SuperWitch:

Mathilda's Book of Shadows

Mathilda The Rise of the Dark Lord

Misted Pines Series

The Girl in the Mist

The Girl in the Woods

Moonlight and Motor Oil Series:

The Hookup

The Slow Burn

The Rising Series:

The Beginning of Everything

The Plan Commences

The Dawn of the End

The Rising

The River Rain Series:

After the Climb

After the Climb Special Edition

Chasing Serenity

Taking the Leap

Making the Match

The Three Series:

Until the Sun Falls from the Sky

With Everything I Am

Wild and Free

The Unfinished Hero Series:

Knight

Creed

Raid

Deacon

Sebring

Wild West MC Series:

Still Standing

Smoke and Steel

Other Titles by Kristen Ashley:

Heaven and Hell

Play It Safe

Three Wishes

Complicated

Loose Ends

Fast Lane

Perfect Together

Too Good To Be True